# Rapture in Death

*Nora Roberts*

writing as

*J.D. Robb*

**PIATKUS**

# 🎗 Visit the Piatkus website!

Piatkus publishes a wide range of bestselling fiction and non-fiction, including books on health, mind, body & spirit, sex, self-help, cookery, biography and the paranormal.

*If you want to:*

- read descriptions of our popular titles
- buy our books over the internet
- take advantage of our special offers
- enter our monthly competition
- learn more about your favourite Piatkus authors

VISIT OUR WEBSITE AT: www.piatkus.co.uk

Copyright © 1996 by Nora Roberts
Material excerpted from *Ceremony in Death* by Nora Roberts writing as J.D. Robb copyright
© 1996 by Nora Roberts

This edition published in Great Britain in 2003 by
Piatkus Books Ltd of
5 Windmill Street, London WIT 2JA
email: info@piatkus.co.uk

Reprinted 2005, 2006

First published in the United States in 1996 by Berkley Publishing Group, a division of
Penguin Putnam Inc., New York.

**The moral right of the author has been asserted**

*A catalogue record for this book is available from the British Library*

ISBN 0 7499 3411 5

Typeset in Times by Palimpsest Book Production Limited,
Polmont, Stirlingshire

Printed and bound in Great Britain by
Mackays of Chatham Ltd, Chatham Kent

But I do nothing upon myself,
And yet am mine own Executioner.

JOHN DONNE

There is rapture on the lonely shore

LORD BYRON

# Chapter One

The alley was dark and stank of piss and vomit. It was home for quick-footed rats and the bony, hungry-eyed felines who hunted them. Red eyes glinted in the dark, some of them human, all of them feral.

Eve's heart tripped lightly as she slipped into the fetid, damp-edged shadows. He'd gone in, she was sure of it. It was her job to follow, to find him, to bring him in. Her weapon was in her hand, and her hand was steady.

'Hey, sweetcakes, wanna do it with me? Wanna do it?'

Voices out of the dark, harsh with chemicals or cheap brews. Moans of the damned, giggles of the mad. The rats and cats didn't live here alone. The company of the human garbage that lined the sweating brick walls was no comfort.

She swung her weapon, crouched as she sidestepped a battered recycling unit that, from the smell of it, hadn't worked in a decade. The stench of food gone over smeared the humid air and turned it into a greasy stew.

Someone whimpered. She saw a boy, about thirteen, all but naked. The sores on his face were festering; his eyes were slits of fear and hopelessness as he scrabbled like a crab back against the filthy wall.

Pity stirred in her heart. She had been a child once, hurt and terrified, hiding in an alley. 'I won't hurt you.' She kept her voice quiet, barely a murmur, kept her eyes on his, maintaining contact as she lowered her weapon.

And that's when he struck.

He came from behind, a roar of motion and sound. Primed to kill, he swung the pipe. The whistle of it stung her ears as she whirled, dodged. There was barely time to curse herself for losing her concentration, forgetting her primary target as two hundred fifty pounds of muscle and mean sent her flying to the bricks.

Her weapon flew out of her hand and clattered into the dark.

She saw his eyes, the glint of mayhem heightened by the chemical, Zeus. She watched the pipe raised high, timed it, and rolled seconds before it cracked against brick. With a pump of her legs, she dived headfirst into his belly. He grunted, staggered, and as he reached for her throat, she brought her fist up hard, smashing it under his jaw. The force of the blow radiated pain and power up her arm.

People were screaming, scrambling for safety in a narrow world where nothing and no one was safe. She spun, used the impetus of the turn to deliver a roundhouse kick that shattered her adversary's nose. Blood fountained, adding to the sick miasma of odors.

His eyes were wild, but he barely jerked at the blow. Pain was no match for the god of chemicals. Grinning as blood poured down his face, he smacked the thick pipe on his palm.

'Kill you. Kill you, cop bitch.' He circled her, swinging the pipe like a whistling whip. Grinning, grinning as he bled. 'Break your head open and eat your brains.'

Knowing he meant it pumped her adrenaline to flash point. Live or die. Her breath came in pants, the sweat pouring like oil down her skin. She dodged the next blow, went down on her knees. Slapping a hand on her boot, she came up grinning.

'Eat this instead, you son of a bitch.' Her backup weapon was in her hand. She didn't bother with stun. The stun setting

2

would do little more than tickle a two hundred fifty pound man flying on Zeus. It was set to terminate.

As he lunged toward her, she hit him with full power. His eyes died first. She'd seen it happen before. Eyes that turned to glass like a doll's, even as he charged her. She sidestepped, prepared to fire again, but the pipe slipped from his fingers. His body began that jerky dance as his nervous system overloaded.

He fell at her feet, a mass of ruined humanity who had played god.

'You won't be sacrificing any more virgins, asshole,' she muttered, and as that wild energy drained, she rubbed a hand over her face. Her weapon arm dropped.

The faint scrape of leather on concrete alerted her. She started her spin, weapon rising, but arms clamped her, lifted her to her toes.

'Always watch your back, Lieutenant,' the voice whispered just before teeth nipped lightly at her earlobe.

'Roarke, goddamn it. I nearly zapped you.'

'You didn't even come close.' With a laugh, he turned her in his arms, and his mouth was on hers, hot, hungry. 'I love watching you work,' he murmured and his hand, clever hand, slid up her body to cup her breast. 'It's . . . stimulating.'

'Cut it out.' But her heart was thundering in reaction, and the order was halfhearted. 'This is no place for a seduction.'

'On the contrary. A honeymoon is a traditional place for a seduction.' He drew her back, kept his hands on her shoulders. 'I wondered where you'd gone off to. I should have known.' He glanced down at the body at their feet. 'What did he do?'

'He had a predilection for beating the brains out of young women, then eating them.'

'Oh.' Roarke winced, shook his head. 'Really, Eve, couldn't you have come up with something a little less revolting?'

'There was a guy on the Terra Colony a couple of years

3

back who fit the profile, and I wondered . . .' She trailed off, frowning. They were standing in a stinking alley, death at their feet. And Roarke, gorgeous, dark angel Roarke, was wearing a tuxedo and a diamond stud. 'What are you all dressed up for?'

'We had plans,' he reminded her. 'Dinner?'

'I forgot.' She tucked her weapon away. 'I didn't think this would take so long.' She blew out a breath. 'I guess I should clean up.'

'I like you the way you are.' He moved into her again, took possession. 'Forget dinner . . . for now.' His smile was slow and irresistible. 'But I do insist on slightly more aesthetic surroundings. End program,' he ordered.

The alley, the smells, and the huddle of bodies winked away. They stood in a huge, empty room with equipment and blinking lights built into the walls. Both floor and ceiling were glass-mirrored black to better project the holographic scenes available on the program.

It was one of Roarke's newest, most sophisticated toys.

'Begin Tropical Setting 4-B. Maintain dual control status.'

In response came the whoosh of waves, the sprinkle of starlight on water. Beneath her feet was white sugar sand, and palm trees waved like exotic dancers.

'That's more like it,' Roarke decided, then began unbuttoning her shirt. 'Or it will be when I get you naked.'

'You've been getting me naked every time I blink for nearly three weeks.'

He arched a brow. 'Husband's privilege. Complaints?'

*Husband.* It was still a jolt. This man with the warrior's mane of black hair, the poet's face, the wild Irish blue eyes was her husband. She'd never get used to it.

'No. Just an—' Her breath hitched as one of his long-fingered hands skimmed over her breasts. 'An observation.'

'Cops.' He smiled, unfastened her jeans. 'Always observing. You're off duty, Lieutenant Dallas.'

4

'I was just keeping my reflexes sharp. Three weeks away from the job, you get rusty.'

He slid a hand between her naked thighs, cupped her, watched her head fall back on a moan. 'Your reflexes are just fine,' he murmured and pulled her down to the soft white sand.

*His wife.* Roarke liked to think about that as she rode him, as she moved under him, as she lay spent beside him. This fascinating woman, this dedicated cop, this troubled soul belonged to him.

He'd watched her work through the program, the alley, the chemical-mad killer. And he'd known she would face the reality of her work with the same tough, terrifyingly courageous determination that she'd possessed in the illusion.

He admired her for it, however many bad moments it gave him. In a few days, they would go back to New York and he would have to share her with her duties. For now, he wanted to share her with nothing. With no one.

He was no stranger to back alleys that reeked of garbage and hopeless humanity. He'd grown up in them, escaped into them, and eventually had escaped from them. He had made his life into what it was – and then she had come into it, sharp and lethal as an arrow from a bow, and had changed it again.

Cops had once been the enemy, then an amusement, and now he was bound to one.

Just over two weeks before, he had watched her walk toward him in a flowing gown of rich bronze, flowers in her hands. The bruises on her face a killer had put there only hours before had been softened under cosmetics. And in those eyes, those big brandy-colored eyes that showed so much, he'd seen nerves and amusement.

*Here we go, Roarke.* He'd nearly heard her say it as she put her hand in his. *For better or worse I'll take you on. God help us.*

Now she wore his ring, and he hers. He'd insisted on

5

that, though such traditions weren't strictly fashionable in the middle of the twenty-first century. He'd wanted the tangible reminder of what they were to each other, the symbol of it.

Now he picked up her hand, kissed her finger above the ornately etched gold band he'd had made for her. Her eyes stayed closed. He studied the sharp angles of her face, the overwide mouth, the short cap of brown hair tousled into spikes.

'I love you, Eve.'

Faint color bloomed on her cheeks. She was so easily moved, he thought. He wondered if she had any idea how huge was her own heart.

'I know.' She opened her eyes. 'I'm, ah, starting to get used to it.'

'Good.'

Listening to the song of water lapping on sand, of balmy breezes whispering through feathery palms, she lifted a hand, brushed the hair back from his face. *A man like him*, she thought, *powerful, wealthy, impulsive, could call up such scenes at the snap of a finger.* And he'd done it for her.

'You make me happy.'

His grin flashed, making her stomach muscles curl in delight. 'I know.' With easy, effortless strength, he lifted her up and over until she straddled him. He skimmed his hands idly up her long, slim, muscled body. 'Are you ready to admit you're glad I shanghaied you off planet for the last part of our honeymoon?'

She grimaced, remembering her panic, her dug-in-at-the-heels refusal to board the transport he'd had waiting, and how he had roared with laughter and had tossed her over his shoulder, climbing on board with her cursing him.

'I liked Paris,' she said with a sniff. 'And I loved the week we had on the island. I didn't see any reason for us to come to some half-finished resort in space when we were going to spend most of our time in bed anyway.'

6

'You were scared.' It had delighted him that she'd been unnerved by the prospect of her first off planet voyage, and it had pleasured him to keep her occupied and distracted for the bulk of the trip.

'I was not.' *Boneless*, she thought. *Scared boneless*. 'I was justifiably annoyed that you'd made the plans without discussing them with me.'

'I seem to recall someone being involved with a case and telling me to plan whatever suited me. You were a beautiful bride.'

It made her lips curve. 'It was the dress.'

'No, it was you.' He lifted a hand to her face. 'Eve Dallas. Mine.'

Love swamped her. It always seemed to come in huge, unexpected waves that left her flailing helplessly. 'I love you.' She lowered herself to him, brought her mouth to his. 'Looks like you're mine.'

It was midnight before they had dinner. On the moon-washed terrace of the towering spear that was the nearly completed Olympus Grand Hotel, Eve dug into stuffed lobster and contemplated the view.

The Olympus Resort would be, with Roarke pulling the strings, completed and fully booked within a year. For now, they had it to themselves – if she ignored the construction crews, staff, architects, engineers, pilots, and other assorted inhabitants who shared the massive space station.

From the small glass table where they sat, she could sec out over the hub of the resort. The lights brightly burned for the night crew, the quiet hum of machinery spoke of round-the-clock labor. The fountains, the lances of simulated torchlight and rainbows of color running fluidly through the spewing waters, were for her, she knew.

He'd wanted her to see what he was building and perhaps to begin to understand what she was a part of now. As his wife.

*Wife*. She blew out a breath that fluttered her bangs and sipped the icy champagne he'd poured. It was going to take some time to understand just how she'd gone from being Eve Dallas, homicide lieutenant, to become the wife of a man who some claimed had more money and power than God.

'Problem?'

She flicked her eyes over his face, smiled a little. 'No.' With intense concentration, she dipped a bit of lobster in melted butter – real butter, no simulation for Roarke's table – and sampled it. 'How am I going to face the cardboard they pass off as food at the Eatery once I'm back on the job?'

'You eat candy bars on the job in any case.' He topped off her wine, lifted a brow when she narrowed her eyes.

'You trying to get me drunk, pal?'

'Absolutely.'

She laughed, something he noted she did more easily and more often these days, and with a shrug, picked up her glass. 'What the hell, I'll oblige you. And when I'm drunk' – she gulped down the priceless wine like water – 'I'll give you a ride you won't soon forget.'

Lust he'd thought sated for the moment crawled edgily into his belly. 'Well, in that case' – he poured wine into his own glass, teasing it to the rim – 'let's both get drunk.'

'I like it here,' she announced. Pushing back from the table, she carried her glass to the thick railing of carved stone. It must have cost a fortune to have it quarried, then shipped – but he was Roarke, after all.

Leaning over, she watched the light and water show, scanned the buildings, all domes and spears, all glossy and elegant to house the sumptuous people and the sumptuous games they would come to play.

The casino was completed and glowed like a golden ball in the dark. One of the dozen pools was lighted for the night and the water glimmered cobalt blue. Skywalks zigzagged between buildings and resembled silver threads. They were empty now, but she imagined what they would be like in six months, a year: crammed with people who shimmered in silks, glowed with jewels. They would come to be pampered within the marble walls of the spa with its mud baths and body enhancement facilities, its soft-spoken consultants and solicitous droids. They'd come to lose fortunes in the casino, to drink exclusive liquor in the clubs, to make love to the hard and soft bodies of licensed companions.

Roarke would offer them a world, and they could come. But it wouldn't be her world when they filled it. She was more comfortable with the streets, the noisy half world of law and crime. Roarke understood that, she thought, as he'd come from the same place as she. So he had offered her this when it was only theirs.

'You're going to make something here,' she said and turned to lean back against the rail.

'That's the plan.'

'No.' She shook her head, pleased that it was already starting to swim from the wine. 'You'll make something that people will talk about for centuries, that they'll dream of. You've come a long way from the young thief who ran the back alleys of Dublin, Roarke.'

His smile was slow and just a little sly. 'Not so very far, Lieutenant. I'm still picking pockets — I just do it as legally as I can. Being married to a cop limits certain activities.'

She frowned at him now. 'I don't want to hear about them.'

'Darling Eve.' He rose, brought the bottle with him.

'So by-the-book. Still so unsettled that she's fallen madly in love with a shady character.' He filled her glass again, then set the bottle aside. 'One that only months ago was on her short list of murder suspects.'

'You enjoy that? Being suspicious?'

'I do.' He skimmed a thumb over a cheekbone where a bruise had faded away — except in his mind. 'And I worry about you a little.' *A lot*, he admitted to himself.

9

'I'm a good cop.'

'I know. The only one I've ever completely admired. What an odd twist of fate that I would have fallen for a woman so devoted to justice.'

'It seems odder to me that I've linked up with someone who can buy and sell planets at a whim.'

'Married.' He laughed. Turning her around, he nuzzled the back of her neck. 'Go on, say it. We're married. The word won't choke you.'

'I know what we are.' Ordering herself to relax, she leaned back against him. 'Let me live with it for a while. I like being here, away with you.'

'Then I take it you're glad you let me pressure you into the three weeks.'

'You didn't pressure me.'

'I had to nag.' He nipped her ear. 'Browbeat.' His hands slid up to her breasts. 'Beg.'

She snorted. 'You've never begged for anything. But maybe you did nag. I haven't had three weeks off the job in . . . never.'

He decided against reminding her she hadn't had it now, precisely. She rarely went through a twenty-four-hour period without running some program that put her up against a crime. 'Why don't we make it four?'

'Roarke—'

He chuckled. 'Just testing. Drink your champagne. You're not nearly drunk enough for what I have in mind.'

'Oh?' Her pulse leaped, making her feel foolish. 'And what's that?'

'It'll lose in the telling,' he decided. 'Let's just say I intend to keep you occupied for the last forty-eight hours we have here.'

'Forty-eight hours?' With a laugh, she drained her glass. 'When do we get started?'

'There's no time like—' He broke off, scowling when the

10

doorbell sounded. 'I told the staff to leave the clearing up. Stay here.' He snugged together her robe, which he'd just untied. 'I'll send them away. Far away.'

'Get another bottle while you're at it,' she told him, grinning as she shook the last drops into her glass. 'Someone drank all of this one.'

Amused, he slipped back inside, crossed the wide living space with its clear glass ceiling and feather-soft carpets. He wanted her there, to start, he decided, on that yielding floor with the ice-edged stars wheeling overhead. He plucked a long white lily out of a porcelain dish, imagining how he would show her just what a clever man could do to a woman with the petals of a flower.

He was smiling as he turned into the foyer with its gilded walls and sweeping marble staircase. Flipping on the view screen, he prepared to send the room service waiter to perdition for the interruption.

With some surprise he saw the face of one of his assistant engineers. 'Carter? Trouble?'

Carter rubbed a hand over a face that was dead pale and damp with sweat. 'Sir. I'm afraid there is. I need to speak with you. Please.'

'All right. Just a moment.' Roarke let out a sigh as he flicked off the screen, disengaged the locks. Carter was young for his position, in his middle twenties, but he was a genius at design and execution. If there was a problem with the construction, it was best to deal with it now.

'Is it the sky glide at the salon?' Roarke asked as he opened the door. 'I thought you'd worked out the kinks there.'

'No – I mean, yes, sir, I have. It's working perfectly now.'

The man was trembling, Roarke realized, and forgot his annoyance. 'Has there been an accident?' He took Carter's arm, steered him into the living area, nudged him into a chair. 'Has someone been hurt?'

'I don't know – I mean, an accident?' Carter blinked, stared

11

glassily. 'Miss. Ma'am. Lieutenant,' he said as Eve came in. He started to rise, then fell weakly down again when she gave him a quick push.

'He's in shock,' she said to Roarke, her voice brisk. 'Try some of that fancy brandy you've got around here.' She crouched down, kept her face level with his. His pupils were pinpricks. 'Carter, isn't it? Take it slow.'

'I . . .' His face went waxy now. 'I think I'm going to be—'

Before he could finish, Eve whipped his head down between his knees. 'Breathe. Just breathe. Let's have that brandy, Roarke.' She held out a hand, and he was there with a snifter.

'Pull it together, Carter.' Roarke eased him back onto the cushions. 'Take a swallow of this.'

'Yes, sir.'

'For Christ's sake, stop sirring me to death.'

Color came back into Carter's cheeks, either from the brandy or from embarrassment. He nodded, swallowed, let out a breath. 'I'm sorry. I thought I was okay. I came right up. I didn't know if I should – I didn't know what else to do.' He spread a hand over his face like a kid at a horror video. He hitched in a breath and said it quickly. 'It's Drew, Drew Mathias, my roomie. He's dead.'

Air exploded out of his lungs, then shuddered back in. He took another deep gulp of brandy and choked on it.

Roarke's eyes went flat. He pulled together a picture of Mathias: young, eager, red hair and freckles, an electronics expert with a specialty in autotronics. 'Where, Carter? How did it happen?'

'I thought I should tell you right away.' Now there were two high bruising red flags riding on Carter's pasty cheeks. 'I came right up to tell you – and your wife. I thought since she's – she's the police, she could do something.'

'You need a cop, Carter?' Eve took the snifter out of his unsteady hand. 'Why do you need a cop?'

12

'I think – he must have – he killed himself, Lieutenant. He was hanging there, just hanging there from the ceiling light in the living room. And his face . . . Oh God. Oh Jesus.'

Eve left Carter to bury his own face in his hands and turned to Roarke. 'Who's got authority on site for something like this?'

'We've got standard security, most of it automated.' Accepting, he inclined his head. 'I'd say it's you, Lieutenant.'

'Okay, see if you can put together a field kit for me. I need a recorder – audio and video – some Seal It, evidence bags, tweezers, a couple of small brushes.'

She hissed out a breath as she dragged a hand through her hair. He wasn't going to have the equipment lying around that would pinpoint body temperature and time of death. There would be no scanner, no sweepers, none of the standard chemicals for forensics she carried habitually to crime scenes.

They'd have to wing it.

'There's a doctor, right? Call him. He'll have to stand in as the ME. I'll get dressed.'


Most of the techs made use of the completed wings of the hotel for living quarters. Carter and Mathias had apparently hit it off well enough to share a spacious two-bedroom suite during their shift on the station. As they rode down to the tenth floor, Eve handed Roarke the palm recorder.

'You can run this, right?'

He lifted a brow. One of his companies had manufactured it. 'I think I can manage.'

'Fine.' She offered a weak smile. 'You're deputized. You hanging in, Carter?'

'Yeah.' But he walked out of the elevator into the hallway on ten like a drunk trying to pass a competency test. He had to wipe his sweaty hand twice on his slacks to get a clear reading on the palm screen. When the door slid open, he stepped back. 'I'd just as soon not go in again.'

13

'Stay here,' she told him. 'I may need you.'

She stepped inside. The lights were blinding bright, up to full power. Music blared out of the wall unit: hard, clashing rock with a screeching vocalist that reminded Eve of her friend Mavis. The floor was tiled in a Caribbean blue and offered the illusion of walking on water.

Along the north and south walls, banks of computers were set up. Workstations, she assumed, cluttered with all manner of electronic boards, microchips, and tools.

She saw clothes heaped on the sofa, VR goggles lying on the coffee table with three tubes of Asian beer – two of them flattened and already rolled for the recycler – and a bowl of spiced pretzels.

And she saw Drew Mathias's naked body swaying gently from a makeshift noose of sheets hitched to the glittering tier of a blue glass chandelier.

'Ah, hell.' She sighed it out. 'What is he, Roarke, twenty?'

'Not much more than.' Roarke's mouth thinned as he studied Mathias's boyish face. It was purple now, the eyes bulging, the mouth frozen into a hideous, gaping grin. Some vicious whim of death had left him smiling.

'All right, let's do what we can. Dallas, Lieutenant Eve, NYPSD, standing in until proper interspace authorities can be contacted and transported. Suspicious, unattended death. Mathias, Drew, Olympus Grand Hotel, Room ten thirty-six, August 1, 2058, one hundred hours.'

'I want to take him down,' Roarke said. It shouldn't have surprised him how quickly, how seamlessly she'd shifted from woman to cop.

'Not yet. It doesn't make any difference to him now, and I need the scene recorded before anything's moved.' She turned in the doorway. 'Did you touch anything, Carter?'

'No.' He scrubbed the back of his hand over his mouth. 'I opened the door, just like now, and walked in. I saw him right away. You . . . you see him right away. I guess I stood

14

there a minute. Just stood there. I knew he was dead. I saw his face.'

'Why don't you go through the other door into the bedroom.' She gestured to the left. 'You can lie down for a while. I'll need to talk to you.'

'Okay.'

'Don't call anyone,' she ordered.

'No. No, I won't call anyone.'

She turned away again, secured the door. Her gaze shifted to Roarke's, and their eyes held. She knew he was thinking, as she was, that there were some – like her – who had no escape from death.

'Let's get started,' she told him.

# Chapter Two

The doctor's name was Wang, and he was old, as most medicals were on off planet projects. He could have retired at ninety, but like others of his ilk, he had chosen to bump from site to site, tending the scrapes and bruises, passing out drugs for space sickness and gravity balance, delivering the occasional baby, running required diagnostics.

But he knew a dead body when he saw one.

'Dead.' His voice was clipped, faintly exotic. His skin was parchment yellow and as wrinkled as an old map. His eyes were black, almond shaped. His head was glossy and slick, lending him the appearance of an ancient, somewhat battered billiard ball.

'Yeah, I got that much.' Eve rubbed her eyes. She'd never had to deal with a space med, but she'd heard about them. They didn't care to have their cushy routine interrupted. 'Give me the cause and the time.'

'Strangulation.' Wang tapped one long finger against the vicious marks on Mathias's neck. 'Self-induced. Time of death I would say between ten and eleven P.M. on this day, in this month, in this year.'

She offered a thin smile. 'Thank you, Doctor. There aren't any other signs of violence on the body, so I lean toward your diagnosis of self-termination. But I want the results of the drug run. Let's see if it was chemically induced. Did you treat the deceased for anything?'

'I cannot say, but he looks unfamiliar. I would have his records, of course. He would have come to me for the standard diagnostic upon arrival.'

'I'll want those as well.'

'I will do my best to accommodate you, Mrs Roarke.'

Her eyes narrowed. 'Dallas, Lieutenant Dallas. Put a rush on it, Wang.' She looked down at the body again. *Small man*, she thought, *thin, pale. Dead.*

Pursing her lips, she studied the face. She'd seen what odd tricks death, particularly violent death, could play with expressions, but she'd never seen anything like that wide, goggle-eyed grin. It made her shudder.

The waste, the pathetic waste of such a young life made her unbearably sad.

'Take him with you, Wang. Get me the reports. You can shoot his basic paperwork to the tele-link in my suite. I need the next of kin.'

'Assuredly.' He smiled at her. 'Lieutenant Roarke.'

She smiled back, showed her teeth, and decided she didn't want to play the name game. Standing, she put her hands on her hips as Wang directed his two assistants to transport the body.

'You find that amusing,' she muttered to Roarke.

He blinked, all innocence. 'What?'

'Lieutenant Roarke.'

Roarke touched her face because he needed to. 'Why not? Both of us could use some comic relief.'

'Yeah, your Dr Wang's a chuckle a minute.' She watched the doctor sail out in front of the dead boy on a gurney. 'It pisses me off. It fucking pisses me off.'

'It's not such a bad name.'

'No.' She nearly did laugh as she rubbed her hands over her face. 'Not that. The boy. A kid like that tossing out his next hundred years of life. That pisses me off.'

'I know.' He reached out to rub her shoulders. 'You're sure it was suicide?'

17

'No sign of struggle. No additional insults to the body.' She shrugged under his hands. 'I'll interview Carter and talk to some others, but the way I see it, Drew Mathias came home, turned on the lights, the music. He drank himself a couple beers, maybe took a VR trip, ate a few pretzels. Then he went in, stripped the sheets off his bed, made himself a rope, fashioned a very precise, professional noose.'

She turned away, scanning the room, letting the scene into her head. 'He took off his clothes, tossed them aside. He climbed up on the table. You can see the smears from his feet. He tied the rope to the light, probably gave it a good tug or two to make sure it was secure. Then he slipped his head into the noose, used the remote to raise the light, and choked himself to death.'

She picked up the remote she'd already bagged for evidence. 'It wouldn't have been quick. It's a slow ascent, not enough to give him a nice clean broken neck, but he didn't struggle, didn't change his mind. If he had, you'd see scrapes from his nails on his neck and throat from where he'd tried to claw free.'

Roarke's brow knit. 'But wouldn't it be instinctive, involuntary to do just that?'

'I don't know. I'd say it depended on how strong a will he had, how much he wanted to die. And why. Could have been cruising on drugs. We'll know that soon enough. The right mix of chemicals, the mind doesn't register pain. He might even have enjoyed it.'

'I won't deny there's some illegals floating around here. It's impossible to regulate and supervise every staff member's habits and personal choices.' Roarke shrugged, frowned up at the gorgeous blue chandelier. 'Mathias doesn't strike me as the type for a habitual, even an occasional user.'

'People are a constant surprise, and it's an unending wonder what they'll pump into their bloodstreams.' Eve jerked her own shoulders in turn. 'I'll give the place the standard toss for illegals, and I'll see what I can find out from Carter.' She dragged her hair back with a hand. 'Why don't you go back up, get some sleep?'

'No, I'll stay. Eve,' he said before she could argue, 'you deputized me.'

It made her smile a little. 'Any decent adjutant would know I need coffee to get through this.'

'Then I'll see that you get some.' He framed her face in his hands. 'I wanted you away from this for a while.' He let her go and walked into the adjoining kitchen to see about her coffee.

Eve stepped into the bedroom. The lights were low and Carter was sitting on the side of the bed, his head in his hands. He jerked straight when he heard her come in.

'Take it easy, Carter, you're not under arrest yet.' When his cheeks paled, she sat beside him. 'Sorry, bad cop humor. I'm recording this, okay?'

'Yeah.' He swallowed hard. 'Okay.'

'Dallas, Lieutenant Eve, interview with Carter – what's your full name, Carter?'

'Ah, Jack. Jack Carter.'

'Carter, Jack, regarding the unattended death of Mathias, Drew, Carter, you shared suite ten thirty-six with the deceased.'

'Yeah, for the past five months. We were friends.'

'Tell me about tonight. What time did you get home?'

'I don't know. About twelve thirty, I guess. I had a date. I've been seeing someone – Lisa Cardeaux – she's one of the landscape designers. We wanted to check out the entertainment complex. They were showing a new video. After that, we went to the Athena Club. It's open to the complex employees. We had a couple of drinks, listened to some music. She's got an early day tomorrow, so we didn't stay late. I took her home.' He smiled weakly. 'Tried to talk her into letting me come up, but she wasn't having any.'

19

'Okay, so you struck out with Lisa. Did you come straight home?'

'Yeah. She's just over at the staff bungalow. She likes it there. Doesn't want to close herself up in a hotel room. That's what she says. It only takes a couple minutes on the glide to get back here. I came up.' He drew a breath, rubbed a hand over his heart as if to calm it. 'Drew had the door secured. He had a thing about that. Some of the crew leave the locks off, but Drew had all that equipment, and he was paranoid about anybody messing with it.'

'Is the palm plate coded for anyone but the two of you?'

'No.'

'Okay, then what?'

'I saw him. Right away. That's when I went up to you.'

'All right. When's the last time you saw him alive?'

'This morning.' Carter rubbed his eyes, trying to visualize the normality of it. Light, food, mumbling conversation. 'We had some breakfast.'

'How was he? Upset, depressed?'

'No,' Carter's eyes focused then, and were for the first time animated. 'That's what I can't get through my head. He was fine. He was joking around, yanking my chain about Lisa because I haven't – you know – scored. We were needling each other, just friendly shit. I said he hadn't scored in so long he wouldn't know it if he did. And why didn't he get himself a woman and come along with us tonight to see how it was done.'

'Was he seeing anyone?'

'No. He always talked about this babe he was hung up on. She wasn't on the station. The babe. That's what he called her. He was going to use his next free cycle to pay her a visit. He said she had it all, brains, beauty, body, and a sex drive that wouldn't quit. Why should he play with lesser models when he had state of the art?'

'You don't know her name?'

20

'No. She was just The Babe. To be honest, I figure he made her up. Drew wasn't what you'd call babe material, you know. And he was shy around women and really into fantasy games and his autotronics. He was always working on something.'

'What about other friends?'

'He didn't have many. He was quiet around a lot of people, internal, you know?'

'He use chemicals, Carter?'

'Sure, your basic stimulant if he was pulling an all-nighter.'

'Illegals, Carter. Did he use?'

'Drew?' His tired eyes popped wide. 'No way. Absolutely no way. He was a total arrow, straight as they come. He wouldn't mess with illegals, Lieutenant. He had a good mind, and he wanted to keep it that way. And he wanted to keep his job, move up. You get tossed for that kind of shit. Only takes one time on a spot check.'

'Are you sure you'd have known if he decided to experiment?'

'You know someone you hang with for five months.' Carter's eyes went sad again. 'You get used to them – habits and everything. Like I said, he didn't hang with other people much. He was happier alone, fiddling with his equipment, diving into his role-playing programs.'

'A loner then, internal.'

'Yeah, that was his way. But he wasn't upset, he wasn't depressed. He kept saying that he was onto something big, some new toy. He was always onto a new toy,' Carter murmured. 'He said just last week that he was going to make a fortune this time, and give Roarke a run for his money.'

'Roarke?'

'He didn't mean anything by it,' Carter said quickly, defending the dead. 'You've got to understand, Roarke – to a lot of us – well, he's ice, you know? Solid ice. Rolling in credits, mag clothes, outstanding digs, power plus, sexy new wife—' He broke off, flushing. 'Excuse me.'

'No problem.' She'd decide later if she was amused or flabbergasted that a boy barely twenty considered her sexy.

'It's just that a lot of us techs – well, a lot of people altogether – sort of aspire. Roarke's like the epitome. Drew totally admired him. He had ambitions, Mrs – Lieutenant. He had goals and plans. Why would he do this?' Suddenly his eyes swam. 'Why would he do this?'

'I don't know, Carter. Sometimes you never know why.'

She led him back, guided him through, until she had a picture of Drew Mathias that gelled. An hour later, there was nothing left for her to do but put together a report for whoever would be transported in to close the case.

She leaned against the mirrored wall of the elevator as she and Roarke rode back to the penthouse. 'It was good thinking to put him in another room on another floor. He may sleep better tonight.'

'He'll sleep better if he takes the tranqs. How about you? Will you sleep?'

'Yeah. I'd turn it over easier if I had a glimmer of what was troubling him, what pushed him to it.' She stepped out into the corridor, waited while Roarke disengaged security to their suite. 'The picture I've got is of your average tech nerd with grand aspirations. Shy of women, into fantasy. Happy in his work.' She lifted her shoulders. 'There weren't any incoming or outgoing calls on his 'link, no E-mail sent or received, no messages recorded, and the security on the door was engaged at sixteen hundred hours by Mathias, disengaged at oh thirty-three by Carter. He didn't have any visitors, didn't go out. He just settled in for the evening, then hanged himself.'

'It's not a homicide.'

'No, it's not a homicide.' Did that make it better, she wondered, or worse? 'Nobody to blame, nobody to punish. Just a dead kid. A life wasted.' She turned to him suddenly, wrapped her arms tightly around him. 'Roarke, you changed my life.'

22

Surprised, he tipped up her face. Her eyes weren't wet, but dry and fierce and angry. 'What's this?'

'You changed my life,' she said again. 'At least part of it. I'm beginning to see it's the best part of it. I want you to know that. I want you to remember that when we get back and things settle into routine, if I forget to let you know what I feel or what I think or how much you mean to me.'

Touched, he pressed his curved lips to her brow. 'I won't let you forget. Come to bed. You're tired.'

'Yeah, I am.' She skimmed her hair back from her face as they started toward the bedroom. Less than forty-eight hours left, she remembered. She wouldn't let useless death mar the last hours of their honeymoon.

She angled her head, fluttered her lashes. 'You know, Carter thinks I'm sexy.'

Roarke stopped. He narrowed his eyes. 'I beg your pardon?'

Oh, she loved it when that lilting Irish voice turned arrogant. 'You're ice,' she continued, circling her head on her tensed shoulders as she unbuttoned her shirt.

'Am I? Am I really?'

'Solid ice, which is, as Mavis would say, mag. And part of the reason you're ice, in case you're wondering, is because you have a sexy new wife.'

Naked to the waist, she sat on the bed and tugged off her shoes. She flicked a glance over at him and saw that he'd tucked his hands in his pockets and was grinning. Her lips curved as well. It felt very good to smile.

'So, ice man' – she cocked her head, lifted a brow – 'what are you going to do about your sexy new wife?'

Roarke ran his tongue over his teeth, then stepped forward. 'Why don't I demonstrate?'

She thought it would be better, facing the trip back, being flung through space like a kid's ray ball. She was wrong.

Eve argued, using what she considered very logical reasons why she shouldn't get into Roarke's private transport.

'I don't want to die.'

He laughed at her, which had her eyes kindling, then he simply scooped her up and carried her on board. 'I'm not staying.' Her heart jittered into her chest as he stepped into the plush cabin. 'I mean it. You'll have to knock me out to get me to stay on this flying death trap.'

'Mmm-hmm.' He chose a wide, scoop-shaped chair in buttery black leather, kept her in his lap and, moving quickly, strapped her in, trapping her arms to limit any possible reprisals.

'Hey. Stop it.' Panicked, she struggled, wiggled, swore. 'Let me out. Let me off.'

Her snug butt jiggling on his lap gave him a solid clue as to how he intended to spend the initial hours of the trip. 'Take off as soon as you have clearance,' Roarke ordered the pilot, then smiled at the flight attendant. 'We won't need you for a while,' he told her and engaged the locks on the cabin doors the moment she made a discreet exit.

'I'm going to hurt you,' Eve promised. When she heard the hum of engines gearing up, felt the faint vibration under her feet that signaled imminent takeoff, she seriously considered gnawing at the safety harness with her teeth. 'I'm not doing this,' she said definitely. 'I am not doing this. Tell him to abort.'

'Too late.' He wrapped his arms around her, nuzzled her neck. 'Relax, Eve. Trust me. You're safer here than you are driving through midtown.'

'Bullshit. Oh Christ.' She squeezed her eyes tight as the engine let out a powerful roar. The shuttle seemed to shoot straight up, leaving her stomach flopping on the ground below. The g's slapped her back, plastering her against Roarke.

She was barely breathing by the time the ride smoothed out and she discovered that the pressure in her chest was caused by the fact that she was holding her breath. She let it out in a whoosh, then sucked in air like a diver surfacing from a great depth.

She was still alive, she told herself. And that was something. Now, she would have to kill him. It was then she realized that not only was she unstrapped, but her shirt was unbuttoned and his hands were on her breasts.

'If you think we're going to have sex after you—'

He merely swiveled her to face him. She caught the glint of humor and lust in his eyes just before his mouth closed cagily over her breast.

'You bastard.' But she laughed as pleasure speared into her, and she cupped her hands behind his head to urge him on.

She'd never take for granted what he could do to her, do for her. Those wild floods of pleasure, the slow, thrilling glide of it. She rocked against him, let herself forget everything but the way his teeth nipped, his tongue licked.

So it was she who pulled him onto the thick, soft carpet, she who dragged his mouth to hers. 'Inside me.' She tugged at his shirt, wanting that hard, muscled flesh under her hands. 'I want you inside me.'

'We have hours yet.' He dipped to her breasts again, so small, so firm, already warm from his hands. 'I need to taste you.'

He did, lavishly. The subtle variety of flavors, from mouth to throat, from throat to shoulder, shoulder to breast. He sampled with tenderness, with finesse, with a quiet concentration focused on mutual pleasure.

He felt her begin to tremble under his hands and mouth.

Her skin grew damp as he roamed to her belly, easing her slacks down, nibbling his way between her thighs. His tongue flicked there, making her moan. Her hips arched for him even as he cupped them, lifted them, opened her. When

25

his tongue slid lazily into the heat, he felt the first orgasm rip through her.

'More.' Greedy now, he devoured. She would let go for him as she had for no one else, he knew. She would lose herself in what they made together.

When she was shuddering, when her hands lay limp on the carpet, he slid up her body, slipped into her. Mated.

Her eyes fluttered open, met his. Concentration was what she saw there. Absolute control. She wanted, needed to destroy it, to know she could, as he could destroy her.

'More,' she insisted, hooking her legs around his waist to take him deeper. She saw the flicker in his eyes, the deep, dark need that lived inside him and, pulling his mouth to hers, scraping her teeth over those beautifully formed lips, she moved under him.

He fisted his hands in her hair, his breath quickening as he rammed himself into her, harder, faster, until he thought his heart would burst from the ferocity of it. She matched him, beat for beat, thrust for thrust, those short, unpainted nails digging into his back, his shoulders, his hips. Delicious little bites of pain.

He felt her come again, the violent contraction of her muscles fisting over him like glory. *Again*, was all he could think. *Again and again and again*, as he hammered into her, swallowing her gasps and moans, shuddering from the thrilling sound of flesh slapping wetly against flesh.

He felt her body tense again, revving toward peak. As that long, low, throaty moan slipped through her lips, he pressed his face into her hair, and with one final thrust, he emptied himself.

He collapsed onto her, his mind fuzzed, his heart thundering. She was limp as water beneath him but for the rage of her heart against his.

'We can't keep this up,' she managed after a moment. 'We'll kill each other.'

He managed a wheezing laugh. 'We'll die well, in any case. I had intended a bit more romance – some wine and music to cap off the honeymoon.' He lifted his head, smiled down at her. 'But this worked, too.'

'It doesn't mean I'm not still pissed off at you.'

'Naturally. We've had some of our best sex when you're pissed off at me.' He caught her chin between his teeth, flicked his tongue along the slight dent in the center. 'I adore you, Eve.'

While she was adjusting to that, as she always did, he rolled off, got lightly to his feet, and walked naked to a mirrored console between two chairs. He laid his palm on it, and a door slid open. 'I have something for you.'

She eyed the velvet box with suspicion. 'You don't have to get me presents. You know I don't want you to.'

'Yes. It makes you uncomfortable and uneasy.' He grinned. 'Perhaps that's why I do it.' He sat beside her on the floor, handed her the box. 'Open it.'

She imagined it would be jewelry. He seemed to thrive on giving her body decorations: diamonds, emeralds, ropes of gold that left her stunned and feeling awkward. But when she opened it, she saw only a simple white blossom.

'It's a flower?'

'From your wedding bouquet. I had it treated.'

'A petunia.' She found herself sentimentally teary-eyed as she picked it out of the box. Simple, basic, ordinary, one that might grow in any garden. The petals felt soft, dewy, and fresh.

'It's a new process one of my companies has been working on. It preserves without changing the basic texture. I wanted you to have it.' He closed a hand over hers. 'I wanted both of us to have it, so we could be reminded that some things last.'

She raised her eyes to his. They had both come from misery, she thought, and survived it. They had been drawn together through violence and tragedy, and had overcome

27

it. They walked different paths and had found a mutual route.

*Some things last*, she thought. *Some ordinary things. Like love.*

# Chapter Three

Three weeks hadn't changed Cop Central. The coffee was still poisonous, the noise abominable, and the view out of her stingy window was still miserable.

She was thrilled to be back.

The cops in her unit had arranged for a message to await her. Since it was blinking slyly on her monitor when she walked in, she figured she had her old pal Feeney, the electronics whiz, to thank for bypassing her code.

> WELCOME BACK, LIEUTENANT LOVEJOY
> Hubba-hubba

*Hubba-hubba?* She snorted out a laugh. Sophomoric humor, maybe, but it made her feel at home.

She glanced over the mess on her desk. She hadn't had time to clear anything up between the unexpected closing of a case during her bachelor party and her wedding day. But she noted the neatly sealed disc, competently labeled, sitting atop her stack of old work.

That would be Peabody's doing, Eve concluded. Sliding the disc into her desk unit, she cursed once and slapped the drive to cure the razzing hiccups it emitted, and saw that the ever-reliable Peabody had indeed written the arrest report, filed it, and logged it.

It couldn't, Eve mused, have been easy on her. Not when she'd been sharing a bed with the accused.

Eve glanced at the old work again, grimaced. She could see she had court dates stuffed and layered together over the next few days. The schedule juggling she'd had to do to accommodate Roarke's demand for three weeks away had had a price. It was time to pay up.

Well, he'd done plenty of juggling as well, she reminded herself. And now it was back to work and reality. Rather than review the cases she would soon give testimony for, she bumped up her 'link and put out a search for Officer Peabody.

The familiar, serious face with its dark helmet of hair fizzed onto her monitor. 'Sir. Welcome back.'

'Thank you, Peabody. My office, please. ASAP.'

Without waiting for a reply, Eve switched off the unit and smiled to herself. She'd seen to it that Peabody had been transferred to the homicide division. Now she intended to take it a bit further. She engaged the 'link again.

'Lieutenant Dallas. Is the commander free?'

'Lieutenant.' The commander's secretary beamed at her. 'How was your honeymoon?'

'It was very nice.' She felt a quick flush of heat at the gleam in the woman's eye. Hubba-hubba had amused her. This dreamy look made her want to squirm. 'Thank you.'

'You were a lovely bride, Lieutenant. I saw the pictures and there were several news runs on the event and the gossip channels were full of it. We saw clips of you in Paris, too. It looked so romantic.'

'Yeah.' *The price of fame*, Eve thought. *And Roarke*. 'It was . . . nice. Ah, the commander?'

'Oh, of course. One moment please.'

As the unit buzzed, Eve rolled her eyes. She could accept being in the spotlight, but she was never going to enjoy it.

'Dallas.' Commander Whitney's grin was an acre wide, and he had an odd look on his hard, dark face. 'You look . . . well.'

'Thank you, sir.'

'You enjoyed your honeymoon?'

Christ, she thought, when was someone going to ask if she'd enjoyed being fucked around the world and into outer space? 'Yes, sir. Thank you. I assume you've already read Officer Peabody's report on the closing of the Pandora case.'

'Yes, very complete. The PA is going for the maximum on Casto. You ran a close one there, Lieutenant.'

She was very well aware how close she'd come to not only missing her wedding day, but the rest of her life. 'It stings when it's another cop,' she said. 'I was rushed, sir, and only had time to give you my recommendation for Peabody's transferral, permanently, to my unit. Her assistance, in this matter and others, has been invaluable.'

'She's a good cop,' Whitney agreed.

'I agree. I have a request, Commander.'

Five minutes later, when Peabody stepped into her crammed office, Eve was tipped back in her chair, scanning the data on her monitor. 'I've got court in an hour,' Eve said without preliminary. 'On the Salvatori case. What do you know about that, Peabody?'

'Vito Salvatori is being tried for multiple murder, with the added circumstance of torture. He is an alleged distributor of illegal substances and stands accused of the murder of three other known dealers of Zeus and TRL. The victims were burned alive in a small rooming house on the Lower East Side last winter – after their eyes and tongues were cut out. You were primary.'

Peabody recited the data matter-of-factly while she stood at attention in her shipshape uniform.

'Very good, Officer. Did you read my arrest report on the case?'

'Yes, Lieutenant, I did.'

Eve nodded. An airbus boomed by the window, spewing noise and displacing air. 'Then you know that before I restrained Salvatori, I broke his left arm at the elbow, his jaw, and relieved him of several teeth. His lawyers are going to try to fry me for excessive force.'

'They'll have a rough time of that, sir, as he was trying to burn down the building around you when you cornered him. If you hadn't restrained him in whatever manner was possible, *he'd* have been fried. So to speak.'

'Okay, Peabody. I've got this and several others to go over before the week's up. I need all the cases on my court schedule downloaded and condensed. You can meet me with the requested data in thirty minutes, east exit.'

'Sir. I'm on assignment. Detective Crouch has me chasing down vehicle registrations.' Only the faintest sneer in her voice indicated Peabody's feeling about Crouch and the garbage assignment.

'I'll handle Crouch. The commander's cleared my request. You're assigned to me. So pass off whatever grunt work that's been dumped on you and get your ass in gear.'

Peabody blinked. 'Assigned to you, sir?'

'Your hearing go bad while I was away?'

'No, sir, but—'

'Have you got a thing for Crouch?' It delighted Eve to see Peabody's serious mouth drop open.

'Are you kidding? He's—' She caught herself, stiffened up. 'He's hardly my type, Lieutenant. I believe I've learned my lesson about romantic attachments on the job.'

'Don't beat yourself up over that one, Peabody. I liked Casto, too. You did a hell of a job on that one.'

It helped to hear it, but the wound was still raw. 'Thank you, Lieutenant.'

'Which is why you are now assigned to me as my permanent aide. You want a detective shield, Officer?'

Peabody knew what she was being given: the opportunity, the gift out of nowhere. She closed her eyes a moment until she had her voice under control. 'Yes, sir, I do.'

'Good. You'll work your ass off for it. Get the data I requested, and let's move.'

'Right away.' At the door, Peabody paused, turned back. 'I'm very grateful for the chance you're giving me.'

'Don't be. You earned it. And if you screw up, I'll bust you down to traffic.' Eve smiled thinly. 'Air traffic.'

Court testimony was part of the job, and so, Eve reminded herself, were high-class weasels like S. T. Fitzhugh, attorney for the defense. He was slick and he was savvy, a man who defended the lowest of lowlifes – as long as their credits held out. His success in assisting drug lords, murderers, and molesters into slithering out of the grip of the law was such that he could easily afford the cream-colored suits and hand-tooled shoes he affected.

He made a dashing figure in the courtroom, his melted-chocolate skin a fine contrast to the soft colors and fabrics he habitually wore. His long, aesthetic face was smooth as the silk of his jacket, thanks to the three-times-weekly treatments at Adonis, the city's top enhancement salon for men. His figure was trim – narrow at the hips, broad at the shoulders – and his voice was the deep, rich baritone of an opera singer.

He courted the press, socialized with the criminal elite, owned his own Jet Star.

It was one of Eve's small pleasures to despise him.

'Let me try to get a clear picture, Lieutenant.' Fitzhugh lifted his hands, bringing his thumbs together to form a bracket. 'A clear picture of the circumstances that led to you attacking my client in his place of business.'

The prosecuting attorney objected. Fitzhugh graciously rephrased. 'You did, Lieutenant Dallas, cause my client great bodily harm on the night in question.'

He glanced back at Salvatori, who had costumed himself for the occasion in a simple black suit. Following his attorney's advice, he had skipped his last three months of cosmetic and

33

youth restoration treatments. There was gray in his hair, a sag to his face and body. He looked old, defenseless.

The jury would make the comparison, Eve imagined, between the young, fit cop and the delicate old man.

'Mr Salvatori resisted arrest and attempted to ignite an accelerant. It was necessary to restrain him.'

'To restrain him?' Slowly, Fitzhugh walked back, passing the recorder droid, moving down the jury box, drawing one of the six automated cameras with him as he laid a supporting hand on Salvatori's thin shoulder. 'You had to restrain him, and that restraint resulted in a fractured jaw and a shattered arm.'

Eve flicked a glance toward the jury. Several members of the panel were looking entirely too sympathetic. 'That's correct. Mr Salvatori refused my request to exit the building – and to put down the cleaver and acetylene torch in his possession.'

'You were armed, Lieutenant?'

'I was.'

'And you carry the standard weapon issued to members of the NYPSD?'

'I do.'

'If, as you claim, Mr Salvatori was armed and resisting, why did you fail to administer the accepted stun?'

'I missed. Mr Salvatori was feeling pretty spry that night.'

'I see. In your ten years on the police force, Lieutenant, how many times have you found it necessary to employ maximum force? To terminate?'

Eve ignored the jitter in her stomach. 'Three times.'

'Three?' Fitzhugh let the word hang, let the jury study the woman in the witness chair. A woman who had killed. 'Isn't that a rather high ratio? Wouldn't you say that percentage indicates a predilection for violence?'

The PA surged to his feet, objecting bitterly, going into the standard line that the witness was not on trial. But of course she was, Eve thought. Cops were always on trial.

'Mr Salvatori was armed,' Eve began coolly. 'I had a

warrant for his arrest in the torture murders of three people. The three people whose eyes and tongues were cut out before they were set on fire and for which crime Mr Salvatori now stands accused in this courtroom. He refused to cooperate by flinging a cleaver at my head, which threw my aim off. He then charged, knocking me to the ground. I believe his words were, "I'm going to cut out your cop-bitch heart," at which time we engaged in hand to hand. At that time I broke his jaw, knocked out several of his teeth, and when he swung the torch in my direction, I broke his goddamn arm.'

'And you enjoyed that, Lieutenant?'

She met Fitzhugh's eyes straight on. 'No, sir, I didn't. But I enjoyed staying alive.'

'Slime,' Eve muttered as she climbed into her vehicle.

'He won't get Salvatori off.' Peabody settled in and, to take the edge off the furnace heat trapped inside, fiddled with the temperature control unit. 'The evidence is too clear cut. And you didn't let him shake you.'

'Yes, I did.' Eve scooped a hand through her hair, then headed into late-afternoon midtown traffic. The streets were choked enough to make her grit her teeth, but overhead, the sky was crisscrossed with airbuses, tourist vans, and midday commuters. 'We limp along, getting pricks like Salvatori off the street, and men like Fitzhugh make fortunes slipping them back out.' She jerked a shoulder. 'Sometimes it pisses me off.'

'Whoever slips them back out, we still limp along and slap them back in again.'

With a half laugh, Eve glanced at her companion. 'You're an optimist, Peabody. I wonder how long that'll last. I'm going to make a detour before we log back on,' she said, changing direction on impulse. 'I want to get the air of that courtroom out of my lungs.'

'Lieutenant? You didn't need me in court today. Why was I there?'

35

'If you're going after that detective shield, Peabody, you need to see what you're up against. It's not just killers and thieves and chemi-heads. It's the lawyers.'

It didn't surprise her to find the streets clogged and parking nonexistent. Philosophically, Eve nosed into an illegal zone, flipped the on-duty light on.

As she stepped out of the car, she gave a hustler on a glide-board a mild stare. He grinned, winked cheekily, then zoomed away toward more conducive surroundings.

'This area's loaded with hustlers and dealers and off-license hookers,' Eve said conversationally. 'That's why I love it.' She opened the door to the Down and Dirty Club, stepped inside to air thick with the sour smells of cheap liquor and bad food.

Privacy rooms lining one wall were open, airing out the musky stink of stale sex.

It was a joint – one that enjoyed being seamy and just skirted the edge of health and decency laws. A holographic band had the stage and was playing listlessly for the smattering of disinterested customers.

Mavis Freestone was in an isolation booth in the back, her hair a purple fountain, two scraps of glowing silver cloth strategically draped over her small, sassy body. The way her mouth was moving, her hips swiveling, Eve was certain she was rehearsing one of her more interesting vocals.

Eve stepped up to the glass, waiting until Mavis's rolling eyes circled around and landed on her. Mavis's mouth, the same searing purple as her hair, rounded into a huge circle of delight. She did a fast boogie, then shoved the door open. An ear-shattering blast of screaming guitars burst out of the booth with her.

Mavis launched herself into Eve's arms, and though she was shouting, Eve caught only every other word over the thundering music.

'What?' Laughing, Eve slammed the door shut, shook the echo out of her head. 'Christ, Mavis, what was that?'

'My new number. It's going to knock them unconscious.'

'I believe it.'

'You're back.' Mavis gave Eve two smacking and unavoidable kisses. 'Let's sit down. Let's have a drink. Tell me every detail. Leave nothing out. Hey, Peabody. Man, aren't you steaming in that uniform?'

She dragged Eve to a sticky table, punched up the menu. 'What do you want? It's on me. Crack pays me pretty solid for the couple gigs a week I do here. He's going to be dredged that he missed you. Oh, I'm so glad to see you. You look terrific. You look happy. Doesn't she look terrific, Peabody? Sex is so, like, therapeutic, right?'

Eve laughed again, knowing she'd come just for this. Mindless entertainment. 'Just a couple of fizz waters, Mavis. We're on duty.'

'Oh, like somebody in here's going to report you. Unbutton that uniform some, Peabody. I'm getting hot just looking at you. How was Paris? How was the island? How was the resort? Did he fuck your brains out everywhere?'

'Beautiful, wonderful, interesting, and yeah, he did. How's Leonardo?'

Mavis's eyes went dreamy. She smiled and poked a silver-tipped nail onto the menu board. 'He's terrific. Cohabitating's better than I thought it would be. He designed this costume for me.'

Eve studied the thin silver straps that almost covered Mavis's tidy apple breasts. 'Is that what you call it?'

'I've got this new number, see. Oh, I've got so much to tell you.' She snagged the fizz water when it plopped through the slot. 'I don't know where to start. There's this guy, this music engineer. I'm working with him. We're doing a disc, Eve – full treatment. He's sure he can peddle it. He's great, Jess Barrow. He was blazing a couple years back with his own stuff. Maybe you heard of him.'

'No.' Eve knew that, for a woman who'd lived on the streets

37

a large portion of her life, Mavis remained stunningly naive about certain matters. 'How much are you paying him?'

'It's not like that.' Mavis's lips moved into a pout. 'I've got to dish up the recording fee, sure. That's the way it works; and if we hit, he takes sixty percent for the first three years. After that we renegotiate.'

'I've heard of him,' Peabody commented. She'd unfastened her collar button – a tribute to her fondness for Mavis. 'He had a couple of major hits a couple years ago, and he was hooked up with Cassandra.' At Eve's arched brow, she shrugged. 'The singer, you know.'

'You a music lover, Peabody? You never fail to amaze me.'

'I like to listen to tunes,' Peabody muttered into her bubbly water. 'Like anyone.'

'Well, the Cassandra connection's dumped,' Mavis said cheerfully. 'He's been looking for a new vocalist. And that's me.'

Eve wondered what else he might be looking for. 'What does Leonardo think?'

'He thinks it's mag. You've got to come to the studio, Eve, catch us in action. Jess is a certified genius.'

She intended to catch them in action. The list of people Eve loved was very short. And Mavis was on it.

She waited until she was back in the car with Peabody, heading to Cop Central. 'Run a make on Jess Barrow, Peabody.'

Without surprise, Peabody took out her diary, plugged in the order. 'Mavis isn't going to like that.'

'She doesn't have to know, does she.'

Eve veered around a glide-cart offering frozen fruit on a stick, then swung onto Tenth where automated jackhammers were tearing up the street again. Overhead, an ad blimp hawked a shoppers' special at Bloomingdale's. Preseason sale on winter coats in the men's, women's, and unisex department, twenty percent off. Such a deal.

38

She spotted the man in the trench coat shambling toward a trio of girls and sighed.

'Shit. There's Clevis.'

'Clevis?'

'This is his turf,' Eve said simply as she pulled into a loading zone. 'I used to do this drag when I was in uniform. He's been around for years. Come on, Peabody, let's spare the little children.'

She stepped onto the sidewalk, skirting a pair of men arguing over baseball. From the smell of them, she judged they'd been standing in the heat arguing for much too long. She shouted once, but the jackhammers swallowed her voice. Resigned, she picked up her pace and intercepted Clevis before he reached the unsuspecting, pink-cheeked girls.

'Hey, Clevis.'

He blinked at her through the pale lenses of sunscreens. His hair was sandy blond and curly around a face as innocent as a cherub's. He was eighty, if he was a day. 'Dallas. Hey, Dallas. I haven't seen you in a big blue moon.' He flashed big white teeth as he sized up Peabody. 'Who's this?'

'Peabody, this is Clevis. Clevis, you aren't going to bother those little girls, are you?'

'No, shit, uh-uh. I wasn't going to bother them.' He wiggled his brows. 'I was just going to show 'em, is all.'

'You don't want to do that, Clevis. You ought to get inside, out of this heat.'

'I like it hot.' He wheezed out a chuckle. 'There they go,' he said with a sigh, as the trio of girls ran laughing across the street. 'Guess I won't be able to show 'em today. I'll show you.'

'Clevis, don't—' Then Eve huffed out a breath. He'd already pulled his trench coat apart. Under it, he was naked but for a bright blue bow tied celebrationally around his withered cock. 'Very nice, Clevis. That's a good color for you. Matches your

39

eyes.' She put a companionable hand on his shoulder. 'Let's take a ride, okay?'

'Okeedokee. Do you like blue, Peabody?'

Peabody nodded solemnly as she opened the back door of the unit, helped him inside. 'Blue's my favorite color.' She shut the door of the vehicle, met Eve's laughing eyes. 'Welcome back, Lieutenant.'

'It's good to be back, Peabody. All in all, it's good to be back.'

It was also good to be home. Eve drove through the high, iron gates that guarded the towering fortress. It was less of a shock now, to glide along the curving drive through those well-tended lawns and flowering trees toward the elegant stone and glass house where she now lived.

The contrast of where she worked and where she lived no longer seemed quite so jarring. It was quiet here – the kind of quiet in a massive city only the very rich could afford. She could hear birdsong, see the sky, smell the sweet aroma of freshly shorn grass. Minutes away, only minutes, was the teeming, noisy, sweating mass of New York.

Here, she supposed, was sanctuary. As much for Roarke as for herself.

Two lost souls. He'd once called them that. She wondered if they'd stopped being lost when they'd found each other.

She left her car at the front entrance, knowing its battered body and tasteless shape would offend Summerset, Roarke's poker-backed butler. It was a simple matter to switch it to automatic, send it around the house and into the slot reserved for her unit in the garage, but she enjoyed her petty needling when it came to Summerset.

She opened the door and found him standing in the grand foyer with a sniff in his nose and a sneer on his lips.

'Lieutenant, your vehicle is unsightly.'

'Hey, it's city property.' She reached down to pick up the

40

fat, odd-eyed cat who'd come to greet her. 'You don't want it there, move it yourself.'

She heard a trill of laughter float down the hall, lifted a brow. 'Company?'

'Indeed.' With his disapproving eye, Summerset scanned her wilted shirt and slacks, skimmed over the weapon harness still strapped to her side. 'I suggest you bathe and change before meeting your guests.'

'I suggest you kiss my ass,' she said cheerfully and strolled by him.

In the main salon, filled with treasures Roarke had collected from around the known universe, an elegant, intimate party was happening. Glossy canapés sat elegantly on silver trays, pale gold wine filled sparkling crystal. Roarke was a dark angel in what he would have seen as casual attire. The black silk shirt open at the collar, the perfectly draped black trousers cinched with a belt gleaming silver at the buckle suited him perfectly, made him look exactly as he was: rich, gorgeous, dangerous.

Only one couple joined him in the spacious room. The man was as bright as Roarke was dark. Long golden hair flowed over the shoulders of a snug blue jacket. The face was square and handsome with lips just slightly too thin, but the contrast of his dark brown eyes kept the observer from noticing.

The woman was stunning. A sweep of deep red hair the color of rich wine was scooped up into curls that tumbled flirtatiously down the nape of her neck. Her eyes were green, sharp as a cat's, and over them were shapely brows as black as ink. She had skin like alabaster creamed over high cheek-bones and a sensually generous mouth.

Her body matched it and was currently poured into a clinging column of emerald that left strong shoulders bare and dipped between her staggering breasts to the waist.

'Roarke.' She let out that fluid laugh again, slid one slim white hand into Roarke's mane of hair and kissed him silkily. 'I have missed you dreadfully.'

41

Eve thought about the weapon strapped to her side and how, on even its lowest setting, it would send the bombshell redhead into a jittery dance. *Just a passing thought*, Eve assured herself, and set Galahad the cat down before she squeezed through the layers of fat and cracked one of his ribs.

'You didn't miss him that time,' Eve said casually as she stepped inside. Roarke, damn him, glanced over and grinned at her.

*We'll just have to wipe that smug look off your face, pal*, she thought. *Real soon.*

'Eve, we didn't hear you come in.'

'Obviously.' She snagged an unidentifiable canapé from the tray and stuffed it into her mouth.

'I don't believe you've met our guests. Reeanna Ott, William Shaffer, my wife, Eve Dallas.'

'Watch yourself, Ree, she's armed.' With a chuckle, William crossed over to extend a hand. He moved in a lope, like a thin horse going out to pasture. 'A pleasure to meet you, Eve. A genuine pleasure. Ree and I were so disappointed we were unable to attend your wedding.'

'Devastated.' Reeanna smiled at Eve, her green eyes sparkling. 'William and I were desperate to meet, face to face, the woman who brought Roarke to his knees.'

'He's still standing.' Eve flicked Roarke a glance as he handed her a glass of wine. 'For now.'

'Ree and William were in the lab on Tarus Three, working on some projects for me. They've just gotten back on planet for some well deserved R and R.'

'Oh?' Like she gave a rat's skinny ass.

'The on-the-board project's been a particular pleasure,' William said. 'Within a year, two at most, Roarke Industries will introduce new technology that will revolutionize the entertainment and amusement world.'

'Entertainment and amusement.' Eve smiled thinly. 'Well, that's earth shattering.'

'Actually, it has the potential to be just that.' Reeanna sipped her wine and sized Eve up: attractive, irritated, competent. Tough. 'There are potential medical breakthroughs as well.'

'That's Ree's end.' William lifted his glass to her with easy, intimate affection in his eyes. 'She's the med expert. I'm just a fun guy.'

'I'm sure, after putting in a long day, Eve doesn't want to hear us talk shop. Scientists,' Reeanna said with an apologetic smile. 'We're so tedious. You're just back from Olympus.' Silk whispered as Reeanna shifted that staggering body. 'William and I were part of the team that designed the amusement and medical centers there. Did you have time to tour them?'

'Briefly.' She was being rude, Eve reminded herself. She would have to become accustomed to coming home and finding elegant company, to seeing gorgeous women drool over her husband. 'Very impressive, even at midconstruction stage. The medical facility will be more so when it's staffed. Was the hologram room in the main hotel yours?' Eve asked William.

'Guilty,' he said with a sparkle. 'I love to play. Do you?'

'Eve considers it work. As it happens, we had an incident while we were there,' Roarke put in. 'A suicide. One of the autotronic techs. Mathias?'

William's brow furrowed. 'Mathias . . . young, red hair, freckles?'

'Yes.'

'Good God.' He shuddered, drank deeply. 'Suicide? Are you sure it wasn't an accident? My recollection is of an enthusiastic young man with big ideas. Not one who'd take his own life.'

'That's what he did,' Eve said shortly. 'He hanged himself.'

'How horrible.' Pale now, Reeanna sat on the arm of a couch. 'Did I know him, William?'

'I don't think so. You might have seen him at one of the clubs while we were there, but I don't remember him as much of a socializer.'

43

'I'm terribly sorry, in any case,' Reeanna said. 'And how awful for you to deal with such a tragedy on your honeymoon. Let's not dwell on it.' Galahad leaped onto the couch, skimmed his head under Reeanna's elegant hand. 'I'd so much rather hear about the wedding we missed.'

'Stay for dinner.' Roarke gave Eve's arm an apologetic squeeze. 'We'll bore you to tears with it.'

'I wish we could.' William offered Reeanna's shoulder the same smooth stroke as she gave the cat's head. 'We're due at the theater. We're already late.'

'You're right, as always.' With obvious regret, Reeanna rose. 'I hope you'll give us a rain check. We'll be on planet for the next month or two, and I'd so love the opportunity to get to know you, Eve. Roarke and I go back . . . a long way.'

'You're welcome any time. And I'll see you both in the office tomorrow, for a full report.'

'Bright and early.' Reeanna set her glass aside. 'Perhaps we can have lunch someday soon, Eve. Just females.' Her eyes twinkled with such easy humor that Eve felt foolish. 'We can compare notes on Roarke.'

The invitation was too friendly to give offense. Eve found herself smiling. 'That should be interesting.' She walked them to the door with Roarke, waved them off. 'Just how many notes,' she said as she stepped back, 'would there be to compare?'

'It was a long time ago.' He snagged her by the waist for a delayed welcome-home kiss. 'Years. Eons.'

'She probably bought that body.'

'I'd have to term it an excellent investment.'

Eve lifted her chin to eye him sourly. 'Is there any beautiful woman who hasn't bounced on your bed?'

Roarke cocked his head, narrowed his eyes in consideration. 'No.' He laughed when she took a swing at him. 'You didn't mean that, or you'd have hit me.' Then he grunted when her fist plowed into his gut. He rubbed it, grateful she'd pulled the punch. 'I should have quit while I was ahead.'

'Let that be a lesson to you, lover boy.' But Eve let him sweep her off her feet and over his shoulder.

'Hungry?' he asked her.

'Starving.'

'Me, too.' He started up the stairs. 'Let's eat in bed.'

# Chapter Four

Eve awoke with the cat stretched over her chest and the bedside 'link beeping. Dawn was just breaking. The light through the sky window was thin and gray from the storm rolling in with morning. With her eyes half closed, she reached out to answer.

'Block video,' she ordered, clearing sleep from her voice. 'Dallas.'

'Dispatch, Dallas, Lieutenant Eve. Suspicious death, Five oh oh two Madison Avenue, Unit Thirty-eight hundred. See resident Foxx, Arthur. Code four.'

'Dispatch, received. Contact Peabody, Officer Delia, to assist. My authorization.'

'Confirmed. Transmission terminated.'

'Code four?' Roarke had shifted the cat and was sitting up in bed, lazily stroking Galahad into feline ecstasy.

'It means I have time for a shower and coffee.' Eve didn't spot a robe handy, so she walked toward the bathroom naked. 'There's a uniform on the scene,' she called out. She stepped into the shower unit, rubbing her gritty eyes. 'Full power all jets, one hundred two degrees.'

'You'll boil.'

'I like to boil.' She let out an enormous sigh of pleasure as pulsing jets of steamy water battered her from all sides. Tapping a glass block, she dispensed a palm full of dark green liquid soap. By the time she stepped out of the shower, she was awake.

Her brow lifted as she saw Roarke standing in the doorway, holding a cup of coffee. 'For me?'

'Part of the service.'

'Thanks.' She took the cup into the drying tube, sipping while warm air swirled around her. 'What were you doing, watching me shower?'

'I like to watch you. Something about long, lean women when they're wet and naked.' He stepped into the shower himself and called for sixty-eight degrees.

It made Eve shiver. She couldn't understand why a man with all the luxuries in the world at his fingertips would actually choose cold showers. She opened the drying tube and combed her fingers through her unstyled cap of hair. She used some of the face glop that Mavis was always pushing at her, brushed her teeth.

'You don't have to get up because I am.'

'I'm up,' Roarke said simply and chose a heated towel rather than the drying tube. 'Do you have time for breakfast?'

Eve watched his reflection in the mirror: gleaming hair, gleaming skin. 'I'll catch something later.'

He hooked the towel around his waist, shook back his dripping mane of hair, cocked his head. 'Yeah?'

'I guess I like looking at you, too,' she muttered and went into the bedroom to dress for death.

Street traffic was light. Airbuses rumbled overhead through the sizzling rain, carting night shift workers home, dragging day shifters to work. Billboards were quiet and the ubiquitous glida grills and carts with their offerings of food and drink were already setting up for the day. Smoke billowed through the vents in streets and sidewalks from the underground world of transportation and retail. The air steamed.

Eve headed across town, making good time.

The section of Madison where a body waited for her was pocked with exclusive boutiques and silvery spears of buildings fashioned to house those who could afford to shop there. The skywalks were glassed in to separate the clientele from the elements and from the noise that would begin to boom within an hour or two.

Eve passed a taxi with a lone passenger. The elegant blonde wore a glittery jacket, a sparkling rainbow of color in the dingy light. *Licensed companion*, Eve mused, *heading home after an all-nighter*. The wealthy could afford to buy fancy sex along with their fancy clothes.

Eve swung into an underground garage at the scene, flashed her badge for the security post. It scanned it, scanned her, then the light blinked from red to green and flashed the number of the empty space assigned to her.

It was, of course, at the far end of the facility from the elevator. *Cops*, she thought with resignation as she hoofed it, *aren't given optimum spaces*.

Eve recited the number of the unit into the speaker box and was whisked up.

There had been a time, not so long before, when she would have been impressed with the sumptuous foyer on the thirty-eighth floor, with its pool of scarlet hibiscus and bronze statuary. That was before she'd entered Roarke's world. She scanned the small, tinkling fountains flanking the entrance and realized that it was highly possible that her husband owned the building.

She spotted the uniform guarding the door of 3800, flipped up her badge.

'Lieutenant.' The cop shifted subtly to attention, sucking in her stomach. 'My partner's inside with the deceased's housemate. Mr Foxx, on discovering his companion's body, called for an ambulance. We responded in addition, as per procedure. The ambulance is on hold, sir, until you clear the scene.'

'Is it secured?'

'It is now.' Her gaze flicked toward the door. 'We weren't able to get much out of Foxx, sir. He's a bit hysterical. I can't be sure what he might have disturbed – other than the body.'

'He moved the body?'

'No, sir. That is, it's still in the tub, but he attempted to, ah, revive the deceased. Had to be in shock to attempt it. There's enough blood in there to swim in. Slashed wrists,' she explained. 'From a visual confirmation, he'd been dead at least an hour before his housemate discovered the body.'

Eve took a firmer grip on her field kit. 'Has the ME been notified?'

'On the way, sir.'

'Fine. Clear Officer Peabody in when she arrives, and continue to stand. Open it,' she added and waited for the uniform to slide her master key in the slot. The door slid open into the wall. Eve immediately heard the hard, ragged sobs of terrible grief.

'He's been like that since we arrived,' the uniform murmured. 'Hope you can tranq him soon.'

Saying nothing, Eve walked in, letting the door slide shut and lock at her back. The entranceway was elaborate in black and white marble. Spiraling columns were draped in some sort of flowering vine, and overhead, a black glass chandelier dripped in five ornate tiers.

Through the portico was a living area that followed the theme. Black leather sofas, white floors, ebony wood tables, white lamps. Drapes striped in black and white were drawn shut, but lights showered from the ceiling, spotlighted up from the floor.

An amusement screen was switched off but hadn't been slipped back into its recess. Glossy white stairs angled up to a second floor, which was ringed with white banisters, atrium style. Lush green ferns hung in enameled pots from the lofted ceiling.

49

Money might drip, she mused, but death had no respect for it. It was a club without a class system.

The sounds of grief echoed and drew her into a small den lined with antique books and cushy with deep chairs the color of good burgundy.

Sunk into one was a man. His handsome face was pale gold and ravaged from tears. His hair was gold as well, the glint of new coin, and was tufted in spikes from his hands. He wore a white silk robe that was spotted and smeared with drying blood. His feet were bare, and his hands were studded with rings that sparkled as his fingers trembled. There was a tattoo of a black swan on his left ankle.

The uniform who was sitting miserably beside the man glanced over at Eve, started to speak.

Eve shook her head quickly, keeping her badge in plain sight. She gestured toward the ceiling, cocking her head in question.

He nodded, jerked his thumb up, then shook his head.

Eve slipped back out. She wanted to see the body, view the scene before she dealt with the witness.

There were several rooms off the second floor. Still, it was simple enough to find her way. She simply followed the trail of blood. She stepped into a bedroom. Here the scheme was soft greens and blues, so that it felt like floating underwater. The bed was an oblong of blue satin sheets, mountained with pillows.

There was statuary here as well, of the classic nude variety. Drawers were built into the walls, giving it an uncluttered – and to Eve – an unlived-in appearance. The ocean blue carpet was soft as a cloud and spotted with blood.

She followed the trail into the master bath. Death didn't shock her, but it appalled her, and she knew it always would: the waste of it, the violence and cruelty of it. But she lived with it too much to be shocked, even by this.

Blood had spurted, showered, streamed on gleaming tiles

of ivory and seafoam green. It had fountained over glass, pooled over the mirrored floor from the gaping wound in the wrist of the hand that hung limply over the lip of a huge clear-sided tub.

The water inside was a dark, nasty pink, and the metallic smell of blood hung in the air. Music was playing, something with strings – perhaps a harp. Fat white candles had been lighted and still burned at both the foot and the head of the long oval tub.

The body that lay in that cloudy pink water had its head resting on a gilt-edged bath pillow, its gaze lifted and fixed on the feathery tails of a fern that hung from the mirrored ceiling. He was smiling, as if he'd been desperately amused to watch himself die.

It didn't shock her, but she sighed as she coated her hands and feet with clear seal, engaged her recorder, and carried her kit inside to stand over the body.

Eve had recognized him. Naked, bled almost dry, and smiling up at his own reflection was the renowned defense attorney S. T. Fitzhugh.

'Salvatori's going to be very disappointed in you, Counselor,' she murmured as she got to work.

Eve had taken a sample of the bloody bathwater, done her initial scan to estimate time of death, bagged the deceased's hands, and recorded the scene when Peabody appeared, slightly out of breath at the doorway.

'I'm sorry, sir. I had some trouble getting uptown.

'It's all right.' She passed Peabody the ivory-handled buck knife she'd secured in clear plastic. 'Looks like he did it with this. It's an antique, I'd guess. Collector's item. We'll run it for prints.'

Peabody tucked the knife in her evidence kit, then narrowed her eyes. 'Lieutenant, isn't that—'

'Yeah, it's Fitzhugh.'

'Why would he kill himself?'

51

'We haven't determined that he did. Never make assumptions, Officer,' she said mildly. 'First rule. Call in the sweepers, Peabody, and let's get the scene tagged. We can release the body to the ME. I'm done with it for now.' Eve stepped back with blood smearing her sealed hands. 'I want you to take a prelim from the two uniforms who responded while I talk to Foxx.'

Eve glanced back at the body, shook her head. 'That's just the way he'd grin at you in court when he figured he'd tripped you up. The son of a bitch.' Still studying the body, she used the cleaner from her kit to remove the blood, tucked the soiled wipe into a bag as well. 'Tell the ME I want toxicology ASAP.'

She left Peabody and followed the blood trail back downstairs.

Foxx was down to choking, whimpering sobs now. The uniform looked ridiculously relieved when Eve reappeared. 'Wait for the ME and my adjutant outside, Officer. Give Officer Peabody your report. I'll speak with Mr Foxx now.'

'Yes, sir.' With almost unseemly delight, he fled the room.

'Mr Foxx, I'm Lieutenant Dallas. I'm sorry for your loss.' Eve located the button that released the drapes, pushed it to let watery light into the room. 'You need to talk to me. You need to tell me what happened here.'

'He's dead.' Foxx's voice was faintly musical, accented. Lovely. 'Fitz is dead. I don't know how that can be. I don't know how I can go on.'

*Everyone goes on*, Eve thought. *There's little choice.* She sat and put her recorder on the table in plain sight. 'Mr Foxx, it would help us both if you talked to me now. I'm going to give you the standard caution. It's just a matter of procedure.'

She recited the revised Miranda while his sobs trickled off, he lifted his head, and aimed swollen, red-rimmed golden eyes at her.

'Do you think I killed him? Do you think I could hurt him?'

'Mr Foxx—'

'I loved him. We've been together for twelve years. He was my life.'

*You still have your life*, she thought. *You just don't know it yet.* 'Then you'll want to help me do my job. Tell me what happened.'

'He – he's been having trouble sleeping lately. Doesn't like to take tranqs. He can usually read, listen to music, spend an hour with VR or one of his games, whatever, to relax. This case he's working on worried him.'

'The Salvatori case.'

'Yes, I believe, yes.' Foxx wiped at his eyes with a damp and bloodied sleeve. 'We didn't discuss his cases in any depth. There was privilege, and I'm not a lawyer. I'm a nutritionist. That's how we met. Fitz came to me twelve years ago for help with his diet. We became friends, we became lovers, then we simply became.'

She would need to know all of that, but for the moment, she wanted to see the events leading up to that last bath. 'He's been having trouble sleeping,' she prompted.

'Yes. He's often plagued with insomnia. He gives so much to his clients. They prey on his mind. I'm accustomed to him getting up in the middle of the night and going into another room to program a game or doze in front of the view screen. Sometimes he'd take a warm bath.' Foxx's already ravaged face blanched. 'Oh God.'

The tears started again, flowing hotly down his cheeks. Eve took a quick look around and spotted a small serving droid in the corner of the room. 'Bring Mr Foxx some water,' she ordered, and the little droid scooted away to comply.

'Is that what happened?' she continued. 'Did he get up in the middle of the night?'

'I don't even remember.' Foxx lifted his hands, let them fall. 'I sleep soundly, never have a bit of trouble. We'd gone

53

to bed just before midnight, watched some of the late news, had a brandy. I woke early. I tend to.'

'What time was that?'

'Perhaps five, five fifteen. We both like early starts, and it's my habit to program the morning meal personally. I saw that Fitz wasn't in bed, assumed he'd had a bad night and that I'd find him downstairs or in one of the spare bedrooms. Then I went into the bath, and I saw him. Oh God. Oh God, Fitz. All the blood. It was like a nightmare.'

His hand pressed against his mouth, all glittering rings and trembles. 'I ran over, I beat on his chest, tried to revive him. I suppose I went a little mad. He was dead. I could see he was dead; still, I tried to pull him out of the water, but he's a very big man, and I was shaking. Sick.' He dropped his hand from mouth to stomach, pressed. 'I called for an ambulance.'

She'd lose him if she couldn't manage to rein him in. Tranquing him wasn't an option until she had the facts. 'I know this is difficult for you, Mr Foxx. I'm sorry we have to do this now, but it's easier, believe me, if we can.'

'I'm all right.' He reached for the glass of water atop the droid. 'I want to get it over.'

'Can you tell me his frame of mind last night? You said he was worried about a case.'

'Worried, yes, but not depressed. There was a cop he couldn't shake on the stand, and it irritated him.' He took a gulp of water, then another.

Eve decided it was best not to mention she was the cop who had irritated him.

'And there were a couple of other cases pending that he was plotting out the defense for. His mind was often too busy for sleep, you see.'

'Did he receive any calls, make any calls?'

'Certainly, both. He often brought work home with him. Last night he spent a couple of hours in his office upstairs.

He arrived home about five thirty, worked until nearly eight. We had dinner.'

'Did he mention anything that was troubling him besides the Salvatori case?'

'His weight.' Foxx smiled a little. 'Fitz hated to put on an extra pound. We discussed him increasing his exercise program, perhaps having some body adjustment work done when he had the time. We watched a comedy on screen in the living room, then went to bed, as I told you.'

'Did you argue?'

'Argue?'

'You have bruises on your arm, Mr Foxx. Did you and Mr Fitzhugh fight last night?'

'No.' He paled even more, and his eyes glittered with the threat of another bout of weeping. 'We never fought physically. Certainly we argued from time to time. People do. I – I suppose I might have gotten the bruises on the tub when I was – when I tried to—'

'Did Mr Fitzhugh have a relationship with anyone else other than yourself?'

Now those swollen eyes went cool. 'If you mean did he have outside lovers, he did not. We were committed to each other.'

'Who owns this unit?'

Foxx's face went rigid, and his voice was cold. 'It was put in our joint names ten years ago. It belonged to Fitz.'

*And now it belongs to you*, Eve thought. 'I would assume Mr Fitzhugh was a wealthy man. Do you know who inherits?'

'Other than charitable bequests, I would inherit. Do you think I would kill him for money?' There was disgust in his tone now, rather than horror. 'What right do you have to come into my home at such a time and ask me such horrible questions?'

'I need to know the answers, Mr Foxx. If I don't ask them here, I'll have to ask them at the station house. I believe

55

this is more comfortable for you. Did Mr Fitzhugh collect knives?'

'No.' Foxx blinked, then went pasty. 'I do. I have a large collection of antique blades. Registered,' he added quickly. 'They're duly registered.'

'Do you have an ivory-handled knife, straight blade, about six inches long in your collection?'

'Yes, it's nineteenth century, from England.' His breath began to hitch. 'Is that what he used? He used one of my knives to—? I didn't see. I only saw him. Did he use one of my knives?'

'I've taken a knife into evidence, Mr Foxx. We'll run tests. I'll give you a receipt for it.'

'I don't want it. I don't want to see it.' He buried his face in his hands. 'Fitz. How could he have used one of my knives?'

He fell to weeping again. Eve heard the voices and hums from the next room and knew the sweepers had arrived. 'Mr Foxx.' She rose. 'I'm going to have one of the officers bring you some clothes. I'm going to ask that you stay here for a little while longer. Is there someone I can call for you?'

'No. No one. Nothing.'

'I don't like it, Peabody,' Eve muttered as they rode down to her car. 'Fitzhugh gets up in the middle of an ordinary night, gets an antique knife, runs himself a bath. He lights the candles, puts on the music, then carves up his wrists. For no particular reason. Here's a man at the height of his career with a shit load of money, plush digs, clients beating down his door, and he just decides, "What the hell, I think I'll die"?'

'I don't understand suicide. I guess I don't have the personality for big highs and lows.'

Eve understood it. She'd even considered it briefly during her stint in state-run homes – and before that, in the dark time before that, when death had seemed a release from hell.

That was why she couldn't accept it for Fitzhugh.

'There's no motivation here, at least none that shows yet.

But we have a lover who collected knives, who was covered with blood, and who will inherit a sizable fortune.'

'You're thinking maybe Foxx killed him.' Peabody mulled it over when they reached garage level. 'Fitzhugh's nearly twice his size. He wouldn't have gone without a fight, and there wasn't any sign of struggle.'

'Signs can be erased,' Eve muttered. 'He had bruises. And if Fitzhugh was drugged or chemically impaired, he wouldn't have put up too much of a struggle. We'll see the tox report.'

'Why do you want it to be a homicide?'

'I don't. I just want it to make sense, and the self-termination doesn't fit. Maybe Fitzhugh couldn't sleep; maybe he got up. Someone was using the relaxation room. Or it was made to seem so.'

'I've never seen anything like that,' Peabody mused, thinking back. 'All those toys in one place. That big chair with all the controls, the wall screen, the autobar, the VR station, the mood tube. Ever use a mood tube, Lieutenant?'

'Roarke's got one. I don't like it. I'd rather have my moods come and go naturally than program them.' Eve spotted the figure sitting on the hood of her car and hissed, 'Like now, for example. I can feel my mood shifting. I think I'm about to be pissed off.'

'Well, Dallas and Peabody, together again.' Nadine Furst, top on-air reporter for Channel 75, slid gracefully from the car. 'How was the honeymoon?'

'Private,' Eve snapped.

'Hey, I thought we were pals.' Nadine winked at Peabody.

'You didn't waste any time putting our little get-together on the air, pal.'

'Dallas.' Nadine spread her pretty hands. 'You bag a killer and close a very public and intense case at your own bachelor party celebration, to which I was invited, it's news. The public not only has the right to know, they eat it up with a spoon. Ratings rocketed. Now look at this, you're barely back and right in the middle of something else big. What's the deal with Fitzhugh?'

'He's a dead man. I've got work to do, Nadine.'

'Come on, Eve.' Nadine plucked at Eve's sleeve. 'After all we've been through together? Give me a nibble.'

'Fitzhugh's clients had better start looking for another lawyer. That's all I've got to give you.'

'Come on. Accident, homicide, what?'

'We're investigating,' Eve said shortly and coded open her locks.

'Peabody?' But Peabody just grinned and shrugged her shoulders. 'You know, Dallas, it's common knowledge that you and the dearly departed weren't fans of each other. The top sound bite after court yesterday was him referring to you as a violent cop who used her badge as a blunt instrument.'

'It's a shame he won't be able to give you and your associates such catchy quotes anymore.'

As Eve slammed the car door, Nadine leaned doggedly in the window. 'So you give me one.'

'S. T. Fitzhugh is dead. Police are investigating. Back off.' Eve started the engine, torpedoed out of the slot so that Nadine had to dance back to save her toes. At Peabody's chuckle, Eve slid a stony glance in her direction. 'Something funny?'

'I like her.' Peabody couldn't resist looking back, and she noted that Nadine was grinning. 'So do you.'

Eve smothered a chuckle. 'There's no accounting for taste,' she said and drove out into the rainy morning.

It had gone perfectly. Absolutely perfectly. It was an exciting, powerful feeling to know that you had the controls. The reports coming from various news agencies were all duly logged and recorded. Such matters required careful organization and were added to the small but satisfactorily growing pile of data discs.

It was such fun, and that was a surprise. Fun had certainly not been the prime motivator of the operation. But it was a delightful side effect.

Who would succumb next?

At the flick of a switch, Eve's face flashed onto a monitor, all pertinent data split-screened beside her. A fascinating woman. Birthplace and parents unknown. The abused child discovered hiding in an alley in Dallas, Texas, body battered, mind blanked. A woman who couldn't remember the early years of her own life. The years that formed the soul. Years when she had been beaten and raped and tormented.

What did that sort of life do to the mind? To the heart? To the person?

It had made the girl a social worker and had made Eve Dallas into a woman who had become a cop. The cop with the reputation for digging deep, and who had come into some notoriety the previous winter during the investigation of a sensitive and ugly case.

That was when she had met Roarke.

The computer hummed, sliced Roarke's face onto the screen. Such an intriguing couple. His background was no prettier than the cop's had been. But he'd chosen, at least initially, the other side of the law to make his mark. And his fortune.

Now they were a set. A set that could be destroyed on a whim.

But not yet. Not for some little time yet.

After all, the game had just begun.

# Chapter Five

'I just don't buy it,' Eve muttered as she called up data on Fitzhugh. She studied his bold, striking face as it flashed onto her monitor, shook her head. 'I just don't buy it,' she repeated.

She scanned his date and place of birth, saw that he'd been born in Philadelphia during the last decade of the previous century. He'd been married to a Milicent Barrows from 2033 to 2036. Divorced, no children.

He'd moved to New York the same year as his divorce, established his criminal law practice, and as far as she could see, had never looked back.

'Annual income,' she requested.

Subject Fitzhugh, annual income for last tax year. Two million, seven hundred USD.

'Bloodsucker,' she murmured. 'Computer, list and detail any arrests.'

Searching. No police record on file.

'Okay, so he's clean. How about this? List all civil suits filed against subject.'

She got a hit on that, a short list of names, and she ordered a hard copy. She requested a list of cases Fitzhugh had lost over the last ten years, noted the names that mirrored the suits filed against him. It made her sigh. It was typical litigation of the era. Your lawyer doesn't get you off, you sue the lawyer. It gave another jab to her hopeful theory of blackmail.

'Okay, so maybe we're going about this the wrong way. New subject, Foxx, Arthur, residence Five oh oh two Madison Avenue, New York.'

Searching.

The computer blipped and whined, causing Eve to slap the unit with the heel of her hand to jog it back. She didn't bother to curse budget cuts.

Foxx appeared on screen, wavering a bit until Eve gave the computer another smack. More attractive, she noted, when he smiled. He was fifteen years younger than Fitzhugh, had been born in East Washington, the son of two career military personnel, had lived in various points of the globe until he had settled in New York in 2042 and joined the Nutrition for Life organization as a consultant.

His annual income just tipped into the six figures. The record showed no marriages but the same-sex license he shared with Fitzhugh.

'List and detail any arrests.'

The machine grumbled as if it were tired of answering questions, but the list popped. One disorderly conduct, two assaults, and one disturbing the peace.

'Well, now we're getting somewhere. Both subjects, list and detail any psychiatric consults.'

There was nothing on Fitzhugh, but she got another hit on Foxx. With a grunt, she ordered a hard copy, then glanced up as Peabody entered.

'Forensics? Toxicology?'

'Forensics isn't in, but we've got tox.' Peabody handed Eve

a disc. 'Low level alcohol, identified as Parisian brandy, 2045. Not nearly enough to debilitate. No other drug traces.'

'Shit.' She'd been hopeful. 'I might have something here. Our friend Foxx spent a lot of his childhood on the therapist's couch. He checked himself into the Delroy Institute just two years ago for a month. And he's done time. Piss away time, but time nonetheless. Ninety days lockup for assault. And he had to wear a probie bracelet for six months. Our boy has some violent tendencies.'

Peabody frowned at the data. 'Military family. They tend to be resistant to homosexuality still. I bet they tried to head shrink him into hetero.'

'Maybe. But he's got a history of mental heath problems and a criminal record. Let's see what the uniforms turned up when they knocked on doors in Fitzhugh's building. And we'll talk to Fitzhugh's associates in his firm.'

'You're not buying suicide.'

'I knew him. He was arrogant, pompous, smug, vain.' Eve shook her head. 'Vain, arrogant men don't choose to be found naked in the bathtub, swimming in their own blood.'


'He was a brilliant man.' Leanore Bastwick sat in her custom-made leather chair in the glass-walled corner office of Fitzhugh, Bastwick, and Stern. Her desk was a glass pool, unsmudged and sparkling. *It suited,* Eve thought, *her icy and stunning blond beauty.* 'He was a generous friend,' Leanore added and folded her perfectly manicured hands on the edge of the desk. 'We're in shock here, Lieutenant.'

It was hard to see shock on the polished surface of it all. New York's steel forest rose up glittering behind Leanore's back, lending the lofty illusion that she was reigning over the city. Pale rose and soft gray added elegant muted color to an office that was as meticulously decorated as the woman herself.

'Do you know of any reason why Fitzhugh would have taken his own life?'

'Absolutely none.' Leanore kept her hands very still, her eyes level. 'He loved life. His life, his work. He enjoyed every minute of every day as much as anyone I've ever met. I have no idea why he would choose to end it.'

'When was the last time you saw or spoke with him?'

She hesitated. Eve could almost see wheels working smoothly behind those heavily lashed eyes. 'Actually, I saw him briefly last night. I dropped a file off for him, discussed a case. That discussion is, of course, privileged.' Her slicked lips curved. 'But I will say he was his usual enthusiastic self, and he was very much looking forward to dueling with you in court.'

'Dueling?'

'That's how Fitz referred to cross-examination of expert and police witnesses.' A smile flickered over her face. 'It was a match, in his mind, of wits and nerve. A professional game for an innate game player. I don't know of anything he enjoyed so much as being in court.'

'What time did you drop off the file last night?'

'I'd say about ten. Yes, I think it was around ten. I'd worked late here and slipped by on my way home.'

'Was that usual, Ms. Bastwick, you slipping by to see him on your way home?'

'Not unusual. We were, after all, professional associates, and our cases sometimes overlapped.'

'That's all you were? Professional partners?'

'Do you assume, Lieutenant, that because a man and woman are physically attractive and on friendly terms that they can't work together without sexual tension?'

'I don't assume anything. How long did you stay – discussing your case?'

'Twenty minutes, a half hour. I didn't time it. He was fine when I left, I'll tell you that.'

'There was nothing he was particularly concerned about?'

'He had some concerns about the Salvatori matter – and

63

others, as well. Nothing out of the ordinary. He was a confident man.'

'And outside of work. On a personal level?'

'A private man.'

'But you know Arthur Foxx.'

'Of course. In this firm we take care to know and socialize at least lightly with the spouses of partners and associates. Arthur and Fitz were devoted to each other.'

'No . . . spats?'

Leanore cocked a brow. 'I wouldn't know.'

*Sure you would*, Eve thought. 'You and Mr Fitzhugh were partners, you had a close professional and apparently a close personal relationship. He must have discussed his homelife with you from time to time.'

'He and Arthur were very happy.' Leanore's first sign of irritation showed in the gentle tapping of a coral-toned nail against the edge of glass. 'Happy couples occasionally have arguments. I imagine you argue with your husband from time to time.'

'My husband hasn't recently found me dead in the bath-tub,' Eve said evenly. 'What did Foxx and Fitzhugh argue about?'

Leanore let out an annoyed huff of breath. She rose, punched in a code on her AutoChef, took out a steaming cup of coffee. None was offered to Eve. 'Arthur had periodic bouts of depression. He is not the most self-confident of men. He tended to be jealous, which exasperated Fitz.' Her brows knit. 'You're probably aware that Fitz was matried before. His bisexuality was somewhat of a problem for Arthur, and when he was depressed, he tended to worry about all the men and women Fitz came into contact with in the course of his work. They rarely argued, but when they did, it was generally about Arthur's jealousy.'

'Did he have reason to be jealous?'

'As far as I know, Fitz was completely faithful. It's not always an easy choice, Lieutenant, being in the spotlight as he was, and given his lifestyle. Even today, there are some who are – let's say – uncomfortable with less-than-traditional sexual preferences. But Fitz gave Arthur no reason to be anything less than content.'

'Yet he was. Thank you,' Eve said as she rose. 'You've been very helpful.'

'Lieutenant,' Leanore began as Eve and the silent Peabody started for the door. 'If I thought for one instant that Arthur Foxx had anything to do with—' She stopped, sucked in a breath. 'No, it's simply impossible to believe.'

'Less possible than believing Fitzhugh slashed his own wrists and let himself bleed to death?' Eve waited a beat, then left the office.

Peabody waited until they'd stepped out onto the skywalk that ribboned the building. 'I don't know whether you were planting seeds or digging for worms.'

'Both.' Eve looked through the glass of the tube. She could see Roarke's office building, shooting tall and polished ebony among the other spears. At least he had no connection with this case. She didn't have to worry about uncovering something he'd done or someone he'd known too well. 'She knew both the victim and the suspect. And Foxx didn't mention her slipping by to discuss work last night.'

'So you've bumped Foxx from witness to suspect?'

Eve watched a man in a tailored robe squawk bad temperedly into a palm 'link as he glided by. 'Until we prove conclusively it was suicide, Foxx is the prime – hell, the only – suspect. He had the means. It was his knife. He had the opportunity. They were alone in the apartment. He had the motive. Money. Now we know he has a history of depression, a record of violence, and a jealous streak.'

'Can I ask you something?' Peabody waited for Eve's nod. 'You didn't care for Fitzhugh on a professional or a personal level.'

'I hated his fucking guts. So what?' Eve stepped off the

skywalk and onto the street level where she'd been lucky enough to find a parking spot. She spied a glida grill, smoking soy dogs and potato rings, and made a beeline through the heavy pedestrian traffic. 'You think I've got to like the corpse? Give me a couple of dogs and a scoop of potatoes. Two tubes of Pepsi.'

'Diet for me,' Peabody interrupted and rolled her eyes over Eve's long, lean form. 'Some of us have to worry about weight.'

'Diet dog, Diet Pep.' The woman running the cart had a dingy CZ stud in the center of her top lip and a tattoo of the subway system on her chest. The A line veered off and disappeared under the loose gauze covering her breasts. 'Reg Dog, Reg Pep, hot potatoes. Cash or credit?'

Eve shoved the limp cardboard holding the food at Peabody and dug for her tokens. 'What's the damage?'

The woman poked a grimy purple-tipped finger at her console, sent it beeping. 'Twenty-five.'

'Shit. You blink and dogs go up.' Eve poured credits into the woman's outstretched hand, grabbed a couple of wafer-thin napkins.

She worked her way back, plopped down on the bench circling the fountain in front of the law building. The panhandler beside her looked hopeful. Eve tapped her badge; he grinned, tapped the beggar's license hung around his neck.

Resigned, she dug out a five credit chip, passed it over. 'Find someplace else to hustle,' she ordered him, 'or I'll run that license and see if it's up to date.'

He said something uncomplimentary about her line of work, but he pocketed the credit and moved on, giving room to Peabody.

'Leanore doesn't like Arthur Foxx.'

Peabody swallowed gamely. Diet dogs were invariably grainy. 'She doesn't?'

'A high-class lawyer doesn't give that many answers unless

66

she wants to. She fed us that Foxx was jealous, that they argued.' Eve held out the scoop of greasy potatoes. After a brief internal struggle, Peabody dug in. 'She wanted us to have that data.'

'Still isn't much. There's nothing in Fitzhugh's records that implicates Foxx. His diary, his appointment book, his 'link logs. None of the data I scanned points the finger. Then again, none of it indicates a suicidal bent, either.'

Contemplatively, Eve sucked on her tube of Pepsi, watched New York lumber by with all its noise and sweat. 'We'll have to talk to Foxx again. I've got court again this afternoon. I want you to go back to Cop Central, get the door-to-door reports, nag the ME for the final autopsy. I don't know what the hang-up is there, but I want the results by end of shift. I should be out of court by three. We'll do another walk-through of Fitzhugh's apartment and see why he omitted Bastwick's little visit.'

Peabody juggled food and duly programmed the duties into her day log. 'What I asked before – about you not liking Fitzhugh. I just wondered if it was harder to push all the buttons when you had bad feelings about the subject.'

'Cops don't have personal feelings.' Then she sighed. 'Bullshit. You put those feelings aside and push the buttons. That's the job. And if I happen to think a man like Fitzhugh deserved to end up bathing in his own blood, it doesn't mean I won't do what's necessary to find out how he got there.'

Peabody nodded. 'A lot of other cops would just file it. Self-termination. End of transmission.'

'I'm not other cops, and neither are you, Peabody.' She glanced over, mildly interested at the explosive crash as two taxis collided. Pedestrian and street traffic barely hitched as smoke billowed, Duraglass pinged, and two furious drivers popped like corks out of their ruined vehicles.

Eve nibbled away at her lunch as the two men pushed, shoved, and shouted imaginative obscenities. She imagined they were obscenities, anyway, since no English was exchanged.

She looked up but didn't spot one of the hovering traffic copters. With a thin smile, she balled up the card-board, rolled up the empty tube, passed them to Peabody.

'Dump these in the recycler, will you, then come back and give me a hand breaking up those two idiots.'

'Sir, one of them just pulled out a bat. Should I call for backup?'

'Nope.' Eve rubbed her hands together in anticipation as she rose. 'I can handle it.'

Eve's shoulder was still smarting when she walked out of court a couple of hours later. She imagined the cab drivers would have been released by now, which wasn't going to happen to the child killer Eve had just testified against, she thought with satisfaction. She'd be in high security lockup for the next fifty years minimum. There was some satisfaction in that.

Eve rolled her bruised shoulder. The cabbie really hadn't been swinging at her, she thought. He'd been trying to crack his opponent's head open, and she'd just gotten in the way. Still, it wasn't going to hurt her feelings that both of them would have their licenses suspended for three months.

She climbed into her car and, favoring her shoulder, put the vehicle on auto to Cop Central. Overhead, a tourist tram blatted out the standard spiel about the scales of justice.

*Well*, she mused, *sometimes they balanced. If only for a short time*. Her 'link beeped.

'Dallas.'

'Dr Morris.' The medical examiner had heavy-lidded hawk eyes in a vivid shade of green, a squared-off chin that was generously stubbled, and a slicked-back mane of charcoal hair. Eve liked him. Though she was often frustrated by his lack of stellar speed, she appreciated his thoroughness.

'Have you finished the report on Fitzhugh?'

'I have a problem.'

'I don't need a problem, I need the report. Can you transmit it to my office 'link? I'm on my way there.'

'No, Lieutenant, you're on your way here. I have something I need to show you.'

'I don't have time to come by the morgue.'

'Make time,' he suggested and ended the transmission.

Eve ground her teeth once. Scientists were so damned frustrating, she thought as she redirected her unit.


From the outside, the Lower Manhattan City Morgue resembled one of the beehive-structured office buildings that surrounded it. It blended, that had been the point of the redesign. Nobody liked to think of death, to have it spoil their appetite as they scooted out of work at lunchtime to grab a bite at a corner deli. Images of bodies tagged and bagged on refrigerated slabs tended to put you off your pasta salad.

Eve remembered the first time she'd stepped through the black steel doors in the rear of the building. She'd been a rookie in uniform shoulder to shoulder with two dozen other rookies in uniforms. Unlike several of her comrades, she'd seen death up close and personal before, but she'd never seen it displayed, dissected, analyzed.

There was a gallery above one of the autopsy labs and there students, rookies, and journalists or novelists with the proper credentials could witness firsthand the intricate workings of forensic pathology.

Individual monitors in each seat offered close-up views to those with the stomach for it.

Most of them didn't come back for a return trip. Many who left were carried out.

Eve had walked out on her own steam, and she'd been back countless times since, but she never looked forward to the visits.

Her target this time wasn't what was referred to as The Theater, but Lab C, where Morris conducted most of his work.

69

Eve passed down the white tiled corridor with its pea green floors. She could smell death there. No matter what was used to eradicate it, the sulky stink of it slid through cracks, around doorways, and it tainted the air with the grinning reminder of mortality.

Medical science had eradicated plagues, a host of diseases and conditions, extending life expectancy to an average of one hundred fifty years. Cosmetic technology had insured that a human being could live attractively for his century and a half.

You could die without wrinkles, without age spots, without aches and pains and disintegrating bones. But you were still going to die sooner or later.

For many who came here, that day was sooner.

She stopped in front of the door at Lab C, held her badge up to the security camera, and gave her name and ID number to the speaker. Her palm print was analyzed and cleared. The door slid open.

It was a small room, windowless and depressing, lined with equipment, beeping with computers. Some of the tools ranged neat as a surgeon's tray on the counters were barbaric enough to make the weak shudder. Saws, lasers, the glinting blades of scalpels, hoses.

In the center of the room was a table with gutters on the side to catch fluids and run them into sterilized, airtight containers for further analysis. On the table was Fitzhugh, his naked body bearing the scars of the recent insult of a standard Y cut.

Morris was sitting on a rolling stool in front of a monitor, face pushed close to the screen. He wore a white lab coat that fluttered to the floor. It was one of his few affectations, the coat that flapped and swirled like a highwayman's cape whenever he walked down the corridors. His slicked-back hair was snugged into a long ponytail.

Eve knew, since he'd called her in directly rather than passing her off to one of his techs, that it was something unusual.

'Dr Morris?'

'Hmm. Lieutenant,' he began without turning around. 'Never seen anything like it. Not in thirty years of exploring the dead.' He swung around with a flutter of his lab coat. Beneath it he wore stovepipe pants and a T-shirt in loud, clashing colors. 'You're looking well, Lieutenant.'

He gave her one of his quick, charming smiles, and her lips curved up in response. 'You're looking pretty good, yourself. You lost the beard.'

He reached up, rubbed a hand over his stubbly chin. He'd sported a precise goatee until recently. 'Didn't suit me. But Christ, I hate to shave. How was the honeymoon?'

Automatically, she tucked her hands in her pockets. 'It was good. I've got a pretty full plate right now, Morris. What do you have to show me you couldn't show me on screen?'

'Some things take personal attention.' He rode his stool over to the autopsy table until he pulled up with a slight squeal of wheels at Fitzhugh's head. 'What do you see?'

She glanced down. 'A dead guy.'

Morris nodded, as if pleased. 'What we would call a normal, everyday dead guy who expired due to excessive blood loss, possibly self-inflicted.'

'Possibly?' She leaped on the word.

'From the surface, suicide is the logical conclusion. There were no drugs in his system, very little alcohol, he shows no offensive nor defensive wounds or bruising, the blood settlement was consistent with his position in the tub, he did not drown, the angle of the wrist wounds . . .'

He bumped closer, picked up one of Fitzhugh's limp, beautifully manicured hands where on the wrist the carved wounds resembled some intricate, ancient language. 'They are also very consistent with self-infliction: a right-handed man, reclining slightly.' He demonstrated, holding an imaginary blade. 'Very quick, very precise slashes to the wrist, severing the artery.'

71

Though she'd already studied the wounds herself, and photographs of them, she stepped closer, looked again. 'Why couldn't someone have come up from behind him, leaned over, slashed down at that same angle?'

'It's not beyond the realm of possibility, but if that were the case, I'd expect to see some defensive wounds. If someone snuck into your bath and sliced your wrist, you'd be inclined to become annoyed, quarrelsome.' He beamed a smile. 'I don't think you'd just settle back in the tub and bleed to death.'

'So you're going with self-termination.'

'Not so fast. I was prepared to.' He tugged on his bottom lip, let it snap back into place. 'I ran the standard brain analysis required with any self-termination or suspected self-termination. That's the puzzle here. The real puzzle.'

He scooted his stool over to his workstation, gestured over his shoulder for her to follow. 'This is his brain,' he said, tapping a finger on the organ floating in clear liquid and attached to wire thin cables that fed into the mainframe of his computer. 'Abby Normal.'

'I beg your pardon.'

Morris chuckled, shook his head. 'Obviously you don't make time to watch enough classic videos. That's from a takeoff on the Frankenstein myth. What I'm saying is, this brain is abnormal.'

'He had brain damage?'

'Damage – well, it seems an extreme word for what I've found. Here, on the screen.' He swiveled around, tapped some keys. A close-up view of Fitzhugh's brain flashed on. 'Again, on the surface, completely as expected. But we show the cross section.' He tapped again, and the brain was sliced neatly in half. 'So much went on in this small mass,' Morris murmured. 'Thoughts, ideas, music, desires, poetry, anger, hate. People speak of the heart, Lieutenant, but it's the brain that holds all the magic and mystery of the human species. It elevates us, separates us, defines us as individuals.

72

And the secrets of it – well, it's doubtful we'll ever know them all. See here.'

Eve leaned closer, trying to see what he indicated with the tap of a finger on the screen. 'It looks like a brain to me. Unattractive but necessary.'

'Not to worry, I nearly missed it myself. For this imaging,' he went on while the monitor whirled with color and shapes, 'the tissue appears in blues, pale to dark, the bone white. Blood vessels are red. As you can see, there are no clots or tumors that would indicate neurological disorders in the making. Enhance quadrant B, sections thirty-five to forty, thirty percent.'

The screen jumped and a section of the image enlarged. Losing patience, Eve started to shrug, then leaned in. 'What is that? It looks like . . . What? A smudge?'

'It does, doesn't it?' He beamed again, staring at the screen where a faint shadow no bigger than a flyspeck marred the brain. 'Almost like a fingerprint, a child's oily finger. But when you enhance again' – he did so with a few brief commands, popping the image closer – 'it's more of a tiny burn.'

'How would you get a burn inside your brain?'

'Exactly.' Obviously fascinated, Morris swiveled toward the brain in question. 'I've never seen anything like that tiny pinprick mark. It wasn't caused by a hemorrhage, a small stroke, or an aneurism. I've run all the standard brain imaging programs and can find no known neurological cause for it.'

'But it's there.'

'Indeed, it is. It could be nothing, no more than a faint abnormality that caused the occasional vague headache or dizziness. It certainly wouldn't be fatal. But it is curious. I've sent for all of Fitzhugh's medical records to see if there were any tests run or any data on this burn.'

'Could it cause depression, anxiety?'

'I don't know. It flaws the left frontal lobe of the right cerebral hemisphere. Current medical opinion is that certain aspects, such as personality, are localized in this specific

73

cerebral area. So it does appear in the section of the brain that we now believe receives and deploys suggestions and ideas.'

He moved his shoulders. 'However, I can't document that this flaw contributed to death. The fact is, Dallas, at the moment, I'm baffled but fascinated. I won't be releasing your case until I find some answers.'

*A burn in the brain*, Eve mused as she uncoded the locks on Fitzhugh's condo. She'd come alone, wanting the emptiness, the silence, to give her own brain time to work. Until she had cleared the scene, Foxx would have other living quarters.

She retraced her steps upstairs, studied the grisly bath again.

*A burn in the brain*, she thought again. Drugs seemed the most logical answer. If they hadn't showed on tox, it could be it was a new type of drug, one that had yet to be registered.

She walked into the relaxation room. There was nothing there but the expensive toys of a wealthy man who enjoyed his leisure time.

*Couldn't sleep*, she mused. *Came in to relax, had a brandy. Stretched out in the chair, watched some screen.* Her lips pursed as she picked up the VR goggles beside the chair. *Took a quick trip. Didn't want to use the chamber for it, just kicked back.*

Curious, she slipped on the goggles, ordered the last scene played. She was popped into a swaying white boat on a cool green river. Birds soared overhead, a fish bulleted up, flashed silver, and dove again. On the banks of the river were wildflowers and tall, shielding trees. She felt herself floating, let her hand dip into the water to trail a quiet wake. It was nearly sunset, and the sky was going pink and purple in the west. She could hear the low hum of bees, the cheerful chirp of crickets. The boat rocked like a cradle.

Stifling a yawn, she pulled the goggles off again. A harmless, sedative scene, she decided and set the goggles down.

Nothing that would have induced a sudden urge to slash one's wrists. But the water might have prompted the urge for a hot bath, so he'd taken one. And if Foxx had crept in, had been quiet enough, quick enough, he could have done it.

It was all she had, Eve decided, and took out her communicator to order a second interview with Arthur Foxx.

# Chapter Six

Eve studied the reports on the knock-on-doors from uniforms. Most of them were what she'd expected. Fitzhugh and Foxx were quiet, kept to themselves, yet friendly with their neighbors in the building. But she latched on to the statement of the droid on doorman duty that placed Foxx at leaving the building at twenty-two thirty and returning at twenty-three hundred hours.

'He didn't mention he went out, did he, Peabody? Not a word about a little jaunt in the evening on his own.'

'No, he didn't mention it.'

'Have we got the security discs logged yet from the lobby and elevator cameras?'

'I loaded them in. They're under Fitzhugh ten-fifty-one on your unit.'

'Let's take a look.' Eve booted her machine, leaned back in her chair.

Peabody scanned the monitor over her shoulder and resisted mentioning that both of them were now officially off duty. It was exciting, after all, working side by side with the top homicide detective at Cop Central. Dallas would sneer at that, Peabody thought, but it was true. She'd been following the career of Eve Dallas for years, and there was no one she admired or wished more to emulate.

The biggest shock of Peabody's life was that somehow, over

the course of a few short months, they had come to be friends as well.

'Stop.' Eve sat up straight as the transmission froze. She studied the classy blonde entering the building at twenty-two fifteen. 'Well, well, there's our Leanore, slipping by.'

'She had the time fairly close. Ten fifteen.'

'Yeah, she's on the mark.' Eve ran her tongue around her teeth. 'What do you think, Peabody? Business or pleasure?'

'Well, she's dressed for business.' Peabody cocked her head and allowed a faint trail of envy to curl up her spine at Leanore's spiffy three-piece suit. 'She's carrying a briefcase.'

'A briefcase – and a bottle of wine. Enhance quadrant D, thirty to thirty-five. An expensive bottle of wine,' Eve murmured when the screen popped and displayed the label clearly. 'Roarke's got some of that little number in the wine cellar. I think it goes for about two hundred.'

'A bottle? Wow.'

'A glass,' Eve corrected, amused when Peabody goggled. 'Something doesn't fit. Resume normal size and speed, shift to elevator camera. Hmm. Yeah, yeah, she's primping,' Eve murmured, watching as Leanore took a gold compact out of her embossed briefcase, powdered her nose, freshened her lipstick as the elevator climbed. 'And lookie there, just flipped open the top three buttons of her blouse.'

'Getting ready for a man,' Peabody said, and shrugged when Eve slanted a look at her. 'I'd guess.'

'I'd guess, too.' Together, they watched Leanore stride down the foyer on the thirty-eighth floor and buzz herself into Fitzhugh's apartment. Eve increased the time delay until Foxx strode out fifteen minutes later. 'Doesn't look happy, does he?'

'No.' Peabody narrowed her eyes. 'I'd say he looks ticked off.' She lifted her brows when Foxx kicked bad temperedly at the elevator door. 'Very ticked off.'

They waited for the drama to resume. Leanore left twenty-two minutes later, color high on her cheeks, eyes glittering.

She jabbed a finger at the elevator, hitched her briefcase on her shoulder. A short time after, Foxx returned carrying a small parcel.

'She didn't stay twenty or thirty minutes, but more than forty-five. What went on inside that apartment that night?' Eve wondered. 'And just what did Foxx bring back with him? Contact the law offices. I want Leanore in here for questioning. I've got Foxx at nine-thirty. Get her in here at the same time. We'll team play them.'

'You want me to interrogate?'

Eve disengaged her machine, rolled her shoulders. 'It's a good place to start. We'll meet here at eight-thirty. No, come by my home office at eight. That'll give us more time.' She glanced at her 'link as it beeped, considered ignoring it, then gave in.

'Dallas.'

'Hey!' Mavis's bright face filled the screen. 'I was hoping I'd catch you before you left. How's it going?'

'Well enough. I'm just about to log out. What's up?'

'Good timing. Great timing. Mag. Listen, I'm at Jess's studio. We're going to do a session. Leonardo's here. We're going to make it a party, so come on by.'

'Hey, listen, Mavis, I've put in a full day. I just want to—'

'Come on.' There were nerves as well as enthusiasm. 'We're going to get food in, and Jess's got the most rocking brew here. It'll debrain you in seconds. He thinks if we can lay something decent down tonight, we could run with it. I'd really like you around. You know, moral support shit. Can't you just stop by for a while?'

'I guess I could.' *Damn it. No backbone.* 'I'll let Roarke know I'll be late. But I can't stay.'

'Hey, I gave Roarke a buzz already.'

'You – what?'

'I 'linked him just a bit ago. Hey, you know, Dallas, I've never been by that meg-cool office of his. He had like the

UN or something in there, all these off country guys. Wild. Anyway, they put me through to the inner sanctum because I was a pal of yours, and I talked to him. So,' Mavis chirped on over Eve's heaved sigh, 'I told him what was up and coming, and he said he'd stop around after the meeting or summit or whatever he was into.'

'Looks like it's all settled.' Eve watched her fantasy involving a whirlpool, a glass of wine, and a fat slab of steak go up in smoke.

'Too tops. Hey, is that Peabody? Hey, Peabody, you come, too. We'll party. See you soon, right?'

'Mavis.' Eve caught her seconds before she disengaged. 'Where the hell are you?'

'Oh, didn't I say? The studio's at Eight Avenue B, street level. Just beat on the door. Somebody'll let you in. Gotta go,' she shouted as something that might have been music boomed. 'They're tuning up. Catch ya.'

Eve blew out a breath, scooped her hair out of her eyes, and glanced over her shoulder. 'Well, Peabody, want to go to a recording session, get your ears fried, eat bad food, and get drunk on bad brew?'

Peabody didn't have to think twice. 'As a matter of fact, Lieutenant, I'd love to.'

It took a lot of banging on a gray steel door that looked as though it had been on the wrong end of a battering ram somewhere along the line. The rain from that morning had turned into steam that smelled unpleasantly of street oil and the recycling units that never seemed to be in full repair in that part of town.

With more resignation than energy, Eve watched two chemi-heads make deals under the dirty light of a street-lamp. Neither of them so much as blinked at Peabody's uniform. Eve turned when one of the powder junkies took a hit less than five feet away.

79

'Damn it, that's just too arrogant. Bust him.'

Resigned Peabody headed over. The chemi-head focused, swore and, swallowing the paper his powder had been cupped in, swung around to run. He skidded on the wet pavement and banged face first into the lamppost. By the time Peabody reached him, he was flat on his back and bleeding, profusely from the nose.

'He's out cold,' she called to Eve.

'Idiot. Call it in. Get a cruiser over here to haul him into the tank. You want the collar?'

Peabody considered, then shook her head. 'Not worth it. The beat cop can take it.' She pulled out her communicator, gave the location as she walked back to Eve. 'The dealer's still across the street,' she commented. 'He's got air blades, but I could try to chase him down.'

'I sense a lack of enthusiasm.' Eve narrowed her eyes, scanned the dealer hulking across the street, air blades steaming. 'Hey, asshole,' she called out. 'You see this uniform here?' She jerked a thumb at Peabody. 'Take your business someplace else, or I'll tell her to bump her weapon up to level three and watch you piss your pants.'

'Cunt,' he shouted back and whizzed off on his blades.

'You've got a real way with community relations, Dallas.'

'Yeah, it's a gift.' Eve turned back, prepared to beat on the door again, and found herself facing a female of massive proportions. She was easily six five, with shoulders wide as a highway. They rose out of a sleeveless leather vest and rippled with muscles and tattoos. Beneath, she wore a unisuit, snug as skin and the color of a healing bruise. She sported a copper nose ring and close-cropped hair fashioned into tight, glossy black curls.

'Fucking drug pushers,' she said in a voice like a cannon boom. 'Stink up the neighborhood. You Mavis's cop?'

'That's right, and I brought my cop with me.'

The woman sized Peabody up out of milky blue eyes. 'Solid. Mavis says you're right. I'm Big Mary.'

80

Eve angled her head. 'Yes, you are.'

It took about ten seconds, then Big Mary's moon-sized face creased in a knife-edged grin. 'Come on in. Jess is just heating up.' By way of welcome, she took Eve's arm and lifted her up and into the short hallway. 'Come on, Dallas's cop.'

'Peabody.' With a cautious glance, Peabody kept warily out of Big Mary's reach.

'Pea body. Yeah, you ain't much bigger than a pea.' Roaring at her own joke, Big Mary carted Eve into a padded elevator, waited for the door to close. They were cocooned together, tight as fish in a pan as Mary directed the unit to take them up one level. 'Jess, he says to take you up to control. You got money?'

It was hard to maintain dignity of any kind when Eve's nose was pressed in Mary's armpit. 'What for?'

'We got food coming. You gotta plunk in your share for the eats.'

'All right. Is Roarke here yet?'

'Ain't seen no Roarke. Mavis says you can't miss him 'cause he is fine and prime.'

The padded door opened, and Eve let out the breath she'd been holding. Even as she sucked in air, her ears were assaulted. Mavis's high, wild voice was screeching to the accompaniment of blistering noise.

'She's got a groove going.'

Only deep affection for Mavis prevented Eve from leaping back into the soundproofing. 'Apparently.'

'I'll get your drinks. Jess, he brought the brew.'

Mary hulked off, leaving Eve and Peabody in a glass-walled control booth that curved in a semicircle a half level above a studio where Mavis was singing her heart and lungs out. With a grin, Eve moved closer to the glass, the better to see.

Mavis had scooped up her hair so that it spewed in a purple fountain out of a multicolored band. She was wearing modified overalls, the black leather straps running up the center of her bare breasts. The rest of the material was a shimmering kaleidoscope that started at the midriff and ended barely south of the crotch. She danced to the beat on a fashionable pair of slides that left the feet bare and propped them onto four-inch stilts.

Eve had no doubt that Mavis's lover had designed the costume for her. She spotted Leonardo in a corner of the studio, glowing like a sunbeam at Mavis and wearing a body-skimming jumpsuit that made him look like an elegant grizzly.

'What a pair,' she murmured and hooked her thumbs in the back pockets of her battered jeans. She turned her head to speak to Peabody, but noted her companion's attention was riveted to the left, and the look on Peabody's face, Eve noted with some curiosity, managed to combine shock, admiration, and lust.

Following Peabody's distracted gaze, Eve had her first view of Jess Barrow. He was beautiful. A painting in motion with a long, shining mane of hair the color of polished oak. His eyes were nearly silver, thickly lashed, intensely focused, as he worked the controls of an elaborate console. His complexion was flawless, tanned to bronze, set off by rounded cheekbones and a strong chin. His mouth was full and firm, and his hands, as they flew over the controls, were as finely sculptured as marble.

'Roll up your tongue, Peabody,' Eve suggested, 'before you step on it.'

'God. Holy God. He's better in person. Don't you just want to bite him?'

'Not particularly, but you go ahead.'

Catching herself, Peabody flushed to the roots of her hair. She shifted on her sturdy legs. This was, she reminded herself, her superior. 'I admire his talent.'

'Peabody, you're admiring his chest. It's a pretty good one, so I can't hold it against you.'

'I wish he would,' she murmured, then cleared her throat

as Big Mary stomped back with two dark brown bottles. 'Jess gets this brew from his family down South. It's fine.'

Since it was also unmarked and unlabeled, Eve prepared to sacrifice a few layers of stomach lining. She was pleasantly surprised when the liquid slid mellowly down her throat. 'It is fine. Thanks.'

'You add to the kitty, you can have more. I'm supposed to go down to wait for Roarke. I hear he's got money to roll in. How come you're not wearing some flash, you linked up with a rich man?'

Eve decided not to mention the baby-fist-sized diamond resting between her breasts under her shirt. 'My underwear's solid gold. It chafes some, but it makes me feel secure.'

After another brief processing delay, Mary hooted with laughter, slapped Eve on the back hard enough to bop her head into the glass, then headed off in her rock-breaking stride.

'We ought to sign her up,' Eve muttered. 'She wouldn't need a weapon or body armor.'

The music built to an ear-scorching crescendo, then cut off as if severed with a knife. Below, Mavis let out a squeal and launched herself into Leonardo's open arms.

'That was a nice take, sugar.' Jess's voice flowed out like top cream and drifted lazily with a Southern drawl. 'You take ten and rest that golden throat for me.'

Mavis's idea of resting her throat was to let out another scream, then wave desperately at Eve. 'Dallas, you're here. Wasn't that mag? I'm coming up, don't go anywhere.' She scrambled through a door on her trendy stilts.

'So this is Dallas.' Jess pushed away from his console. His body was trim and showed off to advantage in jeans as battered as Eve's and a simple cotton shirt that would retail for a beat cop's monthly paycheck. He wore a diamond stud in his ear that glinted as he crossed the booth and a braided gold chain around his wrist that slid fluidly as he held out one of those beautiful hands. 'Mavis is brimming over with stories about her cop.'

'Mavis brims over habitually. It's part of her charm.'

'That it is. I'm Jess, and I'm delighted to meet you at last.' With his hand still cupped over Eve's, he turned that slow, heart-thudding smile onto Peabody. 'And it seems we have two cops for the price of one.'

'I – I'm a huge fan,' Peabody managed and fought against the nervous stutter. 'I have all of your discs, audio and video. I've seen you in concert.'

'Music buffs are always welcome.' He released Eve's hand to take hers. 'Why don't I show you my favorite toy?' he suggested, leading her toward the console. Before Eve could follow, Mavis burst in.

'What did you think? Did you like it? I wrote it. Jess orchestrated it, but I wrote it. He thinks it could hit.'

'I'm really proud of you. You sounded great.' Eve returned Mavis's enthusiastic embrace and grinned at Leonardo over her shoulder. 'How does it feel to be hooked up with a rising music legend?'

'She's wonderful.' He leaned in to give Eve a one-armed squeeze. 'You look terrific. I noticed on some news clips that you wore a number of my designs. I'm grateful.'

'I'm grateful,' Eve said and meant it. Leonardo was a talented and emerging genius of clothing design. 'I didn't look like Roarke's rag-picking cousin.'

'You always look like yourself,' Leonardo corrected, but he narrowed his eyes and flipped his fingers through her untidy hair. 'You need some work here. If you don't have it styled every few weeks, it loses shape.'

'I was going to trim it up some, I just—'

'No, no.' He shook his head solemnly, but his eyes twinkled at her. 'The days of you hacking at it yourself are over. You call Trina, have her do you.'

'We'll have to drag her again.' Mavis grinned at everything.

'She'll keep making excuses and start clipping at it with kitchen shears when it gets in her eyes.' She giggled when Leonardo shuddered. 'We'll get Roarke to hound her.'

'I'd be delighted to.' He stepped out of the elevator, walked straight to Eve and, framing her face in his hands, kissed her. 'What am I hounding you about?'

'Nothing. Have a drink.' She passed him her bottle.

Instead of drinking, he kissed Mavis in greeting. 'I appreciate the invitation. This is quite a setup.'

'Isn't it mag? The sound system's ace of the line, and Jess works all kinds of magic with the console. He's got like six million instruments programmed in. He can play them all, too. He can do anything. The night he came into the D and D changed my life. It was like a miracle.'

'Mavis, you're the miracle.' Smoothly, Jess led Peabody back toward the group. She was flushed and glassy-eyed. Eve could see the pulse in her throat pounding to its own rhythm.

'Down, girl,' she muttered, but Peabody only rolled her eyes.

'You met Dallas and Peabody, right? And this is Roarke.' Mavis bounced on her stilts. 'My closest friends.'

'It's a genuine pleasure.' Jess offered one of his finely boned hands to Roarke. 'I admire your success in the business world and your taste in women.'

'Thank you. I tend to be careful with both.' Roarke scanned the area, inclined his head. 'Your studio's impressive.'

'I love showing it off. It's been in the planning stages for some time. Mavis is actually the first artist to use it, other than myself. Mary's going to order food. Why don't I show you my prize creation before I put Mavis back to work?'

He led the way back to the console, sat at it like a captain at the helm. 'The instruments are programmed in, of course. I can call up any number of combinations and vary pitch and speed. It's accessed for voice command, but I rarely use that. Distracts me from the music.'

He slid controls and had a simple backbeat playing. 'Recorded vocals.' He tapped his fingers over buttons and Mavis's voice punched out, surprisingly gritty and rich. A monitor displayed the sounds with washing of colors and shapes. 'I use that for computer analysis. Musicologists' – he flashed a charming, self-deprecating smile – 'we can't help ourselves. But that's another story.'

'She sounds good,' Eve commented, pleased.

'And she'll sound better. Overdubbing.' Mavis's voice split, layered over itself in close harmony. 'Layers and fill.' Jess's hands danced over the controls, drawing out guitars, brass, the jingle of a tambourine, the searing wail of a sax. 'Cool it down.' Everything slowed, mellowed. 'Heat it up.' Went into double time, blasted.

'That's all very basic, as is having her duet with recording artists of the past. You'll have to hear her version of "Hard Day's Night" with the Beatles. I can also code in any sound.' With a smile flirting around his mouth, he spun a dial, and skimmed his fingers over the keys. Eve's voice whispered out.

'Down, girl.' The words melded into Mavis's vocal, repeating, echoing, drifting.

'How did you do that?' Eve demanded.

'I'm miked,' he explained, 'and hooked into the console. Now that I have your voice on program, I can have your voice replace Mavis's.' He skimmed the controls again, and Eve winced when she heard herself singing.

'Don't do that,' she ordered, and laughing, Jess switched it back.

'Sorry, I can't resist playing. Want to hear yourself croon, Peabody?'

'No.' Then she gnawed her lip. 'Well, maybe.'

'Let's see, something smoky, understated, and classic.' He

worked for a moment, then sat back. Peabody's eyes rounded when she heard herself quietly torching through 'I've Got You Under My Skin.'

'Is that one of your songs?' she asked. 'I don't recognize it.'

Jess chuckled. 'No, it's before my time. You've got a strong voice, Officer Peabody. Good breath control. Want to quit your day job and join the party?'

She flushed and shook her head. Jess cut out the vocals, tuned the console to a bluesy instrumental. 'I worked with an engineer who designed some autotronics for Disney-Universe. It took nearly three years to complete this.' He patted the console like a well-loved child. 'Now that I have the prototype and a working unit, I'm hoping to manufacture more. She works on remote, too. I can be anywhere and link up, run the board. I got specs on a smaller, portable unit, and I've been working on a mood enhancer.'

He seemed to catch himself, shook his head. 'I get carried away. My agent's starting to complain that I'm spending more time working on electronics than recording.'

'Food's here!' Big Mary bellowed.

'Well, then.' Jess smiled, scanned his audience. 'Let's dig in. You've got to keep your energy level up, Mavis.'

'I'm starving.' She grabbed Leonardo's hand and headed for the door. Below, Mary was carting bags and boxes into the studio.

'Go help yourselves,' Jess told them. 'I've got a little fiddling to do. I'll be right along.'

'What do you think?' Eve murmured to Roarke as they headed down, trailed by Peabody.

'I think he's looking for an investor.'

Eve sighed, nodded. 'Yeah, that was my take. I'm sorry.'

'It's not a problem. He's got an interesting product.'

'I had Peabody run a make on him. Nothing's come up. But I don't like to think of him using you – or Mavis.'

'That's yet to be seen.' He turned her into his arms as they stepped into the studio, ran his hands over her hips. 'I missed you. I miss spending large quantities of time with you.'

She felt the heat kindle between her thighs, hotter, lustier than the moment called for. Her breasts tingled with it. 'I missed you, too. Why don't we figure out how to cut the evening short, go home, and fuck like rabbits?'

. He was hard as iron. As he leaned down to nip at her ear, he found himself struggling not to tug at her clothes. 'Good thought. Christ, I want you.'

The hell with where they were, Roarke thought and dragged her head back by the hair to plunder her mouth.

At the console, at the controls, Jess watched them and smiled. Another few minutes, he mused, and they could very well be on the floor, mindlessly mating. Better not. With deft fingers, he skimmed buttons, changed the program. More than satisfied, he rose and started downstairs.

Two hours later, driving home through the dark streets that ran with colors from flashing billboards, Eve pushed her cruiser past the limits of the law. Need was a low, throbbing beat between her thighs, an itch desperate to be scratched.

'You're breaking the law, Lieutenant,' Roarke said mildly. He was rock hard again, like a teenager cruising on hormones.

The woman who prided herself on never abusing her badge muttered, 'Bending it.'

Roarke reached over, cupped her breast. 'Bend it more.'

'Oh Jesus.' She could already imagine what he'd feel like inside her, so she punched the accelerator and shot like a bullet down Park.

A glide-cart operator flipped up her middle finger as Eve screamed around a curb and headed east. Cursing lightly, Eve switched on her duty light, popped up the red and blue globe, and had it flashing.

'I can't believe I'm doing this. I never do this.'

Roarke slid his hand down to her thigh. 'Do you know what I'm going to do to you?'

She gave a hoarse laugh, swallowed hard. 'Don't tell me, for God's sake. I'll kill us.'

Her hands were glued to the wheel and trembling, her body vibrating like a string already plucked. Her breath was already hitching. Clouds slipped past the moon and freed its light.

'Hit the remote for the gate,' she panted. 'Hit the remote. I'm not slowing down.'

He coded it quickly. The iron gate eased majestically open, and she burst through with inches to spare. 'Excellent job. Stop the car.'

'Just a minute, just a minute.' She rocketed up the drive, flying past the gorgeous trees and musical fountains.

'Stop the car,' he demanded again and pressed his hand to her crotch.

She came instantly, violently, barely managing to keep from steering into an oak. Gasping for air, she pulled the vehicle to a stop, fishtailing and ending in a drunken diagonal across the drive.

She flew at him.

They tore at clothes, fighting to find each other in the narrow confines of the car. She bit his shoulder, yanked his trousers open. He was cursing, she was laughing, when he dragged her out of the car. They fell on the grass in a tangle of limbs and twisted clothing.

'Hurry up, hurry up.' It was all she could manage through the unbearable pressure. His mouth was on her breast through her torn shirt, teeth scraping. She pulled at his trousers, dug her fingers into his hips.

His breathing was fast, rough, the raw need clawing through him as urgently as her nails clawed at his back. He could feel his blood roaring, a tidal wave through his veins. His hands bruised her as he rocked her legs back, drove deep inside her.

She screamed, a wild, savage sound of pleasure, her nails raking his back, her teeth fixing on his shoulder. She could feel him pulsing inside her, filling her with each desperate thrust. The punch of the orgasm was painful and did nothing to lessen the monstrous need.

She was wet, hot, her muscles vising over him like teeth with each pump of hips. He couldn't stop, couldn't think, and plunged again and again like a stud covering a mare in heat. He couldn't see her through the red haze that clouded his vision, he could only feel her, racing with him, pistoning her hips. Her voice buzzed in his ears, all whimpers and moans and gasps.

Each sound beat in his blood like a primal chant.

It shattered without warning, beyond his control. His body simply peaked like an engine on maximum power, battered into hers, then erupted. The hot wave of release swamped him, swallowed him, drowned him. It was the only time since he'd first touched her that he didn't know if she had followed him over the edge.

He collapsed, rolled weakly away to try to find air for his overtaxed lungs. In the glowing moonlight, they sprawled on the grass, sweaty, half-dressed, shuddering, like the lone survivors of a particularly vicious war.

With a groan, she rolled over on her stomach, let the grass cool her burning cheeks. 'Christ, what was that?'

'Under other circumstances, I'd call it sex. But . . .' He managed to open his eyes. 'I don't have a word for it.'

'Did I bite you?'

A few aches were making themselves known as his body recovered. He twisted his head, glanced at his shoulder, and saw the imprint of her teeth. 'Someone did. I think it was probably you.'

He watched a star fall, shooting silver from sky to earth. It had been much like that, he thought, like plunging helplessly to oblivion. 'Are you okay?'

'I don't know. I have to think about it.' Her head was still spinning. 'We're on the lawn,' she said slowly. 'Our clothes are torn. I'm pretty sure I have the imprint of your fingers dented into my butt.'

'I did my best,' he murmured.

She snickered first, then chuckled, then broke into fits of giddy, hiccupping laughter. 'Jesus, Roarke, Jesus Christ, look at us.'

'In a minute. I think I'm still partially blind.' But he was grinning as he shifted. She was still shaking with laughter. Her hair stuck up at odd angles, her eyes were glassy, and there were grass stains as well as bruises on her pretty ass. 'You don't look much like a cop, Lieutenant.'

She rolled to sit up as he had, angled her head. 'You don't look much like a rich guy, Roarke.' She tugged on his sleeve – it was all that was left of his shirt. 'But it's an interesting look. How are you going to explain that to Summerset?'

'I'll simply tell him my wife is an animal.'

She snorted. 'He's already decided that for himself.' Blowing out a breath, she looked toward the house. Lights glimmered on the lower level to welcome them home. 'How are we going to get into the house?'

'Well . . .' He found what was left of her shirt, tied it around her breasts, and made her giggle helplessly. They managed to tug on ruined slacks, then sat looking at each other. 'I can't carry you to the car,' he told her. 'I was hoping you'd carry me.'

'We have to get up first.'

'Okay.'

Neither of them moved. The laughter started again, continued as they grabbed onto each other like drunks and staggered to their feet. 'Leave the car,' he decided.

'Uh-huh.' They limped off, weaving. 'Clothes? Shoes?'

'Leave them, too.'

'Good plan.'

Snickering like children breaking curfew, they stumbled

91

up the steps, shushing each other as they fell through the door.

'Roarke!' Shocked tones, rushing feet.

'I knew it,' Eve muttered dourly. 'I just knew it.'

Summerset rushed out of the shadows, his normally set face alive with shock and worry. He saw tattered clothes, bruised skin, wild eyes. 'Was there an accident?'

Roarke straightened up, kept his arm around Eve's shoulders as much for balance as support. 'No. It was on purpose. Go to bed, Summerset.'

Eve glanced over her shoulder as she and Roarke helped each other up the stairs. Summerset stood at the base, gaping. The picture pleased her so much, she snickered all the way to the bedroom.

They fell into bed, exactly as they were, and slept like babies.

# Chapter Seven

At shortly before eight the next morning, a bit sore and fuzzy-brained, Eve sat at her desk in her home office. She considered it more of a sanctuary than an office, really, the apartment Roarke had built for her in his home. Its design was similar to the apartment where she had lived when she'd met him, which she'd been reluctant to give up.

He'd provided it so that she could have her own space, her own things. Even after all the time she'd lived there, she rarely slept in their bed when he was away. Instead, she curled into the relaxation chair and dozed.

The nightmares came less often now, but crept back at odd moments.

She could work here when it was convenient, lock the doors if she wanted privacy. And as it had a fully operational kitchen, she often chose her AutoChef over Summerset when she was alone in the house.

With the sun streaming through the view wall at her back, she reviewed her caseload, juggled legwork. She knew she didn't have the luxury of focusing exclusively on the Fitzhugh case, particularly since it was earmarked a probable suicide. If she didn't turn up hard evidence in the next day or two, she'd have no choice but to lower its priority.

At eight sharp there was a brisk knock on the door.

'Come on in, Peabody.'

'I'll never get used to this place,' Peabody said as she walked inside. 'It's like something out of an old video.'

'You should get Summerset to take you on a tour,' Eve said absently. 'I'm pretty sure there are rooms I've never seen. There's coffee.' Eve gestured toward the kitchen alcove and continued to frown at her logbook.

Peabody wandered off, scanning the entertainment units lining the wall, wondering what it would be like to be able to afford any amusement available: music, art, video, holograms, VR, meditation chambers, games. Play a set of tennis with the latest Wimbledon champ, dance with a hologram of Fred Astaire, or take a virtual trip to the pleasure palaces on Regis III.

Daydreaming a bit, she turned into the kitchen. The AutoChef was already programmed for coffee, so she ordered two, carried the steaming mugs back into the office. She waited patiently while Eve continued to mutter.

Peabody sipped her coffee. 'God. Oh God. It's real.' Blinking in shock, she cupped both hands reverently around the mug. 'This coffee is real.'

'Yeah, you get spoiled. I can hardly stomach the slop down at Cop Central anymore.' Eve glanced up, caught Peabody's dazed expression, and grinned. It hadn't been so long before that she'd had a similar reaction to Roarke's coffee. And to Roarke. 'Pretty great, huh?'

'I've never had real coffee before.' As if sipping liquid gold – and with the depletion of the rain forests and plantations it was equally dear – Peabody drank slowly. 'It's amazing.'

'You've got a half hour to OD on it while we work out the day's strategy.'

'I can have more?' Peabody closed her eyes and just inhaled the scent. 'You're a god, Dallas.'

With a snort, Eve reached for her beeping 'link. 'Dallas,' she began, then her face lit with a grin. 'Feeney.'

'How's married life, kid?'

'It's tolerable. Pretty early in the day for you electronic detectives, isn't it?'

'Got a hot one working. A scramble at the chief's office. Some joker hacked into his mainframe and nearly fried the whole system.'

'They got in?' Her eyes widened in surprise. She wasn't sure even Feeney, with his magic touch, could break the security on the Chief of Police and Security's system.

'Looks that way. Tangled shit all to hell and back. I'm unknotting it,' he said cheerfully. 'Thought I'd check in, see what's what since I haven't heard from you.'

'I hit the ground running.'

'You don't know any other speed. You primary on Fitzhugh?'

'That's right. Something I should know?'

'No. Smart money's that he iced himself, and nobody around here's too sorry. That oil slick loved squeezing cops on the stand. Funny though, second big suicide in a month.'

Eve's interest spiked. 'Second?'

'Yeah. Oh, that's right, you were off honeymooning and making cow's eyes.' He wiggled his bushy red eyebrows. 'Senator in East Washington a couple weeks ago. Jumped out the window of the Capitol Building. Politicians and lawyers. They're crazy anyway.'

'Yeah. Could you get me the data on it when you have the chance? Transfer it to my office unit.'

'What, you going to keep a scrapbook?'

'Just interested.' The feeling was back in her gut. 'I'll pick up the tab next time we're in the Eatery.'

'No problem. As soon as I get this system unknotted, I'll feed it to you. Don't be a stranger,' he told her and signed off.

Peabody continued to take miserly sips of coffee. 'You think there's a connection between Fitzhugh and the senator who took the dive?'

'Lawyers and politicians,' Eve murmured. 'And autotronic engineers.'

'What?'

Eve shook her head. 'I don't know. Disengage,' she ordered her unit, then swung her bag over her shoulder. 'Let's go.'

Peabody struggled not to pout about the lack of another cup of coffee. 'Two suicides in two different cities in a month isn't such a weird thing,' she began, lengthening her stride to catch up with Eve.

'Three. There was a kid on Olympus who hanged himself while we were there. Mathias, Drew. I want to see if you can find a connection, anything that ties them together. People, places, habits, education, hobbies.' She rushed down the stairs, gearing up.

'I don't know the politician's name. I didn't pay attention to the reports on the East Washington suicide.' Busily, Peabody tugged out her personal palm computer and began searching for data.

'Mathias was in his early twenties, autotronics engineer. He worked for Roarke. Shit.' She had a bad feeling she was going to be forced to drag Roarke into her work once again. 'If you run into a snag, ask Feeney. He can pop the data handcuffed and drunk, faster than either of us.'

Eve wrenched open the door, scowled when she didn't see her car at the top of the drive. 'Goddamn Summerset. I've told him to leave my car when I park it.'

'I think he did.' Peabody flipped on her sunshades, pointed. 'It's blocking the drive, see?'

'Oh, yeah.' Eve cleared her throat. The car was just as she'd left it, and fluttering in the mild breeze were a few torn articles of clothing. 'Don't ask,' she muttered and started to hoof it down the drive.

'I wasn't going to.' Peabody's voice was smooth as silk. 'Speculation's more interesting.'

'Shut up, Peabody.'

'Shutting up, Lieutenant.' With a smirk, Peabody climbed in the car and swallowed a laugh when Eve swung the vehicle around and cruised down the drive.

Arthur Foxx was sweating. It was subtle, just a faint sheen over his top lip, but Eve found it satisfying. She hadn't been surprised to discovered his chosen representative was an associate of Fitzhugh's, a young eager beaver in a pricey suit with trendy medallions decorating the slim lapels.

'My client is understandably upset.' The lawyer folded his youthful face into somber lines. 'The memorial service for Mr Fitzhugh is scheduled for one P.M. this afternoon. You've chosen an inappropriate time for this interview.'

'Death chooses the time, Mr Ridgeway, and it's usually inappropriate. Interview with Authur Foxx, re Fitzhugh, case number three oh oh nine one-ASD, conducted by Dallas, Lieutenant Eve. Date August 24, 2058, time oh nine thirty-six. Will you state your name for the record?'

'Arthur Foxx.'

'Mr Foxx, you are aware that this interview is being recorded.'

'I am.'

'You have exercised your right to counsel and understand your additional rights and responsibilities?'

'That's correct.'

'Mr Foxx, you gave an earlier statement regarding your activities on the night of Mr Fitzhugh's death. Do you wish to view a replay of that statement?'

'It's not necessary. I told you what happened. I don't know what else you expect me to tell you.'

'To begin, tell me where you were between twenty-two thirty and twenty-three hundred on the night of the incident.'

'I've already told you. We had dinner. We watched a comedy, we went to bed and caught a bit of the late news.'

'You remained at home all evening?'

'That's what I've said.'

'Yes, Mr Foxx, that's what you've said, on record. But that's not what you did.'

'Lieutenant, my client is here voluntarily. I see no—'

'Save it,' she suggested. 'You left the building at approximately ten thirty P.M. and returned some thirty minutes later. Where did you go?'

'I—' Foxx tugged at the silver string of his tie. 'I stepped out for a few minutes. I'd forgotten.'

'You'd forgotten.'

'My mind was confused. I was in shock.' His tie made wispy sounds as his fingers worked over it. 'I didn't remember something as unimportant as taking a quick walk.'

'But you remember now? Where did you go?'

'Just for a walk. Around the block a few times.'

'You returned with a parcel. What was in it?'

She saw the moment he realized the security cameras had nailed him. His gaze shifted past her and the fingers on his tie became busier. 'I stopped into a 24/7, picked up a few things. Veggie-Smokes. I have the urge for one occasionally.'

'It's a simple matter to check with the 24/7 and determine exactly what you purchased.'

'Some tranqs,' he spit out. 'I wanted to tranq out for the night. I wanted a smoke. There's no law against it.'

'No, but there is a law against giving false statements in a police investigation.'

'Lieutenant Dallas.' The lawyer's voice was still smooth but a bit frayed around the edges with annoyance. It gave Eve the clue that Foxx had been no more forthcoming with his representative than he had with the police. 'The fact that Mr Foxx left the premises for a short time is hardly germane to your investigation. And discovering a loved one's body is a more than reasonable excuse for neglecting to remember a minor detail.'

'One minor detail, maybe. You didn't mention, Mr Foxx,

that you and Mr Fitzhugh had a visitor on the evening of his death.'

'Leanore is hardly a visitor,' Foxx said stiffly. 'She is – was Fitz's partner. I believe they had some business to discuss, which is another reason I went for a walk. I wanted to give them a few moments of privacy to discuss the case.' He took a shallow breath. 'I generally found that more convenient for everyone.'

'I see. So now your statement is that you left the apartment in order to provide your spouse and his partner with privacy. Why didn't you mention Ms Bastwick's visit in your earlier statement?'

'I didn't think of it.'

'You didn't think of it. You stated that you ate dinner, watched a comedy, and went to bed, but you neglected to add in these other events. What other events have you neglected to tell me, Mr Foxx?'

'I have nothing more to say.'

'Why were you angry when you left the building, Mr Foxx? Did it annoy you to have a beautiful woman, a woman with whom Mr. Fitzhugh works closely, drop by your home so late in the evening?'

'Lieutenant, you have no right to imply—'

She barely spared the lawyer a glance. 'I'm not implying, Counselor, I'm asking, in a very straightforward manner, if Mr Foxx was angry and jealous when he stormed out of his building.'

'I did not storm, I walked.' Foxx fisted a hand on the table. 'And I had absolutely no reason to be angry or jealous of Leanore. However often she chose to throw herself at Fitz, he was completely disinterested in her on that level.'

'Ms Bastwick threw herself at Mr Fitzhugh?' Eve lifted her brows. 'That must have ticked you off, Arthur. Knowing that your spouse had no sexual preference between women or men, knowing they were together hours every day during the work week, having her come by, flaunt herself in front of him in your own home. No wonder you were angry. I'd have wanted to deck her.'

'He thought it was amusing,' Foxx blurted out. 'He was actually flattered to have someone so much younger and so attractive playing for him. He laughed when I complained about her.'

'He laughed at you?' Eve knew how to play the game. Sympathy dripped in her voice. 'That must have infuriated you. It did, didn't it? It ate at you, didn't it, Arthur, imagining them together, him touching her, and laughing at you.'

'I could have murdered her.' Foxx exploded with it, batting away his lawyer's restraining hands as fury spurted color into his face. 'She thought she could lure him away from me, make him want her. She didn't give a damn that we were married, that we were committed to each other. All she wanted to do was win. Fucking lawyer.'

'You don't care much for lawyers, do you?'

His breath was shuddering. He caught it, let it shudder out until it was even again. 'No, as a rule, I don't. I didn't think of Fitz as a lawyer. I thought of him as my spouse. And if I'd been disposed to committing murder that night or any other, Lieutenant, I would have murdered Leanore.'

He unfisted his hands, folded them together. 'Now, I have nothing more to say.'

Gauging it to be enough for the time being, Eve terminated the interview, rose. 'We'll be talking again, Mr Foxx.'

'I'd like to know when you're going to release Fitz's body,' he said, getting stiffly to his feet. 'I've decided not to postpone the service today, though it feels unseemly to go on with it with his body still being held.'

'That's the decision of the medical examiner. His tests are still incomplete.'

'Isn't it enough that he's dead?' Foxx's voice trembled. 'Isn't it enough that he killed himself without you dragging it out, pulling out the small and sordid personal details of our lives?'

'No.' She walked to the door, released the code. 'No, it's not.' She hesitated, decided to take a stab in the dark. 'I imagine Mr Fitzhugh was very shocked and very upset by the recent suicide of Senator Pearly.'

Foxx only jerked his head in a formal nod. 'He was shocked, certainly, though they barely knew each other.' Then a muscle jerked in his cheek. 'If you're implying that Fitz took his own life because he was influenced by Pearly, it's ridiculous. They had no more than a slight acquaintance. They rarely communicated.'

'I see. Thank you for your time.' She ushered them out, glanced down the corridor to the adjoining interview room. Leanore should certainly be inside by now, waiting.

Taking her time, Eve strolled down the corridor to a vending unit, contemplated her choices, jingled loose credits in her pocket. She settled on a Chewy Bar and a half tube of Pepsi. The unit delivered the goods, droned out the standard request to recycle, and offered the consumer a mild warning on sugar intake.

'Mind your own business,' Eve suggested. Leaning back against the wall, she lingered over her snack, dumped the trash into the recycle chute, then walked leisurely down the hall.

She'd estimated the twenty-minute wait would steam Leanore. She was right on target.

The woman was pacing like a cat, elegant legs eating up the worn flooring with quick steps. The minute Eve opened the door, she whirled.

'Lieutenant Dallas, my time is extremely valuable, even if yours is not.'

'Depends on how you look at it,' Eve said easily. 'I don't get to log in billable hours at two K a pop.'

Peabody cleared her throat. 'For the record, Lieutenant Eve Dallas has entered Interview Room C to conduct the remainder of the proceedings. The subject has been informed of all rights and has chosen self-representation during this interview. All data has been logged in record.'

'Fine.' Eve sat, indicated the chair across from her. 'Whenever you've finished prowling, Ms Bastwick, we can get started.'

'I was ready to begin this procedure at the appropriate time.' Leanore sat, crossed her satiny legs. 'With you, Lieutenant, not your subordinate.'

'Hear that, Peabody, you're my subordinate.'

'Duly recorded, sir,' Peabody said dryly.

'Though I consider it insulting and unnecessary.' Leanore brushed at the cuffs of her trim black suit. 'I'm attending Fitz's memorial in a few hours.'

'You wouldn't be here, being unnecessarily insulted, if you hadn't lied in your previous statement.'

Leanore's eyes went glacial. 'I assume you can substantiate that accusation, Lieutenant.'

'You stated for the record that you had gone to the deceased's residence last evening on a professional matter. That you remained, discussing a case, for twenty to thirty minutes.'

'More or less,' Leanore said, her voice frosty around the edges.

'Tell me, Ms Bastwick, do you always take a bottle of vintage wine to a business meeting and groom yourself for said meeting in the elevator like a prom queen?'

'There's no law against good grooming, Lieutenant Dallas.' Her gaze flicked dismissively over Eve's untidy hair down to her battered boots. 'You might try it yourself.'

'Aw, now you've hurt my feelings. You polished yourself up, flicked open the top three buttons of your blouse, and brought along a bottle of wine. Sounds like seduction time to me, Leanore.' Eve shifted closer, nearly winked. 'Come on, we're all girls. We know the drill.'

Leanore took her time, studied a minute chip in her manicure. She remained icy. Unlike Foxx, the woman didn't break a sweat. 'I dropped by that evening to consult with Fitz on a professional matter. We had a brief meeting, and I left.'

'You were alone with him during that time.'

'That's right. Arthur got into one of his snits and went out.'

'One of his snits?'

'It was typical of him.' There was a sneer in her voice now, light and disdainful. 'He was outrageously jealous of me, certain I was trying to lure Fitz away from him.'

'And were you?'

A slow, feline smile curved Leanore's lips. 'Really, Lieutenant, if I'd put any effort into it, don't you think I would have succeeded?'

'I'd say you put effort into it. And not succeeding would have really burned you.'

Leanore lifted a shoulder. 'I'll admit I was giving it some consideration. Fitz was wasting himself on Arthur. Fitz and I had a great deal in common, and I found him very attractive. I was very fond of him.'

'Did you act on your attraction and your fondness that evening?'

'You could say I made it clear that I was open to a more intimate relationship with him. He wasn't immediately receptive, but it was only a matter of time.' She moved her shoulders, a quick, confident movement. 'Arthur would have known that.' Her eyes went cold again. 'And that's why I believe he killed Fitz.'

'Quite a piece of work, isn't she?' Eve muttered when the interview was completed. 'Doesn't see anything wrong with trying to lure a man into adultery, break apart a longstanding relationship. More, she's convinced there isn't a man in the world who could resist her.' She sighed heavily. 'Bitch.'

103

'Are you going to charge her?' Peabody wondered.

'For being a bitch?' With a small smile, Eve shook her head. 'I could try to nail her on the false statement, and she and her legal pals would brush it off like lint. Not worth the time. We can't place her at the scene at time of death or hang any kind of motive on her. And I can't see that self-absorbed bimbo sneaking up on a two hundred fifty pound man and slashing his wrists. She wouldn't have wanted to get all that blood on her nifty suit.'

'So you're back to Foxx?'

'He was jealous, he was pissed, he inherits all the toys.' Eve rose, paced to the door and back. 'And we've got nothing.' She pressed her fingers to her eyes. 'I've got to go with what he said when he lost it during interview. He'd have killed Leanore, not Fitzhugh. I'm going to review the data on the two previous suicides.'

'I haven't got much yet,' Peabody began as she followed Eve out of the interview room. 'There wasn't time.'

'There's time now. And Feeney's probably come through. Get me what you've got, then get me more,' Eve demanded and swung into her office. 'Engage,' she ordered the computer as she plopped down in front of it. 'Play new communications.'

Roarke's face swam onto the screen. 'I assume you're out fighting crime. I'm on my way to London, a little glitch that requires personal attention. I don't imagine it will take long. I should be back by eight, which will give us plenty of time to fly out to New Los Angeles for the premiere.'

'Shit, I forgot.'

On screen, his image smiled. 'I'm sure you've conveniently forgotten the engagement, so consider this a gentle reminder. Take care of yourself, Lieutenant.'

Flying to California to spend the evening rubbing elbows with puffed-up video types, eating the glossy little vegetables people out there considered food, tolerating reporters sticking recorders in her face and asking lame questions was not her idea of an entertaining evening.

The second communication was from Commander Whitney, ordering her to prepare a statement for the media on several ongoing cases. *Hot damn*, she thought sourly. *More headlines.*

Then the data from Feeney flashed on screen. Eve rolled her shoulders, hunkered down, and got to work.

At two, she walked into the Village Bistro. Her shirt was sticking to her back as the temperature control on her unit had once again died an unnatural death. The air inside the tony restaurant was ocean breeze cool. Soft, loving zephyrs flitted through, teasing the feathery palms, which grew in huge, white china pots. Glass tables were arranged on two levels, cleverly situated near a small, black water lagoon or in front of a wide-view screen of a white sand beach. Servers wore short uniforms in tropical hues and threaded their way through the tables with offerings of colorful drinks and artistically arranged dishes.

The maître d' was a droid dressed in a flowing white jumpsuit and programmed with a snooty French accent. He took one look at Eve's worn jeans and limp shirt and wrinkled his prominent nose.

'Madam, I am afraid we have no tables available. You would perhaps prefer the delicatessen on the next block north.'

'Yeah, I would.' Because his attitude annoyed her, she stuck her badge in his face. 'But I'm eating here. I don't give a shit if that puts your chips in a twist, pal. Where's Dr Mira's table?'

'Put that away,' he hissed, looking everywhere at once and fluttering his hands. 'Do you wish my customers to lose their appetites?'

'They'll really lose them if I take my weapon out, which is what I'll do if you don't show me Dr Mira's table and see that I've got a glass of iced fizzy water in the next twenty seconds. Got that program?'

His lips clamped together and he nodded. Stiff-backed, he led the way up a swing of faux stone steps to the second level, and then onto an alcove fashioned to resemble an ocean terrace.

'Eve.' Mira rose immediately from her pretty table and took both of Eve's hands. 'You look wonderful.' To Eve's faint surprise, Mira kissed her cheek. 'Rested. Happy.'

'I guess I am.' After a brief hesitation, Eve leaned forward and touched her lips to Mira's cheek in turn.

The droid had already snapped to a server. 'Dr Mira's companion wishes a fizzy water.'

'Iced,' Eve added, curling her lip at the maître d'.

'Thank you, Armand.' Mira's soft blue eyes twinkled. 'We'll order shortly.'

Eve took another quick scan of the restaurant, the diners in their summer pastels and pricey cottons. She shifted on her padded chair. 'We could have met in your office.'

'I wanted to take you to lunch. This is one of my favorite spots.'

'The droid's an asshole.'

'Well, perhaps Armand is a bit overprogrammed, but the food is wonderful. You should try the Clams Maurice. You won't regret it.' She settled back when Eve's water was served. 'Tell me, how was your honeymoon?'

Eve gulped down half the water and felt human again. 'Tell me how long I can expect people to ask me that question?'

Mira laughed. She was a pretty woman with soft sable hair swept back from a quietly attractive face. She wore one of her habitually elegant suits, this one in pale yellow. She appeared polished and tidy. She was one of the leading behavioral psychiatrists in the country, and was often consulted by the police about the most vicious crimes.

Though Eve was unaware of it, Mira's feelings toward her were strong and deeply maternal.

'It embarrasses you.'

'Well, you know. Honeymoon. Sex. Personal.' Eve rolled her eyes. 'Stupid. I guess I'm just not used it. To being married. To Roarke. To the whole business.'

'You love each other and make each other happy. There's no need to get used to it, only to enjoy it. You're sleeping well?'

'Mostly.' And because Mira knew her deepest and darkest secrets, Eve dropped her guard. 'I still have nightmares, but not as often. The memories come and go. None of it's as bad now that I've dealt with it.'

'Have you dealt with it?'

'My father raped me, abused me, beat me,' Eve said flatly. 'I killed him. I was eight years old. I survived. Whoever I was before I was found in that alley doesn't matter now. I'm Eve Dallas. I'm a good cop. I've made myself.'

'Good.' *There would be more*, Mira thought. Traumas such as the one Eve had lived through cast echoes that never completely faded. 'You still put the cop first.'

'I am a cop first.'

'Yes.' Mira smiled a little. 'I suppose you always will be. Why don't we order, then you can tell me why you called.'

# Chapter Eight

Eve chose Mira's recommendation of clams, then treated herself to some of the real yeast bread set in a silver basket on the table. As she ate, she gave Mira a profile of Fitzhugh and the details of his death.

'You'd like me to tell you if he was capable of taking his own life. Disposed to it, emotionally, psychologically.'

Eve cocked a brow. 'That's the plan.'

'Unfortunately, I can't do that. I can tell you that everyone is capable of it, given the right circumstances and emotional state.'

'I don't believe that,' Eve said so firmly, so decisively, that Mira smiled.

'You're a strong woman, Eve. Now. You've made yourself strong, rational, tough-minded. You're a survivor. But you remember despair. Helplessness. Hopelessness.'

Eve did; too well, too clearly. She shifted in her chair. 'Fitzhugh wasn't a helpless man.'

'The surface can hide a great deal of turmoil.' Dr Mira held up a hand before Eve could interrupt again. 'But I agree with you. Given your profile of him, his background, his lifestyle, I wouldn't tag him as a likely candidate for suicide – certainly not one of such an abrupt and impulsive nature.'

'It was abrupt,' Eve agreed. 'I dealt with him in court right before this happened. He was as smug and arrogant and full of his own sense of importance as ever.'

'I'm sure that's true. I can only say that some of us – many of us – confronted with some crisis, some personal upheaval of the heart or mind, choose to end it rather than live through it or change it. You and I can't know what Fitzhugh might have found himself confronted with on the night of his death.'

'That isn't a hell of a lot of help,' Eve muttered. 'Okay, let me give you two more.' Briskly, with a cop's dispassion, she related the other suicides. 'Pattern?'

'What did they have in common?' Mira tossed back. 'The lawyer, the politician, and the tech.'

'A blip in the brain. Maybe.' Tapping her fingers on the cloth, Eve frowned. 'I've got some chains to pull to get all the data, but it could be the motive. The reason behind it all might be physiological rather than psychological. If there's a connection, I've got to find it.'

'You're veering out of my field, but if you find data linking the three cases, I'd be happy to do a workup.'

Eve smiled. 'I was counting on it. I don't have a lot of time. The Fitzhugh case can't stay a priority for much longer. If I can't nail something down soon and use it to convince the commander to keep the file open, I'll have to move on. But for now—'

'Eve?' Reeanna slipped up to the table, looking stunning in an ankle-skimming robe of bleeding rainbow colors. 'Well, how nice. I was lunching with an associate and thought I recognized you.'

'Reeanna.' Eve worked up a smile. She didn't mind looking like a street hawker next to the glamorous redhead, but she did mind having her consult lunch interrupted. 'Dr Mira, Reeanna Ott.'

'Dr Ott.' Gracious, Mira offered a hand. 'I've heard of your work and admired it.'

'Thank you, and I'll say the same. It's an honor to meet one of the top psychiatrists in the country. I've scanned a number of your papers and found them fascinating.'

'You flatter me. Won't you sit down, join us for some dessert?'

'I'd love to.' Reeanna flicked a questioning glance at Eve. 'If I'm not interrupting official business.'

'We seem to be finished with that part of the program.' Eve looked up at the waiter summoned by a discreet flick of Mira's finger. 'Just coffee. House brand. Black.'

'I'll have the same,' Mira said. 'And a dish of the Blueberry Trifle. I'm weak.'

'So am I.' Reeanna beamed at the waiter as though he would personally prepare her selection. 'A double latte, and a slice of Chocolate Sin. I'm so tired of processed food,' she confided to Mira. 'I intend to gorge myself while I'm in New York.'

'And how long will you be in town?'

'It depends a great deal on Roarke' – she smiled at Eve – 'and how long he finds it useful to have me here. I have a feeling he'll be shipping both William and me off to Olympus within a few weeks.'

'The Olympus Resort's quite an undertaking,' Mira commented. 'All the blips I've seen on the news and entertainment channels have been fascinating.'

'He'd like to have it up and fully operational by next spring.' Reeanna ran her hand up and down the trio of gold links she wore around her neck. 'We'll see. Roarke usually gets what he wants. Wouldn't you agree, Eve?'

'He didn't get where he is by taking no for an answer.'

'No, indeed. You were just on the resort. Did he give you a tour of the Autotronics Arcade?'

'Briefly.' Eve's lips quirked a little. 'We had . . . a lot of ground to cover in a short time.'

Reeanna's smile was slow and sly. 'I imagine you did. But I hope you tried a few of the programs that are in place. William's so proud of those games. And you did mention you'd seen the hologram room in the Presidential Suite of the hotel.'

110

'I did. Made use of it several times. Very impressive.'

'Most of that's William's doing – the design – but I will take partial credit. We plan to utilize that new system to enhance the treatment of addicts and certain psychoses.' She shifted as their coffee and dessert was served. 'That might be of interest to you, Dr Mira.'

'It certainly would. It sounds fascinating.'

'It is. Wickedly expensive right now, but we hope to refine and bring the cost down. But for Olympus, Roarke wanted the best – and he's getting it. Such as the Lisa droid.'

'Yeah.' Eve remembered the stunning female droid with the sultry voice. 'I've seen her.'

'She'll be in PR and customer service. A very superior model that took months to perfect. Her intelligence chips are unmatched by anything on the market. She'll have decision making and personality capabilities well beyond the current available units. William and I—' She broke off, chuckled at herself. 'Listen to me. I just can't get away from work.'

'It's fascinating.' Mira dipped delicately into her trifle. 'Your study of brain patterns and their genetic thrust on personality, and their application to electronics is compelling, even to a dug-in-at-the-roots psychiatrist such as myself.' She hesitated, glanced at Eve. 'As a matter of fact, your expertise might lend a new angle on a particular case Eve and I were discussing.'

'Oh?' Reeanna forked up some chocolate and all but hummed over it.

'Hypothetical.' Mira spread her hands, well aware of the official ban of layman consults.

'Naturally.'

Eve drummed her fingers on the table again. She preferred Mira's take, but weighing the options, decided to expand.

'Apparent self-termination. No known motive, no known predisposition, no chemical inducement, no family history. Behavioral patterns up to point of termination normal. No substantiated signs of depression or personality fluctuations. Subject is a sixty-two-year-old male, professional, high-end education, successful, financially solvent, bisexual, with long-term same-sex marriage.'

'Physical disabilities?'

'None. Clean health card.'

Reeanna's eyes narrowed in concentration, either over the profile or the dessert she was slowly spooning into her mouth. 'Any psychological defects, treatment?'

'No.'

'Interesting. I'd love to see the brain wave pattern. Available?'

'Currently classified.'

'Hmm.' Reeanna sipped her latte contemplatively. 'Without any known physical or psychiatric abnormalities, no chemical addictions or usage, I'd lean toward a brain blip. Possible tumor. Yet I assume none showed up in autopsy?'

Eve thought of the pinprick, but shook her head. 'Not a tumor, no.'

'There are cases of predisposition that slide through genetic scanning and evaluation. The brain is a complicated organ and still baffles even the most elaborate technology. If I could see his family history . . . Well, to take a wild guess, I'd say your man had a genetic time bomb that went undetected through normal analysis. He'd reached the point in his life where the fuse ran short.'

Eve cocked a brow. 'So he just blew?'

'In a manner of speaking.' Reeanna leaned forward. 'We're all coded in, Eve, in the womb. What we are, who we are. Not just the color of our eyes, our build, our skin tones, but our personalities, our tastes, our intellect, and our emotional scale. The genetic code is stamped on us at the moment of conception. It can be altered to a certain extent, but the basis of what we are remains. Nothing can change it.'

'We are what we're born?' Eve thought of a filthy room, a

112

blinking red light, and a young girl curled into a corner with a bloody knife.

'Precisely.' Reeanna's smile beamed out.

'You don't take into account environment, free will, the basic human drive to better oneself?' Mira objected. 'To consider us merely physical creatures without heart, soul, and a range of choices to be made over a lifetime lowers us to the level of animals.'

'And so we are,' Reeanna said with a sweep of her fork. 'I understand your viewpoint as a therapist, Dr Mira, but mine, as a physiologist, runs down a different lane, so to speak. The decisions we make throughout our life, what we do, how we live, and what we become were printed on our brains while we swam in the womb. Your subject, Eve, was fated to take his life at that time, in that place, and in the manner he chose. Circumstances might have altered it, but the results would have been the same, eventually. It was, in essence, his destiny.'

*Destiny?* Eve thought. Had it been hers to be raped and abused by her own father? To become less than human, to fight her way through that abyss?

Mira shook her head slowly. 'I can't agree. A child born in poverty on the edge of Budapest, taken from the mother at birth and raised in privilege, with love and care in Paris, would reflect that upbringing, that education. The emotional nest,' she insisted, 'and the basic human drive to better oneself can't be discounted.'

'I agree, to a point,' Reeanna qualified. 'But the stamp of the genetic code – that which predisposes us to achievement, failure, good or evil, if you will – overrides all else. Even with the most loving and nurturing of backgrounds, monsters breed; and in the toilets of the universe, goodness, even greatness survives. We are what we are – the rest is window dressing.'

'If I subscribe to your theory,' Eve said slowly, 'the subject in question was fated to take his life. No circumstances, no twists or turns of environment would have prevented it.'

113

'Precisely. The predisposition was there, lurking. Likely an event set it off, but it may have been a minor thing, something easily passed off in another brain pattern. Research still under way at the Bowers Institute has compiled strong evidence of genetic brain patterns and their unassailable influence on behavior. I can get you discs on the subject, if you like.'

'I'll leave the head studies to you and Dr Mira.' Eve shoved her coffee aside. 'I've got to get back to Cop Central. I appreciate the time, Dr Mira,' she said as she rose. 'And the theories, Reeanna.'

'I'd love to discuss them further. Any time.' Reeanna lifted a hand and shook Eve's warmly. 'Do give my best to Roarke.'

'I will.' Eve shifted slightly on her feet when Mira rose to kiss her cheek. 'I'll be in touch.'

'I hope you will, and not just when you've a case to discuss. Tell Mavis hello for me when you see her.'

'Sure.' Hitching her bag on her shoulder, Eve swung her way out, pausing briefly to sneer at the maître d'.

'A fascinating woman.' Reeanna slid her tongue in one long, slow lick over the back of her spoon. 'Controlled, a little angry underneath, straight focused, and unused and vaguely uncomfortable with casual displays of affection.' She laughed lightly at Mira's lifted brow. 'Sorry, professional pitfall. It drives William mad. I didn't mean any offense.'

'I'm sure you didn't.' Mira's lips curved, and her eyes warmed with understanding. 'I often find myself doing the same. And you're right, Eve is a very fascinating woman. Quite self-made, which, I'm afraid, might unbalance your genetic printing theory.'

'Really?' Obviously intrigued, Reeanna leaned forward. 'You know her well?'

'As well as possible. Eve is a . . . contained individual.'

'You're very fond of her,' Reeanna commented with a nod. 'I hope you won't take it the wrong way if I say she wasn't at all what I expected when I learned Roarke was to marry. That he was to marry at all was a surprise, but I imagined his spouse as a woman of polish and sophistication. A homicide detective who wears her shoulder harness as another woman might an heirloom necklace wasn't my conception of Roarke's choice. Yet they look right together, suited. One might even say,' she added with a smile, 'destined.'

'That I can agree with.'

'Now, tell me, Dr Mira, what is your opinion of DNA harvesting?'

'Oh, well now . . .' Happily, Mira settled down for a lively busman's holiday.

At her desk unit, Eve juggled the data she'd compiled on Fitzhugh, Mathias, and Pearly. She could find no link, no common ground. The only real correlation between the three was the fact that none of them had exhibited any suicidal tendencies before the fact.

'Probability the subject cases are related?' Eve demanded.

Working Probability five point two percent

'In other words, zip.' Eve blew out a breath, scowling automatically when an airbus rumbled by, rattling her stingy window. 'Probability of homicide in the matter of Fitzhugh using currently known data.'

With currently known data, probability of homicide is eight point three percent.

'Give it up, Dallas,' she told herself in a mutter. 'Let it go.'

Deliberately, she swiveled in her chair, watching the air traffic clog the sky outside her window. Predestination. Fate. Genetic imprint. If she were to believe in any of that, what was

115

the point of her job – or her life, for that matter? If there was no choice, no changing, why struggle to save lives or stand for the dead when the struggle failed?

If it was all physiologically coded, had she simply followed the pattern by coming to New York, fighting her way out of the dark to make something decent out of herself? And had it been a smear on that code that had blocked out those early years of her life, that continued to shadow bits and pieces of it even now?

And could that code kick in, at any given moment, and make her a reflection of the monster who had been her father?

She knew nothing of her other blood kin. Her mother was a blank. If she had siblings, aunts, uncles, or grandparents, they were all lost in that dark void in her memory. She had no one to base her genetic code on but the man who had beaten and raped her throughout childhood until in terror and pain she had struck back.

And killed.

Blood on her hands at eight years of age. Is that why she'd become a cop? Was she constantly trying to wash away that blood with rules and law and what some still called justice?

'Sir? Dallas?' Peabody laid a hand on Eve's shoulder and jumped when Eve jolted. 'Sorry. Are you all right?'

'No.' Eve pressed her fingers to her eyes. The discussion over dessert had troubled her more than she'd realized. 'Just a headache.'

'I've got some departmental-issue painkillers.'

'No.' Eve was afraid of drugs, even officially sanctioned doses. 'It'll back off. I'm running out of ideas on the Fitzhugh case. Feeney fed me all known data on the kid on Olympus. I can't find any correlation between him and Fitzhugh or the senator. I've got nothing but piddly shit to hang on Leanore and Arthur. I can request truth detection, but I won't get it. I'm not going to be able to keep it open more than another twenty-four hours.'

'You still think they're connected?'

'I want them to be connected, and that's a different thing. I haven't exactly given you an impressive lift on with your first assignment as my permanent aide.'

'Being your permanent aide is the best thing that ever happened to me.' Peabody flushed a little. 'I'd be grateful if we got stuck shoveling through inactives for the next six months. You'd still be training me.'

Eve leaned back in her chair. 'You're easily satisfied, Peabody.'

Peabody shifted her gaze until her eyes met Eve's. 'No, sir, I'm not. When I don't get the best, I get real cranky.'

Eve laughed, dragged a hand through her hair. 'You sucking up, Officer?'

'No, sir. If I was sucking up, I'd make some personal observation, such as marriage obviously agrees with you, Lieutenant. You've never looked lovelier.' Peabody smiled a little when Eve snorted. 'That's how you'd know I was sucking up.'

'So noted.' Eve considered a moment, then cocked her head. 'Didn't you tell me your family are Free-Agers?'

Peabody didn't roll her eyes, but she wanted to. 'Yes, sir.'

'Cops don't usually spring from Free-Agers. Artists, farmers, the occasional scientist, lots of craft workers.'

'I didn't like weaving mats.'

'Can you?'

'If held at laser point.'

'So, what? Your family pissed you off and you decided to break the mold, go into a field dramatically removed from pacifism?'

'No, sir.' Puzzled at the line of questioning, Peabody shrugged. 'My family's great. We're still pretty tight. They're not going to understand what I do or want to do, but they never tried to block me. I just wanted to be a cop, the same way my brother wanted to be a carpenter and my

117

sister a farmer. One of the strongest tenets of Free-Ageism is self-expression.'

'But you don't fit the genetic code,' Eve muttered and drummed her fingers on her desk. 'You don't fit. Heredity and environment, gene patterns – they all should have influenced you differently.'

'The bad guys wished I had been,' Peabody said soberly. 'But I'm here, keeping our city safe.'

'If you get an urge to weave a mat—'

'You'll be the first to know.'

Eve's unit beeped twice, signaling incoming data. 'Additional autopsy report on the kid.' Eve gestured for Peabody to come closer. 'List any abnormal brain pattern,' she ordered.

Microscopic abnormality, right cerebral hemisphere, frontal lobe, left quadrant. Unexplained. Further research and testing under way.

'Well, well, I think we just caught a break. Display visual of frontal lobe and abnormality.' The cross section of the brain popped on screen. 'There.' A quick surge of excitement churned in her belly as Eve tapped the screen. 'That shadow – pinprick. See it?'

'Barely.' Peabody leaned closer until she was all but cheek to cheek with Eve. 'Looks like a flaw on the display.'

'No, a flaw in the brain. Increase quadrant six, twenty percent.'

The picture shifted, and the section with the shadow filled the screen. 'More of a burn than a hole, isn't it?' Eve said half to herself. 'Hardly there, but what kind of damage, what kind of influence would it have on behavior, personality, decision making?'

'I pretty well dumped my required Abnormal Physiology at the Academy.' Peabody moved her sturdy shoulders. 'I did better in Psych, better yet in Tactics. This is over my head.'

118

'Mine, too,' Eve admitted. 'But it's a link, our first one. Computer, cross section of brain abnormality, Fitzhugh, file one two eight seven one. Split screen with current display.'

The screen jittered, went to fuzzy gray. Eve swore, smacked it with the heel of her hand, and bumped out a shaky image blurred across the center.

'Son of a bitch. Son of a bitch. This cheap shit we have to use around here. It's a wonder we can close a case on jaywalking. Download all data, you bastard, on disc.'

'Maybe if you sent this unit into Maintenance,' Peabody suggested and received a snarl.

'It was supposed to be overhauled while I was away. The fuckers in Maintenance have their fingers up their butts. I'm going to run this through one of Roarke's units.' She caught Peabody's lifted brow and tapped her foot as she waited for the wheezy machine to download. 'You got a problem with that, Officer?'

'No, sir.' Peabody tucked her tongue in her cheek and decided against mentioning the series of codes Eve was about to break. 'No problem here.'

'Fine. Get to work on the red tape and get me the brain scan of the senator for comparison.'

Peabody's smug little smile fell away. 'You want me to bump heads with East Washington?'

'Your head's hard enough to handle it.' Eve ejected the disc and pocketed it. 'Call me when you get it. The minute you get it.'

'Yes, sir. If we get a link there, we're going to need an expert analyst.'

'Yeah.' Eve thought of Reeanna. 'I might just have one. Get moving, Peabody.'

'Moving, Lieutenant.'

119

# *Chapter Nine*

Eve wasn't one for breaking rules, yet she found herself standing outside the locked door of Roarke's private room. It was disconcerting to realize that after a decade of going by the book, she could find it so easy to circumvent procedure.

*Do the ends justify the means?* she wondered. *And are the means really so out of line?* Maybe the equipment in the room beyond was unregistered and undetectable to Compuguard and therefore illegal, but it was also top of the line. The pathetic electronics budgeted to the Police and Security Department had been antiquated nearly before it was installed, and Homicide's slice of the budget pie was stingy and stale.

She tapped her fingers on her pocket where the disc rested and shifted her feet. *The hell with it,* she decided. She could be a law-abiding cop and walk away or she could be a smart one.

She placed her hand on the security screen. 'Dallas, Lieutenant Eve.'

The locks disengaged with a quiet snick and opened into Roarke's huge data center. The long curve of windows, which were shielded against sun and flybys, kept the room in shadows. She ordered lights, secured the door, and walked over to face the wide, U-shaped console.

Roarke had programmed her palm and voice print into the system months before, but she'd never used the equipment alone. Even now that they were married, she felt like an intruder.

She made herself sit, snugged the chair into the console. 'Unit one, engage.' She heard the silky hum of high-level equipment responding and nearly sighed. Her disc slid in smoothly, and within seconds had been decoded and read by the civilian unit. 'And so much for our elaborate security at NYPSD,' she muttered. 'Wall screen on full. Display data, Fitzhugh File H-one two eight seven one. Split screen with Mathias File S-three oh nine one two.'

Data flowed like water onto the huge wall screen facing the console. In her admiration, Eve forgot to feel guilty. She leaned forward, scanning birth dates, credit ratings, purchasing habits, political affiliations.

'Strangers,' she said to herself. 'You couldn't have had less in common.' Then her lips pursed as she noted correlations on a section of purchasing habits. 'Well, you both liked games. Lots of on-line time, lots of entertainment and interactive programs.' Then she sighed. 'Along with about seventy percent of the population. Computer, split screen display, brain scan both loaded files.'

With an almost seamless segue, Eve was studying the images. 'Increase and highlight unexplained abnormalities.'

The same, she mused, eyes narrowed. Here the two men were the same, like brothers, twins in the womb. The burn shadow was precisely the same size and shape, in precisely the same location.

'Computer, analyze abnormality and identify.'

Working ... Incomplete data ... Searching medical files. Please wait for analysis.

'That's what they all say.' She pushed away from the console to pace while the computer juggled its brain. When the door opened, she spun around on her heel and very nearly flushed when Roarke walked in.

'Hello, Lieutenant.'

'Hi.' She dipped her hands in her pockets. 'I – ah – had some trouble with my unit at Cop Central. I needed this analysis, so I . . . I can put a hold on it if you need the room.'

'No need for that.' Her obvious discomfort amused him. He strolled to her, leaned down, and kissed her lightly. 'And no need for you to fumble through an explanation as to why you're using the equipment. Digging for secrets?'

'No. Not the way you mean.' The fact that he was grinning at her increased the embarrassment level. 'I needed something a little more competent than the tin cans we have at Cop Central, and I figured you'd be gone for a couple more hours.'

'I got an early transport back. Need some help with this?'

'No. I don't know. Maybe. Stop grinning at me.'

'Was I?' His grin only widened as he slid his arms around her and tucked his hands in the back pockets of her jeans. 'How was your lunch with Dr Mira?'

She scowled. 'Do you know everything?'

'I try. Actually, I had a quick meeting with William, and he mentioned that Reeanna had run into you and the doctor. Business or pleasure?'

'Both, I guess.' Her brows lifted as his hands got busy on her butt. 'I'm on duty, Roarke. Your hands are currently rubbing the ass of a working cop.'

'That only makes it more exciting.' He shifted to nibble her neck. 'Want to break a few laws?'

'I already am.' But she turned her head instinctively to give him better access.

'Then what are a few more?' he murmured and slid his hand out of her pocket and around her body to cup her breast. 'I love the feel of you.' His mouth was trailing along her jawline toward her mouth when the computer beeped.

Analysis complete. Display or audio?

'Display,' Eve ordered and wiggled free.

'Damn,' Roarke sighed. 'I was so close.'

'What the hell is this?' Hands fisted on her hips, Eve scanned the display on the view screen. 'It's gibberish. Fucking gibberish.'

Resigned, Roarke sat on the edge of the console and studied the display himself. 'It's technical; medical terms, primarily. A bit out of my realm. A burn, electronic in origin. Does that make sense?'

'I don't know.' Thoughtfully, she tugged on her ear. 'Does it make sense for a couple of dead guys to have an electric burn hole in the frontal lobe of their brains?'

'Some fumbling with the equipment during autopsy?' Roarke suggested.

'No.' Slowly, she shook her head. 'Not on two of them, examined by different MEs in different morgues. And they're not surface flaws. They're inside the brain. Microscopic pin-pricks.'

'What's the relationship between the two men?'

'None. Absolutely none.' She hesitated, then shrugged. He was already involved in a peripheral manner, why not drag him into the center? 'One of the men is yours,' she told him. 'The autotronics engineer from the Olympus Resort.'

'Mathias?' Roarke pushed off the console, his half-amused, half-intrigued expression going dark. 'Why are you investigating a suicide on Olympus?'

'I'm not officially. It's a hunch, that's all. The other brain your fancy equipment's analyzing is Fitzhugh's. And if Peabody can untangle the red tape, I'll plug in Senator Pearly's.'

'And you expect to find this microscopic burn in the senator's brain?'

'You're a quick study, Roarke. I've always admired that about you.'

'Why?'

123

'Because it's annoying to have to explain everything step by step.'

His eyes narrowed. 'Eve.'

'All right.' She held up her hands, let them fall. 'Fitzhugh just didn't strike me as the type to do himself. I couldn't close the case until I'd explored all the options. I've been running out of options. I might have put it to bed anyway, but I kept thinking about that kid hanging himself.'

She began to pace restlessly. 'No predisposition there, either. No obvious motive, no known enemies. He just has himself a snack and makes a noose. Then I heard about the senator. That makes three suicides without logical explanations. Now, for people like Fitzhugh and the senator, with their kind of financial base, there's counseling at the snap of a finger. Or in cases of terminal illness – physical or emotional – voluntary self-termination facilities. But they took themselves out in bloody and painful ways. Doesn't fit.'

Roarke nodded. 'Go on.'

'And the ME on Fitzhugh came up with this unexplained abnormality. I wanted to see if, on the off chance, the kid had anything like it.' She gestured to the screen. 'He does. Now I need to know what put it there.'

Roarke shifted his eyes back to the screen. 'Genetic flaw?'

'Possibly, but the computer says unlikely. At least it's never come across anything like it before – through heredity, mutation, or outside causes.' She moved behind the console, scrolled the screen. 'See there, in the projection of possible mental affects? Behavioral alterations. Pattern unknown. A lot of help that is.'

She rubbed her eyes, thought it through. 'But that says to me that the subject could, and likely would, behave out of pattern. Suicide would be out of pattern for these two men.'

'True enough,' Roarke agreed. Leaning back against the console, he crossed his legs at the ankles. 'But so would

124

dancing naked in church or kicking elderly matrons off a skywalk. Why did they both choose self-termination?'

'That's the question, isn't it? But this gives me enough, once I figure out how to spin it to Whitney, to keep both cases open. Download data to disc, print hard copy,' she ordered, then turned to Roarke. 'I've got a few minutes now.'

His brow quirked, a habitual gesture she secretly adored. 'Do you?'

'Which laws did you have in mind to break?'

'Several, actually.' He glanced at his watch as she stepped forward to unbutton his elegant linen shirt. 'We have a premiere in California tonight.'

Her fingers stopped, her face fell. 'Tonight.'

'But I think we have time for a few misdemeanors first.' With a laugh, he scooped her off her feet and laid her back on the console.

Eve was tugging on a floor-length, siren-red sheath and complaining bitterly about the impossibility of wearing so much as a scrap of underwear under the clinging material when her communicator beeped. Naked to the waist, with the flimsy bodice hanging to her knees, she pounced.

'Peabody?'

'Sir.' Several expressions passed over Peabody's face before it went carefully blank. 'That's a lovely dress, Lieutenant. Are you premiering a new style?'

Baffled, Eve looked down, then rolled her eyes. 'Shit. You've seen my tits before.' But she set the communicator down and struggled the bodice into place.

'And may I say, sir, they're quite lovely.'

'Sucking up, Peabody?'

'You bet.'

Eve stifled a chuckle and sat on the edge of the sofa in the dressing room. 'Report?'

'Yes, sir. I . . . ah . . .'

Noting that Peabody's eyes had shifted and glazed over, Eve glanced over her shoulder. Roarke had just walked into the room, damp from his shower, tiny beads of water glistening on his bare chest, a white towel barely hitched at his hips.

'Stay out of view, will you, Roarke, before my aide goes brain dead.'

He looked toward the communicator screen, grinned. 'Peabody, hello.'

'Hi.' Even over the unit, her swallow was audible. 'Nice to see you – I mean, how are you?'

'Very well, and you?'

'What?'

'Roarke.' Eve heaved a sigh. 'Give Peabody a break, will you, or I'll have to block video.'

'You don't have to do that, Lieutenant.' Voice rusty, Peabody deflated as Roarke slipped out of view. 'Jesus,' she said under her breath and grinned foolishly at Eve.

'Settle your hormones, Peabody, and report.'

'Settling, sir.' She cleared her throat. 'I've untangled most of the bureaucratic tape, Lieutenant. Just a couple more snags. At this juncture, we should have the requested data by oh nine hundred. But we have to go to East Washington to view it.'

'I was afraid of that. All right, Peabody. We'll catch the shuttle at oh eight hundred.'

'Don't be foolish,' Roarke said from behind her while he critically studied the lines of the dinner jacket he held. 'Take my transport.'

'It's police business.'

'No reason to squeeze yourselves into a tuna can. Traveling in comfort doesn't make it less official. In any case, I've some business I can see to in East Washington myself. I'll take you.' He leaned over Eve's shoulder, smiled at Peabody. 'I'll have a car sent for you. Seventy forty-five? Is that convenient?'

'Sure.' She wasn't even disappointed that he was now wearing a shirt. 'Great.'

126

'Listen, Roarke—'

'Sorry, Peabody.' He cut Eve off smoothly. 'We're running a bit late here. See you in the morning.' Reaching over, he manually disengaged the communicator.

'You know, it really pisses me off when you do that kind of thing.'

'I know,' Roarke said equably. 'That's why it's irresistible.'

'I've spent half my life on one sort of transport or another since I met you,' Eve grumbled as she settled into her seat in Roarke's private Jet Star.

'Still cranky,' he observed, and signaled the flight attendant. 'My wife needs another dose of coffee, and I'll join her.'

'Right away, sir.' She slipped into the galley with silent efficiency.

'You really get a bang out of saying that, don't you? My wife.'

'I do, yes.' Roarke tipped her face up with a fingertip and kissed the shallow dent in her chin. 'You didn't sleep enough,' he murmured, rubbing his thumb under her eye. 'You so rarely turn off that busy brain of yours.' He flicked a glance up at the flight attendant as she set steaming coffee on the table in front of them. 'Thank you, Karen. We'll take off as soon as Officer Peabody arrives.'

'I'll inform the pilot, sir. Enjoy your flight.'

'You don't really have to go to East Washington, do you?'

'I could have handled it from New York.' He shrugged, lifted his coffee. 'Personal attention always has more impact. And I have the added benefit of watching you work.'

'I don't want you involved in this.'

'You never do.' He lifted her cup, handed it to her with an easy smile. 'However, Lieutenant, I'm involved with you, and therefore you can't shut me out.'

'You mean you won't be shut out.'

'Precisely. Ah, here's the redoubtable Peabody now.'

She came aboard pressed and polished, but spoiling the effect with her jaw hanging open as she swiveled her head right and left in an attempt to see everything at once.

The cabin was as plush and sumptuous as a five-star hotel, with deep, cushy seats and gleaming tables, the glint of crystal holding flowers so fresh they gleamed with dew.

'Stop gaping, Peabody, you look like a trout.'

'Nearly finished, Lieutenant.'

'Don't mind her, Peabody, she woke up surly.' Roarke rose, disconcerting Peabody until she realized he was offering her a seat. 'Would you care for coffee?'

'Well, ah, sure. Thanks.'

'I'll fetch it and leave you two to discuss your work.'

'Dallas, this is . . . ultra.'

'It's just Roarke,' Eve muttered into her coffee.

'Yeah, like I said. Ultra.'

Eve glanced up as he came in with more coffee. *Dark and gorgeous and just a bit wicked*, she thought. *Yeah*, she supposed, *ultra was the word all right*. 'Well, strap in, Peabody, and enjoy the ride.'

The takeoff was smooth, and the trip was short, providing Peabody with just enough time to fill Eve in on the details. They were to report to the office of the Chief of Security for Government Employees. All data would be viewed in house, and nothing could be transferred or transported.

'Fucking politics,' Eve complained as they jumped into a cab. 'Who are they protecting, for Christ's sake? The man's dead.'

'Standard CYA procedure. And there are always plenty of asses to cover in East Washington.'

'Fat asses.' Eve eyed Peabody consideringly. 'Been to East Washington before?'

'Once, when I was a kid.' Peabody moved her shoulders.

128

'With my family. The Free-Agers staged a silent protest against artificial insemination of cattle.'

Eve didn't bother to muffle a snort. 'You're full of surprises, Peabody. Since you haven't been here in a while, you may want to take in the scenery. Check out the memorials.' She gestured as they whizzed by the Lincoln Memorial and its throng of tourists and street hawkers.

'I've seen plenty of videos,' Peabody began, but Eve lifted her brows.

'Check out the scenery, Peabody. Consider it an order.'

'Sir.' With what on another face might have been considered a pout, Peabody turned her head.

Eve nipped a card recorder out of her bag and tucked it under her shirt. She doubted security was so tight it would involve X rays or a strip search And if it did, she'd simply claim she always carried her spare on her person. Eve flipped a glance at the driver, but the droid had her eyes bland and on the road.

'Not a bad town for sightseeing,' Eve commented as they veered onto the vehicle bypass of the White House where the old mansion could just be seen through reinforced gates and steel bunkers.

Peabody swiveled her head, looked dead into Eve's eyes. 'You can trust me, Lieutenant. I thought you knew that.'

'It's not a matter of trust.' Because she heard the hurt in Peabody's voice, Eve spoke gently. 'It's a matter of not being willing to put anyone's ass but my own in a sling.'

'If we're partners—'

'We're not partners.' Eve inclined her head, and there was authority in her tone now. 'Yet. You're my aide, and you're in training. As your superior, I decide how far your butt sticks out in the wind.'

'Yes, sir,' Peabody said stiffly and made Eve sigh.

'Don't get your briefs in a twist, Peabody. There'll come a time when I'll let you take your lumps with the commander. And believe me, he's got a hell of a punch.'

129

The cab pulled over to the curb outside the gates of the Security Building. Eve shoved credits through the safety slot, climbed out, and approached the view screen. She placed her palm on the plate, slipped her badge into the identification slot, and waited for Peabody to mirror the procedure.

'Dallas, Lieutenant Eve, and aide, appointment with Chief Dudley.'

'One moment for verification. Authorization confirmed. Please place all weapons in holding bin. Warning. It is a federal offense to bring any weapons into the facility. Any individual entering with a weapon in his or her possession will be detained.'

Eve slipped her police issue out of her holster, then, with some regret, bent down to take her clinch piece out of her boot. At Peabody's bland look, she shrugged. 'I started carrying a spare after my experience with Casto. A clinch piece might have saved me some grief.'

'Yeah.' Peabody dumped her standard-issue stunner in the bin. 'I wish you'd blasted the son of a bitch.'

Eve opened her mouth, closed it again. Peabody had been careful not to mention the Illegals detective who'd charmed her, bedded her, and used her while he'd killed for profit.

'Look,' Eve said after a moment. 'I'm sorry about the way things went down there. If you want to vent about it sometime—'

'I'm not much of a venter.' Peabody cleared her throat. 'Thanks, anyway.'

'Well, he'll be stretching those long legs of his in lockup into the next century.'

Peabody's mouth curved grimly. 'There is that.'

'You are cleared to enter. Please step through the gate, proceed to the autotram on the green line for transport to second level clearing.'

'Jesus, you'd think we were going to see the president instead of some suit-and-tie cop.' Eve walked through the gate that efficiently shut and bolted behind them. She and Peabody settled down on the stiff plastic seats of the tram. With a mechanical hum, it sped them through bunkers and into a steel-walled passageway that angled down until they were ordered to step out into an anteroom filled with harsh, artificial light and walls of view screens.

'Lieutenant Dallas, Officer.' The man who approached wore the smoke gray uniform of Government Security with the rank of corporal. His blond hair was buzz cut so close his pale white scalp peeked through. His thin face was equally pale, the skin tone of a man who spent his time indoors and underground.

His uniform shirt bulged under hefty mountains of biceps.

'Leave your bags with me, please. No electronic or recording devices are permitted beyond this point. You are under surveillance and will remain so until you leave the facility. Understood?'

'Understood, Corporal.' Eve handed him her bag, then Peabody's, and pocketed the receipts he gave her. 'Some place you've got here.'

'We're proud of it. This way, Lieutenant.'

After depositing the bags in a bomb-safe lockup, he led them to an elevator, programmed it for Section Three, Level A. The doors closed without a sound; the car ran with barely a trace of movement. Eve wanted to ask how much the taxpayers had paid for the luxury, but decided the corporal wouldn't appreciate the irony.

She was certain of it when they were deposited in a wide lobby decorated with foam scoop chairs and potted trees. The carpet was thick and undoubtedly wired for motion detection. The console at which three clerks busily worked was equipped with a full range of computers, monitors, and communications systems. The piped-in music was beyond soothing and edging toward mind dulling.

The clerks weren't droids, but they were so stiff and polished, so radically conservative in dress, that she thought

131

they'd have been better off as automatons. Mavis, she thought with deep affection, would have been appalled at the lack of style.

'Reconfirmation of palm prints, please,' the corporal requested, and obediently, Eve and Peabody laid their right hands flat on the plate. 'Sergeant Hobbs will escort you from here.'

The sergeant, tucked neatly into her uniform, stepped from behind the console. She opened another reinforced door and led the way down a silent corridor.

At the last checkpoint, there was a final screen for weapons, then they were key-coded into the chief's office.

Here was a sweeping view of the city. Eve supposed, after one glance at Dudley, that he considered it his city. His desk was as wide as a lake, and one wall flashed with screens spot-checking various areas of the building and grounds. On another were photos and holograms of Dudley with heads of state, royalty, ambassadors. His communications center rivaled the control room at NASA Two.

But the man himself cast the rest in shadow.

He was enormous, easily six seven and a beefy two seventy. His wide, rawboned face was weathered and tanned, with his brilliantly white hair cropped short. On hands as big as Virginia hams, he wore two rings. One was the symbol of military rank; the other was a thick gold wedding band.

He stood poker straight and studied Eve out of eyes the color and texture of onyx. For Peabody, he never spared a glance.

'Lieutenant, you're inquiring into the death of Senator Pearly.'

So much for amenities, Eve thought and answered in kind. 'That's affirmative, Chief Dudley. I'm investigating the possibility that the senator's death is connected to another case on which I am primary. Your cooperation in this matter is duly noted and appreciated.'

'I find the possibility of a connection slim to none. However, after reviewing your record with NYPSD, I found no objection to allowing you to view the senator's file.'

'Even a slim possibility bears investigating, Chief Dudley.'

'I agree, and I admire thoroughness.'

'Then, might I ask if you knew the senator personally?'

'I did, and though I did not agree with his politics, I considered him a dedicated public servant and a man with a strong moral base.'

'One who would take his own life?'

Dudley's eyes flickered for a moment. 'No, Lieutenant, I would say not. Which is why you're here. The senator has left behind a family. In the area of family, the senator and I were in harmony. Therefore, his apparent suicide does not fit the man.'

Dudley touched a control on his desk, inclined his head to the view wall. 'On screen one, his personal file. On screen two, his financial records. Screen three, his political file. You'll have one hour to review data. This office will be under electronic surveillance. Simply request Sergeant Hobbs when you've completed your hour.'

Eve's opinion of Dudley was a little hum in her throat as he left the office. 'He's making it easy for us. If he didn't particularly like Pearly, I'd say he respected him. Okay, Peabody, let's get to work.'

She scanned the screens as her cop's eyes had already scanned the room. She was nearly certain she'd spotted all the security cameras and recorders, and taking a chance on a very uncomfortable detention, shifted so that her body was partially blocked by Peabody's.

She pulled the diamond Roarke had given her from under her shirt, ran it idly along its chain, and with her free hand slid the small recorder out, kept it pressed just at her throat as she aimed it at the screens.

'A clean life,' she said aloud. 'No criminal record whatsoever. Parents married, still living, still based in Carmel. His father did military time, ranked colonel, served during the Urban Wars. Mother an MT with time off as professional parent. That's a pretty solid upbringing.'

Peabody kept her eyes on the screen and off the recorder. 'Solid education, too. Graduate of Princeton, with postgrad work at the World Learning Center on Space Station Freedom. That was right at its conception, and only the top students could get in. Married at thirty, just before his first run for office. Adjusted Population advocate. Requisite one child, male.'

She shifted her gaze to another screen. 'His politics are dead center Liberal Party. Butted heads with your old friend DeBlass over the appeal of the Gun Ban and the Morality Bill DeBlass was pushing.'

'I have a feeling I would have liked the senator.' Eve turned slightly. 'Scroll personal data to medical history.'

The screen flipped, and the technical terms made her eyes want to cross. She'd have them translated later, she thought, if she managed to get out of the facility with the recorder.

'Looked like a healthy specimen. Physical and mental records show no abnormality. Tonsils treated in childhood, a broken tibia in his twenties as a result of a sport injury. Sight correction, standard, in middle forties. A permanent sterilization procedure during the same period.'

'This is interesting.' Peabody continued to scan the political screen. 'He was endorsing a bill that would require all legal representatives and technicians to be rescreened every five years, at their own expense. That wouldn't sit too well with the legal community.'

'Or with Fitzhugh,' Eve murmured. 'Looks like he was after the electronic empire, too. Tougher testing requirements for new devices, new licensing laws. That wouldn't have made him Mister Popularity, either. Autopsy report,' she demanded, then narrowed her eyes when it flashed on screen.

She skimmed through the jargon, shook her head. 'Boy, was he a mess when they scraped him up. Didn't leave them a hell

134

of a lot to work with. Brain scan and dissection. Nothing,'
she said after a moment. No report here of an abnormality
or flaw.'

'Display,' she demanded, and stepped closer to the screen
to study the visual herself. 'Cross section. Side view, enhance.
What do you see, Peabody?'

'Unattracive gray matter, too damaged for transplant.'

'Enhance right hemisphere, frontal lobe. Jesus, what a
fucking mess he made out of himself. You just can't see.
Can't be sure.' She stared until her eyes burned. Was that
a shadow, or was it simply part of the trauma caused when
a human skull smashed brutally into concrete?

'I don't know, Peabody.' She had all she needed, and she
slid the recorder under her shirt again. 'But I do know that
there's no motive or predisposition for self-destruct in this
data. And that makes three. Let's get the hell out of this
place,' she decided. 'It gives me the creeps.'

'I'm with you all the way on that one.'


They got tubes of Pepsi and what passed for a hash sandwich at
a glide-cart on the corner of Pennsylvania Avenue and Security
Row. Eve was just about to hail a transport back to the airport
when a sleek black limo glided to the curb. The rear window
slid down, and Roarke smiled out at them.

'Would you ladies like a lift?'

'Wow,' was all Peabody could manage as she scanned the
car from bumper to bumper. It was a gleaming antique, a
luxury from another era, and as romantic and tempting as
sin.

'Don't encourage him, Peabody.' When Eve started to climb
in, Roarke took her hand and tumbled her into his lap. 'Hey.'
Mortified, she jabbed with her elbow.

'I love to fluster her when she's on duty,' Roarke said,
wrestling Eve back onto his lap. 'And how was your day,
Peabody?'

135

Peabody grinned, delighted to see her lieutenant flushed and cursing. 'It just got better. If this thing has a privacy screen, I can leave you two alone.'

'I said not to encourage him, didn't I?' This time her elbow had better aim, and Eve managed to slide off onto the seat. 'Idiot,' she muttered at Roarke.

'She dotes on me so.' He sighed, settled back. 'It's almost smothering. If you've finished your police business, can I offer you a tour of the city?'

'No,' Eve said before Peabody could open her mouth. 'Straight back to New York. No detours.'

'She's a real party animal, too,' Peabody said soberly, then neatly folded her hands and watched the city stream by.

# *Chapter Ten*

Before Eve left for home, she perfected a detailed report on the similarities in the alleged suicides and why her suspicions that the senator's death was due to the same as yet unknown causes. She transferred her findings to the commander's unit, with a flag to his home 'link.

Unless his wife was hosting one of her ubiquitous dinner parties, she knew Whitney would review the report before morning. With that hope, she took the sky glide from homicide to the Electronic Detective Division.

She found Feeney at his desk, his stubby fingers holding delicate tools, microglasses turning his eyes to saucers as he stripped down a miniboard.

'You doing repair and maintenance these days?' She eased a hip on the edge of his desk, careful not to jar his rhythm. She'd expected no more than the grunt she received in response and waited while he transferred a sliver of something onto a clear dish.

'Somebody's having fun and games,' he muttered. 'Managed to get a virus of some kind right into the chief's unit. Memory's been boosted, the GCC compromised.'

She glanced at the silver sliver and imagined that was the GCC. Computers weren't her forte. 'Got a line on it?'

'Not yet.' With tiny tweezers, he lifted the sliver, studied it through his glasses. 'But I will. I found the virus, dosed it, that's first priority. This poor little bastard's dead, though. When I autopsy it, we'll see.'

She had to smile. It was so like Feeney to think of his components and chips in human terms. He replaced the sliver, sealed the dish, then tugged off his glasses.

His eyes shrank, blinked, refocused. And there he was, Dallas thought, rumpled, wrinkled, and baggy, just as she liked him best. He'd made her a cop, giving her the kind of in-the-field training she could never have learned through discs or VR. And though he'd transferred from Homicide to captain in EDD, she continued to depend on him.

'So,' she began. 'Did you miss me?'

'Were you gone?' He grinned at her, reached a hand into a bowl for some candied almonds. 'Did you like your fancy honeymoon?'

'Yeah, I did.' She took a nut herself. It had been a long time since lunch. 'Even with a body at the end of it. I appreciate the data you dug up for me.'

'No problem. A lot of fuss for self-terminations.'

'Maybe.' His office was larger than hers, due to his rank and his love of space. His boasted a view screen which, as usual, was tuned to a classic film channel. Just now Indiana Jones was being lowered into a pit of asps. 'It's got a few interesting aspects, though.'

'Want to share?'

'That's why I'm here.' She'd copied the data she'd taken from the senator's file and took the disc from her pocket. 'I've got a brain dissection on here, but the picture's a little rough. Can you clean it up, boost it some?'

'Can bears shit in the reforested park?' He took the disc, swiveled to his unit, and loaded it. Moments later, he was scowling over the image. 'Pitiful imaging. What did you do, use a portable to record off screen?'

'It would be better if we didn't get into that.'

He turned his head, studied her with that same scowl. 'You teetering on a line, Dallas?'

'My balance is good.'

138

'Let's hope so.' Preferring to work manually, he slid out a keyboard. His workingman's fingers danced over keys and controls like a master harpist's over strings. He jerked a shoulder when she leaned close. 'Don't crowd me, kid.'

'I need to see.'

Under his expertise the picture was clearing, contrasts sharpening. She struggled for patience as he fine tuned, diddled, humming to himself as he worked. Behind her all hell was breaking loose between Harrison Ford and the snakes.

'That's about the best we can do on this unit. You want more, I have to take it into master.' He flicked a glance up at her. 'You gotta log on for master. Technically.'

She knew he'd bypass regulations for her and risk an interview with IAD. 'Let's go with this for now. You see that, Feeney?' She tapped a finger against the screen just under the tiny shadow.

'I see a hell of a lot of trauma. This brain must have been bashed good and proper.'

'But this.' She could just make it out. 'I've seen this before. On two other scans.'

'I'm no neurologist, but I'd guess it's not supposed to be there.'

'No.' She straightened. 'It's not supposed to be there.'


She got home late and was met by Summerset at the door. 'There are two . . . gentlemen to see you, Lieutenant.'

With a quick jolt, she thought of the data she'd commandeered. 'Are they wearing uniforms?'

Summerset's pursed mouth pruned further. 'Hardly. I've put them in the front parlor. They insisted on waiting, though you had not indicated when you would arrive, and Roarke is detained at the office.'

'Okay, I'll handle it.' She wanted a huge plate of anything edible, a hot bath, and some thinking time. Instead, she wound her way down to the parlor and found Leonardo and

Jess Barrow. Relief came first, then annoyance. Summerset, the creep, knew Leonardo and could have told her who was waiting to see her.

'Dallas.' Leonardo's moon-sized face creased into a grin when he spotted her. He swept across the room, a giant in a magenta skin suit overbloused with emerald gauze. No wonder Mavis adored him. He caught Eve up in a bone crushing hug, then narrowed his eyes. 'You haven't dealt with your hair yet. I'll call Trina myself.'

'Oh. Well.' Intimidated, Eve raked her fingers through her short, messy cap of hair. 'I don't really have time right now to—'

'You have to make time for personal appearance. Not only are you an important public figure in your own right, but you're Roarke's wife.'

She was a cop, damn it. Suspects and victims didn't give a rat's ass about her hairdo. 'Right. As soon as—'

'You're neglecting your treatments,' he accused her, simply rolling over her excuses like a big smooth boulder down a bumpy slope. 'Your eyes are strained and your brows need shaping.'

'Yeah, but—'

'Trina will be in touch to set up a session. Now then.' He propelled her across the room, all but dumped her into a chair. 'Relax,' he ordered. 'Put your feet up. You've had a long day. Can I get you anything?'

'No, really. I'm—'

'Some wine.' Inspired, he beamed, gave her shoulder a quick rub. 'I'll see to it. And don't worry. Jess and I won't keep you long.'

'No use arguing with a born nurturer,' Jess commented as Leonardo moved off to order the wine for Eve. 'Nice to see you, Lieutenant.'

'Aren't you going to tell me I've lost weight, or gained it, or need a facial?' But she blew out a breath and leaned back. It

140

did feel incredibly good to sit in a chair that wasn't designed to torture the ass. 'Okay, let's have it. Something must be up for you to tolerate Summerset insulting you until I got home.'

'Actually, he just looked appalled and closed us in here. I do think he's going to run a room scan after we're gone to be sure we didn't lift any of the knickknacks.' Jess sat down, cross-legged, on the cushion at her feet. His silver eyes were smiling, his voice smooth as Bavarian cream. 'Great knickknacks, by the way.'

'We like them. If you'd wanted the tour, you should have said so before Leonardo set me down. I'm going to stay here awhile.'

'Looking at you will do just fine. I hope you don't mind me saying you're the most attractive cop I've ever . . . . rubbed shoulders with.'

'Have we rubbed shoulders, Jess?' Her brows lifted, disappearing under her bangs. 'I hadn't noticed.'

He chuckled, patted her knee with one of his beautiful hands. 'I would love that tour, sometime or other. But right now we have a favor to ask.'

'Got a traffic blot you need fixing?'

His lovely face beamed. 'Well, now that you mention it—'

Leonardo carried the crystal glass filled with pale gold wine across the room himself. 'Don't tease her, Jess.'

Eve accepted the glass, glanced up at Leonardo. 'He's not teasing me, he's flirting with me. He likes to live dangerously.'

Jess let out an appealingly musical laugh. 'Caught. Happily married women are the safest to flirt with.' He spread his hands as she sipped, considered him. 'No harm, no foul.' He picked up her hand, ran a fingertip along the intricate carving on her wedding ring.

'The last man who messed with me is doing life in lockup,' Eve said casually. 'That's after I beat the crap out of him.'

141

'Oops.' Chuckling, Jess released her hand. 'Maybe I'd better let Leonardo ask for the favor.'

'It's for Mavis,' Leonardo said, and his eyes became warm and liquid as he spoke her name. 'Jess thinks the demo disc is ready. Music and entertainment is a tough field, you know. Crowded, competitive, and Mavis has her heart set on making it. After what happened with Pandora—' He shuddered delicately. 'Well, after what happened before, and Mavis being arrested, fired from the Blue Squirrel, going through all of that . . . It's been rough on her.'

'I know.' The guilt set in again, for her part in it. 'It's behind her now.'

'Thanks to you.' Though Eve shook her head, Leonardo insisted. 'You believed her, you worked for her, you saved her. Now I'm going to ask you for something else because I know you love her as much as I do.'

Eve's eyes narrowed. 'You're boxing me in very neatly, aren't you?'

He didn't bother to suppress the smile. 'I hope so.'

'It's my idea,' Jess interrupted. 'Leonardo had to be nudged some to approach you with it. He didn't want to take advantage of your friendship or your position.'

'My position as a cop?'

'No.' Jess smiled, reading her reaction perfectly. 'As Roarke's wife.' *Oh, she didn't care for that*, he thought, amused. This was a woman who wanted to stand firm, on her own. 'Your husband has a great deal of influence, Dallas.'

'I know what Roarke has.' It wasn't precisely true. She didn't have a clue as to the full extent of his holdings and operations. She didn't want to. 'What do you want from him?'

'Just a party,' Leonardo said quickly.

'A what?'

'A party for Mavis.'

'A splashy one,' Jess put in, grinning. 'A busting one.'

'An event.' Leonardo shot Jess a warning look. 'A stage, so to speak, where Mavis can mingle with people, perform. I haven't mentioned the idea to her in case you objected. But we thought if Roarke could invite . . .' There was obvious embarrassment now as she only stared at him. 'Well, he knows so many people.'

'People who buy performance discs, go to clubs, look for entertainment.' Not embarrassed in the least, Jess smiled winningly. 'Maybe we should get you some more wine.'

Instead, she set the barely touched glass aside. 'You want him to give a party.' Wary of a trap, she scanned both faces. 'That's it?'

'More or less.' Hope sprang in Leonardo's chest. 'We'd like to run the demo during it, have Mavis give a live performance as well, I know it's an expense. I'm more than willing to pay—'

'It won't be the money that concerns him.' Eve considered, tapped her fingers on the arm of the chair. 'I'll talk to him about it and get back to you. I guess you want it soon.'

'As soon as possible.'

'I'll get back to you,' she repeated, then rose.

'Thank you, Dallas.' Leonardo bent in several places to kiss her cheek. 'We'll get out of your way.'

'She's going to be a huge hit,' Jess predicted. 'She just needs a liftoff.' He took a disc out of his pocket. 'This is a copy of the demo,' he told her. *A specially doctored copy*, he thought, *just for the lieutenant*. 'Give it a try. See what we've come up with.'

She smiled at it, thinking of Mavis. 'I will.'

Upstairs, alone, Eve programmed the AutoChef and came up with a steaming plate of pasta and what was certainly fresh sauce from garden-grown tomatoes and herbs. It never ceased to amaze her what Roarke had access to. She wolfed it down

143

while she ran a bath. As an afterthought, she tossed in some of the foaming salts he'd bought her in Paris.

She thought they smelled like her honeymoon: rich and romantic. She sank into a tub the size of a small lake and sighed greedily. *Blank the mind before thinking*, she decided and popped open the control panel in the wall. She'd already loaded the demo in the bedroom unit and switched it to play on the recessed screen in the bathroom.

She settled back into hot, frothy water, a second glass of vintage wine in her hand, and shook her head. What the hell was she doing here? Eve Dallas, a cop who'd come up the hard way; a nameless kid found in an alley, abandoned and abused, with a murder on her hands blocked from her memory.

Even a year before, that memory had been patchy and her life had been one of work, survival, and more work. Standing for the dead was her business, and she was good at her job. That had been enough. She'd made it enough.

Until Roarke. The glitter of the ring on her finger continued to puzzle her.

He loved her. He wanted her. He, the competent, successful, and enigmatic Roarke, even needed her. That was the biggest puzzle of all. And maybe, since she couldn't seem to solve it, she would eventually learn to simply accept it.

She brought the wine to her lips, sank a little lower into the water, and hit the remote.

Instantly, color and sound exploded into the room. In defense, she lowered the volume before her eardrums burst. Then Mavis swirled across the screen, as exotic as a sprite, potent as straight whiskey. Her voice was a screech, but it was appealing, nonetheless, and it suited her as well as the music Jess had designed to showcase the vocals.

It was hot, ruthless, and raw. Very much Mavis. But as Eve soaked it in, she realized that the sound and the show had more polish. Oh, there had always been flash and sparkle

144

when it came to Mavis's work, but now there was a thin sheen of gloss she had lacked before.

*Production values*, she supposed. *Orchestration. And someone who has the eye to recognize a rough diamond and the talent and willingness to help buff it up.*

Eve's opinion of Jess took a step up. Maybe he'd looked like a cocky boy showing off on his complicated console, but he obviously knew how to make it work. More, he understood Mavis, Eve realized. He appreciated her for what she was and what she wanted to do, and he'd found a way for her to do it well.

Eve chuckled to herself and lifted her glass in toast to her friend. It looked like they were going to have a party at that.

In his studio downtown, Jess reviewed the demo. He sincerely hoped that Eve was watching the disc. If she did, her mind would be open. Wide open to dreams. He wished he knew what they would be, where they would take her. Then he could see what she would see. He could document. Relive. But his research hadn't yet allowed him to find the path into the dreams. *One day*, he thought, *one day*.

Eve's dreams took her back into the dark, into the dread. They were jumbled, then shockingly clear, then scattered again like leaves in the wind. It was terrifying. She dreamed of Roarke, and that was soothing. Watching an explosive sunset with him in Mexico, making reckless love in the dark, bubbling water of a lagoon. Hearing his voice in her ear when he was inside her, urging her to let go. Just let go.

Then it was her father, holding her down, and she was a child, helpless, hurting, frightened.

*Please don't.*

The smell of him was there, candy over liquor. Too sweet, too strong. She was gagging on it and weeping, and his hand was over her mouth to stifle her screams when he raped her.

145

*Our personalities are programmed at conception.* Reeanna's voice floated in, cool and sure. *We are what we are made. Our choices are already set at birth.*

And she was a child, in a terrible room, a cold room that smelled of garbage and urine and death. And there was blood on her hands.

Someone was holding her, pinning her arms, and she fought like a wild thing, like a terrified, desperate child would fight.

'Don't. Don't. Don't.'

'Ssh, Eve, it's a dream.' Roarke gathered her closer, rocked, while the clammy sweat on her skin soaked into his shirt and broke his heart. 'You're safe.'

'I killed you. You're dead. *Stay dead.*'

'Wake up now.'

He pressed his lips to her temple, struggling to find the right way to soothe her. If he'd had the power, he would have gone back in time and cheerfully murdered what haunted her.

'Wake up, darling. It's Roarke. No one's going to hurt you. He's gone,' he murmured when she stopped fighting him and began to shudder. 'He's never coming back.'

'I'm all right.' It humiliated her, always, to be caught in the grip of a nightmare. 'I'm okay now.'

'I'm not.' He continued to hold her, stroking until her tremors eased. 'It was a bad one.'

She kept her eyes shut, tried to concentrate on the scent of him: clean and male. 'Remind me not to go to bed after gorging on spiced spaghetti.' She realized he was fully dressed and the bedroom lights were on low. 'You haven't been to bed.'

'I just got in.' He eased her back to study her face and brushed a drying tear from her cheek. 'You're still pale.' It tore at him, and his voice was edgy. 'Why the hell won't you take a soother at least?'

'I don't like them.' As usual, the nightmare had left her with the dull throb of a headache. Knowing he would see it if he looked too closely, she shifted away. 'I haven't had

146

one in a while. Weeks really.' Calmer now, she rubbed her tired eyes. 'That one was all jumbled up. Strange. Maybe it was the wine.'

'And maybe it's stress. You will work until you collapse.'

She angled her head, glanced at the watch on his wrist. 'And who's just coming in from the office at two A.M.?' She smiled, wanting to erase the worry from his eyes. 'Buy any small planets lately?'

'No, just a few minor satellites.' He rose, stripped off his shirt, then lifted a brow when he caught the considering look she gave his bare chest. 'You're too tired.'

'I don't have to be. You could do all the work.'

Laughing, he sat to take off his shoes. 'Thank you very much, but why don't we wait until you have the energy to participate?'

'Christ, that's so married.' But she slid down in the bed, exhausted. The headache was just on the edge of her brain, cannily waiting to strike. When he slipped into bed beside her, she rested her tender head on his shoulder. 'I'm glad you're home.'

'So am I.' He brushed his lips over her hair. 'You'll sleep now.'

'Yeah.' It soothed her to feel the rhythm of his heart under the palm of her hand. She only felt slightly ashamed of needing it there, needing him there. 'Do you think we're programmed at conception?'

'What?'

'I wonder.' She was drifting into that twilight sleep already, and her voice was thick and slow. 'Is it just the luck of the draw, the gene pool, what slips in with egg and sperm? Is that it? What does that make us, Roarke, you and me?'

'Survivors,' he said, but he knew she was asleep. 'We survived.'

He lay awake a long time, listening to her breathe, watching the stars. When he was certain she slept without scars, he let himself follow.

She was awakened at seven by a communiqué from Commander Whitney's office. She'd been expecting the summons. She had two hours to prep for the face-to-face report.

It didn't surprise her that Roarke was already up, dressed, and sipping coffee while he scanned the stock reports on his monitor. She grunted at him, her usual morning greeting, and took coffee into the shower with her.

He was on the 'link when she came back. His broker, she imagined from the bits and pieces of conversation she caught. She snagged a muffin, intending to stuff it into her mouth as she dressed, but Roarke grabbed her hand, pulled her down on the sofa.

'I'll get back to you by noon,' he told his broker, then ended transmission. 'What's your hurry?' he asked Eve.

'I've got to meet Whitney in an hour and a half and convince him there's a link between three unrelated victims, talk him into letting me pursue the matter, and to accept data I accessed illegally. Then I'm due in court, again, to testify so that a lowlife pimp, who ran an unlicensed stable of minors and beat one of them to death with his hands, goes into a cage and stays there.'

He kissed her lightly. 'Just another day at the office. Have some strawberries.'

She had a weakness for them and plucked one out of the bowl. 'We don't have any – you know – *thing* scheduled for tonight, do we?'

'No. What did you have in mind?'

'I was thinking we could just hang.' She moved her shoulders. 'Unless I'm in Interview being kicked because of breaching government security.'

'You should have let me do it for you.' He grinned at her. 'A little time, and I could have accessed the data from here.'

148

She closed her eyes. 'Don't tell me that. I really don't want to know that.'

'What do you say to watching some old videos, eating popcorn, and necking on the sofa?'

'I say, thank you, God.'

'It's a date then.' He topped off their coffee. 'Maybe we'll even manage to have dinner together. This case – or these cases – are troubling you.'

'I can't get a hook, a focal point. There's no why, there's no how. Other than Fitzhugh's spouse and his associate, no one's been even one step out of line. And they're both just idiots.' She moved her shoulders. 'It's not homicide when it's self-termination, but it feels like homicide.' She huffed out a disgusted breath. 'And if that's all I've got to convince Whitney, I'm going to be dragging my ass out of his office after he stomps it.'

'You trust your instincts. He strikes me as a man who's smart enough to trust them as well.'

'We'll soon see.'

'If they arrest you, darling, I'll wait for you.'

'Ha ha.'

'Summerset said you had visitors last night,' Roarke added as she rose to go to the closet.

'Oh, shit, I forgot.' Dumping the robe on the floor, she pawed naked through her clothes. It was a process Roarke never failed to enjoy. She found a shirt of plain blue cotton, shrugged it on. 'I had a couple of guys over for a quick orgy after work.'

'Did you take pictures?'

She chuckled and found some jeans, remembered court, and switched to tailored slacks. 'It was Leonardo and Jess. They're looking for a favor. From you.'

Roarke watched as Eve started to pull on the slacks, remembered underwear, and yanked open a drawer. 'Oh-oh. Will it hurt?'

'I don't think so. And actually, I'm kind of for it. They were thinking you could throw a party for Mavis here. Let her perform. The demo disc is done. I watched it myself last night and it's really good. It would give her a chance to, like, premiere it before they start hawking it.'

'All right. We could probably do it in a week or two. I'll check my schedule.'

Half dressed, she turned to him. 'Just like that?'

'Why not? It's not a problem.'

She pouted a little. 'I figured I'd have to persuade you.'

Anticipation lit wickedly in his eyes. 'Would you like to?'

She fastened her slacks, kept her face bland. 'Well, I really appreciate it. And since you're being so accommodating, I guess this is a good time to hit you with part two.'

Idly, he poured more coffee, flicked a glance at the monitor as the off planet agriculture reports began to scroll. He'd recently bought a minifarm on Space Station Delta.

'What's part two?'

'Well, Jess has worked out this one number. He ran it by me last night.' She looked at Roarke, making it up as she went along. 'It's a duet, really impressive. And we thought, if for the party – the live portion of the performance – you could do it with Mavis.'

He blinked, lost all interest in crops. 'Do what with Mavis?'

'Perform it. Actually it was my idea,' she continued, nearly losing it when he paled. 'You've got a nice voice. In the shower, anyway. The Irish comes out. I mentioned it, and Jess thought it was fabulous.'

He managed to shut his mouth, but it wasn't easy. Slowly he reached over to disengage the monitor. 'Eve—'

'Really, it would be great. Leonardo has a terrific design for your costume.'

'For my—' Thoroughly shaken, Roarke got to his feet. 'You want me to wear a costume and sing a duet with Mavis? In public?'

'It would mean so much to her. Just think of the press we could get.'

'Press.' Now he blanched. 'Christ Jesus, Eve.'

'It's really a sexy number.' Testing them both, she walked over, began to toy with the buttons of his shirt as she looked hopefully up into his eyes. 'It could put her right over the top.'

'Eve, I'm fond of her, really I am. I just don't think—'

'You're so important.' She trailed her finger down the center of his chest. 'So influential. And so . . . gorgeous.'

It was just a little too thick. He narrowed his eyes, caught the laughter in hers. 'You're putting me on.'

Her laughter burst out. 'You bought it. Oh, you should have seen your face.' She pressed a hand to her belly, yelping when he yanked her ear. 'I would have talked you into it.'

'I don't think so.' Not at all sure of himself, he turned away, started to reach for his coffee again.

'I could have. You'd have done it if I'd played it right.' All but doubled over with laughter, she threw her arms around him, hugged herself to his back. 'Oh, I love you.'

He went very still as emotion delivered a hard, bruising punch to his heart. Shaken, he turned, gripped her arms.

'What?' The laughter died out of her face. He looked stunned, and his eyes were dark and fierce. 'What is it?'

'You never say it.' Swamped, he dragged her close and buried his face in her hair. 'You never say it,' he repeated.

She could do nothing but hold on, rocked by the emotions pulsing from him. *Where had this come from?* she wondered. *Where had he hidden it?* 'Yes, I do. Sure I do.'

'Not like that.' He hadn't known how much he'd needed to hear her say it, just like that. 'Not without prompting. Without thinking about it first.'

She opened her mouth to deny it, then closed it again. It was true, and it was foolish, cowardly. 'I'm sorry. It's hard

151

for me. I do love you,' she said quietly. 'Sometimes it scares me because you're the first. And the only.'

He held her there until he was sure he could speak, then eased her back, looked into her eyes. 'You've changed my life. Become my life.' He touched his lips to hers, let the kiss deepen slowly, silkily. 'I need you.'

She linked her arms around his neck, pressed close. 'Show me. Now.'

# Chapter Eleven

Eve started off to work humming. Her body felt soft and strong, her mind rested. She took it as an omen when her vehicle purred to life on the first attempt, and the temperature control hung at a pleasant seventy-two degrees.

She felt ready to face her commander and convince him she had a case to pursue.

Then she got to Fifth and Forty-seventh and hit the jam. Street traffic was stopped, air traffic was circling like vultures, and no one was paying any heed to the noise pollution laws. The horns, shouts, curses, catcalls screamed out and echoed. The minute she stopped, her temperature control gleefully pumped up to ninety-five.

Eve slammed out of her car and joined the melee.

The glide-cart hawkers were taking advantage of the moment, slipping and sliding through the pack and doing a monster business on frozen fruit sticks and coffee. She didn't bother to flash her badge and remind any of them they weren't allowed the vend off the curbs. Instead, she snagged a vendor, bought a tube of Pepsi, and asked what the hell was going on.

'Free-Agers.' Eyes shifting for more customers, he slid her credits into his safe slot. 'Protest on conspicuous consumption. Hundreds of 'em, stretched across Fifth like a pretty ribbon. Singing. Want a wheat muffin to go with that? Fresh.'

'No.'

'Gonna be here awhile,' he warned and stepped onto his cart to glide through standing traffic.

'Son of a bitch.' Eve scanned the scene. She was blocked in on all sides by furious commuters. Her ears were ringing and heat was pumping out of her car like a furnace.

She slammed back in, beat on the control panel with her fist, and managed to knock the temperature down to a brisk sixty. Overhead, a tourist blimp trundled by, full of gawkers.

With no faith whatsoever in her vehicle, Eve rammed it into vertical lift and hit her official warning siren. The siren wheezed on, no match for the cacophony of noise, but she managed a shaky lift. Her wheels missed the roof of the car in front of her by at least an inch as her vehicle coughed and choked its way into the air.

'Next stop, recycling heap. I swear it,' she muttered and she punched at her communicator. 'Peabody, what the fuck is going on here?'

'Sir.' Peabody popped on screen, eyes bland, mouth sober. 'I believe you've encountered the jam incited by the protest on Fifth.'

'That wasn't scheduled. I know damn well it wasn't on the boards for this morning. They can't have a permit.'

'Free-Agers don't believe in permits, sir.' She cleared her throat when Eve snarled. 'I believe if you head west, you'll have better luck on Seventh. Traffic is heavy there, but it's moving. If you check your dash monitor—'

'Yeah, like that's going to work in this piece of shit. Call Maintenance and tell them they're meat. Then contact the commander, explain that I may be a few minutes late for the meeting.' As she spoke, she wrestled with the car, which tended to dip and cause both pedestrians and other drivers to stare up in terror. 'If I don't fall on someone, I should be there in twenty minutes.'

She avoided, barely, the edge of a billboard hologram touting the delights of private air travel. She and the Jet

154

Star headed in opposite directions with varying degrees of success. She nicked the curb as she set down on Seventh and couldn't blame the suit and tie pumping up his air skates for flipping her the bird.

But she'd missed him, hadn't she?

She was just indulging in a sigh of relief when her communicator shrilled.

'Any unit, any unit. Twelve seventeen, roof of Tattler Building, Seventh and Forty-second. Respond immediately. Unidentified female, considered armed.'

*Twelve seventeen*, Eve thought. Self-termination threat. What the hell was this? 'Dispatch, Dallas, Lieutenant Eve, responding. ETA five minutes.'

She beat her siren into life and hit vertical again.

The Tattler Building, home of the nation's most popular tabloid, was shiny and new. The buildings on its former site had been razed in the thirties for the urban beautification program, which was a euphemism for the decay of infrastructure and construction that had plagued New York during the period.

It speared up in silvery steel, bullet-shaped, and was ringed by circling skywalks and glides with a fresh-air restaurant spilling out from its base.

Eve double parked, grabbed her field kit, and pushed her way through the crowd gathered on the sidewalk. She flipped her badge at the security guard and watched relief drown his face.

'Thank Christ. She's up there, holding everybody off with antimugging spray. Got Bill dead in the eyes when he tried to grab her.'

'Who is she?' Eve demanded as he hustled his way toward the interior elevator banks.

'Cerise Devane. She owns the fucking place.'

'Devane?' Eve knew her vaguely. Cerise Devane, CEO of Tattler Enterprises, was one of the privileged and influential people who sauntered in Roarke's circles. 'Cerise Devane is

155

on the roof threatening to jump? What is this, some sort of insane publicity stunt to bump up their circulation?'

'Looks real to me.' He puffed out his cheeks. 'She's buck ass naked, too. That's all I know,' the guard claimed as the elevator shot upward. 'Her assistant made the call. Frank Rabbit. You can get more out of him – if he's conscious by now. Guy keeled right over when she went out on the ledge. That's what I heard.'

'You call for psych?'

'Somebody did. We got the company shrink up there now, and a specialist in self-termination is on the way. Fire department, too, and air rescue. Everything's backed up. Bad traffic jam on Fifth.'

'Tell me about it.'

The doors opened onto the roof, and Eve stepped out into a brisk, cooling wind that hadn't been able to find its way through the towering walls of buildings to the valley of the streets. She took a quick scan.

Cerise's office was built onto the roof, or more accurately, into it. Slanted walls of treated glass formed a peak and would afford the CEO a three hundred sixty degree view of the city and people she loved to dish up in her paper.

Through the glass, Eve could see the artwork, decor, and equipment designed for a top-flight office. And on the U-shaped lounging sofa, a man was stretched out with a compress on his forehead.

'If that's Rabbit, tell him to pull himself together and get out here to fill me in. And get anyone who isn't essential off this roof. Clear that crowd off the streets. If she goes off, we don't need her squashing bystanders.'

'I just don't have the man power,' the guard began.

'Get Rabbit out here,' she repeated and called Cop Central. 'Peabody, I've got a situation.'

'I heard. What do you need?'

'Get down here, send a crowd dispersal unit to move those

156

people off the street. Bring me all available data on Cerise Devane. See if Feeney can put a freeze on her 'links – home, personal, and portable – for the last twenty-four hours. Make it snappy.'

'Done,' Peabody responded and broke transmission.

She turned as the guard all but carried a young man across to her. Rabbit's company tie was loose, his stylishly shaped hair was mussed and matted. His hands, neatly manicured, shook.

'Tell me exactly what happened,' she snapped. 'Make it fast, and make it clear. You can fall apart when I'm finished with you.'

'She just – just walked out of the office.' His voice hitched and dipped and he sagged weakly against the supporting arm of the guard. 'She looked so happy. She was almost dancing. She – she'd taken off her clothes. She'd taken them off.'

Eve cocked a brow. At the moment, Rabbit seemed more shocked by his boss's sudden whim for exhibitionism than the possibility of her death. 'What led up to it?'

'I don't know. I swear, I have no idea. She'd wanted me to come in early, about eight. She was upset over one of the lawsuits. We're always getting sued. She was smoking and gulping coffee and pacing. Then she sent me out to light a fire under Legal and said she was going to take a few minutes to relax and level out.'

He stopped, covered his face with his hands. 'Fifteen minutes later she walked out, smiling and – and nude. I was so stunned, I just sat there. Just sat there.' His teeth began to chatter. 'I've never even seen her without her shoes.'

'Being naked's not her big problem now,' Eve pointed out. 'Did she speak to you, say anything?'

'I, well, I was so stunned, you see. I said something, something like, 'Ms Devane, what are you doing? Is something wrong?' And she just laughed. She said it was perfect. She had it all figured out now, and everything was wonderful. She was going to sit out on the ledge awhile before she jumped.

I thought she was joking, and I was nervous so I laughed a little.'

His eyes were stricken. 'I laughed, and then I saw her go to the edge of the roof. Jesus. She just popped over the side. I thought she'd jumped, and I ran out and over. There she was, sitting on the ledge, swinging her legs and humming. I asked her please to come back up before she lost her balance. She just laughed, spritzed a little of the spray at me, and told me she'd just found her balance and to go away like a good boy.'

'She get any calls, make any?'

'No.' He wiped his mouth. 'Any transmissions would have gone through my unit. She's going to jump, I tell you. She leaned over while I was watching, nearly went over then. And she said what a nice trip it was going to be. She's going to jump.'

'We'll see about that. Stay available.' Eve turned away. The company shrink was easy enough to spot. He was dressed in a knee-length white smock and black pipestem pants. His comforting gray hair was twisted into a neat queue, and he was leaning over the edge of the roof, his posture transmitting anxiety.

Even as Eve started toward him, she swore. She heard the whirl of flybys, then cursed the media again as she spotted the first air van. Channel 75, naturally, she mused. Nadine Furst was always first out of the gate.

The shrink straightened, smoothed down his smock for the cameras. Eve decided she was going to detest him. 'Doctor?' She held up her badge and noticed the undisguised excitement in his eyes. All Eve could think was, a company the size and strength of Tattler could afford better.

'Lieutenant, I believe I'm making some progress with the subject.'

'She's still on the ledge, isn't she?' Eve pointed out and brushed past him to lean over. 'Cerise?'

'More company?'

Sleek and pretty, skin the color of blushing rose petals, her well-toned legs swinging merrily, Cerise looked up. Her hair was jet black, its carefully groomed waves blowing in the breeze. She had a foxy, intelligent face and sharp green eyes. Just now, those eyes were soft and dreamy.

'Why, it's Eve, isn't it? Eve Dallas, the new bride. Lovely wedding, by the way. Really the social event of the year. We moved thousands of units with our coverage.'

'Good for you.'

'You know, I had research and data search busting butt to try to get the honeymoon itinerary. I don't think anybody but Roarke could have managed a full media blackout.' She wagged her finger playfully, and her perky breasts swayed. 'You could have shared, just a little. The public's dying to know.'

She giggled at that, shifted, and nearly overbalanced. 'We're all dying to know. Whoops. Not yet. Too much fun, don't want to rush it.' Straightening, she waved at the air vans. 'Usually I hate the damn visual media. Can't think why, just now. I love everybody!' She shouted the last, tossing her arms wide.

'That's nice, Cerise. Why don't you come back up for a minute. I'll give you some data on the honeymoon. Exclusive.'

Cerise smiled slyly. 'Uh-uh-uh.' The refusal was playful again, almost a giggle. 'Why don't you come down and join me? You can go with me. I'm telling you, it's the ultimate.'

'Now, Ms Devane,' the shrink began, 'all of us have moments of despair. I understand. I'm with you. I hear your sorrow.'

'Oh stuff it.' Cerise brushed him back with a gesture. 'I'm talking to Eve. Come on down, sweetie. But not too close.' She shook the spray and giggled. 'Come on and join the party.'

'Lieutenant, I don't recommend that you—'

'Shut up and go wait for my aide,' Eve told him as she swung a leg over the steel safety wall, lowered herself over the edge.

The wind didn't seem quite so pleasant when she was dangling seventy stories over the street, nudged on a steel ledge barely two feet wide. Here it buffeted and swirled, aided by the backwash from the air vans. It plucked at the clothes and slapped the skin. She ordered her heart to stop jumping and pressed her back to the building.

'Isn't it beautiful,' Cerise sighed. 'I'd love to have some wine now, wouldn't you? No, a big flute of champagne. Roarke's Reserve forty-seven would go down smooth right now.'

'I think we've got a case at home. Let's go open one.'

Cerise laughed, turned her head, and smiled hugely. And it was the smile, Eve realized as her heart lurched again, she'd seen on the face of a young man hanging from a homemade noose. 'I'm already drunk on happiness.'

'If you're happy, why are you sitting naked on a ledge considering taking the last leap?'

'That's what makes me happy. I don't know why you don't understand.' Cerise lifted her face to the sky, closed her eyes. Eve risked shifting a few inches closer. 'I don't know why everyone doesn't understand. It's so beautiful. It's so thrilling. It's everything.'

'Cerise, you go off this ledge, it's nothing. It's over.'

'No, no, no.' She opened her eyes again, and they were glazed. 'It's just the beginning, don't you see? Oh, we're all so blind.'

'Whatever's wrong can be fixed. I know.' Carefully, Eve laid a hand on Cerise's. She didn't grip, didn't want to risk it. 'Surviving's what counts. You can change things, make things better, but you have to survive to do it.'

'Do you know how much work that is? And what's the point when there's so much pleasure just waiting. I feel so good. Don't.' Chuckling, Cerise aimed the spray at Eve's face. 'Don't spoil it now. I'm having such a nice time.'

'You have people who are worried about you. You have

family, Cerise, who love you.' Eve strained to remember. Was there a child, a spouse, parents? 'If you do this, you'll hurt them.'

'Only until they understand. The time's coming when everyone will understand. It's going to be better then. Beautiful then.' She looked dreamily into Eve's eyes, that beaming and terrifying smile on her lips. 'Come with me.' She grabbed Eve's hand, clutched. 'It's going to be wonderful. You only have to let go.'

Sweat snaked a line down Eve's back. The woman's grip was like a vise, and a struggle for freedom could doom them both. She forced herself not to resist, to ignore the twisting wind and the hum of the air vans documenting every movement. 'I don't want to die, Cerise,' she said calmly. 'And neither do you. Self-termination is for cowards.'

'No, it's for explorers. But suit yourself.' Cerise patted Eve's hand, released it, and gave a long, trilling laugh to the wind. 'Oh God, I'm so happy,' she said and, throwing her arms wide, leaned forward into space.

Instinctively, Eve grabbed. She nearly lost her perch as her fingertips brushed the trim line of Cerise's hip. She banged onto her side, fought the roll forward as wind and space pulled at her. Gravity worked fast, mercilessly. Eve stared down into that wildly smiling face until it was only a blur.

'Jesus God. Oh, Jesus God.' Dizzy with reaction, she pushed herself up, leaned her head back, shut her eyes. Screams and shouts rained on her, and the air displaced by the media van coming in for a close-up struck her cheeks.

'Lieutenant. Dallas.'

The voice was like a bee buzzing in her ears, and Eve simply shook her head.

On the roof, Peabody stared down and fought against the nausea rising into her throat. All she could see now was that Eve was pressed on the ledge, white as a sheet, and one careful move would send her after the woman she'd tried

161

to save. Taking a deep breath, Peabody trained her voice to sharp, professional tones.

'Lieutenant Dallas, you're needed here. I require your recorder for a full report.'

'I hear you,' Eve said wearily. Keeping her eyes straight ahead, she reached behind to grip the edge of the roof. As a hand locked over hers, she got to her feet. Turning her back to the fall, she looked dead into Peabody's eyes, read the fear. 'The last time I thought about jumping, I was eight.' Though her legs shook a bit, she swung back onto the roof. 'I won't go that way.'

'Jesus, Dallas.' Forgetting herself for a moment, Peabody gave Eve a hard hug. 'You scared the hell out of me. I thought she was going to pull you off.'

'So did I. She didn't. Get a grip here, Peabody. The press is having a field day.'

'Sorry.' Peabody pulled back, coloring a bit. 'Sorry.'

'No problem.' Eve looked over to where the shrink was standing at the edge, one hand to his heart in a pose for the busy cameras. 'Asshole,' she muttered. She dug her hands into her pockets. She needed a minute, just another minute, to settle. 'I couldn't stop her, Peabody. I couldn't find the right button to push.'

'Sometimes there isn't one.'

'There was one that switched her onto this.' Eve said quietly. 'There had to be one to switch her off.'

'I'm sorry, Dallas. You knew her.'

'Not really. Just one of the people who walk past a corner of your life.' She pushed it away, had to push it away. Death, however it came, always left responsibilities. 'Let's see what we can do here. Did you tag Feeney?'

'Affirmative. He locked on her 'links from EDD and said he would head over personally. I downloaded data on the subject, didn't take time to scan it.'

They walked toward the office. Through the glass, Rabbit

162

could be seen sitting with his head between his knees. 'Do me a favor, Peabody. Pass that limp rag off to a uniform for a formal statement. I don't want to deal with him right now. I want her office secured. Let's see if we can figure out what the hell she was doing that set her off.'

Peabody marched in, had Rabbit up and out with a uniform in seconds. With wicked efficiency, she cleared the room, sealed the outer doors. 'It's all ours, sir.'

'Haven't I told you not to call me sir?'

'Yes, sir,' Peabody said with a smile she hoped would lift the heavy mood.

'There's a smart-ass lurking under that uniform.' Eve blew out a breath. 'Recorder on, Peabody.'

'Already on.'

'Okay, here she is. She's in early, pissed off. Rabbit says she was hyped about some litigation. Get data on that.' As she spoke, Eve wandered the room, absorbing details. Sculptures, mostly mythological figures in bronze. Very stylized. Deep blue carpet to match the sky, the desk in rose tones with a mirror gloss. Office equipment sleek and modern and tinted that same flowery shade. A huge copper urn exploded with exotic blooms, and Eve noticed a pair of potted trees.

She crossed to the computer, took her master pass out of her field kit, and called for the last use report.

Last use, 8: 10 a.m., call for file number 3732-L Legal, Custler v Tattler Enterprises.

'That'd be the lawsuit she was pissed about,' Eve concluded. 'Jibes with Rabbit's earlier statement.' She glanced down at a marble ashtray loaded with a half dozen cigarette butts. Using tweezers, she picked one up, examined it. 'Caribbean tobacco. Web filter. Pricey. Bag these.'

'You think they might be laced with something?'

'She was laced with something. Her eyes were wrong.' She

163

wouldn't forget them, Eve knew, for a long, long time. 'We can hope there's enough left of her for a tox report. Take a sample of those coffee dregs, too.'

But Eve didn't think they would find what she was looking for in the tobacco or the coffee. There had been no chemical trace in any of the other suicides.

'Her eyes were wrong,' Eve repeated. 'And her smile. I've seen that smile before, Peabody. A couple of times now.'

As she tucked the evidence bags away, Peabody glanced up. 'You think this is connected with the others?'

'I think Cerise Devane was a successful, ambitious woman. And we'll go through procedure, but I'm willing to lay odds we won't find a motive for self-termination. She sends Rabbit out,' Eve continued, pacing the office. Annoyed by the constant hum, she glanced up, scowled at the air van still hovering. 'See if you can find the privacy shields. I'm tired of those jerks.'

'A pleasure.' Peabody hunted up the control panel. 'I thought I saw Nadine Furst in one of them. The way she was leaning out, it was a good thing she was wearing a harness. She might have ended up as the lead on her own newscast.'

'At least she'll get it right,' Eve said half to herself and nodded when the privacy shields slid into place and closed off the glass. 'Good. Lights,' she ordered, and brought the brightness back up. 'She wanted to relax, level herself off for the rest of the day.'

Eve poked into a cold box, found soft drinks, fruit, wine. One of the wine bottles had been opened and air sealed, but there was no glass to indicate Cerise had started drinking early. And it wasn't a couple of belts that had put that look in her eyes, Eve mused.

In the adjoining bath, complete with whirlpool, personal sauna, and mood enhancer tube, she found a cupboard filled with soothers and tranqs and legalized lifters. 'A big believer in chemical assistance, our Cerise,' she commented. 'Take them in for testing.'

'Jesus, she's got her own pharmacy. The mood tube's set on concentration mode, and the last use was yesterday morning. She didn't take a spin this morning.'

'So what does she do to relax?' Eve stepped into an adjoining room, which was a small sitting room, she noted, complete with full entertainment unit, sleep chair, serving droid.

A lovely, sage-green suit was neatly folded on a small table. Matching shoes stood on the floor under it. Jewelry – a heavy linked gold chain, complicated twists of earrings, a slim bracelet watch-recorder – had been slipped tidily in a glass bowl.

'She undressed in here. Why? What was the point?'

'Some people relax better without the confines of clothes,' Peabody said, then flushed when Eve cast a considering glance over her shoulder. 'I've heard.'

'Yeah. Maybe. But it doesn't suit her. She was a real put-together woman. Her assistant told me he'd never even seen her without shoes, and suddenly she's a closet nudist. I don't think so.'

Her gaze landed on the VR goggles on the arm of the sleep chair. 'Maybe she took a trip after all,' Eve murmured. 'She's frazzled, wants to smooth the edges. So she comes in here, stretches out, programs something, and takes a little ride.'

Eve sat, picked up the goggles. *VR goggles*, she mused. Fitzhugh and Mathias had taken trips before death as well. 'I'm going to see where she went and when. Ah, if I appear to have any suicidal urges after I'm done – or decide I can relax better without the confines of my clothes – you're ordered to knock me cold.'

'Without hesitation, sir.'

Eve cocked a brow. 'But you're not expected to enjoy it.'

'I'll hate every minute of it,' Peabody promised, and folded her hands.

With a weak laugh, Eve slipped the goggles on. 'Display

log,' she ordered. 'Bull's-eye. She went VR at 8:17 this morning.'

'Dallas, if that's the case, maybe you shouldn't do this. We can take it in and test it under controlled conditions.'

'You're my control, Peabody. If I look too happy to live shortly, zap me. Replay last run program,' Eve ordered and settled back. 'Jesus.' She hissed it out as two young studs walked toward her. Dressed only in strips of glossy black leather studded with silver, they were oiled, muscled, and fully aroused.

Her environment was now a white room, mostly bed, and there was satin under her naked body, gauze draped overhead to filter the candlelight from a soaring chandelier of glittery crystal.

Music, something low and pagan, throbbed on the air. She was draped over a mountain of feather pillows, and as she started to shift, the first young god straddled her.

'Hey, listen, pal—'

'For your pleasure only, mistress,' he crooned and rubbed her breasts with scented oil.

*This is a bad idea*, she thought as little involuntary shivers of pleasure centered in her gut. Oil was slicked over her stomach, her thighs, down her legs to her toes.

She could understand how the current situation could make a woman strip and smile, but not how it could drive her to suicide.

*Stick it out*, she ordered herself and turned her mind to something else. She thought of the report she needed to give her commander. Of unexplained shadows on the brain.

Teeth closed delicately over her nipple, a tongue slid wetly over the captured point. She arched in reaction, but the hand she shot out in protest slipped off a taut, oil-slicked shoulder.

Then the second stud knelt between her legs and went to work on her with his mouth.

166

She came before she could stop herself, a small pop of release. Panting, she ripped the goggles off and found Peabody gaping at her.

'It wasn't a walk on a quiet beach,' Eve managed.

'I could see that. What was it, exactly?'

'A couple of mostly naked guys and a big satin bed.' Eve blew out a breath, set the goggles down. 'Who'd have thought she relaxed with sex fantasies?'

'Ah, Lieutenant. Sir. As your aide, I believe it's my responsibility to test that unit. For evidence control.'

Eve tucked her tongue in her cheek. 'Peabody, I couldn't let you take that kind of risk.'

'I'm a cop, sir. Risk is my life.'

Eve rose, held out the goggles as Peabody's eyes lit. 'Bag it, Officer.'

Deflated, Peabody dumped the goggles into a seal. 'Hell. Were they good looking?'

'Peabody, they were gods.' She stepped back into the office proper, gave it one more scan. 'I'm going to order in sweepers, but I don't think they'll find anything. I'll take the disc you downloaded into Central, contact next of kin – though the media will already have this all over the fucking airwaves.'

She hitched up her field kit. 'I don't feel at all suicidal.'

'I'm relieved to hear it, Lieutenant.'

Still, Eve frowned at the goggles. 'How long was I riding that, five minutes?'

'Nearly twenty.' Peabody gave a sour smile. 'Time flies when you're having sex.'

'I wasn't having sex.' Guilt had her worrying her wedding ring. 'Exactly. If there'd been something in that program, I should have felt it, so that looks like a dead end. Have it analyzed anyway.'

'Will do.'

'You wait for Feeney. Maybe he'll find something interesting on her 'link logs. I'm going to go grovel to the commander.

When you finish here, deliver the bags to the lab, then report to my office.' Eve started for the door, tossed a look over her shoulder. 'And Peabody, no playing with the evidence.'

'Spoilsport,' she muttered when Eve was out of earshot.

# Chapter Twelve

Commander Whitney sat behind his massive, well-organized desk and listened. He appreciated the fact that his lieutenant delivered a clean and concise report, and he admired that she could omit certain details without a flicker.

A good cop had to stand cool under fire. Eve Dallas, he was pleased to know, was ice.

'You had the autopsy data on Fitzhugh analyzed outside the department.'

'Yes, sir.' She didn't blink. 'The analysis required more sophisticated equipment than NYPSD currently has access to.'

'And you had access to this more sophisticated equipment.'

'I was able to gain access.'

'And run the analysis?' he asked, quirking a brow. 'Computer science is not your strong suit, Dallas.'

She looked him dead in the eye. 'I've been working on improving my skills in that area, Commander.'

He doubted that, sincerely. 'Subsequently, you gained entry to the files at the Government Security Center, and there, confidential reports fell into your hands.'

'That's correct. I don't wish to reveal my source.'

'Your source?' he repeated. 'Are you telling me you have a weasel at GSC?'

'There are weasels everywhere,' Eve said coolly.

'That might fly,' he murmured. 'Or you might find yourself facing a subcommittee back in East Washington.'

Eve's stomach shimmied, but her voice stayed steady. 'I'm prepared for that.'

'You'd better be.' Whitney sat back, steepled his hands, tapped his fingertips against his chin. 'The case on the Olympus Resort. You also accessed data there. That's quite a bit out of your jurisdiction, Lieutenant.'

'I was on scene during that incident, and I reported my findings to interspace authorities.'

'Who then took over the disposition of the matter,' Whitney added.

'I'm authorized to request data when an outside case relates to one of mine, Commander.'

'That's yet to be substantiated.'

'The data's necessary for me to substantiate the connection.'

'That would hold, Dallas, if there was a homicide.'

'I believe there are four of them, including Cerise Devane.'

'Dallas, I've just viewed the recording of that incident. I saw a cop and a jumper on a ledge, the cop attempting to talk the subject in, and the subject choosing the leap. She was not pushed, she was not coerced, she was not threatened in any way.'

'It's my professional opinion that she was coerced.'

'How?'

'I don't know.' And for the first time, frustration leaked through. 'But I'm sure, dead sure, that if they had enough of her brain to scrape up off the street for analysis, they'd find that same burn on the frontal lobe. I know it, Commander. I just don't know how it's getting there.' She waited a beat. 'Or being put there.'

His eyes flickered. 'Are you theorizing that someone is influencing certain individuals to self-termination through some sort of brain implant?'

170

'I can't find any genetic link among the subjects. No social group, education sphere, or religious affiliation. They didn't grow up in the same town, they didn't drink the same water, attend the same health clubs or centers. But they all had the same flaw in the brain. That's beyond coincidence, Commander. It was caused, and if by being caused it coerced those people to end their lives, then it's murder. And it's mine.'

'You're walking a thin wire, Dallas,' Whitney said after a moment. 'The dead have families, and the families want this put away. Your continued investigation extends the grieving process.'

'I'm sorry for that.'

'It's also raising questions from The Tower,' he added, referring to the Chief of Police and Security.

'I'm willing to present my report to Chief Tibble, if directed.' But she hoped she wouldn't be. 'I'll stand on my record, Commander. I'm not a rookie playing terrier with a dead case.'

'Even experienced cops overfocus, make mistakes.'

'Then let me make them.' She shook her head before he could speak. 'I was on that ledge today, Commander. I looked at her face, into her eyes when she went off. And I know.'

He folded his hands on the edge of the desk. Administration was always a struggle in compromise. He had other cases, and he needed her on them. The budget was thin, and there was never enough time or man power. 'I can give you a week, no more. If you don't have the right answers by then, you close the files.'

She drew a breath. 'And the chief?'

'I'll speak with him personally. Get me something, Dallas, or be prepared to move on.'

'Thank you, sir.'

'Dismissed,' he said, then added when she reached the door. 'Oh, and Dallas, if you're going to go outside the official

171

sphere for . . . research, watch your step. And give my best to your husband.'

She colored slightly. He'd pinned her source, and they both knew it. She mumbled something and escaped. Dodged that stun stream, she thought and dragged a hand through her hair. Then, with an oath, she dashed toward the nearest down glide. She was going to be late for court.

She was approaching the end of her shift when she made it back to her office and found Peabody settled at the desk, a cup of coffee in her hand.

Eve leaned against the doorjamb. 'Comfortable, Officer?'

Peabody jerked, sloshed a little coffee, cleared her throat. 'I didn't know your ETA.'

'Apparently. Something wrong with your unit?'

'Ah, no. No, sir. I thought it more efficient to enter the new data directly into yours.'

'That's a good story, Peabody, you stick with it.' Eve walked to her AutoChef and programmed coffee for herself. It was Roarke's blend rather than the poison served in the bull pen area, which explained Peabody cozying up at her superior's desk.

'What new data?'

'Captain Feeney pulled all communications on Devane's 'links. Doesn't appear to be anything that relates, but it's all here. We have her personal datebook with all appointments and the most current data from her last health exam.'

'She have any problems there?'

'Not a one. She was a tobacco addict, registered, and took regular anticancer injections. She had no sign of disease: physical, emotional, or mental. Tended toward stress and overwork, which was counteracted with soothers and tranqs. She was cohabitating, happily, by all reports. Her partner is currently off planet. You have the name of next of kin, her son from a previous partnership.'

172

'Yeah, I contacted him. He's based at the Tattler offices in New L.A. He's coming in.' Eve angled her head. 'Comfortable, Peabody?'

'Yes, sir. Oh, sorry.' She got up quickly from behind the desk and resettled in the ratty chair beside it. 'Your meeting with the commander?'

'We've got a week,' Eve said briskly as she sat. 'Let's make the most of it. ME's report on Devane?'

'Not yet available.'

Eve turned to her 'link. 'Let's see if we can give him a little shove.'

By the time she got home, she was staggering. She'd missed dinner, which she thought was just as well since she'd ended the day at the morgue viewing what was left of Cerise Devane.

Even the stomach of a veteran cop could turn.

And she would get nothing there, nothing at all. She doubted even Roarke's equipment could reconstruct enough of Devane to be of any help.

She walked in, nearly tripped over the cat who was stretched at the threshold, and drummed up the energy to bend down and lift him. He studied her, annoyance gleaming in his bicolored eyes.

'You wouldn't get kicked, pal, if you draped your fat ass somewhere else.'

'Lieutenant.'

She shifted the cat, looked over at Summerset who, as usual, had appeared out of nowhere. 'Yeah, I'm late,' she snapped. 'Give me a demerit.'

He didn't add his normal withering remark. He had seen the clips on the news channel, and he had watched her on the ledge. He had seen her face. 'You'll want dinner.'

'No, I don't.' She wanted bed and headed for the stairs.

'Lieutenant.' He waited for her bad-tempered oath, waited

until she'd turned her head to scowl at him. 'A woman who steps out on a ledge is either very brave or very stupid.'

The scowl turned into a sneer. 'I don't have to ask what category you put me in.'

'No, you don't.' He watched her climb up and thought her courage was terrifying.

The bedroom was empty. She told herself she'd run a house scan for Roarke's location in just a minute, then fell facedown on the bed. Galahad wiggled out of the crook of her arm and climbed onto her butt to circle and knead his way to comfort.

Roarke found her there minutes later, sprawled out in exhaustion, a sausage-shaped cat guarding her flank.

He simply studied her for a while. He, too, had seen the news clips. They had paralyzed him, dried the saliva in his mouth, and turned his bowels to water. He knew how often she faced death – others' and her own – and told himself he accepted it.

But that morning he had watched, helpless, while she'd teetered on the brink. He'd looked into her eyes, seen the grit and the fear. And he had suffered.

Now she was here, home, a woman with more bone and muscle than curves, with hair that badly needed tending and boots worn out at the heels.

He walked over, sat on the edge of the bed, and laid a hand over the one curled loosely on the spread.

'I'm just getting my second wind,' she murmured.

'I can see that. We'll go dancing in a minute.'

She managed a chuckle. 'Can you move that boulder off my butt?'

Obligingly, Roarke picked up Galahad, smoothed the ruffled fur. 'You've had quite a day; Lieutenant. The media's been full of you.'

She rolled over but kept her eyes shut a minute longer. 'I'm glad I missed it. You know about Cerise then.'

'Yes, I had Channel 75 on while I was preparing for my first meeting this morning. I caught it all live.'

She heard the strain in his voice and opened her eyes. 'Sorry.'

'You'll say you were doing your job.' He set the cat aside and brushed the hair back from Eve's cheek. 'But it was above and beyond, Eve. She could have taken you with her.'

'I wasn't ready to go.' She cupped a hand over the one he held to her cheek. 'I had a flash when I was up there. Memory flash of when I was a kid, standing at the window of some filthy flop he'd booked us into. I thought about jumping then, just getting it the hell over with. I wasn't ready to go. I'm still not.'

Galahad climbed out of Roarke's lap and stretched his bulk over Eve's belly. It made Roarke smile. 'Looks like we both intend to keep you here for a while. What have you eaten today?'

She pursed her lips. 'Is this a quiz?'

'Nothing to speak of,' he decided.

'Food's not high on my list right now. I've just come from the morgue. Contact with concrete after seventy-story flights does unattractive things to flesh and bone.'

'I don't imagine there was enough to scan for comparison with the others.'

Despite the grisly image, she grinned, sat up, and gave him a quick, loud kiss. 'You're cued up, Roarke. That's one of the things I like best about you.'

'I thought it was my body.'

'That's right up on the list,' she told him as he rose and went over to the recessed AutoChef. 'No, there isn't going to be enough, but there has to be a connection. You see it, don't you?'

He waited until the protein drink he'd ordered came through. 'Cerise was an intelligent, sensible, and driven woman. She was often selfish, continually vain, and could be an enormous pain in the ass.' He came back to the bed, held out the glass. 'She wasn't the type to jump off the roof of her own building – and let the visual media scoop her own organization.'

'I'll add that to my data.' She frowned at the creamy, mint-colored drink in her hand. 'What is this?'

'Nutrition. Drink it.' He tipped it up to her lips. 'All.'

She took the first sip out of self-defense, decided it wasn't altogether hideous, and gulped it down. 'There. Feel better now?'

'Yes. Did Whitney give you room to pursue?'

'I've got a week. And he knows I've been using your . . . facilities. He's pretending he doesn't.' She set the glass aside, started to stretch back out, then remembered. 'We were supposed to watch videos, eat popcorn, and neck.'

'You stood me up.' He tugged on her hair. 'I'll have to divorce you.'

'God, you're strict.' Suddenly nervous, she rubbed her hands together. 'While you're in that mode, I guess I'd better come clean.'

'Oh, were you out necking with someone else?'

'Not exactly.'

'I beg your pardon?'

'You want a drink? We've got some wine up here, don't we?' She started to get off the bed, but she wasn't at all surprised to have his hand snake out and grip her arm.

'Clarify.'

'I'm going to. I just think it might go down better with some wine. Okay?' She tried a smile but knew it fell far short of charming when he met it with a long, steely stare. His grip loosened enough for her to scoot up and hurry over to the bedroom cold box. She took her time pouring it, and kept her distance as she began.

'Peabody and I were doing the first sweep of Devane's office and quarters. She has a relaxation room.'

'I'm aware of that.'

'Sure you are.' She took a sip first to fortify her for confession before she crossed back. 'Anyway, I noticed she had VR goggles on the arm of her sleep chair. Mathias had been on VR before he hanged himself. Fitzhugh liked to use VR. It's a slim link, but I figured it was better than no link.'

'Over ninety percent of the population of this country has at least one VR per household,' Roarke pointed out, eyes still narrowed on her face.

'Yeah, but you have to start somewhere. This is a brain flaw, VR links to the brain as well as the senses. It occurred to me that if there was a defect, intentional or accidental, in the goggles, it might have caused the suicidal urge.'

He nodded slowly. 'All right. I follow that.'

'So I tried her set.'

'Wait.' He held up a hand. 'You suspected the goggles were a contributor to her death, so you merrily put them on yourself. Are you out of your mind?'

'Peabody was there as control, with orders to stun me if necessary.'

'Well then.' Disgusted, he flung up a hand. 'That's just fine. That's perfectly reasonable then. She'd knock you unconscious before you jumped off the roof.'

'There you are.' She sat down beside him, handed him his glass. 'I checked the last use log. She'd gone VR minutes before she walked out and onto that ledge. I was sure I was going to find something in whatever program she'd been on.' She paused to scratch the back of her neck. 'You know, I figured it would be some relaxation program. Maybe a meditation run, your standard sea cruise, or a country meadow.'

'I take it it wasn't.'

'No, it wasn't. It was, ah, a fantasy run. You know, a sexual fantasy.'

Intrigued now, he folded his legs under him, cocked his head. His mouth remained sober, his Irish blue eyes bland.

177

'Was it really?' He took a casual sip of wine before setting the glass aside. 'And consisted of?'

'Well, there were these guys.'

'Plural?'

'Just two.' She could feel the heat rising up to her throat and detested it. 'It was an official investigation.'

'Were you naked?'

'Jesus, Roarke.'

'I believe it's a perfectly reasonable question.'

'Maybe for a minute, okay? It was the program, and I had to test the program, and it wasn't my fault these guys were all over me – and I aborted it before, well almost before . . .'

She stumbled to a guilty halt and saw with shock that he was grinning at her. 'You think it's funny?' Bunching her fist, she punched him in the shoulder. 'I've been feeling like slime all day, and you think it's funny.'

'Before what?' he asked, nipping the glass out of her hand before she could upend it over his head. He set it down beside his own. 'You aborted the program almost before what, precisely?'

Her eyes went to slits. 'They were great. I'm getting a copy of the program for my personal use. I won't need you anymore, because I've got a couple of love slaves.'

'Wanna bet?' He pushed her back on the bed, wrestled with her, and managed to get her shirt over her head.

'Cut it out. I don't want you. My love slaves keep me satisfied.' She flipped him, nearly had him pinned when his mouth closed over her breast, and his hand slid neatly down to cup her over the thin wool snug at her crotch.

Heat speared through her like lightning.

'Damn it.' She gasped out a breath. 'I'm just pretending to enjoy this.'

'Okay.'

He tugged the slacks over her hips, then skimmed his fingertips over her. She was already wet, luring him in. His

178

teeth closed over her nipple, tugged, just as he nudged her to peak.

It wasn't a gentle pop this time. The orgasm came in one hard, fast wave that swamped her, drowned her, then tossed her helplessly over the next crest.

She moaned out his name. It was always his name. But when she reached for him, he cuffed her wrists, drew her arms over her head. 'No.' His own breathing was uneven and thick as he stared down at her. 'Just take it. Take me.'

He slipped inside her slowly, inch by inch, watching her eyes go blind and dark as he moved. Clamping down on the urge to ravish, to answer the sudden wild pistoning of her hips, he let her drive herself over the next edge.

And when she was limp and her breathing in tatters, he shifted to long, steady strokes. 'Take more,' he murmured, swallowing her groans, holding her captive, hands, mouth, loins. 'And more.'

Her system was overloaded, scrambled like her pulse. Her body was under siege, her sex so sensitized the wild pleasure was akin to pain. And still he moved slowly, lazily. 'I can't,' she managed, and her head whipsawed even as her hips arched for more. 'It's too much.'

'Let go, Eve.' He was holding onto control by his fingernails. 'Once more.'

He didn't let himself fall until she did.

Her head was still spinning when she managed to push herself up on her elbows. Amazingly, they were both still half dressed and on top of the spread. From the corner of the bed, Galahad sat watching her with feline disgust. Or maybe it was envy.

Roarke had rolled over on his back and had what could only be interpreted as a smug smile on his lips.

'I guess that flexed your testosterone.'

His smile spread wider. She jabbed a finger into his ribs.

'If that was to punish me, you missed the target.'

179

Now he opened his eyes and they were filled with warm amusement. 'Darling Eve, did you really think I'd consider your little adventure some sort of virtual adultery?'

She pouted a little. However ridiculous it was, she was miffed that he wasn't at all jealous. 'Maybe.'

With a long sigh, he sat up, set his hands on her shoulders. 'You can indulge in fantasy professionally or personally. I'm not your keeper.'

'It doesn't bother you?'

'Not in the least.' He gave her a friendly kiss, then caught her chin firmly in his hand. 'Try it in the flesh, even once, and I'll have to kill you.'

Her pupils widened, and foolishly her heart gave a pleased little leap. 'Oh, well, that's fair.'

'That's fact,' he said simply. 'Now that we have that straightened out, you should get some sleep.'

'I'm not tired anymore.' She tugged her slacks back over her hips and made him sigh again.

'I suppose that means you want to work.'

'If I could use your system, just for a couple of hours, I could get a jump on my legwork tomorrow.'

Resigned, he pulled on his own slacks. 'Let's go then.'

'Thanks.' She tucked her hand in his companionably as they walked toward the private elevator. 'Roarke, you wouldn't really kill me, would you?'

'Oh yes, I would.' Smiling easily, he nudged her into the car. 'But, given our relationship, I would trouble to do so quickly, and with as little pain as possible.'

She shot him a glance. 'Then I'll have to say same goes.'

'Naturally. East wing, third level,' he ordered, and gave her hand a companionable squeeze. 'I wouldn't have it any other way.'

# Chapter Thirteen

For the next few days, Eve beat her head against the wall of every dead end. When she needed a change of pace to clear her mind, she beat Peabody's head against the wall. She hounded Feeney to eke out whatever free time he could to find her something. Anything.

She gritted her teeth when other cases landed on her desk, and she worked overtime.

When the lab boys dragged their feet, she hopped on their backs and rode them mercilessly. It got to the point that the lab began to dodge her communications. To combat that, she hauled Peabody down to the lab for a little face-to-face persuasion.

'Don't try to sell me that SOS about backup, Dickie.'

Dickie Berenski, privately known as Dickhead, looked pained. As chief lab tech, he should have been able to delegate a half dozen drones to ward off a personal confrontation with an irate detective, but every one of them had deserted him.

Heads would roll, he thought, and sighed. 'What do you mean SOS?'

'Same old shit, Dickie. It's always SOS with you.'

He scowled but decided to make the acronym his own. 'Listen, Dallas, I got you the breakdown on all the over the counters, didn't I? Flagged them personally as a favor.'

'Favor, my ass, I bribed you with box seats for the Arena Ball play-offs.'

His face went prim. 'I assumed that was a gift.'

'And I'm not bribing you again.' She jabbed a finger into his puny chest. 'What's the deal with the VR goggles? Why haven't I got your report?'

'Because I haven't found anything to report. It's a hot program, Dallas—' His eyebrows did a little suggestive dance. 'But it was clean. No defects. So are all the other options on that unit – clean and up to code. Better than,' he added, his voice whining faintly. 'We should have so good. I had Sheila take the whole unit apart and put it back together. Damn fine equipment, top of the line – higher than top. The technology's off the scale. But that's to be expected. It's a Roarke product.'

'It's a—' She broke off, struggling not to show her surprise or distress at this new tidbit of information. 'Which plant manufactures it?'

'Hell, Sheila's got that data. Off planet, I'm pretty sure. Cheaper labor. And that baby was right off the ship. Hasn't been on the open market more than a month.'

Her stomach had clutched and tightened further. 'But it's not defective?'

'Nope. It's a real honey. I've already put in for one of my own.' He wiggled his brows hopefully. 'Of course, you could probably get me a unit at cost.'

'You get me the report, now, every single detail, and release the unit to me, and I'll think about it.'

'It's Sheila's flex day,' he whined, his mouth stretching down in a search for pity. 'She'll have the report finished up and on your desk by noon tomorrow.'

'Now, Dickie.' A good cop knew her quarry's weaknesses. 'And I'll see about making you a gift of your own unit.'

'Well, in that case . . . hang for ten.' Cheery now, he hurried over to a computer bank tucked in one of the cubbyholes in the lab's beehive.

'Dallas, one of those units probably goes for two thousand,

182

base.' Peabody stared after Dickie in disgust. 'You overbribed him.'

'I want that report.' Eve imagined that Roarke had a case of the units somewhere for promotional giveaways. Giveaways, she thought with a sick roll in her stomach, to politicians, employees, prominent citizens. 'I'm down to three days. And nothing. I won't be able to waltz Whitney toward an extension.' She looked back over as Dickie pushed out of the cubicle.

'Sheila had it almost nailed down.' He offered a sealed disc and a hard copy. 'Look at this. This is a compu-graft of the VR pattern for the last program. Sheila's highlighted a couple of blips.'

'What do you mean, blips?' Eve snatched the page and studied what appeared to be a series of lightning bolts and swirls.

'Can't say for certain. Probably the subliminal relaxation, or in this case, substimulation option. Some of the newer units are offering several extended subliminal packages. You can see these shadow the program, slide in every few seconds.'

'Suggestions?' She felt her energy surge. 'You mean the program was fitted with subliminal suggestions to the user?'

'Common enough practice. It's been used for habit breaking, sexual enhancement, mind expanding, and so on for decades. My old man quit tobacco on subliminals fifty years ago.'

'What about planting urges . . . such as self-termination?'

'Look, subs give you little nudges toward hunger, consumer goods, or aid in habit breaking. That kind of direct suggestion?' He tugged at his lip, shook his head. 'You'd have to go deeper, and I'd say it would take a long series of sessions to make the suggestion stick on a normal brain. Survival instinct's too strong.'

He shook his head again, convinced. 'We played those programs over and over.'

*Particularly the sexual fantasy sequences*, Eve thought.

183

'Ran them on test subjects, into the droid for analysis. We got nobody jumping off the roof. In fact, we got no unusual reaction from anyone or out of the droid. It's just a top flight, that's it.'

'I want a full analysis on the subliminal shadows.'

He'd already anticipated that. 'I need to keep the unit then. Sheila's started on it, as you can see, but it takes time. You've got to run the program, back out the overt VR, expunge the subliminals. Then it takes compu time to test, analyze, and report. A good subliminal, and I guarantee this one's an ace, is subtle. Chasing down its pattern isn't like reading a truth analysis.'

'How much time?'

'Two days, a day and a half if we get lucky.'

'Get lucky,' she suggested and passed the hard copy to Peabody.


Eve tried not to worry about the fact that the VR was one of Roarke's toys, or what the consequences could be if it was indeed found to be part of the coercion. Subliminal shadows. That could be the connection she'd been searching for. The next step was to tag the VR units that had been in Fitzhugh's, Mathias's, and Pearly's possession at time of death.

With Peabody keeping pace, she hustled down the sidewalk. Her vehicle was – still – in Maintenance. Eve didn't think it worth the incredible headache of requisitioning a sub for a three-block hike.

'Autumn's coming.'

'Huh?'

Curious that Eve seemed oblivious to the freshening in the air, the balmy scent on the eastward breeze, Peabody paused to take a deep breath. 'You can smell it.'

'What are you doing?' Eve demanded. 'Are you crazy? Suck in enough of New York and you'll have to spend a day in detox.'

184

'You get past the transport fumes and the body odor and it's wonderful. They might just pass that new fresh air bill this election.'

Eve spared her aide a glance. 'Your Free-Ager's showing, Peabody.'

'Nothing wrong with environmental concerns. If it wasn't for the tree huggers, we'd all be wearing filter masks and sunshades year round.' Peabody looked longingly at a people glide but matched her pace to Eve's long-legged stride. 'Not to put a damper on things, Lieutenant, but you're going to have to do a major tap dance to access those VR units. SOP would be for them to have been returned to the deceaseds' estates by this time.'

'I'll get them – and I want this kept quiet, on a need-to-know basis only – until I sort it out.'

'Understood.' She waited a moment. 'I'd imagine Roarke has so many tentacles out there it would be impossible to know who's doing exactly what at any given time.'

'It's a conflict of interest and we both know it. I'm putting your ass on the line with this.'

'Sorry to disagree, sir, but I'm in charge of my own ass. It's only on the line if I put it there.'

'So noted and appreciated.'

'Then you can also note that I'm a big fan of Arena Ball as well, sir.'

Eve stopped, took a long look, then laughed. 'One ticket or two?'

'Two. I could get lucky.'

They exchanged grins just as a shrill siren split the air. 'Oh hell, oh shit, five minutes either way and we'd have slipped by this.'

Eve drew her weapon and spun on her heel. The alarm pealed from the credit exchange center directly in front of her. 'What fool hits a CEC two blocks from Cop Central? Clear the street, Peabody,' she ordered, 'then cover the back exit.'

The first order was almost unnecessary as pedestrians were already scattering, trampling each other over glides and skywalks in a rush for cover. Eve whipped out her communicator, gave the standard order for backup before she dived through the automatic doors.

The lobby was a mass of confusion. Her only advantage was that the wave of people were rushing out as she rushed in, and they offered some cover. Like most CECs, the lobby area was small, windowless, banked with high counters for personal privacy. Only one of the personal service counters was manned by a human, the other three by droids who had gone into automatic shutdown once the panic button had been pushed.

The lone human was a female, probably midtwenties, with closely cropped black hair, a tidy, conservative white jumpsuit, and an expression of utter terror on her face as she was held through the security port by the throat.

The man who gripped her was busy squeezing off her air and waving what was certainly a homemade explosive with his free hand.

'I'll kill her. I'll fucking stuff it down her throat.'

The threat didn't worry Eve nearly as much as the calm, deliberate manner in which it was delivered. She discounted chemicals and a professional status. From the appearance of his threadbare jeans and shirt, the tired, unshaven face, she concluded she had one of the city's desperately poor on her hands.

'She hasn't done anything to you.' With the first mad rush already out the door, Eve approached slowly. 'She's not responsible. Why don't you let her go?'

'Everyone's done something to me. Everyone's part of the system.' He yanked, pulling the hapless clerk a little farther through the security port. She was wedged now to the shoulders and turning faintly blue. 'Keep back,' he said quietly. 'I've got nothing to lose and nowhere to go.'

'You're choking her. Snuff her and you've got no shield. Ease up a little. What's your name?'

'Names don't count for shit.' But he did loosen his grip enough to have the young clerk wheeze in a desperate breath. 'Money's what matters. I walk out with a bag of credits, nobody gets hurt. Hell, they'll just make more.'

'It doesn't work that way.' Cautious, Eve took another three steps, keeping her eyes on his. 'You know you're not going to get out of here. By now the street's blocked, the security units are deployed. Jesus, pal, the area's lousy with cops any time of the day or night. You could've picked better than this.'

Out of the corner of her eye, she saw Peabody slide through the rear access and take up her position. Neither of them could risk firing while he had the clerk and the explosive in his hands.

'If you drop that thing, even sweat too much, it could blow. Then everybody dies here.'

'Then we'll all die here. It doesn't matter anymore.'

'Let the clerk go. She's a civilian. She's just trying to make a living.'

'So was I.'

She saw it in his eyes just an instant too late. The utter despair. In a blink he tossed the hand-held boomer high and right. Eve's life flashed obscenely before her eyes as she sprinted forward and made the dive. She missed by a fingertip.

Even as she braced for the insult of the blast, the crudely made ball rolled into a corner, bobbled, then settled quietly.

'Dud.' The would-be thief let out a weak laugh. 'Doesn't it just figure?' Then, as Eve popped to her feet, he charged.

She didn't have time to aim, much less fire her weapon. He hit her like a battering ram, driving her back hard into one of the self-service counters. The explosion came now, inside her head as her hip slammed painfully into the edge. Sheer luck had her holding onto her weapon as stars burst in her head.

She hoped the crack she heard was the cheap laminate giving and not bone.

He had her gripped in a pathetically loverlike embrace that was surprisingly effective. It blocked her weapon and pinned against the counter, so she was forced to shift her body weight rather than pivot.

They hit the floor, and this time she was unlucky enough to land first so that his thin, panic-fueled body dropped heavily on hers. Her elbow cracked on the tile, her knee jarred and twisted viciously. With more enthusiasm than finesse, she rammed the side of her weapon against his temple.

The move proved to be as effective as a stun. His eyes rolled up white before she shoved him aside and got to her knees.

Panting, fighting back the nausea that was a result of taking some bony part of his body in the stomach, she blew the hair out of her eyes. Peabody was also on her knees, the boomer in one hand, her weapon in the other.

'I couldn't get a clear shot. I went for the boomer first, thought you could take him.'

'Fine, that's just dandy.' She hurt everywhere, and now her pulse began to hammer at the sight of her aide clutching a bomb. 'Don't move.'

'Not moving. Barely breathing.'

'I'll call the goddamn bomb disposal unit. Get a safe box in here now.'

'I was just about—' Peabody broke off, went pale as death. 'Oh hell, Dallas. It's heating up.'

'Dump it. Dump it now! Take cover.' Swiping out one handed, Eve dragged the unconscious man with her behind the counter, draped herself over him, then locked her arms over the back of her head.

The explosion blasted the air, fumed out a fist of heat and had God knew what raining down on her. The auto fire control system whirled into action, spewing sprays of icy water, shrilling out a new alarm, warning employees and customers to vacate the building in a calm and orderly manner.

She sent up a quick thanks to whoever was listening that she felt no bright pain, and that all her body parts appeared to be attached.

Coughing against the thick wash of smoke, she crawled out from behind what was left of the counter. 'Peabody. Christ.' She hacked, wiped her stinging eyes, and kept crawling over the wet, now filthy floor. Something hot burned the heel of her hand, made her swear again. 'Come on, Peabody. Where the hell are you?'

'Here.' The answer was weak, followed by a fit of throaty coughing. 'I'm okay. I think.'

They met on hands and knees through the curtain of smoke and water and eyed each other's blackened faces. Casually, Eve reached out and rapped Peabody several times on the side of the head. 'Your hair was on fire,' she said mildly.

'Oh. Thanks. How's the asshole?'

'Still unconscious.' Eve sat back on her heels and took a quick self-inventory. She didn't see any blood, which was no small relief. Most of her clothes were still there, which hardly mattered since they were ruined. 'You know, Peabody, I think Roarke owns this building.'

'Then he's probably going to be pissed. Smoke and water damage is a bitch.'

'You're telling me. Let's call it a goddamn day. The credit cops can handle this. I'm giving a party tonight.'

'Yeah.' Mouth twisted, Peabody tugged on the torn sleeve of her uniform. 'I'm looking forward to it.' Then she swayed, squinted. 'Dallas, how many pairs of eyes did you have when we came in here?'

'One. Just one.'

'Shit. Now you've got two. I think one of us has a problem.' With this, Peabody pitched forward into Eve's arms.

There wasn't time to clean up. After she'd hauled Peabody

189

out of the wreckage and dumped her on the medical technicians, she had a report to relay to the officer in charge of the security team, then she fed the same data to the bomb disposal unit. Between reports she harassed the MTs about Peabody's condition and blocked their attempts to treat her to an injury scan.

Roarke was already dressed for the evening when she rushed in the door. He cut off his conversation with Tokyo on his palm link, shifted away from the team of florists currently arranging pink and white hibiscus in the foyer.

'What the hell happened to you?'

'Don't ask.' She raced past him and hit the stairs at a dead run.

She was out of what was left of her shirt by the time he came into the bedroom, closed the door. 'I will ask.'

'The bomb wasn't a dud after all.' Unwilling to sit down and smear whatever was on her slacks onto the furniture, she balanced on one foot and fought off a boot.

Roarke took a deep breath. 'The bomb?'

'Well, a homemade boomer. Very unreliable.' She pried off the second boot, then began to peel off her torn and blackened slacks. 'Guy hits a CEC two blocks from Cop Central. Idiot.' She dumped the tatters on the floor, swung around to head to the bath, only to come up short when Roarke took her arm.

'Name of God.' He turned her to get a closer look at the purpling bruise that spread over her hip. It was bigger than his spread hand. Her right knee was raw and there were more bruises blooming on her arms and shoulders. 'You're a mess, Eve.'

'You should see the other guy. Well, at least he'll get three square and a roof for a few years, courtesy of the state. I've got to get cleaned up.'

He didn't release her, only shifted his gaze to hers. 'I don't suppose you bothered to let the MTs work on you.'

190

'Those butchers?' She smiled. 'I'm fine, just sore. I can get a quick treatment tomorrow.'

'You'll be lucky if you can walk by tomorrow. Come on.'

'Roarke—' But she winced and hobbled, and he pulled her into the bath.

'Sit. Be quiet.'

'We don't have time for this.' She sat, rolled her eyes. 'It's going to take me a couple hours to get the stink and soot off. Christ, those boomers smell.' She turned her head to sniff at her shoulder and grimaced. 'Sulfur.' Then she eyed him warily. 'What's that?'

He approached with a thick pad soaked in something pink. 'The best we can do at the moment. Stop wiggling.' He laid the pad over her injured knee, holding it in place and ignoring her curses.

'That stings. Christ, are you crazy?'

'I'm beginning to think so.' With his free hand, he caught her chin, carefully examined her blackened face. 'At the risk of repeating myself, you're a mess. Hold that pad in place.' He squeezed lightly on her chin. 'I mean it.'

'Okay, okay.' She huffed out a breath and kept the pad over her knee as he walked back to a wall cabinet. The sting was easing. She didn't want to admit that the ripe ache in her knee was backing off. 'What's in this stuff?'

'This and that. It'll ease the swelling and numb the injury for a few hours.' He came back with a small tube of liquid. 'Drink it.'

'Uh-uh, no drugs.'

Very calmly, he laid a hand on her shoulder. 'Eve, if you're not in pain at the moment, it's due to adrenaline. You're going to hurt, and hurt big time, very shortly. I know what it feels like to be bruised and battered all over. Now drink it.'

'I'll be fine. I don't want—' She gasped when he pinched her nose, drew her head back, and poured the liquid down her throat. 'Bastard,' she managed, choking and batting at him.

'That's a good girl. Now, into the shower.' He walked to the glass-enclosed tube and ordered the spray at half force and a soothing eighty-six degrees.

'I'll get you for that. I don't know how, I don't know when, but I'll do it.' She limped into the shower, still muttering. 'Son of a bitch pours drugs down my throat. Treats me like a goddamn imbecile.' The moan of relief came involuntarily as the soft water slid over her abused body.

He watched her, smiling as she braced both hands against the wall and ducked her head under the spray. 'You'll want to wear something loose and floor length. Try the blue ankle sweep Leonardo designed for you.'

'Oh, go to hell. I can dress myself. Why don't you stop staring at me and go order some of your minions around?'

'Darling, they're our minions now.'

She bit off a chuckle and rapped her hand against the shower panel to access the 'link recessed there. 'Brightmore Health Center,' she ordered. 'Fifth floor admissions.' She waited for the connection and managed to soap up her hair one-handed. 'This is Lieutenant Eve Dallas. You have my aide, Officer Delia Peabody. I want status.' She listened to the standard line for approximately five seconds before she cut off the charge nurse. 'Then find out, and find out now. I want her full status, and believe me, you don't want me coming down there to get it.'

It took her an hour, a relatively painless hour, she was forced to admit. Whatever Roarke had made her drink didn't leave her with that helpless, floaty feeling she detested. Instead, she felt alert and only slightly giddy.

It might have been the drug that made her admit, at least to herself, that he'd been right about the dress. It slid weightlessly over her skin, concealing the bruises stylishly with its high neck, long, tapering sleeves, and draping skirt. She added the diamond he'd given her as a symbolic apology for swearing at him – even though he'd deserved it.

With less resentment than usual, she fussed with her face, struggled with her hair. The result, she decided as she gave herself a study in the triple mirrors in the closet, wasn't half bad. She supposed she looked as close to elegant as she was ever going to get.

When she walked onto the roof terrace where the performance session of the party was to take place, Roarke's quick smile agreed with her. 'There she is,' he murmured and walked over to take both of her hands, bringing them to his lips.

'I don't think I'm talking to you.'

'All right.' He lowered his head and, mindful of bruises, kissed her lightly. 'Feel better?'

'Maybe.' She sighed and didn't bother to tug her hands away. 'I guess I'll have to tolerate you, since you're doing all this for Mavis.'

'We're doing it for Mavis.'

'I haven't done anything.'

'You married me,' he pointed out. 'How's Peabody? I heard you calling the health center from the shower.'

'Mild concussion, bumps, and bruises. She was a little shocky, but she's stabilized. She went after the boomer.' Remembering that moment, Eve blew out a slow breath. 'It started to heat up right in her hand. No way I could get to her.' She closed her eyes, shook her head. 'Scared the hell out of me. I thought I'd find pieces of her everywhere.'

'She's tough and smart, and she's learning from the best.'

Eve opened her eyes, narrowed them. 'Flattery isn't going to make me forgive you for drugging me.'

'I'll find something else that will.'

She surprised him by reaching up, framing his face with her hands. 'We're going to talk about that, ace.'

'Anytime. Lieutenant.'

But she didn't smile. Her eyes only went more intense. 'There's another thing we have to talk about. It's serious.'

'I can see that.' Concerned, he glanced around at the bustling caterers, the wait staff already lined up for their final briefing. 'Summerset can handle the last of this. We can use the library.'

'It's bad timing, I know, but it can't be helped.' She took his hand, an instinctive gesture of support, as they headed out of the room and down the wide corridor toward the library.

Inside, he closed the door, ordered lights, then poured drinks. Mineral water for Eve. 'You'll have to forgo alcohol for a few hours,' he told her. 'The painkiller doesn't mix well with it.'

'I think I can restrain myself.'

'Tell me.'

'Okay.' She set the glass aside without drinking, pushed both hands through her hair. 'You've got a new VR unit on the market.'

'I do.' He sat on the arm of a leather sofa, took out a cigarette, and lighted it. 'It hit a month, six weeks ago, depending on region. We've improved a number of the options and programs.'

'With subliminals.'

He blew out smoke thoughtfully. It wasn't difficult to read her, he thought, when you understood her. She was worried, stressed, and the soothing power of the drug couldn't overtake her in that area. 'Naturally. Several of the option packages include a variety of subliminals. They're very popular.' Still watching her, he nodded. 'I take it Cerise had one of the new units and was using it before she jumped.'

'Yeah. The lab hasn't yet been able to identify the subliminal. May turn out to be nothing, but—'

'You don't think so,' he finished.

'Something triggered her. Something triggered all of them. I'm working on confiscating the VR units owned by the other subjects. If it turns out they all owned that new model . . . the investigation's going to circle around your company. On you.'

'I had a sudden urge to encourage self-termination?'

'I know you had nothing to do with it,' she said quickly and fiercely. 'I'm going to do everything I can to keep you out of it. I want—'

'Eve,' he interrupted quietly, shifted to crush out his cigarette, 'you don't have to explain yourself to me.' He reached in his pocket, took out his memo card, and tapped in a code. 'The R and D on that model was done in two locations. In Chicago and on Travis II. Manufacturing was handled by one of my subsidiaries, again on Travis II. The distribution and shipping, on and off planet, by Fleet. The packaging through Trillium, marketing by Top Drawer here in New York. I can have all the data sent to your office unit, if that's most convenient.'

'I'm sorry.'

'Stop.' He tucked the card away and rose. 'There are literally hundreds, perhaps thousands of employees in these companies. I can certainly get you a list, for whatever good that would do.' Then he paused, reached down, and rubbed a thumb over the diamond she wore. 'You should know I personally worked on and approved the design, initialed the schematics. The unit's been in development for more than a year, and I spot-checked every stage at one time or another through that period. My hands are all over it.'

She'd been sure of that, afraid of that. 'It could come to nothing. Dickhead claims my theory of subliminal coercion to self-termination is over the edge of unlikely into the impossible.'

Roarke smiled a little. 'How can one trust a man called Dickhead? Eve, you used the unit yourself.'

'Yeah, which also put a big wrench in my pet theory. All I got out of it was an orgasm.' She couldn't quite bring off a smile herself. 'I want to be wrong, Roarke. I want to be

195

wrong and close these cases as voluntary self-terminations. But if I'm not—'

'We'll deal with it. First thing tomorrow, I'll look into it myself.' She started to shake her head, but he took her hand. 'Eve, I know the drill; you don't. I know my people, at least the department heads in each stage. You and I have worked together before.'

'I don't like it.'

'That's a pity.' He toyed with the diamond between her breasts again. 'I believe I do.'

# Chapter Fourteen

'Roarke sure knows how to dish a party.' Mavis stuffed a deviled quail egg in her mouth and chattered over it. 'Everybody, and I mean everybody's here. Did you see Roger Keene? He's like top hound at Be There Records. And Lilah Monroe? She's tearing them up with her new audience participation show on Broadway. Maybe Leonardo can charm her into using him for new costume design. And there's—'

'Take a breath, Mavis,' Eve advised as her friend babbled and continually pushed canapés into her mouth. 'Adjust the speed.'

'I'm so nervous.' With her hands momentarily free, Mavis pressed them to her stomach – bare but for an artistic rendering of a ripe, red orchid. 'I can't level, you know? When I'm this hyped I've just gotta eat and talk. And eat and talk.'

'And throw up if you don't slow down,' Eve warned. She scanned the room and had to admit that Mavis was right. Roarke knew how to dish up a party.

The room glittered, and so did the people. Even the food seemed to be glossy and polished, almost too ornamental to eat, though you couldn't prove that by Mavis. Since the weather had cooperated, the roof was open, inviting in the fresh breeze and showers of starlight. One wall was filled with a view screen, and Mavis whirled and pranced over it, her music sizzling out into the room.

Roarke had been canny enough to keep the volume muted.

'I'm never going to be able to pay you back for this.'

'Come on, Mavis.'

'No, I mean it.' After sending Leonardo a beaming smile and an exaggerated air kiss, she turned back to Eve. 'You and me, Dallas, we go back awhile. Hell, if you hadn't busted me, I'd probably still be picking pockets and running the grift.'

Eve chose an interesting-looking blot on a cracker for herself. 'That's digging deep, Mavis.'

'Maybe, but it doesn't change the facts. I did a lot to straighten myself out and change direction. I'm kind of proud of it.'

*Remaking ourselves*, Eve thought. *It could happen. It did happen.* She glanced over to where Reeanna and William were chatting with Mira and her spouse. 'You should be. I'm proud of you.'

'But what I'm talking about is this. I want to get it out – okay? – before I get up there and try to blow the diamonds off the ears of this group.' Mavis cleared her throat and promptly forgot the little speech she'd prepared. 'Hell with it. I know you, and I really love you. Like really love you, Dallas.'

'Christ, Mavis, don't start getting me all weepy. Roarke's already drugged me.'

Unashamed, Mavis swiped her hand under her nose.

'You'd have done this for me – if you knew how.' When Eve blinked and frowned, Mavis found her sentiment turning to amusement. 'Shit, Dallas, you wouldn't have the first clue how to order up anything more complicated than soy dogs and veggie hash. Roarke's hands are all over this bash.'

'*My hands are all over it.*' Roarke's words echoed in Eve's mind and made her shudder. 'Yeah, they are.'

'You asked him to do it, and he did it for you.'

Determined to let nothing shadow the evening, Eve shook off the dread. She shook her head. 'He did it for you, Mavis.'

Slowly, Mavis's lips curved and her eyes got misty again.

198

'Yeah, I guess he did. You've got a fucking prince, Dallas. A fucking prince. I've got to go throw up now. Be right back.'

'Sure.' With a half laugh, Eve grabbed some fizzy water from a passing tray and headed for Roarke. 'Excuse me, one minute,' she said and tugged him away from a group of people. 'You're a fucking prince,' she told him.

'Why thank you. I think.' He slid an arm around her waist, gently, put his other hand over hers that held the stem of her glass. He surprised her by moving her into a very smooth dance. 'You have to use your imagination with Mavis's . . . style,' he decided. 'But this one could almost be considered romantic.'

Eve lifted a brow and turned in to Mavis's voice rising over clashing brass. 'Yeah, it's a real old-fashioned, sentimental tune. I'm a lousy dancer.'

'You wouldn't be if you didn't try to lead. I decided since you weren't going to sit down and rest that battered body of yours, you could lean on me a while.' He smiled down at her. 'You're starting to limp again, just a bit. But you do look almost relaxed.'

'The knee's a little stiff,' Eve admitted. 'But I am pretty relaxed. I guess it was listening to Mavis babble. She's throwing up now.'

'Lovely.'

'It's just nerves. Thanks.' She went with impulse and gave him one of her rare public kisses.

'You're welcome. For?'

'For making sure we're not eating soy dogs and veggie hash.'

'My pleasure.' He drew her closer, keeping his arms easy. 'Believe me, it's my pleasure. Well, Peabody wears basic black and a mild concussion well,' he noted.

'What?' Jerking back, Eve followed his gaze and spotted her aide just coming through the wide double doors and snagging a flute off a tray. 'She should be flat on her back,' Eve muttered

199

and pulled away from Roarke. 'Excuse me while I go put her there.'

She stalked across the room, eyes narrowing as Peabody tried out a toothy smile. 'Some party, Lieutenant. Thanks for the invite.'

'What the hell are you doing out of bed?'

'It's just a bump on the head, and all they were doing was poking at me. I wasn't going to let a little thing like an explosion keep me from doing a party at Roarke's.'

'Are you on meds?'

'Just a couple of regulation pain blockers, and—' Her face fell when Eve snatched the champagne out of her hand. 'I was just going to hold it. Really.'

'Hold this,' Eve suggested and shoved her water into Peabody's hand. 'I ought to cart your butt right back to the health center.'

'You didn't go,' Peabody muttered, then lifted her chin. 'And I'm off duty. On personal time. You can't order me back.'

However much she sympathized and admired determination, Eve held firm. 'No liquor,' she snapped out. 'No dancing.'

'But—'

'I hauled you out of that building today, and I can haul you out of here. By the way, Peabody,' Eve added. 'You could lose a few pounds.'

'So my mother's always telling me.' Peabody huffed out a breath. 'No liquor, no dancing. Now, if you've finished with the restrictions, I'm going to go talk to somebody who doesn't know me.'

'Fine. Oh, Peabody?'

Peabody turned, scowling. 'Yes, sir?'

'You did good today. I won't have to think twice about going through the door with you.'

As Eve walked away, Peabody gaped after her. It had been

simply, even casually said, but it was the finest professional compliment she'd ever been given.

Socializing wasn't Eve's favorite pastime, but she did her best. She even resigned herself to dancing when she couldn't slide her way out of it. So she found herself being steered – it was the way she thought about dancing – around the floor by Jess.

'Your pal William?' Jess began.

'More Roarke's pal. I don't know him well.'

'Anyhow, he had some interesting input on designing an interactive to go with this disc. Bring the audience into the music – into Mavis.'

Brow lifted, Eve glanced back to the screen. Mavis was swiveling her barely covered hips and shrieking about burning up in the fire of love while red and gold flames spurted around her.

'You actually think people would want to go in there?'

He chuckled, let his voice cruise deeper south. 'Sugar, they'll trample each other to get in. And pay big for the chance.'

'And if they do,' she said, turning back to him, 'you get a nice fat percentage.'

'That's standard on development deals like this. Check with your man. He'll tell you.'

'Mavis made her choice.' She softened, noting that several guests were absorbed in the screen show. 'I'd say she made a good one.'

'We both did. I think we've got a hit,' he told her. 'And when we give them a taste of the show live and in the flesh – well, if the roof wasn't already off, we'd blow it off.'

'You're not nervous?' She looked at him: confident eyes, cocky mouth. 'No, you're not nervous.'

'I've been playing for my supper for too many years. It's a job.' He smiled at her, walked his fingers casually up her back. 'You don't get nervous tracking killers. Revved, right? Psyched, but not nervous.'

'Depends.' She thought of what she was tracking now, and her stomach fluttered.

'No, you're steel. I could see that the first time I looked at you. You don't give, you don't back off. You don't flinch. It makes your brain, well your makeup, so to speak, a fascination. What drives Eve Dallas? Justice, revenge, duty, morality? I'd say it's a very unique combination of all of those, fueled by a conflict of confidence and self-doubt. You've got a strong sense of what's right, and you're constantly questioning who you are.'

She wasn't sure she liked the turn of the conversation. 'What are you, a musician or a shrink?'

'Creative people study other people; and music is a science as much as an art, an emotion as much as a science.' His silvery eyes stayed on hers as he guided her smoothly around other couples. 'When I design a series of notes, I want it to affect people. I have to understand, even study human nature if I'm to get the right reaction. How will this make them behave, make them think, make them feel?'

Eve spared an absent smile as William and Reeanna danced by, absorbed in each other. 'I thought it was for entertainment.'

'That's the surface. Just the surface.' His eyes were excited, gleaming with it as he spoke. 'Any music hack can run a theme through a computer and come out with a competent tune. The music business has gotten more and more ordinary and predictable because of technology.'

Brows lifted, Eve glanced toward the screen, and Mavis. 'I'd have to say I don't hear anything ordinary or predictable here.'

'Exactly. I've put in time studying how tones, notes, and rhythms affect people, and I know what buttons to push. Mavis is a treasure. She's so open, so malleable.' He smiled when

Eve's eyes hardened. 'I meant that as a compliment, not that she's weak. But she's a risk taker, a woman who's willing to strip herself down and become a vessel for the message.'

'The message is?'

'Depends on the mind of the audience. The hopes and dreams. I wonder about your dreams, Dallas.'

*So do I,* she thought, but she met his gaze blandly. 'I'd rather stick with reality. Dreams are deceptive.'

'No, no, they're revealing. The mind, and the unconscious mind in particular, is a canvas. We paint on it constantly. Art and music can add such colors, such style. Medical science has understood that for decades and uses it to treat and study certain conditions, both psychological and physiological.'

She angled her head. *Was there another message here?* 'You sound more like a scientist than a musician now.'

'I've blended. One day, you'll be able to pick a song personally designed for your own brain waves. The mood enhancement capabilities will be endless and intimate. That's the key. Intimacy.'

She sensed he was making a pitch and stopped dancing. 'I wouldn't think it would be cost effective. And research into technology designed to analyze and coordinate with individual brain waves is illegal. For good reason. It's dangerous.'

'Not at all,' he disagreed. 'It's liberating. New processes, any sort of real progress usually starts out as illegal. As for the cost, it would be high initially, then come down as the design was adjusted for mass production. What's a brain but a computer, after all? You have a computer analyze a computer. What could be simpler?'

He glanced over at the screen. 'That's the intro for the last number. I've got to check my equipment before my cue.' He leaned in, kissed her cheek lightly. 'Wish us luck.'

'Yeah, luck,' she murmured, but her stomach was knotted.

*What was a brain but a computer? Computers analyzing computers. Individualized programs designed for personal brain wave patterns. If it was possible, would it be possible to add suggestive programs linked directly with the user's brain?* She shook her head. Roarke would never have approved it. He wouldn't have taken such a foolish risk. But she made her way through the crowd to him, laid a hand on his arm.

'I need to ask you a question,' she said quietly. 'Have any of your companies been doing under-the-table research on designing VR for personal brain wave patterns?'

'That's illegal, Lieutenant.'

'Roarke.'

'No. There was a time when I would have ventured into any number of not essentially legal areas in business. That wouldn't have been one of them. And no,' he added, anticipating her. 'That VR model is universally, not individually designed. Only the programs can be personalized by the user. What you're talking about is cost prohibitive, logistically tangled, and simply too damn much trouble.'

'Okay, that's what I figured.' Her muscles relaxed. 'But can it be done?'

He paused a moment, then lifted his shoulder. 'I have no idea. You'd have to have the individual's cooperation or access to a brain scan. That also involves personal approval and consent. And then . . . I have no idea,' he repeated.

'If I can get Feeney alone—' She swiveled her head, trying to find the electronics detective in the whirling crowd.

'Take the evening off, Lieutenant.' Roarke slipped an arm around her. 'Mavis is about to get her spotlight.'

'Okay.' She forced herself to push the worry to the back of her mind as Jess settled at his console and gave an introductory riff. *Tomorrow*, she promised herself and led the applause as Mavis spun onto the floor.

Then the worry was gone, melted away by the blast of Mavis's energy and her own wild pleasure as lights, music, and showmanship combined in a dizzy kaleidoscope.

'She's good, isn't she?' She was unaware she'd gripped

Roarke's arm like a mother with a child in the school play. 'Different, weird, but good.'

'She's all of that.' The clashing edge of notes, sound effects, and vocals would never be his music of choice, but he found himself grinning. 'She's caught the crowd. You can relax.'

'I'm relaxed.'

He laughed and hugged her closer. 'If you were wearing buttons, you'd pop them.' He didn't mind the fact that he had to put his mouth on her ear for her to hear him. And since he was there, anyway, he added an inventive suggestion for after the party.

'What?' She went hot all over. 'I believe that particular act is illegal in this state. I'll check my code book and get back to you. Cut it out.' She hunched up her shoulder in reaction as his teeth and tongue got busy on her earlobe.

'I want you.' Lust prickled over his skin like a rash, instant, itchy, immediate. 'Right now.'

'You can't be serious,' she began, but she found he was, fiercely, when his mouth closed over hers in a wild and urgent kiss. Blood thudded her pulse to vibrant life and the muscles in her thighs went limp. 'Get ahold of yourself.' She managed to ease back a half inch and was breathless, shocked, and very near blushing. Not everyone's attention was focused on Mavis. 'We're in the middle of an event here. A public one.'

'Then let's leave.' He was hard as rock, painfully ready. There was a wolf inside him, poised to lunge. 'There are a lot of private rooms in this house.'

She would have laughed if she hadn't felt the need vibrating from him. 'Get a grip, Roarke. This is Mavis's big moment. We're not running off into a closet like a couple of randy teenagers.'

'Yes, we are.' Half blind, he pulled her through the crowd and out of it while she babbled in stunned protest.

'This is nuts. What are you, a pleasure droid? You can damn well hold yourself in check for a couple of hours.'

'The hell with it.' He yanked open the closest door and shoved her inside what was indeed a closet. 'Now, goddamn it.' Her back rapped up against the wall, and before she could so much as gasp, he pulled up her skirts and drove himself into her.

She was dry, unprepared, shocked. *Ravaged*, was all she could think as she bit down on her lip to keep from crying out. He was rough, careless, and sent the bruises singing as he rammed her, over and over, into the wall. Even as she shoved at him, he pounded into her, his hands hiking up her hips, digging in and ripping a startled cry of pain from her throat.

She could have stopped him, her training was thorough. But training had dissolved into sheer feminine distress. She couldn't see his face, wasn't sure she'd recognize it if she could.

'Roarke.' It was shock, bone deep, that quavered in her voice. 'You're hurting me.'

He muttered something, a language she didn't understand and had never heard, so she stopped struggling, gripped his shoulders, and shut her eyes to what was happening to both of them.

Still he plowed into her, hands digging into her hips to keep her open for him, his breath whistling in her ear. He took her brutally, and with none of the finesse or control that was such an innate part of him.

He couldn't stop. Even as part of his brain stepped back, appalled at what he was doing, he simply couldn't stop. The need was like a cancer eating at him and he had to sate it to survive. There was a voice somewhere in his head, greedy and gasping. *Harder. Faster. More.* It drove him, pushed him, until with one final vicious thrust, he emptied.

She held on. It was that or slide to the floor. He was shuddering like a man with a fever and she didn't know whether to soothe him or belt him.

'Goddamn it, Roarke.' But when he pressed a hand to the

wall to keep balance as he swayed, she lost any sense of insult in worry.

'Hey, what is it? How much have you had to drink, anyway? Come on, lean on me.'

'No.' With the violent need met, his mind cleared. And remorse was a hot weight in his belly. He shook off the dizziness and eased himself back. 'Good God, Eve. Good God. I'm sorry. I'm so sorry.'

'Okay. It's okay.' He was sheet white. She'd never seen him look even remotely ill and was terrified. 'I should get Summerset, somebody. You've got to lie down.'

'Stop it.' He very carefully nudged away her stroking hands and stepped back until they were no longer touching. How could she bear to have him touch her? 'For Christ's sake. I raped you. I just raped you.'

'No.' She said it firmly, hoping the tone of her voice would be as effective as a slap. 'You did not. I know what rape is. What you did wasn't rape, even if it was a little overenthusiastic.'

'I hurt you.' When she reached out, he held up his hands to stop her. 'Goddamn it, Eve, you're bruised from head to foot, and I shoved you against the wall in some fucking closet and used you. Used you like a—'

'Okay.' She stepped forward, but he shook his head. 'Don't back away from me, Roarke. That's what will hurt. Don't do that.'

'I need a minute.' He rubbed his hands over his face. He still felt light-headed and queasy, and worse, slightly out of himself. 'Christ, I need a drink.'

'Which brings me back to my question. How much have you had?'

'Not enough. I'm not drunk, Eve.' He dropped his hands and looked around. *A closet*, was all he could think. *For God's pity, a closet.* 'I don't know what happened, what came over me. I'm sorry.'

207

'I can see that.' But she still couldn't see the whole picture. 'You kept saying something. Weird. Like *liomsa*.'

His eyes darkened. 'It's Gaelic. *Mine* it means. I haven't used Gaelic in . . . not since I was a boy. My father used it often when he was . . . on a drunk.'

He hesitated, then he reached out to graze his fingertips over her cheek. 'I was so rough with you. So careless.'

'I'm not one of your crystal vases, Roarke. I can take it.'

'Not like that.' He thought of the whimpers and protests of the alley whores that had come through the thin walls and haunted him when his father had bedded them. 'Never like that. I never thought of you. I didn't care, and there's no excuse.'

She didn't want him humble. It unnerved her. 'Well, you're too busy beating yourself up for me to bother, so let's go back.'

He touched her arm before she could open the door. 'Eve, I don't know what happened. Literally. One minute we were standing there, listening to Mavis, and the next . . . it was overpowering, vicious. Like my life depended on having you. Not just sex, but survival. I couldn't control it. That's not excusing what—'

'Wait.' She leaned back against the door a moment, struggled to separate woman from cop, wife from detective. 'You're not exaggerating?'

'No. It was like a fist around my throat.' He managed a very weak smile. 'Well, perhaps that's the wrong portion of the anatomy. There's nothing I can say or do to—'

'Eject the guilt a minute, will you, and think.' Her eyes were cold now, hard as agate. 'A sudden and irresistible urge – more a compulsion. One you, a very controlled man, couldn't control? You just pounded yourself into me with all the finesse of a sweaty celibate breaking fast with a rented sex droid.'

He winced at that, felt the tear of guilt. 'I'm all too aware of that.'

'And it's not your style, Roarke. You've got moves, I can't keep up with all of them, but they're all slick, practiced. You may get rough, but never mean. And as one who's made love with you in about every way that's anatomically possible, I can certify that you're never selfish.'

'Well.' He wasn't quite certain how to react. 'You humble me.'

'It wasn't you,' she murmured.

'I beg to differ.'

'It wasn't what you've made yourself into,' she corrected. 'And that's what counts. You snapped off. Something inside you snapped off. Or on. That son of a bitch.' Her breath shuddered out as she met Roarke's eyes, and in them she saw the dawning of understanding. 'That son of a bitch has something. He was telling me while we were dancing. He was fucking bragging, and I didn't get it. But he just had to give a little demonstration. And that's what's going to hang him.'

This time Roarke's grip on her arm was firm. 'You're talking about Jess Barrow. About brain scans and suggestions. Mind control.'

'Music should affect how people behave, how they think. How they feel. He said that to me minutes before the performance began. Cocky bastard.'

Roarke remembered the shock in her eyes when he'd thrown her against the wall and driven himself into her like a battering ram. 'If you're right,' his voice was cool now, too cool, 'I want a moment alone with him.'

'It's police business,' she began, but he stepped slightly closer, and his eyes were cold and determined.

'You'll give me a moment alone with him, or I'll find a way to take it. Either way, I'll have it.'

'All right.' She laid a hand over his, not to ease his grip but in solidarity. 'All right, but you'll wait your turn. I have to be sure.'

'I'll wait,' he agreed. But the man would pay, Roarke

promised himself, for wedging even one instant of fear and distrust into their relationship.

'I'll let the performance wind up first,' she decided. 'I'll interview him, unofficially, in my office downstairs, with Peabody as control. Don't make a move on him, Roarke. I mean that.'

He opened the door, let her slip out. 'I said I'd wait.'

The music was still going strong, and it hit them with a high, gritty pitch yards before they reached the doorway. But she had only to step in and through the crowd before Jess's eyes shifted from his controls and met hers.

His smile was quick, cocky, amused.

And she was sure.

'Find Peabody and ask her to go down to my office and set up for a prelim interview.' She stepped in front of Roarke, willed his gaze to move to hers. 'Please. We're not talking about just a personal insult here. We're talking about murder. Let me do my job.'

Roarke turned without a word. The moment she lost him in the crowd, she worked her way through to Summerset. 'I want you to watch Roarke.'

'I beg your pardon?'

'Listen to me.' Her fingers dug through his neat jacket and into bone. 'It's important. He could be in trouble. I don't want you to let him out of your sight until at least an hour after the performance. If anything happens to him, I'll fry your ass. Understood?'

Not in the least, but he did understand her urgency. 'Very well.' He spoke with dignity, crossed the room with grace, but his nerves were shattered.

Confident that Summerset would watch Roarke like a mother hawk, she wound her way through the audience again until she stood on the front edge of the group. She applauded with the rest, schooled herself to flash a supportive smile as Mavis wound up for the encore. And when the next round of applause rang out, she slipped toward Jess and skirted the controls.

'Quite a triumph,' she murmured.

'I told you, she's a treasure.' There was a wicked gleam in his eyes as he smiled up at her. 'You and Roarke missed a couple of numbers.'

'Some personal business,' she said levelly. 'I really need to talk to you, Jess. About your music.'

'Glad to. Nothing I like better.'

'Now, if you don't mind. Let's go someplace a little more private.'

'Sure.' He shut down his console, locked on the code. 'It's your party.'

'Damn right it is,' she murmured, and led the way.

# Chapter Fifteen

She chose the elevator, wanting to move quickly and privately. She programmed it for the short vertical glide, then the horizontal shift from wing to wing.

'I've got to tell you, you and Roarke have a fantastic place here. Just ultra mag.'

'Oh, it'll do until we find something bigger.' She said it dryly and refused to let his laughter grate on her nerves. 'Tell me, Jess, did you decide to work with Mavis, seriously, before or after you knew the connection with Roarke?'

'I told you, Mavis is one in a million. Only had to see her a couple of times, doing a short gig down at the Down and Dirty to know we'd meld well.' The grin flashed. Charming. A choirboy holding a frog under his robe. 'It sure didn't hurt a thing that she had a contact like Roarke on her side. But she had to have the goods.'

'But you knew about the connection before.'

He moved a shoulder. 'I'd heard about it. That's why I went down to see her. That kind of club isn't my usual venue. But she flashed for me. If I can move her into some hot gigs, then if Roarke, or someone of his ilk, let's say, is interested in investing in a coming act, it smooths everybody.'

'You're smooth, Jess.' She stepped out of the car when the doors slid open. 'Real smooth.'

'Like I said, I've been shaking gigs since I was a kid. I think I got it down.' He looked around the corridor as she led the way.

212

Old art, the real thing, he noted, pricey wood, carpet some craftsman had worn his fingers weaving a century before.

This was money, he thought. The kind that built empires.

At the doorway of her office, she turned. 'I don't know how much he's got,' she said, reading him perfectly. 'And I don't really care.'

The smile still in place, he lifted a brow, lowered his gaze to the fat tear-shaped diamond lying against the bodice of soft midnight silk. 'But you ain't wearing paste and rags, sugar.'

'I have, and I might again. And Jess?' She flicked off the coded lock. 'Don't call me sugar.'

Eve glided in, nodded to a puzzled but attentive Peabody. 'Have a seat,' she told Jess and moved directly to her desk.

'Nice milieu. Well, hi, sweetie.' He couldn't for the life of him remember her name, but he beamed at Peabody as if they were old, dear friends. 'Did you catch the act?'

'Most of it.'

He dropped into a chair. 'So, what do you think?'

'I thought it was great. You and Mavis really put on a show.' She risked a smile, not at all sure what Eve wanted from her. 'I'm ready to buy the first disc.'

'That's what I like to hear. Can a guy get a drink in here?' he asked Eve. 'I like to stay dry before a performance, and I'm more than ready to get wet.'

'No problem. What would you like?'

'That champagne looked good.'

'Peabody, there should be a bottle in the kitchen. Pour our guest here a glass of wine, will you? And why don't you get us some coffee?'

She leaned back and considered. Technically, she should record from this point, but she wanted a lead-in before she went on log. 'Someone like you, who designs music and the atmosphere surrounding it, has to be as much technician as artist, right? That's what you were explaining to me before the performance.'

'That's the way the business shakes down now, has for a lot of years.' He flicked one of his beautiful hands, braceleted with gold. 'I'm lucky I've got an aptitude for both and an interest. The days of plucking out a tune on the piano or playing a riff on a guitar have gone the way of fossil fuel. Almost extinct.'

'Where'd you get your tech training? I'd have to say it's way above run of the mill.'

He shot a fresh smile as Peabody came back with the drinks. He was comfortable, relaxed, and assumed he was in the middle of a kind of job interview. 'On the job, mostly, a lot of late-night hacking. But I did a stretch of home ed with MIT.'

She already knew some of the data from Peabody's make, but she wanted to lull him. 'Impressive. You've made a name for yourself both in performance and design. Isn't that right, Peabody?'

'Yeah. I've got all your discs, and I'm looking forward to something new. It's been a while.'

'I heard that somewhere.' Eve picked up the ball Peabody was unaware she'd tossed. 'Have a dry spell, Jess?'

'Not at all. I wanted to take my time perfecting the new equipment, putting together just the right elements. When I hit with the new stuff, it's going to be something no one's ever seen or heard before.'

'And Mavis is like a springboard.'

'In a manner of speaking. She was a lucky break. She'll showcase some of the material that wasn't right for me, and I've individualized some pieces to match her. I figure on doing some of my own sessions in a few months.'

'After everything's in place.'

He toasted her, sipped. 'Exactly.'

'You ever design soundtracks for VR?'

'Now and again. It's not a bad gig, if the program's interesting.'

'And I bet you know how to lay down subliminals.'

He paused, then sipped again. 'Subliminals? That's straight tech.'

'But you're a damn good tech, aren't you, Jess? Good enough to know computers in and out. And brains. A brain's just a computer, isn't it? Isn't that what you told me?'

'Sure.' His focus was all for Eve so that he didn't notice that Peabody had come to attention.

'And you're into mood enhancements, which lead to mood shifts. Behavioral and emotional patterns. Brain wave patterns.' She took a recorder out of her desk, placed it in plain sight. 'Let's talk about that.'

'What the hell is this?' He set down his glass, scooted to the edge of his seat. 'What's the deal?'

'The deal is, I'm going to advise you of your rights, then we're going to have a chat. Officer Peabody, engage backup recording and log on, please.'

'I didn't agree to a fucking interview.' He got to his feet. Eve got to hers.

'That's all right. We can make it obligatory, and take you to Cop Central. There might be a wait. I haven't booked an interview room. But you won't mind spending a few hours in lockup.'

Slowly, he sat again. 'You turn cop fast, Dallas.'

'No, I don't. I stay cop. Always. Dallas, Lieutenant Eve,' she began for the recorder, and fed in time and place before reciting the revised Miranda. 'Do you understand your rights and options, Jess?'

'Yeah, I get it. But I don't know what the hell this is about.'

'I'm going to make that very clear for you. You are being questioned in the matters of the unresolved deaths of Drew Mathias, S. T. Fitzhugh, Senator George Pearly, and Cerise Devane.'

'Who?' He looked convincingly baffled. 'Devane? Isn't that the woman who jumped off the Tattler Building? What am I supposed to have to do with suicide? I didn't even know her.'

'You were unaware that Cerise Devane was CEO and majority stockholder of Tattler Enterprises?'

'No, I guess I knew who she was, but—'

'I imagine you found yourself in *The Tattler* from time to time during your career.'

'Sure, they're always digging for dirt. They've tossed some my way. It's just part of the business.' Fear had backed off and left him mildly irritated. 'Look, the lady jumped. I was downtown, in session, when she took the leap. I've got witnesses. Mavis for one.'

'I know you weren't there, Jess. I was. At least I know you weren't there in the flesh.'

His sculpted mouth curled into a sneer. 'What am I, a goddamn ghost?'

'Do you know or have you ever had contact with an autotronics tech by the name of Drew Mathias?'

'Never heard of him.'

'Mathias also did a pass through MIT.'

'So have thousands. I opted for in-home. I never even set foot on campus.'

'And never had any contact with other students?'

'Sure I did. Over the 'link, E-mail, laser fax, whatever.' He shrugged his shoulders, drummed his fingers over the top of the hand-tooled boot he'd cocked on his knee. 'I don't remember any autotronics tech by that name.'

She decided to change tacks. 'How much work have you done on individualized subliminals?'

'I don't know what you're talking about.'

'You don't understand the term?'

'I know what it means.' This time his shrug was jerky. 'And as far as I know, it's never been done, so I don't know what you're asking me.'

Eve took a chance. She looked over at her aide. 'Do you know what I'm asking him, Peabody?'

'I think it's clear enough, Lieutenant.' She was struggling

216

through the mud of confusion. 'You'd like to know how much work the interview subject has done on individualized subliminals. Perhaps the interview subject should be reminded that it is not currently illegal to research or have an interest in this area. Only development and implementation are against current state, federal, and international laws.'

'Very good, Peabody. Does that help clear things up for you, Jess?'

The byplay had given him enough time to settle. 'Sure, I'm interested in the area. Lots of people are.'

'It's a little out of your field, isn't it? You're just a musician, not a licensed scientist.'

It was exactly the right button. His sat up in his chair, his eyes flashing once. 'I'm fully certified in Musicology. Music isn't just a bunch of notes strung together, sweetheart. It's life. It's memory. Songs trigger specific and often predictable emotional reactions. Music's an expression of emotion, desires.'

'And here I thought it was just a nice way to pass the time.'

'Entertainment is only a slice of the pie. The Celts went to war with bagpipes. They were as much a weapon to them as a broadax. Warring natives in Africa psyched themselves up with drums. Slaves survived on their spirituals, and men have been seducing women to music for centuries. Music plays the mind.'

'Which brings us back to the question. When did you decide to take it a step further and tie in to individual brain patterns? Did you just stumble across it, sort of blind luck, while you were noodling out a tune?'

He gave a short laugh. 'You really think what I do is just a slide, don't you? Just sit down, punch in some notes, and go. It's work. It's hard, demanding work.'

'And you're damned proud of your work, aren't you? Come on, Jess, you wanted to tell me earlier.' Eve rose, came around

217

the desk to sit on the front edge. 'You've been dying to tell me. To tell someone. What good is it, what satisfaction is there in creating something so amazing, then having to keep it to yourself?'

He picked up his glass again, ran his fingers down the long, slim stem. 'This isn't exactly the way I'd pictured this.' He took a sip, considered the consequences – and the rewards. 'Mavis says you can be flexible. It's not just code books and procedure with you.'

'Oh, I can be flexible, Jess.' When it's warranted. 'Talk to me.'

'Well, let's just say that if – hypothetically – I had worked out a technique for individualized subs, mood enhancements on a personal brain pattern, it could be big. People like Roarke and you, with your contacts and financial base, your influence, let's say, could work around a few antiquated laws and make a big pile. Revolutionize the personal entertainment and enhancement industry while you were at it.'

'Is this a business offer?'

'Hypothetically,' he said and gestured with his glass. 'Roarke industries has the R and D, the facilities, the man power, and the credits to take something like this and run with it. And a smart cop, seems to me, could find a way to bend the law, just enough, to make it go down smooth.'

'Gosh, Lieutenant,' Peabody said with a smile that didn't touch her eyes. 'Sounds like you and Roarke are the perfect couple. Hypothetically.'

'And Mavis as the conduit,' Eve murmured.

'Hey, Mavis is chilled. She got what she wanted. After tonight, she's going to cruise.'

'And you figure that evens out using her to get to Roarke.'

He moved a shoulder again. 'Backs gotta be scratched, honey. I gave hers a real full treatment.' The wicked amusement flashed into his eyes again. 'Did you enjoy the informal demonstration of my hypothetical system?'

Not certain even her training could keep the fury off her face, she turned, slipped back behind the desk. 'Demonstration?'

'The night you and Roarke came by the studio to watch the session. Seemed to me you two were pretty eager to leave, to be alone.' His smile sharpened at the corners. 'A little honeymoon revisited?'

She kept her hands behind the desk a moment until she could unclutch her fists. She glanced over toward the door of Roarke's connecting office, and saw with a jolt that the monitoring light blinked green over it.

He was watching, she realized. That was not only illegal, but dangerous under the circumstances. She flicked her eyes back to Jess. She couldn't afford to break rhythm. 'It seems you're unusually interested in my sex life.'

'I told you, you fascinate me, Dallas. You've got a mind. It's fucking steel, with all these dark spaces burned into it I wonder what would happen if you opened those spaces. And sex is a master key.' He leaned forward, eyes locked on hers. 'What do you dream, Dallas?'

She remembered the dreams, the sick horror of them, the night she'd watched the disc of Mavis. The disc he'd given her. Her hands trembled once before she could control them. 'You son of a bitch.' She rose slowly, planted her hands on the desk. 'You like giving demonstrations, asshole? Is that what Mathias was to you? A demonstration?'

'I told you, I don't know who that is.'

'Maybe you needed an autotron tech to perfect your system. Then you tried it out on him. You had his brain waves, so you programmed them in. Did you program in him tying his own noose and slipping it around his neck, or did you leave the method up to him?'

'You just veered way out of orbit.'

'And Pearly? What's the connection there? Political statement? Were you looking ahead? You're a real visionary. He'd

219

have tossed his weight against legalizing your new toy. Why not use it on him?'

'Hold it. Hold it.' He got to his feet. 'You're talking about murder. Christ, you're trying to wrap me up with murder.'

'Then Fitzhugh. Did you need a couple more demonstrations, Jess? Or did you just get a taste for it? Powerful, isn't it, being able to kill without getting your hands bloody?'

'I never killed anyone. You can't wrap this on me.'

'Devane was a bonus, with the media right there. You got to watch. I bet you really love to watch, don't you, Jess? I bet you got hot watching. Like you got hot thinking about where you'd push Roarke tonight with your goddamn toy.'

'That's what's rocking you, isn't it?' Furious, he leaned on the desk. His smile wasn't charming now, but feral. 'You want to sting me because I wired into your man. You should be thanking me. I bet the two of you fucked like wild minks.'

Her hand was in a fist, her fist slamming into his jaw before her brain registered the act. He went down like a stone, face first, arms splayed, and sent her 'link flying.

'Goddamn it.' Breath hitching, she uncurled her fist, clutched it again. 'Goddamn it.'

Peabody's voice came cool and calm through the buzzing in her ears. 'Let the backup record show that subject physically threatened the lieutenant during questioning. As a result, subject lost his balance and struck his head on the desk. He appears to be momentarily stunned.'

While Eve could do no more than stare at her, Peabody rose, stepped over, and dragged Jess up by the collar of his shirt. She held him there a moment, as if considering his condition. His knees sagged, his eyes rolled back white.

'That's affirmative,' she stated, then dumped him into a chair. 'Lieutenant Dallas, I believe your recorder has been damaged.' With a brush of her hand, Peabody tipped Eve's coffee onto the unit, effectively frying its chips. 'Mine is

220

in working order and will be sufficient for reporting this interview. Are you injured?'

'No.' Eve shut her eyes, snapped her control back into place. 'No, I'm fine. Thank you. The interview breaks at oh one thirty-three. Subject Jess Barrow will be transported to the Brightmore Health Center for examination and treatment, and there be detained until nine hundred hours, when this interview will continue at Cop Central. Officer Peabody, please arrange for transport. Subject is to be held for questioning, charges pending.'

'Yes, sir.' Peabody glanced over as the door to Roarke's office slid open. It only took one look at his face to realize that there might be trouble. 'Lieutenant,' she began, careful to keep the recorder turned away. 'I'm getting interference on my communicator, and your 'link may have been damaged when the subject knocked it to the floor. Permission to use another room to send for the MTs.'

'Go ahead,' Eve said and sighed as she watched Roarke come in and Peabody stride out. 'You had no business monitoring this interview,' she began.

'I beg to differ. I had every business.' He glanced down at the chair as Jess moaned and shifted. 'He's coming around. I'd like my moment with him now.'

'Listen, Roarke—'

He cut her off with one swift, ice-edged stare. 'Now, Eve. Leave us alone.'

That was the trouble between them, she decided. Both of them were so used to giving orders that neither of them took orders well. But she remembered the stricken look in his eyes when he'd backed away from her. They had both been used, she thought, but Roarke had been victimized.

'You've got five minutes. That's it. And I'm going to warn you right now. The record shows he's relatively undamaged. If there are marks on him, it's going to swing back on me and compromise my case against him.'

221

His lips twitched in a bare flicker of a smile as he took her arm and led her to the door. 'Lieutenant, give me some credit. I'm a civilized man.' He shut the door in her face, locked it.

And, he thought, he knew how to cause great discomfort to the human body without leaving so much as a dent.

He walked over, hauled Jess out of the chair, and shook him until his eyes blinked into focus. 'Awake now, are you?' Roarke said softly. 'And aware?'

Sweat pooled cold at the base of Jess's spine. He was looking into the face of murder, and he knew it. 'I want a lawyer.'

'You're not dealing with the cops now. You're dealing with me. At least for the next five minutes. And you have no rights or privileges here.'

Jess swallowed, struggled for a show of cool. 'You can't lay a hand on me. If you do, it'll slap right back on your wife.'

Roarke's lips curved and struck a fresh fist of terror in Jess's gut. 'I'm going to show you just how mistaken you are in that.'

His eyes never left Jess's face as he reached down, grabbed onto his penis, and twisted. It was some satisfaction to see every drop of blood drain out of the man's face and watch his mouth work like a guppy's as it gasped for air. With his thumb, he pressed gently on Jess's windpipe and cut off even that thin passage of air until the silver eyes bulged.

'Hell, isn't it, to be led around by the cock?' He gave one last jerk of the wrist before letting Jess collapse into the chair and curl up like a shrimp.

'Now, let's talk,' he said pleasantly enough. 'About private matters.'

Out in the corridor, Eve paced up and down, glancing every few seconds at the thick door. She knew very well if Roarke had implemented the soundproofing, Jess could be shrieking his lungs out and she wouldn't hear.

If he killed him . . . Good God if he killed him, how was

222

she going to handle it? She stopped, appalled, and pressed a hand to her stomach. How could she even consider it? She was duty bound to protect the bastard. There were rules. Whatever her personal feelings, there were rules.

She marched to the door, coded in, and hissed out a breath as her code was denied. 'Son of a bitch. Goddamn it, Roarke.' He knew her too well. With little hope, she raced down the corridor, into his office, and tried the connecting door.

Entrance denied.

She streaked to the monitor, cued up the security camera for her office, and found he'd locked her out of that as well.

'God almighty, he is killing him.' She rushed the door again, beat on it uselessly with her fist. Moments later, like magic, the locks slicked back, and the door slid quietly open. She went through at a dead run and saw Roarke calmly sitting at her desk, smoking.

Her heart pounded as she looked down at Jess. He was pale as death, his pupils the size of pinpricks, but he was breathing. In fact, he was wheezing out air like a faulty temperature control.

'He's unmarked.' Roarke picked up the brandy he'd poured himself. 'And I believe he's begun to see the error of his ways.'

Eve leaned down, peered closely into Jess's eyes, and watched him cringe back into the chair like a kicked dog. The sound he made was barely human. 'What the hell did you do to him?'

He doubted Eve or the NYPSD would approve of the tricks he'd picked up in his more shadowy travels. 'Much less than he deserved.'

She straightened and now took a long, hard look at Roarke. He looked like a man about to entertain late night guests or chair an important business meeting. His suit was unwrinkled, his hair unmussed, his hands perfectly steady. But his eyes, she noted, were just on the down side of wild.

'Christ, you're scary.'

Carefully, he set his brandy down. 'I'll never hurt you again.'

'Roarke.' She pushed back the urge to go to him, close her arms around him. It wasn't what the moment called for, she decided. Or what he wanted. 'This can't be personal.'

'Yes.' He drew in smoke, blew it out slowly. 'It can. And is.'

'Lieutenant.' Peabody stepped in, her face bland. 'The MTs are here. With your permission, I'll accompany the suspect to the health center.'

'I'll go.'

'Sir.' Peabody slid a glance toward Roarke. He'd yet to take his eyes off Eve, she noted. And those eyes looked more than a little dangerous. 'If you'll excuse me, I believe you have more pressing matters here. I can handle this. You still have a number of guests in the house, including the press. I'm sure you'd prefer this matter remain quiet until its disposition.'

'All right. I'll contact Central from here, make the necessary arrangements. Prepare for second phase interview tomorrow, nine hundred hours.'

'I'm looking forward to it.' Peabody glanced over at Jess, lifted a brow. 'He must have hit his head pretty hard. Still looks dazed, skin's clammy.' She offered Roarke a wide smile. 'I know just how that feels.'

Roarke laughed, feeling more of the tension drain away. 'No, Peabody. In this case, I don't believe you do.'

He got up, walked to her and, framing her square face with his elegant hands, kissed her. 'You're beautiful,' he murmured before turning to Eve. 'I'll see to the rest of our guests. Take your time.'

As he walked out, Peabody touched her fingertips to her lips. Pleasure had radiated down to her toes and out through the reinforced tips of her boots. 'Oh wow. I'm beautiful, Dallas.'

'I owe you, Peabody.'

'I think I just got paid.' She stepped back to the door. 'Here come the MTs. We'll get our boy out of here. Tell Mavis she was absolutely ultra.'

'Mavis.' Eve pressed her fingers to her eyes. How was she going to tell Mavis?

'If I were you, Dallas, I'd give her tonight to glow. You can tell her about this later. She'll be fine. In here,' she called, gesturing. 'We got us what looks like a mild concussion.'

# Chapter Sixteen

Getting a warrant for search and seizure at two in the morning was a tricky business. She lacked the straightforward data to cop an automatic clearance and needed a judge. Judges tended to be cranky about calls in the middle of the night. And trying to explain why she needed clearance for a sweep and scan of a music console currently on her own premises was a dicey job.

This being the case, Eve tolerated the clipped, angry lecture from her judge of choice.

'I understand that, Your Honor. But this can't wait until a decent hour in the morning. I have a strong suspicion that the console in question is linked to the deaths of four people. Its designer and operator is currently being detained, and I cannot expect his immediate cooperation.'

'You're telling me music kills, Lieutenant?' The judge snorted. 'I could have told you that. The crap they're pumping out these days could murder an elephant. In my day, we had *music*. Springsteen, Live, Cult Killers. That was music.'

'Yes, sir.' She rolled her eyes. She'd had to pick a classic music buff. 'I really need that warrant, Your Honor. Captain Feeney is available to begin the initial scan. The operator had admitted to using the console illegally, on the record. I need more to tie it to the cases in question.'

'You ask me, those music consoles should be banned and burned. This is piddly shit here, Lieutenant.'

'Not if the evidence bears out my belief that this console and its operator are linked to the death of Senator Pearly and others.'

There was a pause, a wheeze. 'That's a big leap. No pun intended.'

'Yes, sir. I need the warrant to bridge the gap.'

'I'll send it through, but you better have something, Lieutenant. And it better be solid.'

'Thank you. Sorry to have disturbed—' The 'link clicked in her ear, forcefully. 'Your sleep,' she finished, then picked up her communicator and tagged Feeney.

'Hey, Dallas.' His face was flushed with fun, wide with a grin. 'Where ya been, kid? Party's just breaking up. You missed Mavis doing a set with a hologram of the Rolling Stones. You know how I feel about Jagger.'

'Yeah, he's like a father to you. Don't take off, Feeney. I've got a job for you.'

'Job? It's two A.M., and my wife's feeling, you know—' He winked sloppily. 'Interested.'

'Sorry, put the glands on hold. Roarke will arrange to have your wife taken home. I'll be up in ten. Take a dose of Sober-Up if you need it. It could be a long night.'

'Sober-Up?' His face fell into its usual morose lines. 'I've been working all night to get drunk. What's this about?'

'Ten minutes,' she repeated and cut him off.

She took the time to change out of the party dress, and discovered bruises she hadn't been aware of throbbing fresh. She took a quick moment to slap a coat of numbing cream where she could reach and winced her way into a shirt and trousers.

Still, she was true to her word and walked onto the roof terrace ten minutes later.

Roarke had been at work here, she noted, and had cleared out lingering guests. If there were any stragglers, he was dealing with them elsewhere, giving her a clear stage.

Feeney sat alone on a chair beside a decimated buffet spread, glumly eating pâté. 'You sure know how to put me out of a party mood, Dallas. The wife was so dazzled to get a limo ride home, she forgot she was going to jump me. And Mavis was looking all over for you. I think she was a little hurt you didn't hang around to congratulate her.'

'I'll make it up to her.' Her porta-link hummed, signaling an incoming transmission. She read the display, hit print out. 'Here's our warrant.'

'Warrant?' He reached for a truffle and popped it in his mouth. 'For what?'

Eve shifted, gestured toward the console. 'For that. Ready to work your magic?'

Feeney swallowed the truffle, looked toward the console. The light some would have called love gleamed in his eyes. 'You want me to play with that? Hot damn.'

He was up, almost bounding toward the equipment and running reverent hands over it. She heard him mumbling something about TX-42, high velocity sound trips, and mirror merging capabilities. 'The warrant clears me to override his lock off code?'

'It does. Feeney, it's serious.'

'You're telling me.' He lifted his hands, rubbing fingertips together like an old-world safe cracker about to hit the big time. 'This baby is one serious mother. The design's inspired, the payload's off the scale. It's—'

'Very likely responsible for four deaths,' Eve interrupted. She walked over to join him. 'Let me bring you up to date.'

Within twenty minutes, using the portable kit out of his car, Feeney was at work. Eve couldn't understand what he was muttering about, and he didn't take it kindly when she leaned over his shoulder.

That gave her time to pace, then to call in for a report on Jess's status. She had just finished ordering Peabody to turn duty over to a uniform guard and go home to get some sleep when Roarke came in.

'I gave your regrets to our guests,' he told her and helped himself to another brandy. 'I explained that you'd been called to duty suddenly. I had much sympathy on living with a cop.'

'I tried to tell you it was a bad deal.'

He only smiled, but the smile didn't quite reach his eyes. 'It placated Mavis. She's hoping you'll get in touch tomorrow.'

'I will. I'll need to explain things. Did she ask about Barrow?'

'I told her he was . . . indisposed. Rather abruptly.' He didn't touch her. He wanted to, but he wasn't quite ready. 'You're hurting, Eve. I can see it.'

'You pinch my nose again, and I'll flatten you. Feeney and I have a lot of work here, and I have to be sharp. I'm not fragile, Roarke.' The message was in her eyes, asking him to put it aside. 'Get used to it.'

'Not yet.' He put down his brandy, slipped his hands into his pockets. 'I could help there,' he said, inclining his head toward Feeney.

'It's police business. You're not authorized to touch that unit.'

When he only shifted his eyes back to hers with some of the old humor in them, she let out a huge sigh. 'It's up to Feeney,' she snapped. 'He outranks me, and if he wants your fingers in his pie, it's his deal. I don't want to know about it. I've got reports to put together.'

She started out, irritation in every body line. 'Eve.' When she stopped and scowled over her shoulder at him, he shook his head. 'Nothing.' He lifted his shoulders, feeling helpless. 'Nothing,' he said again.

'Put it to bed, goddamn it. You're pissing me off.' She stalked out, nearly making him smile.

'I love you, too,' he murmured, then wandered toward Feeney. 'What have we here?'

'Brings tears to my eyes, I swear it. It's beautiful, brilliant. I tell you the guy's a genius. Certified. Come here and take a look at this image board. Just look at it.'

Roarke slipped off his jacket, hunkered down, and went to work.

She never went to bed. For once, Eve buried her prejudice and took her sanctioned dose of uppers. The Alert All cleared the drag of fatigue and most of the cobwebs from her brain. She used the shower off her office, broke down and wrapped an ice bandage over her sore knee, and told herself she'd deal with the bruises later.

It was six A.M. when she went back to the roof terrace. The console had been methodically taken apart. Wires, boards, chips, discs, drives, panels were arranged over the gleaming floor in what she could only assume were organized piles.

In his elegant silk shirt and tailored slacks, Roarke sat cross-legged among them, diligently entering data in a logbook. He'd tied his hair back, she noted, to keep it from falling over his face. And that face was intense, focused, the dark blue eyes ridiculously alert for the hour.

'I've got that,' he muttered to Feeney. 'Running the components now. I've seen something like this before. Something close. It's calibrating.' He held the logbook out and under the kick panel of the console. 'Have a look.'

A hand shot out, grabbed the logbook. 'Yeah, this could do it. It could fucking do it. Suck my dick.'

'Irishmen have such a way with words.'

At Eve's dry tone, Feeney's head popped up. His hair stuck straight up, as if he'd shocked himself while fiddling with the electronics. His eyes were bright and wild. 'Hey, Dallas. I think we just nailed it.'

'What took you so long?'

'What a kidder.' Feeney's head disappeared again.

Eve exchanged a long, sober study with Roarke. 'Good morning, Lieutenant.'

'You're not here,' she said as she walked past him. 'I don't see you here. What have you got, Feeney?'

'Got a lot of options on this baby,' he began, and popped up again to settle in the molded chair of the console. 'Lotsa doodads, and they are impressive. But the one we had to dig deep to find, under layers of some pretty hunky security, is the honey.'

He ran his hands over the console again, stroking fingers over the smooth surface that now topped empty guts. 'The designer would have made a hell of an E-detective. Most of the guys under me can't do what he can. Creativity, see.' He wagged a finger at her. 'It's not just formulas and boards. Creativity turns the corner into an open field. This guy's walked that field. He fucking owns it. And this is what he'd call his crowning glory.'

He offered the logbook, knowing she'd scowl over the codes and components. 'So?'

'It took some art to get down to that. He had it locked under his private pass, his voice pattern, his palm print. Some layers of fail safe, too. Nearly blew ourselves up about an hour ago, right, Roarke?'

Roarke rose and tucked his hands in his pockets. 'I never doubted you for an instant, Captain.'

'Like hell.' In tune with his man, Feeney grinned. 'If you weren't saying your prayers, boyo, I was saying mine. Still, I can't think of many others I'd be pleased to be blown to hell with.'

'The feeling's nearly mutual.'

'If you two have finished your little male bonding dance, would you care to explain what the hell I'm supposed to be looking at here?'

'It's a scanner. The most intricate I've seen outside of Testing.'

'Testing?'

It was a procedure every cop dreaded, and one every cop faced whenever they were forced to set their weapon on maximum for termination.

'Even though every member of NYPSD's brain pattern is on record, a scan's taken during Testing. Search for damage, flaws, any abnormalities that might have contributed to the use of maximum force. That scan's compared with the last taken, then the subject is taken on a couple of VR rides that use the data downloaded from the scan. Nasty business.'

Feeney had only faced it once and hoped never to go through the process again.

'And he's managed to duplicate or simulate that process?' Eve asked.

'I'd say he's improved on it on a couple of levels.' Feeney gestured toward the stack of discs. 'That's a lot of brain wave patterns. Shouldn't be too difficult to compare them with the victims' and identify.'

Her pattern would be on one, she thought. Her mind, on disc. 'Tidy,' she said half to herself.

'Brilliant, really. And potentially deadly. Our boy's got some spiffy twists on mood sets. They're all tied into musical patterns, you know, notes and chords. He picks the tune, see, then enhances what you'd call the tone of it, to pump along the target's reaction, their state of mind say, their unconscious impulses.'

'So he uses it to get into their head, deep. The subconscious.'

'Got a lot of medical technology I'm not real familiar with, but I'd say that's about it. Heavy into sexual urges,' Feeney added. 'That's our boy's specialty. I've got a little more break-down to do, but I'd say he could program the brain pattern, set the mood enhance, and give the target mind a nice hefty push.'

'Off a ledge?' she demanded.

'That's tricky, Dallas. Where I'm at here is enhancement, suggestive shit. Sure, if somebody was leaning toward the ledge, thinking about going over, this might give them that last nudge. But to coerce a mind to act in a manner completely adverse, completely out of character, I'd have to back off on that for now.'

'They jumped, choked, and bled to death,' she reminded him impatiently. 'Maybe we've all got suicidal urges buried in the subconscious. And this just brings them to the surface.'

'You need Mira for that, not me. I'll keep digging.' He smiled hopefully. 'After breakfast?'

She forced down impatience. 'After breakfast. I appreciate the long night, Feeney, and the quick work. But I needed the best.'

'And you got it. The guy you decided to link yourself up with isn't half bad, either, as a tech. I'd make a decent E-man out of him if he'd give up the drudgery of his lifestyle.'

'My first offer of the day.' Roarke smiled. 'You know where the kitchen is, Feeney. You're welcome to the AutoChef, or you can ask Summerset to arrange for the meal of your choice.'

'Around here, that means real eggs.' He stretched kinks out, popped joints. 'You want me to tell him breakfast for three?'

'You get started,' Roarke suggested. 'We'll be down shortly.' He waited until Feeney had sauntered out, whistling at the thought of eggs Benedict and blueberry pancakes. 'You haven't much time, I know.'

'I have enough, if you have something to say.'

'I do.' It was rare for him to feel awkward. He'd almost forgotten the sensation until it swamped him. 'What Feeney just pointed out to you, about his opinion on the capabilities here. The fact that it's unlikely for the subject to be influenced to act out of character, to do something abhorrent.'

233

She saw immediately where he was going and wanted to curse. 'Roarke—'

'I'll finish this. I've been the man who took you last night. I've lived in that skin, and it hasn't been so long ago that I've forgotten him. I turned him into something else because I wanted to. And I could. Money helped, and a certain need for . . . polish. But he's still there. He's still part of me. I was reminded of that rather violently last night.'

'Do you want me to hate you for it, to blame you for it?'

'No, I want you to understand it, and me. I came from the kind of man who hurt you last night.'

'So did I.'

That stopped him, had emotion swimming back into his eyes. 'Christ, Eve.'

'And it scares me. It wakes me up in the middle of the night, the wondering just what's inside me. I live with it every single day. I knew where you came from when I took you on, and I don't care. I know you've done things, broken laws, lived outside them. But I'm here.'

She huffed out a breath, shifted her feet. 'I love you, okay? That's it. Now, I'm hungry, and I've got a full day ahead of me, so I'm going down before Feeney cleans us out of eggs.'

He stepped in front of her before she could storm out. 'One more minute.' He framed her face with his hands, lowered his mouth to hers, and turned her scowl into a sigh with a kiss so tender it made her throat ache and her toes curl.

'Well,' she managed when he eased back. 'That's better, I guess.'

'Much better.' He linked his fingers with hers. And because he had used it when he'd hurt her, he balanced that out by using it now. '*A ghra.*'

'Huh?' A line appeared between her brows. 'Is that Gaelic again?'

'Yes.' He brought their joined fingers to his lips. 'Love. My love.'

'It's got a nice ring.'

'It does, yes.' He sighed a little. It had been a long time since he'd let himself hear the music of it.

'It shouldn't make you sad,' she murmured.

'It doesn't. Just thoughtful.' He gave her hand a friendly squeeze. 'I'd love to buy you breakfast, Lieutenant.'

'Talked me into it.' Comfortable, she tightened her grip. 'We got any crepes?'


The trouble with chemicals, Eve thought as she set up for the next interview with Jess Barrow, was that no matter how safe, mild, and helpful they claimed to be, they always made her feel false. She knew she wasn't naturally alert, that underneath that surging, induced energy, her body was a mass of desperate fatigue.

She kept imagining her system wearing a huge clown's mask of enthusiasm over a gray, exhausted face.

'Back in the saddle, Peabody?' Eve asked as her aide walked into the white-walled, uncluttered room.

'Yes, sir. I briefed myself via your reports, dropped by your office on the way here. You have a message from the commander on hold, and two from Nadine Furst. I think she smells a story.'

'She'll have to wait. I'll relay to the commander during our first break here. Know anything about baseball, Peabody?'

'I played short for two years at the Academy. Golden Glove.'

'Well, warm up. When I toss you a ball, you field it, zing it back. We're going Tinker to Evers to Chance here, with Feeney coming in before the end of the inning.'

Peabody's eyes lit. 'Hey, didn't know you were a historian.'

'I have many hidden facets. Just field the ball, Peabody. I want to dust this son of a bitch at the plate. You've read the report, you know the drill.' She signaled for the suspect to be brought in. 'Let's cook him. If he lawyers up, we'll have to juggle. But I'm banking on him being too arrogant to go that route initially.'

'Mostly, I like cocky men. I guess I'll have to make an exception here.'

'And he's got such a pretty face,' Eve added, then moved aside as a uniform delivered her man. 'How's it going, Jess? Feeling better today?'

He'd had time to regroup and time to stew. 'I could hang you on undue force. But I'm going to let it pass because before this is done, you'll be the top joke of your idiot department.'

'Yep, he's feeling better. Have a seat.' She stepped to the small table, engaged the recording unit. 'Dallas, Lieutenant Eve, with Peabody, Officer Delia, as aide. The time is oh nine hundred, September 8, 2058. Interview subject Barrow, Jess, file number S-one nine three oh five. Would you please state your name for the record?'

'Jess Barrow. You got that much right.'

'I have, during our previous interview, given you your rights and options under the law, is that correct?'

'You gave me the drill, sure.' For all the good it had done him, he thought, and shifted carefully in his seat. His cock ached like a rotted tooth.

'And you understand those rights and options as stated?'

'I got them then; I get them now.'

'Do you wish, at this time, to make use of your right to an attorney or representative?'

'I don't need anybody but myself.'

'All right then.' Eve sat, linked her fingers, smiled. 'Let's get started. In your previous statement, you admitted to the design and use of equipment built for tampering with personal brain patterns and behavior.'

'I didn't admit to shit.'

She kept smiling. 'That's a matter of interpretation. Do you now deny that during a social gathering at my home last

236

evening, you utilized a program you have designed to make certain suggestions, subliminally, to the subject Roarke?'

'Hey, if your husband took you off and tossed your skirts over your head, it's your business.'

Her smile never faltered. 'It certainly is.' She needed to hang him here, on this one point, to hang him on the rest. 'Peabody, perhaps Jess is unaware of the penalty for giving false statement to a police official during Interview.'

'That penalty,' Peabody said smoothly, 'carries a maximum term of five years in full lockup. Shall I replay the pertinent data from the initial interview, Lieutenant? The subject's memory might be faulty due to the injury received while assaulting an officer.'

'Assault, my ass.' He snarled at Peabody. 'You think you can double-team me this way? She struck me without provocation, then let that bastard she married come in and . . .'

He trailed off, remembering the warning Roarke had issued in a soft, silky voice directly in his ear. While the pain, almost sweet in its intensity, had radiated through his system.

'You wish to make an official complaint?' Eve asked.

'No.' Even now, a light line of sweat beaded on his upper lip and made Eve wonder just what Roarke had done to him. 'I was upset last night. Things got out of hand.' He took a steadying breath. 'Listen, I'm a musician. I take a lot of pride in my work, in the art of it. I like to think what I do influences people, touches them. My pride in that might have given you the wrong impression as to the scope of my work. Basically, I don't know what all the fuss is about.'

He smiled again, with a good deal of his usual charm, and spread his handsome hands. 'Those people you talked about last night. I don't know them. I've heard of some of them, sure, but I didn't know them personally or have anything to do with their decision to self-terminate. I'm against it, myself. In my opinion, life's too short as it is. This is all a misunderstanding, and I'm willing to forget it.'

Eve leaned back in her chair, sent a look toward her aide. 'Peabody, he's willing to forget it.'

'That's generous of him, Lieutenant, and not surprising, under the circumstances. A stretch for breaking the statute on personal privacy through electronics is stringent. And, of course, there's the added charge of designing and implementing equipment designed for individual subliminals. Right there, with the multiple counts, you're looking at a ten-year minimum in the cages.'

'You can't begin to prove any of it. Any of it. You've got no case here.'

'I'm giving you a chance to roll over here, Jess. They go easier on you when you roll. And as to the civil case that my husband and I are entitled to bring against you, I will state here, for the record, that I will waive that right, contingent on your admission of guilt on the criminal charges – if that admission comes in the next thirty seconds. Think about it.'

'I don't have to think about anything, because you've got nothing.' He leaned forward. 'You're not the only one with people behind you. What do you think will happen to your big, bad career if I go to the press with this?'

She said nothing, just watched him, then glanced at the time count on the recorder. 'Offer is rescinded.' Eve nodded at the monitoring camera. 'Peabody, please uncode the door for Captain Feeney.'

When Feeney walked in, he was beaming. He set a disc and file on the table and stuck out his hand to Jess. 'I've got to tell you, your work's the best I've ever seen. It's a real pleasure to meet you.'

'Thanks.' Jess shifted to audience mode, shook hands warmly. 'I love my work.'

'Oh, it shows.' Feeney sat down, made himself comfortable. 'I haven't enjoyed anything for years as much as I did taking that console apart.'

Another time, another place, it might have been comic, the

way Jess's face underwent the transformation from obliging star to blank shock to ripe fury. 'You fucked with my equipment? Took it apart? You had no right laying a hand on it! You're meat! You're dead! You're destroyed!'

'Let the record show the subject is overwrought,' Peabody recited blandly. 'His threats against the person of Captain Feeney are accepted as emotional rather than literal.'

'Well, the first time, anyway,' Feeney said cheerfully. 'You want to watch your step there, friend. Put too much of that on record, and we tend to get pissy. Now.' He leaned forward on his elbows. 'Let's talk shop. You had some great security, admirable. Took me a while to bypass. But then, I've been in the game as long as you've been breathing. Designing that personal brain scanner was some accomplishment. So compact, so delicate to the touch. I gauged its range at two yards. Now, that's damn good for that small and portable a unit.'

'You didn't get into my equipment.' Jess's voice wavered. 'You're bluffing. You couldn't get down to the core.'

'Well, the three fail safes were tricky,' Feeney admitted. 'I spent nearly an hour on the second one, but the last was really just padding. I guess you never figured you'd need anything at that level.'

'Did you run the discs, Feeney?' Eve asked him.

'Started on them. You're on there, Dallas. We don't have Roarke's on file. Civilian, you know. But I found yours and Peabody's.'

Peabody blinked. 'Mine?'

'I'm running comparison checks on the names you requested, Dallas.' He smiled broadly at Jess again. 'You've been busy, collecting specimens. That's a fine storage option you designed, terrific data compression capabilities. It's going to break my heart to destroy that equipment.'

'You can't!' It was sincere pain and distress now. His eyes swam with it. 'I've put everything I've got into that. Not just money, but time and thought and energy. Three years of my life, almost straight through without a break. I stepped back from my career to design it. Do you have any idea what I can accomplish with it?'

Eve picked up the ball. 'Why don't you tell us, Jess? In your own words. We'd love to hear it.'

# Chapter Seventeen

Jess Barrow started slowly, in fits and starts, speaking of his experiments and research, his fascination with the influence of outside stimuli on the human brain; the senses, and the enhancement of the senses through technology.

'What we can do for pleasure, for punishment – we haven't even tapped the surface. That's what I wanted to do,' he explained. 'Tap the surface and go under it. Dreams, Dallas. Needs, fears, fantasies. All my life, music's been what's moved me to . . . everything: hunger, passion, misery, joy. How much more intense would all that be if you could just get inside, really use the mind to exploit and explore?'

'So you worked on it,' she prompted. 'Devoted yourself to it.'

'Three years. More really, but three solid on the design, experimentation, perfecting. Every penny I had went into it. I've got next to nothing left now. That's why I needed backing. Why I needed you.'

'And Mavis was your link to me, and from me to Roarke.'

'Look.' He lifted his hands, rubbed them over his face, dropped them onto the table. 'I like Mavis, and she's got a real spark. Yeah, I'd have used her if she was bland as a droid, but she's not. I didn't do her any harm. If anything, I gave her a boost up. Her ego level was ditch low when we hooked up. Oh, she was masking it pretty good, but she'd lost

241

confidence in herself from what happened before. I gave her confidence a jolt.'

'How?'

He hesitated, decided he'd take a bigger fall by evading. 'Okay, I gave her some subliminal nudges in the right direction. She should be grateful,' he insisted. 'And I worked with her, straight stuff, getting her shined up without taking away her natural edge. You heard her yourself. She's better than she ever was.'

'You experimented on her,' Eve said, and wanted to hang him for that alone, 'without her knowledge or consent.'

'It wasn't like she was some droid rat. Christ, I'd perfected the system.' He jabbed a finger at Feeney. 'You know it's prime.'

'It's beautiful,' Feeney agreed. 'Doesn't make it legal.'

'Shit, genetic engineering was illegal, in vitro work, prostitution. What did that get us? We've come a long way, but we're still in the dark ages, man. This is a benefit, this is a way to push the mind forward into dreams and make what we dream real.'

'Not all of us want our dreams to be reality. What gives you the right to make that choice for someone else?'

'Okay.' He held up a hand. 'Maybe I got over-enthusiastic a few times. You get caught up. But all I did with you was expand on what was there. So I enhanced the lust bars that night in the studio. What did it hurt? Another time I gave your memory a little push, jiggled a few locks. I wanted to be able to prove what could be done, so when the time was right, I could approach you and Roarke with a business proposition. And last night . . .'

He trailed off, knowing he'd miscalculated badly there. 'Okay, last night I went too far, the tone was too dark. I got carried away with it. Performing before a real audience again, it's like a drug. It hypes you. Maybe I punched the power a little hard on him. An honest mistake.' He tried that smile again. 'Look, I've used it on myself, dozens of times. There's no harm, nothing permanent. Just temporary mood enhancement.'

'And you pick the mood?'

'That's part of it. With standard equipment, you don't have as much control, not nearly the depth of field. With what I've developed, you can turn it on and off like a light. Sexual need or satisfaction, euphoria, melancholy, energy, relaxation. Name it, you got it.'

'A death wish?'

'No.' He shook his head quickly. 'I don't play those games.'

'But it's all a game to you, isn't it? You push the buttons, and the people dance. You're the electronic god.'

'You're missing the big picture,' he insisted. 'Do you know what people would pay for this kind of capability? You can feel anything you want.'

Eve opened the file Feeney had brought in. She tossed photos out, faceup. 'What did they feel, Jess?' She pushed the morgue shots of four deaths at him. 'What was the last thing you made them feel so that they killed themselves with smiles on their faces?'

He went white as death itself, eyes glazing before he managed to shut them. 'No. No way. No.' Doubling over, he retched out his health center breakfast.

'Let the record show the suspect is momentarily indisposed,' Peabody said dryly. 'Should I call for maintenance and a health aide, Lieutenant?'

'Christ, yes,' Eve muttered as Jess continued to heave. 'We'll break this interview at oh ten fifteen. Dallas, Lieutenant Eve, record off.'

'Great brain, weak stomach.' Feeney went to the dispenser in the corner and poured a cup of water. 'Here, boy, see if you can choke some of this down.'

Jess's eyes watered. His stomach muscles were raw. Water

sloshed in the cup so that Feeney had to guide it to his mouth. 'You can't hang that on me,' he managed. 'You can't.'

'We'll see about that.' Eve stepped aside so that the incoming aide could cart him off to the infirmary. 'I need some air,' she muttered and walked out.

'Hold on, Dallas.' Feeney hurried after her, leaving Peabody to direct maintenance and gather up the file. 'We need to talk.'

'My office is closer.' She swore lightly as her knee throbbed. The ice bandage was wearing off and needed to be replaced. Her hip was murderous.

'Took a beating with that CEC hit yesterday, didn't you?' Feeney clucked sympathetically as she hobbled. 'Been looked over yet?'

'Later. I've been pressed for time. Let's give the creep an hour to get his stomach back in place, then hit him again. He hasn't cried lawyer yet, but it's coming. Won't matter a damn once we match those brain patterns to the victims.'

'That's the problem. Sit down,' he advised when they stepped into her office. 'Take a load off that leg.'

'It's the knee, and sitting's making it stiffen up. What's the problem?' she asked and headed for the coffee.

'Nothing matches.' He studied her mournfully when she turned. 'Not one match in the whole lot. Plenty as yet unidentified, but I've got the prints on all victims, no autopsy scan on Devane, but I got the one from her last physical. There's no match, Dallas.'

So she did sit, heavily. There was no need to ask if he was sure. Feeney was as thorough as a domestic droid searching for dust in corners. 'Okay, he's got them someplace else. Did we get the warrant for his studio and quarters?'

'A team's going through it right now. I haven't gotten a report.'

'He could have a lock box, some safe hole.' She shut her eyes. 'Shit, Feeney, why would he keep them when he was

244

done with them? He's probably destroyed them. He's arrogant, but he's not stupid. They'd hang him and he'd know it.'

'The possibility's high there. Then again, he could have kept them as souvenirs. It never fails to surprise me what people keep. That guy last year that cut up his wife? Kept her eyes, remember. In a damn music box.'

'Yeah, I remember.' *Where had this headache come from?* she wondered and rubbed uselessly at her temples to erase it. 'So, maybe we'll get lucky. If we don't, we've got plenty now. And a good shot of breaking him.'

'Here's the thing, Dallas.' He sat on the edge of her desk, reached into his pocket for his bag of candied almonds. 'It doesn't feel right.'

'What do you mean, it doesn't feel right? We've got him cold.'

'We've got him cold, all right. But not on murder.' Thoughtfully, Feeney chewed a coated nut. 'I can't resolve myself to it. The guy who designed that equipment is brilliant, twisted some sure, self-absorbed. The guy we just shook down is all of those things, and you can add childish. It is a game to him, one he wants to make a big profit on. But murder . . .'

'You're just in love with his console.'

'That I am,' he admitted without shame. 'He's weak, Dallas, and not just his stomach. How's he going to make himself rich by killing people off?'

She arched a brow. 'I guess you've never heard of murder for hire.'

'That boy doesn't have the guts for it, or the steel.' He ate another nut. 'And where's the motive? Did he pick those people out of a hat? And there's this. What he's got requires proximity to tap the subconscious. You can't place him at any of the scenes.'

'He said something about remote capabilities.'

'Yeah, it had a fine one, but it wouldn't command this option. Not that I can figure.'

She sat back, deflated. 'You're not making my day here, Feeney.'

'Just food for thought. If he's got a hand in it, he's got help. Or a more personal, portable unit.'

'Could it be adjusted into VR goggles?'

The idea intrigued him, made his hangdog eyes gleam. 'Can't say for sure. It'll take some time to work that out.'

'I hope you've got the time. He's all I've got, Feeney. If I can't crack him, he's going to walk on the murders. Tucking him away for ten to twenty on what we've got doesn't do it for me.' She huffed out a breath. 'He'll go for a psych evaluation. He'll go for anything he thinks will buy him a shot. Maybe Mira can pin him.'

'Send him over after the break,' Feeney suggested. 'Let her take him for a few hours, and do yourself a favor. Go home and get some sleep. You run on empty long enough, you drop.'

'Maybe I will. I'll set it up, deal with Whitney. A couple hours off might clear my head. I must be missing something.'


For once, Summerset wasn't hovering. Eve snuck in the house like a thief, limped her way upstairs. She left a trail of clothes on her way to the bed, and she sighed greedily when she fell on it.

Ten minutes later, she was on her back, staring at the ceiling. The aches were bad enough, she thought grumpily. But the stimulator she'd taken hours before hadn't worn off. It was passing, leaving her light-headed with fatigue, while her system still bubbled like a brew.

Sleep was not going to happen.

She found herself picking apart the pieces of the case, putting them back together. Each time the puzzle formed differently until it was a blurred jumble of facts and theories.

At this rate, she wouldn't be close to coherent when she met with Mira.

She considered indulging in a long, hot bath in lieu of sleep.

246

Then, inspired, she popped up and grabbed a robe. She took the elevator, with the purpose of avoiding Summerset, and stepped up on the lower level into the garden path of the solarium. A session in the lagoon pool, she decided, was just the ticket.

She dumped the robe, padded naked to the dark water walled in genuine stone and framed with fragrant blooms. When she dipped a toe, she found it blissfully warm. She sat on the first step and set the control panel for jets and bubbles. As the water began to churn, she started to program music. With a quick grimace, she decided she wasn't in the mood for tunes.

She simply floated at first, grateful there was no one around to hear her whimpering as the pulsing water worked on her aches. She let herself breathe. Floral perfume. She let herself drift. Simple pleasures.

The conflict of fatigue and stimulation balanced out into relaxation. Drugs, she decided, were highly overrated. Water worked wonders. Turning over lazily, she began to swim, slowly at first while her muscles warmed and limbered. Then she put some kick into it, hoping to work off the excess of the stimulant and revive herself with natural exercise.

When the timer clicked and the water calmed, she continued with long, steady strokes, skimmed down to the glossy black bottom until she felt like an embryo in the womb, then broke the surface with a loud, satisfied groan.

'You swim like a fish.'

Instinct had Eve reaching for her side arm only to encounter her own naked ribs. Quickly, she blinked the water out of her eyes and focused on Reeanna.

'It's a cliché.' She walked to the edge of the pool. 'But accurate.' She set her shoes aside, sat, and slid her legs into the water. 'Do you mind?'

'Help yourself.' Eve didn't consider herself fanatically modest, but she dipped a little lower. She hated being caught naked. 'Were you looking for Roarke?'

'No, actually, I've just left him. He and William are still at it upstairs in his office. I was just leaving for a salon appointment.' She tugged at her gorgeous, glossy red curls. 'I've got to do something about this mop. Summerset mentioned you were down here, so I thought I'd just drop in on you.'

Summerset. Even smiled grimly. He'd spotted her after all. 'I had a couple of hours personal time. Thought I'd take advantage of it.'

'And what a lovely spot to take it. Roarke's got such amazing class, doesn't he?'

'Yeah, you could say so.'

'I really just wanted to stop for a moment to tell you how much I enjoyed last evening. I barely got to speak to you – such a crowd. And then you were called away.'

'Cops are lousy socializers,' Eve commented and wondered how to get out and to her robe without feeling like an idiot.

Reeanna reached down, cupped water, and let it pour out of her hand. 'I hope it wasn't anything . . . dreadful.'

'Nobody died, if that's what you mean.' Then Eve made herself smile. She *was* lousy at socializing, and she told herself to make a better effort. 'Actually, I got a break in the case I've been working on. We took a suspect into custody.'

'That's good.' Reeanna tilted her head, her eyes intrigued. 'Would that be the suicide matter we discussed before?'

'I'm not really free to say one way or the other at this time.'

Reeanna smiled. 'Cop talk. Well, one way or the other, I've been giving it quite a bit of thought. Your case, or whatever you'd call it, would make a fascinating paper. I've been so busy with tech, I haven't done any writing in some time. I hope, when you resolve the matter and it's public record, I can discuss it with you in some detail.'

'I can probably do that. If and when.' She bent a little. The woman was an expert, after all, and could be of some help. 'As it happens, the suspect is being evaluated by Dr Mira right about now. Do you ever do behavioral and personality evaluations?'

'I have, certainly. From a different angle than Mira. You'd have to say we're two sides of one coin. Our final diagnosis would often be the same, but we'd use a different process and a different viewpoint.'

'I might need two viewpoints before this one's over,' Eve mused, measuring Reeanna. 'You don't happen to have security clearance, do you?'

'As it happens, I do.' She continued to swing her legs lazily, but her eyes were alert, interested. 'Level Four, Class B.'

'That just skims by. If it comes up, how would you feel about working for the city as a temporary consultant? I can guarantee long hours, lousy conditions, and low pay.'

'Who could resist that kind of offer?' Reeanna laughed, tossed back her hair. 'Actually, I'd love the opportunity for some hands on again. Too long in labs, working with machines. William adores that, you know, but I need people.'

'I might just give you a call.' Deciding it was more foolish to huddle in the water than to climb casually out, Eve stood.

'You know where to reach me – Dear God, Eve, what happened to you?' Instantly, Reeanna was swinging her legs back, rising. 'You're black and blue.'

'Hazards of the job.' She managed to snag one of the body towels stacked near the edge and started to wind it around her when Reeanna tugged it away.

'Let me have a look at you. You haven't been treated.' Her fingers probed at Eve's hip.

'Hey, do you mind?'

'I certainly do.' Impatient, Reeanna lifted her eyes. 'Oh, be still. Not only am I female and have personal knowledge of the female body, but I've got a medical degree. What have you done for that knee? It's looks nasty.'

'Ice bandage. It's better.'

'Then I'd hate to have seen it when it wasn't. Why haven't you been to a health center, or at least an MT stop?'

'Because I hate them. And I haven't had time.'

249

'Well, you've got time now. I want you to lie down on that massage table. I'll get my emergency kit out of the car and deal with this.'

'Look, I appreciate it.' She had to raise her voice as Reeanna was already striding away. 'But they're just bruises.'

'You'll be lucky if you didn't chip a bone in that hip.' With this dark promise, Reeanna stepped into the elevator, and the doors snapped shut.

'Oh, thanks, I feel heaps better now.' Resigned, Eve toweled off, put on her robe, then reluctantly went to the padded table beneath an arbor of wildly blooming wisteria. She'd no more than settled when Reeanna was back, stalking over the tiles with a neat leather case in her hand.

The woman could move, Eve mused. 'I thought you had a salon date.'

'I called, switched times. Lie back, we'll deal with that knee first.'

'You charge extra for house calls?'

Reeanna smiled a little as she opened her case. Eve took one glance inside, turned her head away. Christ but she hated medicine.

'This one's free. We can consider it practice. I haven't worked on a human in nearly two years.'

'That inspires confidence.' Eve closed her eyes as Reeanna took out a miniscanner and examined her knee. 'Why haven't you?'

'Hmm. Well, it's not broken, so that's something. Badly wrenched and inflamed. Why?' She dug into her case again. 'Roarke's part of the reason. He made William and me an offer impossible to refuse. The money was seductive, and Roarke knows which buttons to push.'

Eve hissed as something stingingly cold was pressed to her knee. 'You're telling me.'

'He was aware I had a long, personal interest in behavioral patterns and effects of stimulation. The opportunity to create new technology, working with virtually unlimited funds, was too tempting to miss. Vanity couldn't resist the chance to be a part of something new, and with Roarke behind it, undoubtedly successful.'

Closing her eyes had been a mistake, Eve realized. She was starting to float. The throbbing in her hip slowed. She felt Reeanna's gentle fingers smoothing something cool and slick over it. Her shoulder received the same treatment. The absence of pain was like a tranq and tugged her deeper.

'He never seems to miss.'

'No. Not since I've known him.'

'I've got a meeting in a couple hours,' Eve said thickly.

'Rest first.' Reeanna removed the poultice from Eve's knee and was pleased to see the swelling had already gone down. 'I'm going to put another deep healing poultice on this, then an ice bandage to finish it off. It's still likely to be a bit stiff after prolonged use. I'd advise you to baby it for the next couple of days.'

'Sure. Baby it.'

'Did you get all this last night, rounding up your suspect?'

'No, before. He didn't give me any trouble. Little bastard.' Her brows knit, digging a line between them. 'Can't nail him though. Just can't nail it down.'

'I'm sure you will.' Reeanna's voice was soothing as she continued the treatment. 'You're thorough and involved. I saw you on one of the news channels. Going out on the ledge with Cerise Devane. Risking your life.'

'Lost her.'

'Yes, I know.' Efficiently, Reeanna coated the treated bruises with numbing cream. 'It was horrible. Visually shocking. More so for you, I'd imagine. You'd have seen her face, her eyes, up close, as she went off.'

'She was smiling.'

'Yes, I could see that.'

'She wanted to die.'

251

'Did she?'

'She said it was beautiful. The ultimate experience.'

Satisfied she'd done all she could, Reeanna picked up another towel, spread it over Eve. 'There are some who believe that. Death as the ultimate human experience. No matter how advanced medicine and technology, none of us escape it. Since we're destined for it in any case, why not see it as a goal rather than an obstacle?'

'It's meant to be fought. Every bloody inch of the way.'

'Not everyone has the energy or the need to fight. Some go gently.' She picked up Eve's limp hand, automatically checking the pulse. 'Some go resistantly. But all go.'

'Somebody sent her. That makes it murder. That makes it mine.'

Reeanna tucked Eve's arm under the towel. 'Yes, I suppose it does. Get some sleep. I'll tell Summerset to wake you in time to make your meeting.'

'Thanks. Really.'

'It's nothing.' She touched Eve's shoulder. 'Between friends.'

She studied Eve a moment longer, then glanced at her diamond-studded watch. She was going to have to push to make her rescheduled salon date, but there was just one minor detail to see to yet.

She repacked her kit, left a tube of numbing cream on the table for Eve, and hurried out.

# Chapter Eighteen

Eve paced the soft, pretty carpet in Dr Mira's office, hands jammed in her pockets, head lowered like a bull preparing for the charge.

'I don't get it. How can his profile not fit? I've got him cold on the lesser charges. The little prick's been playing with people's brains, reveling in it.'

'It isn't a matter of fitting, Eve. It's a matter of probabilities.'

Patient, calm, Mira sat in her comfy, body-molding chair and sipped jasmine tea. She needed it, she mused. The air was foaming with Eve's frustration and energy.

'You have his confession and the evidence that he has been experimenting with individualized brain pattern influence. And I quite agree he has a lot to answer for. But as to coercion to self-termination, I can't, in any decisive manner, corroborate your suspicions through my evaluation.'

'Well, that's just great.' She spun on her heel. Reeanna's treatment and the hour's nap had restored her. If anything, her color was high, her eyes overbright. 'Without your corroboration, Whitney's not going to buy the package, which means the PA won't buy it.'

'I can't adjust my report to suit you, Eve.'

'Who's asking you to?' Eve threw up her hands, then dug them into her pockets. 'What doesn't fit, for Christ's sake? The man's got a God complex any idiot before vision reconstruction surgery could spot.'

'I agree that his personality pattern leans toward an excess of ego and his temperament has a high caliber of the artiste under siege.' Mira sighed. 'I wish you'd sit down. You're making me tired.'

Eve dropped into a chair, scowled. 'There, I'm sitting. Explain.'

Mira had to smile. The sheer drive and unrelenting focus was admirable. 'Do you know, Eve, I can never understand why impatience is so attractive on you. And how, with such a high volume of it, you still manage to be thorough in your work.'

'I'm not here for analysis, Doctor.'

'I know. I only wish I could convince you to agree to regular sessions. But that's another subject, for another time. You have my report, but to summarize my findings, the subject is egocentric, self-congratulatory, and one who habitually rationalizes his antisocial behavior as art. He's also brilliant.'

Dr Mira signed a little, shook her head. 'A truly fine mind. He was nearly off the scale in the standard Trislow and Secour tests.'

'Good for him,' Eve muttered. 'Let's put his brain on disc and give *him* a few suggestions.'

'Your reaction is understandable,' Mira said mildly. 'Human nature is resistant to any sort of mind control. Addicts rationalize by deluding themselves that they're in control.' She rolled her shoulders. 'In any case, the subject has an admirable, even astonishing skill for visualization and logic. He's also fully aware, and smug if you will, about those skills. Under the surface charm, he is – to use your unscientific term – a prick. But I cannot, in good conscience, label him a murderer.'

'I'm not worried about your conscience.' Eve set her teeth. 'He's able to design and operate equipment that is capable of influencing behavior in targeted individuals. I have four dead bodies whose minds I believe – no, I know – were influenced to self-termination.'

'And logically, there should be a connection.' Mira sat back, reached over, and programmed tea for Eve. 'But you don't have a sociopath in holding, Eve.' She passed Eve a fragrant, steaming cup they both knew she didn't want. 'As there is, of yet, no clear motive for these deaths, and if they were indeed coerced, it's my considered opinion that it's a sociopath who is responsible.'

'So what separates him?'

'He likes people,' Mira said simply, 'and wants, quite desperately, to be liked and admired by them. Manipulative, yes, but he believes he's created a great boon to humankind. One he'll make a profit on, certainly.'

'So, maybe he just got carried away.' *Isn't that what he called his use of Roarke the night before?* Eve though. *He'd just gotten carried away.* 'And maybe he isn't as much in control of his equipment as he thinks.'

'That's possible. From another angle, Jess enjoys his work; he needs to be a party to the results of it. His ego requires that he see, experience at least a part of what he's caused.'

*He wasn't in the damn closet with us*, Eve thought, but was afraid she understood Mira's meaning: the way Jess had looked for her, at her when they'd come back to the party, the way he'd smiled. 'This isn't what I want to hear.'

'I know that. Listen to me.' Mira set her cup aside. 'This man is a child, an emotionally stunted savant. His vision and his music are more real to him, certainly more important than people, but he doesn't discount people. Overall, I simply find no evidence that he would risk his freedom and his freedom of expression to kill.'

Eve sipped tea out of reflex rather than desire. 'If he had a partner?' she speculated, thinking of Feeney's theory.

'It's possible. He wouldn't be a man who would happily share his accomplishments. Still, he had a great need for both adulation and financial success. It might be possible, if he found himself in need of assistance on some level of his design, he entered into a partnership.'

255

'Then why didn't he roll over?' Eve shook her head. 'He's a coward; he'd have rolled. No way he'd take the heat for this alone.' She sipped again, letting her thoughts play out. 'What if he were genetically imprinted toward sociopathic behavior? He's intelligent, canny enough to mask it, but it's simply part of his makeup.'

'Branded at conception?' Mira nearly sniffed. 'I don't subscribe to that school. Upbringing, environment, education, choices both moral and immoral form us into what we are. We are not born monsters or saints.'

'But there are experts in the field who believe we are.' And she had one, Eve mused, at her disposal.

Mira read her easily enough and couldn't prevent the prick to her pride. 'If you wish to consult with Dr Ott on this matter, it's your privilege. I'm sure she'd be thrilled.'

Eve wasn't sure whether to wince or smile. Mira very rarely sounded testy. 'That wasn't meant as an insult to your skills, Doctor. I need a hammer here; you can't provide it.'

'Let me tell you what I think about the branding at birth issue, Lieutenant. It's a cop-out, plain and simple. It's a crutch. I couldn't help setting fire to that building and burning hundreds of people alive. I was born an arsonist. I couldn't stop myself from battering that old woman to death for her handful of credits. My mother was a thief.'

It quite simply infuriated her to think of that ploy being used to blot out responsibility – and on the other side to scar those who were defenseless against the monsters who bore them.

'It excuses us from humanity,' she continued, 'from morality, from right and wrong. We can say we were marked in the womb and never had a chance.' She angled her head. 'You of all people should know better.'

'This isn't about me.' Eve set her cup down with a snap. 'It isn't about where I came from or what I made myself. It's about four people, that I'm aware of, who weren't given a choice. And someone has to answer for that.'

'One thing,' Mira added as Eve rose. 'Are you focused on this man because of personal insults to you and those you love, or because of the dead you represent?'

'Maybe it's both,' Eve admitted after a moment.

She didn't contact Reeanna, not yet. She wanted a little time to let it stew in her mind. And she was delayed by finding Nadine Furst in her office.

'How'd you get past desk security?' Eve demanded.

'Oh, I have my ways.' Nadine swung her leg, beamed a friendly smile. 'And most of the cops around here know you and I have a history.'

'What do you want?'

'I wouldn't say no to a cup of coffee.'

Grudgingly, Eve turned to the AutoChef, pumped up two cups. 'Make it fast, Nadine. Crime is rampant in our city.'

'And that keeps us both in business. What did you get called out on last night, Dallas?'

'Excuse me?'

'Come on. I was at the party. Mavis was terrific, by the way. First you and Roarke take off.' She sipped delicately. 'It didn't take a sharp reporter like me to get an inkling of what that was about.' She wiggled her brows, chuckling when Eve simply stared. 'But your sex life isn't news – at least on my beat.'

'We were running out of shrimp patties. We ran down to the kitchen and made some up. It would have been so embarrassing.'

'Yeah, yeah.' Nadine waved that away and concentrated on her coffee. Even in the upper echelons of Channel 75 they rarely had access to such potent brew. 'Then I notice, being the keen observer that I am, that you sweep Jess Barrow off and out at the end of the set. Never came back. Either of you.'

'We're having a mad, illicit affair,' Eve said dryly. 'You may want to turn that over to the gossip desk.'

'And I'm boinking a one-armed sex droid.'

'You always were an explorer.'

'Actually, there was this unit once . . . but I digress. Roarke, in his usual charming fashion, manages to move the lingering guests along, herds the hangers-on into the recreation center – great hologram deck, by the way – and gives your regrets. Duty calls?' Nadine angled her head. 'Funny. Nothing shows on my cop scanner that would have pulled our ace homicide detective out at that time of night.'

'Not everything goes out on the scanner, Nadine. And I'm just a soldier. I go when and where I'm told.'

'Sell it to someone else. I know how tight you are with Mavis. Nothing but top level would have pulled you away at her big moment.' She leaned forward. 'Where's Jess Barrow, Dallas? And what the hell has he done?'

'I don't have anything to give you, Nadine.'

'Come on, Dallas, you know me. I'll hold it down until I get the go-ahead. Who'd he kill?'

'Switch the channel,' Eve advised, then pulled out her communicator when it beeped. 'Display only, no audio.'

Quickly, she scanned the transmission from Peabody, manually requested a meeting, including Feeney, in twenty minutes. She set the communicator on the desk, turned back to the AutoChef to see if there were any soy chips available. She needed something to sop up the caffeine.

'I've got work, Nadine,' Eve continued, when she discovered she had nothing but an irradiated egg sandwich in stock. 'And nothing to bump up your ratings.'

'You're holding out on me. I know you've got Jess in custody. I've got sources in Holding.'

Annoyed, Eve turned back. Holding was innately ripe with leaks. 'I can't help you.'

'Are you charging him?'

'The charges are not for broadcast at this time.'

'Damn it, Dallas.'

'I'm on the edge here,' Eve snapped. 'And it could go either way. Don't push me. If and when I'm free to speak to the media on the matter, you'll be the first. You'll have to be satisfied with that.'

'You mean I have to be satisfied with nothing.' Nadine rose. 'You're got something big, or you wouldn't be so snotty about it. I'm only asking for a—'

She broke off as Mavis burst in. 'Jesus, Dallas, Jesus. How could you arrest Jess? What are you doing?'

'Mavis, damn it.' She could visualize Nadine's reporter's ears growing longer and sharper. 'Sit,' she demanded, stabbing a finger at a chair, then at Nadine. 'You, out.'

'Have a heart, Dallas.' Nadine attached herself to Mavis. 'Can't you see how upset she is? Let me get you some coffee, Mavis.'

'I said out, and I mean it.' At her wit's end, Eve rubbed her hands over her face. 'Take off, Nadine, or I'll put you on the blackout list.'

As a threat, it had punch. The blackout list meant there wouldn't be a cop in the homicide division who'd give Nadine the right time, much less a story lead. 'Okay, fine. But I'm not dropping this.' There were other ways to dig, she thought, and other tools to dig with. She snatched up her bag, gave Eve one last bitter look, then flounced out.

'How could you?' Mavis demanded. 'Dallas, how could you do this?'

To insure some level of privacy, Eve shut the door. Her headache had come full circle and was now gleefully throbbing behind her eyes. 'Mavis, this is my job here.'

'Your job?' Her eyes were laser blue today, and redrimmed from weeping. It was touching the way they matched the cobalt streaks in her scarlet hair. 'What about my career? I finally get the break I've been waiting for, working for, and you toss my partner into a cage. And for what?' Her voice hitched. 'Because he came on to you and pissed Roarke off.'

'What?' Her mouth fell open, worked silently before she could get her tongue around words. 'Where the hell did you get that?'

'I just got off the 'link with Jess. He's devastated. I can't believe you'd play this way, Dallas.' Her eyes began to leak again. 'I know Roarke's premiere with you, but we've got history.'

At that moment, with Mavis noisily weeping into her hands, Eve could have cheerfully strangled Jess Barrow. 'Yeah, we've got history, and you should know I don't play that way. I don't toss someone in a cage because I find them a personal annoyance. Would you sit down?'

'I don't need to sit.' She wailed it, made Eve wince as the sound acted as the dull point of an edgy knife on her brain.

'Well, I do.' She dropped into a chair. How much could she safely tell a civilian without crossing the line? And how far over the line was she willing to go? She looked at Mavis again, sighed. As far as it took. 'Jess is the prime suspect in four deaths.'

'What? What bend did you go around since last night? Jess wouldn't—'

'Be quiet,' Eve snapped. 'I haven't got him solid on that yet, but I'm working on it. I do, however, have him on other charges. Serious charges. Now, if you'd stop blubbering and sit the hell down, I'll tell you what I can.'

'You didn't even stay and watch my whole act.' Mavis managed to fall into a chair, but she didn't manage to stop blubbering.

'Oh, Mavis, I'm sorry.' Eve dragged a hand through her hair. She was lousy with weepers. 'I couldn't – there was nothing I could do. Mavis, Jess is into mind control.'

'Huh?' It was such a wild statement coming from the most grounded person she knew that Mavis stopped crying long enough to sniffle and gape. 'Huh?'

'He's developed a program that accesses brain wave patterns

260

and influences behavior. And he's used it on me, on Roarke, and on you.'

'On me? No, he didn't. Get genuine here, Dallas, this is too Frankenstein. Jess isn't a mad scientist. He's a musician.'

'He's an engineer, a musicologist, and a prick.' Eve took a deep breath, then related as much as she felt was necessary. As she spoke, Mavis's tears dried up, hardening her eyes. Her bottom lip quivered once, then thinned.

'He used me to get to you, to get to Roarke. I was just a spring. Then once I'd bounced him to you, he fucked with your mind.'

'This is not your fault. Stop it,' Eve ordered when Mavis's eyes started to shimmer again. 'I mean it. I'm tired, I'm pressed, and my head is about to explode. I don't need this soggy routine from you right now. It's not your fault. You were used, and so was I. He was hoping for Roarke's backing on his project. It doesn't make me less of a cop or you less of a performer. You're good, and you got better. He knew you could, and that's why he used you. He's too damn arrogant about his talent to have linked himself up with a dud. He wanted somebody who could shine. And you did.'

Mavis swiped a hand under her nose. 'Really?'

It was that one word delivered with such shaky hope that made Eve realize how far Mavis's ego had sunk. 'Yeah, really. You were great, Mavis. That's solid.'

'Okay.' She wiped at her eyes. 'I guess my feelings got hurt when you didn't hang for the act. Leonardo said I was being silly. You wouldn't have split if you hadn't had to split.' She took a long breath that lifted her thin shoulders, then dropped them again. 'Then Jess, when he called, he laid all this stuff on me. I shouldn't have bought into it.'

'It doesn't matter. We'll smooth out the rest later. I'm pressed here, Mavis. I don't have much time to wrap this up.'

'You think he killed people?'

'I have to find out.' She looked over at the knock on her door. Peabody stepped in, hesitated.

'Sorry, Lieutenant. Should I wait outside?'

'No, I'm going.' Mavis sniffled, rose, sent Eve a watery smile. 'Sorry about the flood and everything.'

'We'll mop it up. I'll talk to you when I can. Don't worry about this.'

Mavis nodded, and her lowered lashes concealed the quick flare in her eyes. She intended to do more than worry.

'Everything all right here, Lieutenant?' Peabody asked when Mavis left them alone.

'Actually, Peabody, everything's fucked.' Eve sat, tried to drill holes in her temples with her fingers to release the pressure. 'Mira doesn't think our boy has the personality profile for murder. I've insulted her because I'm going for another consultant. Nadine Furst is sniffing too close to the center, and I've just broken Mavis's heart and shattered her ego.'

Peabody waited a beat. 'Well, other than that, how are things?'

'Cute.' But it did prod a reluctant smile. 'Damn, give me a nice clear murder any day over this physiological crap.'

'Those were the good old days, all right.' Peabody shifted to make room as Feeney stepped in. 'Well, the gang's all here.'

'Let's get to work. Status?' Eve asked Feeney.

'Sweepers found more discs at the suspect's studio. So far, no matches on victims. He kept a log of his work.' Uncomfortable, Feeney shifted. Jess had been very explicit in his speculations on results, including the sexual nudge he'd given Eve and Roarke. 'He names names, times, ah, suggestions. There's no mention of any of the four dead. I've been through his communications system. No transmissions to or from any of the victims.'

'Well, that's dandy.'

Feeney shifted his feet again, and his color fluctuated into a blush. 'I've sealed the work log for your eyes only.'

Her brows knit. 'Why?'

'He, ah, talks about you a lot. On a personal level.' He focused his eyes an inch over Eve's head. 'Again, he's very explicit in his speculations.'

'Yeah, he made it clear he was overly interested in my head.'

'He isn't just interested in that part of your anatomy.' Feeney puffed out his cheeks, blew the air out. 'He considered it would be an entertaining experiments to attempt to ah . . .'

'What?'

'Influence your behavior toward him . . . in a sexual manner.'

Eve let out a snort. It wasn't just the words, but Feeney's stiffly formal delivery. 'He figured he could use his toy to get me into the sack? Great. We can lay another charge on him. Intent to sexually molest.'

'Did he say anything about me?' Peabody wanted to know and received a glare from Eve.

'That's sick, Officer.'

'Just wondering.'

'We're adding to his cage time,' Eve continued, 'but we're not pinning him on the big one. And Mira's profile is going to work against us.'

'Lieutenant.' Peabody sucked in her breath and took the chance. 'Have you considered that she's right? That's he's not responsible?'

'Yeah, I have. And that scares the hell out of me. If she's right, there's someone else out there with a brain toy, and we're not even close. So we all better hope we've got our man safely locked away.'

'Speaking of our man,' Feeney broke in. 'You better know he's lawyered himself.'

'I figured he would. Anybody we know?'

'Leanore Bastwick.'

'Well, hell. Small world.'

263

'She wants to make points off of you, Dallas.' Feeney took out his bag of nuts, offered them to Peabody. 'She's raring to go. Wants to set up a media conference. Word is she took him on pro bono, just for the shot at you, and the media coverage this will get once it hits.'

'She can take her shot. We can block the press conference for twenty-four hours. We'd better solidify before then.'

'I pulled a thread loose,' Peabody told her. 'It might unravel more with some tugging. Mathias did indeed attend MIT for two semesters. Unfortunately, his term there was three years after Jess did his at-home degree, but Jess used his alumni status to access data from their files. He also taught an E-class elective on musicology, which the university uploaded into their library curriculum. Mathias took the course during his last semester.'

Eve felt a quick power surge. 'That's something to tug on. Good work. It connects, finally. And maybe we've been looking in the wrong place. Pearly was the first known victim. What if he's the one who was connected with the others? It could be as simple as their common interest in electronic games.'

'We looked there already.'

'So look again,' she told Peabody. 'And look deeper. Not all the clubs and loops are above ground. If Mathias was used to help develop the system, he might have bragged about it. Those hobby hackers use all kinds of compunames. Can you find his?'

'Eventually,' Feeney agreed.

'You can contact Jack Carter. He was his roommate on Olympus. Maybe he can give you a boost on them. Peabody, contact Devane's son, see what you can shake out of him on this angle. I'll work on the Fitzhugh angle.' She glanced at her watch. 'I'll make a stop first. Maybe I can cut through some of the layers.'

*

She felt she was back to square one, looking for the connection. There had to be one, and she was going to have to involve Roarke to find it. She called him from her car 'link.

'Well, hello, Lieutenant. How was your nap?'

'Too short and too long ago. How long are you going to be in midtown?'

'Another few hours at any rate. Why?'

'I'm coming by. Now. Can you squeeze me in?'

He smiled. 'Always.'

'It's business,' she said, and cut him off before she could smile back. Daring her auto-drive, she programmed destination, then used her 'link again. 'Nadine.'

Nadine angled her head, shot Eve a cold look. 'Lieutenant.'

'Nine A.M., my office.'

'Should I bring a lawyer?'

'Bring your recorder. I'll give you a jump on tomorrow's press conference re Jess Barrow.'

'What press conference?' The image and voice quality sharpened as Nadine went immediately to private, dragging headphones over her hair. 'There's nothing on schedule.'

'There will be. You want that jump, and you want the official report from the primary, be there at nine.'

'What's the catch?'

'Senator Pearly. Get me everything. Not the official data, the quiet stuff. His hobbies, playgrounds. His underground connections.'

'Pearly was clean as a church choir.'

'You don't have to be dirty to play underground, you just have to be curious.'

'And what makes you think I can get private data on a government official?'

'Because you're you, Nadine. Feed the data to my home unit, and I'll see you at nine hundred hours. You'll beat the pack by two hours easy. Think of those ratings.'

'I'm thinking. Deal,' she snapped and signed off.

When Eve was able to glide smoothly into the parking facility at Roarke's midtown office, she began to think more kindly toward vehicle maintenance. Her VIP space was waiting, locking its security shield the moment she shut down.

The elevator accepted her palm print and zoomed her up to the top floor in a quiet, dignified ride.

She'd never get used to it.

Roarke's personal assistant beamed at her, welcomed her home, welcomed her in, and escorted her through the plush outer offices, down the streamlined corridor, and into the elegant efficiency of Roarke's private office.

But he wasn't alone.

'Sorry.' She struggled not to frown at Reeanna and William. 'I'm interrupting.'

'Not at all.' Roarke walked over, kissed her lightly. 'We're just finishing up.'

'Your husband's quite the slave driver.' William held out a hand to shake Eve's warmly. 'If you hadn't come along, Reeanna and I would have to do without our dinner.'

'That's William.' Reeanna laughed. 'He's either thinking of electronics or his stomach.'

'Or you. Can you join us?' he asked Eve. 'I thought we'd try the French place on the skyline level.'

'Cops never eat.' Eve tried to adjust herself to the easy social tone. 'But thanks.'

'You need regular fuel to help the healing process.' Reeanna narrowed her eyes for a quick, professional survey. 'Any pain?'

'Not much. I appreciate the personal service. And I wonder if I could speak to you for a few minutes on an official matter – if you have time after your meal.'

'Of course.' Curiosity flitted over her face. 'Could I ask what it's about?'

'The possibility of doing a consult on a case I'm working on. If you're agreeable, I'd need to do it tomorrow, early.'

'A consult on an actual human being? I'm there.'

'Reeanna's weary of machines,' William put in. 'She's been making noises for weeks about going back into private practice.'

'VR, holograms, autotronics.' She rolled her beautiful eyes. 'I long for flesh and blood. Roarke has us set up on the thirty-second level, west wing. I should be able to nudge William through a meal in an hour. Just meet me there.'

'Thanks.'

'Oh, and Roarke,' Reeanna continued as she and William started toward the door. 'We'd love to have that personal take on the new unit as soon as you can manage it.'

'And she calls me a slave driver. Tonight, before I leave.'

'Wonderful. Later, Eve.'

'Food, Reeanna. I'm dreaming of coquille St Jacques.' William was laughing as he pulled her out of the door.

'I didn't mean to break up your meeting,' Eve began.

'You didn't. And you've given me a breather before I have to dig into a mountain of status reports. I've had all the data on that VR unit you're concerned about transmitted. I've skimmed the surface, but I've found nothing out of line so far.'

'That's something.' She'd rest easier once she could eliminate that angle.

'William would be able to spot any problem quicker,' he added. 'But as he and Ree were in on the development, I didn't think you'd care to pass it by him.'

'No. Let's keep it close.'

'Reeanna was concerned about you. So am I.'

'She gave me a going-over. She's good.'

'Yes, she is.' Still, he tipped Eve's face back with a fingertip. 'You've got a headache.'

'What's the point of illegal brain scans when you can already see into my head?' She closed her hand over his wrist before he could drop his arm. 'I can't see into yours. It's annoying.'

'I know.' His lips curved as he pressed them to her brow. 'I love you. Ridiculously.'

'I didn't come here for this,' she murmured when his arms wound around her.

'Take a minute anyway. I need it.' He could feel the outline of the diamond around her neck, one she had worn first reluctantly, and now habitually. 'That'll do it.' He eased her back, pleased that she'd held on another moment. She so rarely held on. 'What's on your mind, Lieutenant?'

'Peabody dug up a thin connection between Barrow and Mathias. I want to see if I can tighten it. How much trouble would it be to access underground transmissions, using MIT's on-line services as a starting point?'

His eyes lighted. 'I love a challenge.' He moved around the desk, engaged his unit, then slid open a hidden panel under it, flicked a switch manually.

'What's that?' Her teeth went on edge. 'Is that a block system? Did you just tune out Compuguard?'

'That would be illegal, wouldn't it?' he said cheerfully. He reached over his shoulder to pat her hand. 'Don't ask the question, Lieutenant, if you don't want to hear the answer. Now, what time period are you interested in, particularly?'

Scowling, she dug out her log, read off the dates of Mathias's attendance at MIT. 'I'm looking for Mathias specifically. I don't know what line names he used yet. Feeney's getting them.'

'Oh, I think I can find them for you. Why don't you see about ordering us a meal? No reason to go hungry.'

'Coquille St Jacques?' she said dryly.

'Steak. Rare.' He slid out a keyboard and began to work manually.

# Chapter Nineteen

Eve ate standing up, breathing down Roarke's neck. When he'd had enough of that, he simply reached around and pinched her.

'Back off.'

'I'm just trying to see.' But she backed off. 'You've been at it a half hour.'

He imagined, with the equipment available at Cop Central, even Feeney would have taken twice as long to get to that same point. 'Darling Eve,' he said, then sighed when she only frowned at him. 'There are layers here, Lieutenant. Layers over layers. That's why they call it underground. I've located two of the coded names our young, doomed autotronics ace used. There'll be more. Still, it takes some doing to unscramble transmissions.'

He turned the machine on auto so he could enjoy his own dinner.

'It's all just games, isn't it?' Eve shifted so she could see the screen run with figures and odd symbols as it worked. 'Just grown-up kids playing games. Secret societies. Hell, they're just high-tech clubhouses.'

'More or less. Most of us enjoy diversions, Eve. Games, fantasies, the anonymity of a computer mask so we can pretend we're someone else for a time.'

*Games*, she thought again. Maybe it all boiled down to games, and she just hadn't looked closely enough at the rules and players. 'What's wrong with being who you are?'

'It's not enough for everyone. And this sort of thing attracts the lonely and the egocentric.'

'And fanatics.'

'Certainly. E-services, particularly underground ones, provide the fanatic with an open forum.' He cocked a brow, cut neatly into his steak. 'They also provide a service – educational for that matter – informative, intellectual. And can be perfectly harmless entertainment. They're legal,' he reminded her. 'Even the underground ones aren't closely regulated. And that stems mainly from the fact that it's nearly impossible to do so. And cost prohibitive.'

'EDD keeps a line on them.'

'To some extent. Look here.' He swung back, tapped out a few keys, and had a display sliding onto one of the wall screens. 'See that? It's nothing more than a somewhat amusing diatribe about a new version of Camelot. A multiuser role playing program, hologram optional,' he explained. 'Everyone wants to be king. And there.' He gestured to another screen. 'A very straightforward advertisement for a partner in Erotica, a sexual fantasy VR program, dual remote controls mandatory.' He grinned at her knitted brow. 'One of my companies manufactures it. It's quite popular.'

'I bet.' She didn't ask if he'd tried it out himself. Some data she didn't need. 'I don't get it. You can rent a licensed companion, probably cheaper than the cost of that program. You get sex in the flesh. Why do you need this?'

'Fantasy, darling. Having control or abdicating it. And you can run the program over and over, with nearly unlimited variations. It's mood again, and mind. All fantasies are mood and mind.'

'Even the fatal ones,' she said slowly. 'Isn't that what this is all about? Having control. Ultimate control over someone else's mood and mind. They don't even know they're playing the game. That's the big kick. You'd need a huge ego and no conscience. Mira says Jess doesn't fit.'

270

'Ah. That's a problem, isn't it?'

She flicked a look down at him. 'You don't sound surprised.'

'He's what, in my alley days in Dublin, we would have called a fug – cross between a fuck and a pug. Lots of mouth and no balls. I never met a fug who could draw blood without whining.'

She cleaned the steak off her plate and set it aside. 'It seems to me that killing in this manner is bloodless. Cowardly. Fuglike.'

He grinned at that. 'Well put, but fugs don't kill, they just talk.'

She hated that she was beginning to agree and had muscled her way down what looked like a dead end with Jess Barrow. 'I've got to have more. How much longer do you figure?'

'Until I'm through. You can keep yourself occupied with the data on the VR unit.'

'I'll come back to it. I'm going to go down to Reeanna's office. I can just leave her a memo about Jess if she's not back from dinner.'

'Fine.' He didn't try to dissuade her. She had to move, he knew. To take some action. 'Will you come back up when you're done, or will I meet you at home?'

'I don't know.' He looked perfect there, she thought, sitting in his snazzy office, manipulating controls. Maybe everyone wanted to be king, she mused, but Roarke was content being Roarke.

His gaze shifted to hers, held. 'Yes, Lieutenant?'

'You're exactly what you want to be. That's a pretty good deal.'

'Most of the time. And so are you what you want to be.'

'Most of the time,' she murmured. 'I'll check in with Feeney and Peabody after I meet with Reeanna. See if anything's come loose. Thanks for dinner – and the computime.'

'You can pay me back.' He took her hand, rose. 'I want, very much, to make love with you tonight.'

'You don't have to ask.' Flustered, she moved her shoulders. 'We got married and everything.'

'Let's say asking is part of the fantasy.' He moved in, just a little; touched his lips to hers, just a whisper. 'Let me woo you tonight, darling Eve. Let me surprise you. Let me . . . seduce you.' He laid a hand on her heart, felt the hard, thick beat of it. 'There,' he murmured. 'I've already started.'

Her knees were quivering. 'Thanks. That's just what I need to keep my mind focused on my work.'

'Two hours.' This time he lingered over the kiss. 'Then let's take something for ourselves.'

'I'll try.' She stepped back while she was sure she still could, walked quickly toward the door. Then she turned back, just looked at him. 'Two hours,' she told him. 'Then you can finish what you started.'

She heard him laugh as she closed the door and hurried toward the elevator. 'Thirty-nine, west,' she ordered, then found herself smiling.

Yes, they'd take something for themselves, she decided. Something Jess and his nasty little toy had tried to steal from them.

Then she stopped, and her smile faded. *Was that the problem here?* she wondered. Was she so focused on that – on a kind of personal retribution – that she was missing something bigger? Or smaller?

If Mira was right, and Roarke with his fug theory was on the mark, then she was off. It was time, she admitted, to pull back a bit. Refocus.

*It was a tech crime*, she mused. *But tech crimes still require the human element: motive, emotion, greed, hate, jealousy, and power.* Which of those – or which combination of those – was at the core of this? She could see both greed and a hunger for power in Jess. But would he kill for them?

272

Steely minded, she replayed his reaction to the morgue shots in her mind. Would a man who had caused that to happen, had directed it to happen, react with such violent distress when faced with the results?

Not impossible, she decided. But it didn't fit her image of the hand on the button.

He enjoyed seeing the results of his work, she remembered. He liked to snicker over them and note them down in his log. Did he have another log, one the sweepers missed? She'd have to take a trip through his studio herself.

Deep in thought, she stepped out on thirty-nine, scanned the shielded glass walls of a lab. It was quiet here, security in full swing as indicated by the cameras in full view, the warning red beep of motion detectors. If there were any drones still at work, they were behind closed doors.

She placed her palm on a plate, received verification, answered the request for voice print by giving her name, then requested the location of Reeanna's office.

You are cleared for top level, Dallas, Lieutenant Eve. Proceed left through breezeway, then right at termination. Dr Ott's office is five meters beyond this point. It will not be necessary to repeat this procedure to gain entry. You are cleared.

She wondered if Roarke or Reeanna had cleared her through and followed the directions. The breezeway impressed her, offering a full view of the city on all sides. She could look between her own feet and see the life bustling on the street below. The music piped in was energetic, and made her think sourly of some musicologist's idea of fueling drones with enthusiasm for their work. *Wasn't that just one more kind of mind control?*

She passed a door bearing an imprint that identified it as William's. A game master, she thought. It might be helpful to get his input, pick his brain, jiggle a few hypotheses out

273

of him. She knocked, watched his recorder light beep red for locked.

I'm sorry, William Shaffer is not currently in his office. Please leave your name and any message. He will respond as soon as possible.

'It's Dallas. Look, William, if you've got a couple minutes when you finish dinner, I've got something I'd like to run by you. I'm going to drop by Reeanna's office now. I'll leave a memo if she's not there. I'll be in the building or at home later if you've got time to talk to me.'

As she turned away, she glanced at her watch. How long did it take to eat, for God's sake? You picked up food, put it in your mouth, chewed, and swallowed.

She found Reeanna's office, knocked. She hesitated for less than five seconds when the recorder light beeped green, then slid the door open. If Reeanna didn't want her inside, she'd have kept it locked, Eve decided, and indulged herself in a thorough study.

It looked like Reeanna, she decided. Polished to a bright sheen, underlying sexual tones in the slashes of fiery red in the laser art against cool white walls.

The desk faced the window to provide Reeanna with a constant view of the busy sky traffic.

The sitting area was plush with a deeply cushioned body-form lounger that still held the imprint of its last occupant. Reeanna's curves were impressive, even in silhouette. The clear Plasticide table was hard as stone and was intricately carved with diamond patterns that caught and refracted the light from an arched-neck lamp with a rose-toned shade.

Eve picked up the VR goggles laid on it, saw they were indeed Roarke's latest model, and set them down again. They still made her uncomfortable.

Turning away, she studied the workstation across the room.

274

Nothing soft or feminine about that area, she noted. It was all business. Slick white counter, muscle flexing equipment even now hard at work. She heard the low hum of a computer on auto, frowned at the symbols flickering on the monitor. They looked similar to what she'd tried to decipher from Roarke's screen.

But then, computer codes all looked the same to her.

Curious, she walked over to the desk, but nothing interesting had been left out to examine. A silver pen, a pair of pretty gold earrings, a hologram of William wearing a flight suit and grinning youthfully. A short printout, again in that baffling computer code.

Eve sat on the edge of the desk. She didn't want to fit her wiry build into the imprint left by Reeanna's. Pulling out her communicator, she tagged Peabody.

'Anything?'

'Devane's son is willing to cooperate. He's aware of the interest she had in games, particularly role playing. It wasn't an interest he shared, but he claims he knows one of her usual partners. He dated her for a short time. I've got her name. She lives right here in New York. I have the data. Should I transmit?'

'I think you can handle an interview solo. Arrange a meet, bring her in only if she refuses to cooperate. Report back.'

'Yes, sir.' Peabody's voice remained sober, but her eyes lighted with the assignment. 'I'm on my way.'

Satisfied, Eve tried for Feeney, hit his frequency occupied recording. She had to settle for leaving a request for contact.

The door opened. Reeanna stopped her rush inside when she spotted Eve at her desk. 'Oh, Eve. I didn't expect you quite yet.'

'Time's part of my problem.'

'I see.' She smiled, let the door shut. 'I suppose Roarke cleared you in.'

'I guess he did. Problem?'

'No, no.' Reeanna waved her hand. 'I'm distracted, I suppose. William went on endlessly about some glitches he's concerned about. I left him brooding over his crème brûlée.' She flicked a glance toward her humming computer. 'The work never stops around here. R and D's a twenty-four/seven proposition.' She smiled. 'Like police work, I imagine. Well, I didn't take time for brandy. Would you like some?'

'No, thanks. On duty.'

'Coffee then.' Reeanna moved over to a counter, requested a snifter of brandy, a cup of black coffee. 'You'll have to excuse my lack of focus. We're a little behind schedule today. Roarke needed data on the new VR model, and he wanted it from conception to implementation.'

'That was yours. I didn't realize that until he mentioned it just now.'

'Oh, William's mostly. Though I had a small part. Now.' She handed Eve the coffee, then took her brandy around the desk to sit. 'What can I do for you?'

'I'm hoping you'll agree to that consult. The subject is currently in custody, now lawyered, but I don't think we'll be blocked there. I need a profile, angling from your particular area of expertise.'

'Genetic branding.' Reeanna tapped her fingers. 'Interesting. What are the charges?'

'I'm not free to discuss that until I have your agreement and clear the session with my commander. Once that's done, I'd like the testing scheduled for seven hundred.'

'Seven A.M.?' Reeanna winced. 'Ouch. And here I'm a night owl rather than a lark. You want me up and running at that hour, give me some incentive.' She smiled a little. 'I can assume you've already had Mira test your subject – and the results weren't to your liking.'

'Second opinions aren't unusual.' It was a defensive answer. She felt defensive. And, Eve realized, she felt guilty.

'No, but Dr Mira's reports are sterling, and they're very rarely questioned. You want him badly.'

'I want the truth badly. To find it, I have to separate theory and lies and deceptions.' She pushed off the desk. 'Look, I thought you were interested in doing this sort of thing.'

'I am, very. But I like to know what I'm dealing with. I'd need the subject's brain scan.'

'I've got it. In evidence.'

'Really?' Her eyes gleamed, catlike. 'It's also important to have all available data on his biological parents. Are they known?'

'We accessed that data for Dr Mira's test. It'll be available to you.'

Reeanna leaned back, swirling her brandy. 'It must be murder.' Her lips twitched at Eve's expression. 'After all, that's your field. The study of the taking of lives.'

'You could put it that way.'

'How do you put it?'

'The investigation of the takers.'

'Yes, yes, but in order to do so, you study the dead – and death itself. How it happened, what caused it, what transpired in those last moments between the taker and the victim. Fascinating. What kind of personality is required to study death routinely, day after day, year after year, as a vocation? Does it scar you, Eve, or harden you?'

'It pisses you off,' she said shortly. 'And I don't have time to philosophize.'

'Sorry, bad habit.' Reeanna let out a sigh. 'William tells me I analyze everything to death.' She smiled. 'Not that it's a crime – that sort of murder. And I am interested in assisting you. Call your commander,' she invited. 'I'll wait and see if clearance is forthcoming. Then we can go over details.'

'I appreciate it.' Eve removed her communicator, turned away, and requested display only. It took longer and was, she felt, less effective. The coding through of information and request. How could you add your instincts, your determination to a display?

But she did her best and waited.

What the hell are you trying to do, Dallas, override Mira?

I want another opinion, Commander. It's well within procedure. I'm pursuing all angles. If I'm unable to convince the PA to charge Jess with coercion to self-terminate, I don't want the lesser charges to slide. I need verification of intent to harm.

It was pushing it, and she knew it. Eve waited with a knotted stomach while Whitney mulled over his decision.

*Just give me the opening,* she thought. *He needs his ears pinned back. He needs to pay.*

You're cleared to proceed on my authorization, Lieutenant. This better not be a waste of budget. We both know Mira's report will weigh heavily.

Understood and appreciated. Dr Ott's report will give Barrow's lawyer a headache, if nothing else. I'm currently working on detailing connection between suspect and victims. Results will be available by nine hundred hours.

Be damn sure of it. My butt is now swinging with yours. Whitney out.

Eve let out a long, quiet breath. She'd bought a little more time, and that was all, she admitted to herself, she was after. With time, she could dig deeper. If Roarke and Feeney couldn't pull out data, there was no one, off or on planet, who could.

Jess would pay, but murder would go unavenged. She closed her eyes a moment. And that was where she stood. Avenging the dead.

She opened her eyes again, wanting to align herself before she relayed the details to Reeanna.

That's when she saw it, in black and white there on the computer monitor.

Mathias, Drew logged as AutoPhile. Mathias, Drew logged as Banger. Mathias, Drew logged as HoloDick.

Her heartbeat jerked, but her hand was steady as a rock as she switched her communicator from off to open, signaling to Peabody and Feeney on code one. Backup required. Respond immediately to transmission source.

She pocketed the card, turned. 'The commander okayed the consult. Reluctantly. I'm going to need results, Reeanna.'

'You'll get them.' Reeanna sipped her brandy, then shifted her gaze to the sleek little unit on her desk. 'Your heart rate just spiked, Eve, and your adrenaline level rose dramatically.' She angled her head. 'Oh dear,' she murmured, and lifted her sparkling hand. It held an official NYPSD stunner. 'That's a problem.'

Several floors above, Roarke scanned the new data on Mathias, hummed over it. *Now we're getting somewhere*, he thought. He switched back to auto and tuned in to the data on the new VR unit. Wasn't it odd, he thought, and interesting, that some of the components on Jess Barrow's magic console so closely mirrored the components of his new unit?

Then he swore softly when his interoffice 'link buzzed.

'I don't want interruptions.'

'I'm sorry, sir. There's a Mavis Freestone here. She claims you'll see her.'

He switched the second computer to auto, blocked both audio and video. 'Let her in, Caro. And you can log out for the day. I won't need you anymore.'

'Thank you. I'll bring her back directly.'

Roarke frowned to himself, idly picked up the VR unit Reeanna had left him to try out. A few adjustments, he mused. Improved for the next release. It was loaded with subliminal options, and could explain the coincidence of similarity. Still, he didn't care for it. He began to consider a possible leak in his R and D division.

He wondered just what William had come up with as alterations for the second manufacturing run and tucked a disc into his alternate unit. It wouldn't hurt to run the data while he saw just what Mavis had on her mind.

His machine beeped acceptance, began to upload as his door opened. Mavis whirled in like a freak storm.

'It's my fault, all my fault, and I don't know what to do.'

Roarke came around the desk, took Mavis's hands, and sent an understanding look at his baffled assistant. 'Go on home. I'll deal with this. Oh, and leave the security open for my wife, please. Sit down, Mavis.' He steered her to a chair. 'Take a breath.' Reading her accurately, he patted her head. 'And don't cry. What's all your fault?'

'Jess. He used me to get to you. Dallas said it wasn't my fault, but I've thought about it, and it is.' She gave one long, heroic sniffle. 'I've got this.' She held up a disc.

'And this is?'

'I don't know. Maybe evidence. You take it.'

'Okay.' He nipped the disc out of her hand as she waved wildly. 'Why haven't you given it to Eve?'

'I would – I was going to. I thought she was here. I don't think I'm supposed to have it. I didn't even tell Leonardo about it. I'm a terrible person,' she finished.

Hysterical women had come his way before. Roarke slipped the disc into his pocket, walked over, and ordered a tall soother of the milder variety. 'Here, drink this. What sort of evidence do you think this is, Mavis?'

'I dunno. You don't hate me, do you?'

'Darling, I adore you. Drink it down.'

'Really?' She gulped obediently. 'I really like you, Roarke, and not just because you're rolling in credits or anything. It's good that you are, 'cause poor sucks, right?'

280

'It does indeed.'

'But either way, you make her so happy. She doesn't even know how happy because she's never been. You know?'

'Yes. Three slow quiet breaths now. Ready? One.'

'Okay.' She took them, very seriously, her eyes on his. 'You're good at this. Calming people down. I bet she doesn't let you do it for her much.'

'No, she doesn't. Or she doesn't know it when I do.' He smiled. 'We know her, don't we, Mavis?'

'We love her. I'm so sorry.' Tears came, but they were soothing and soft. 'I figured it out after I ran the disc I gave you. At least I figured out some of it. It's a copy of the lay down from my video. I ran it off on the sly. I wanted it for posterity, you know? But there's a memo after it.'

She looked down at her hands. 'This is the first time I played it, the first time I heard it all. He gave a copy to Dallas, but he made notes after this version, about . . .' She broke off, lifted suddenly dry eyes. 'I want you to hurt him for this. I want you to hurt him really bad. Play it, from where I've cued it.'

Roarke said nothing, but he rose and slid the disc into his entertainment unit. The screen filled with light, with music, then the volume and intensity lowered as a background for Jess's voice.

'I'm not sure what the results will be. One day I'll find the key to tapping in at the source. For now, I can only specualte. The suggestion is to the memory. The reenactment of trauma. Something's at the core of those shadows on Dallas's mind. Something fascinating. What will she dream tonight after playing the disc? How long will it be before I can seduce her to share it all with me? What secrets does she hide? It's such fun to wonder. I'm just waiting for the chance to tap into Roarke's darker side. Oh, he has one, so close to the surface you can almost see it. Thinking of them together, with just the animal in control, gives me such a rush. I can't think of two more fascinating subjects for this project. God bless Mavis

281

for opening the door. Within six months I'll know these two so well, anticipate their reactions so clearly, I'll be able to lead them right where I want them. Then there's no limit. Fame, fortune, adulation. I'll be the goddamn father of virtual pleasure.'

Roarke remained silent as the disc ran out. He didn't remove it, certain his fingers would crush it like powder.

'I've already hurt him,' he said at length. 'But not enough. Not nearly enough.' He turned to Mavis. She'd risen and stood, small as a fairy, her slip-shouldered dress of pink gauze somehow valiant. 'You aren't responsible for this,' Roarke told her.

'Maybe that's true. I have to work that out. But I know he wouldn't have gotten that close to her, or you, without me. Will that help keep him in a cage?'

'I think he'll hear the lock turn and wait a long time before he hears it open again. You'll leave it with me?'

'Yeah. I'll get out of your hair now.'

'You're always welcome here.'

Her mouth quirked. 'If it wasn't for Dallas, you'd have run like hell in the opposite direction the first time you saw me.'

He came to her, kissed her firmly on that crooked mouth. 'That would have been my mistake – and my loss. I'll call a car for you.'

'You don't have to—'

'A car will be waiting for you at the front entrance.'

She rubbed a hand under her nose. 'One of those mag limos?'

'Absolutely.'

He walked her to the door, closed it thoughtfully behind her. The disc would be enough, he hoped, to drive another nail in Jess. But it still didn't point to murder. He went back, ordered both of his machines to display on screen.

Sitting behind his desk, he picked up the VR goggles and studied the data.

*

Eve lowered her gaze to the stunner. From her angle, she couldn't be sure which setting was clicked. A sudden move, she knew, could result in anything from mild discomfort and partial paralysis to death.

'It's illegal for a civilian to own or operate that weapon,' she said coolly.

'I don't believe that's particularly relevant, under the circumstances. Take yours out, Eve, slowly, and by the fingertips. Then set it on the desk. I don't want to hurt you,' Reeanna added when Eve made no move to obey. 'I never have. Not really. But I'll do whatever's necessary.'

Keeping her eyes on Reeanna's, Eve reached slowly for her side arm.

'And don't think about trying to use it. I don't have this on max, but it is on a very high setting. You won't have use of your extremities for days, and though the possible brain damage isn't necessarily permanent, it is very inconvenient.'

Eve knew very well what the stunner could do, and she took out her weapon carefully, laid it on the corner of the desk. 'You'll have to kill me, Reeanna. But you'll have to do it face to face, in person. It won't be like the others.'

'I'm going to try to avoid that. A short, painless, even enjoyable session on VR, and we can adjust your memory and direct your target. You're well aimed at Jess, Eve. Why don't we just keep it that way?'

'Why did you kill those four people, Reeanna?'

'They killed themselves, Eve. You were right there when Cerise Devane jumped off that building. One has to believe what one sees with one's own eyes.' She sighed. 'Or most do. You're not most, are you?'

'Why did you kill them?'

'I merely encouraged them to end their lives in a certain manner at a certain time. And why?' Reeanna shrugged her lovely shoulders. 'Why, because I could.'

She smiled beautifully and gave her bell tinkle of a laugh.

# Chapter Twenty

It wouldn't take long, Eve calculated, for Peabody or Feeney to home in on her signal. She just needed time. And she had a feeling Reeanna would provide it. Some egos, like some people, fed on regular admiration. Reeanna fit on both levels.

'Did you work with Jess?'

'That amateur.' Reeanna tossed her hair at the idea. 'He's a piano player. Not that he doesn't have a certain talent for basic engineering, but he lacks vision – and guts,' she added with a slow, feline smile. 'Women are so much more courageous and more vicious than men, all in all. Don't you agree?'

'No. I think courage and viciousness have no gender.'

'Well.' Disappointed, Reeanna pursed her lips briefly. 'In any case, I corresponded with him briefly a couple of years ago. We exchanged ideas, theories. The anonymity of underground E-services are handy. I enjoyed his pontificating and was able to flatter him into sharing some of his technical progress. But I was well ahead of him. Frankly, I never thought he'd get as far as he apparently has. Simple mood expanding, I imagine, with some direct suggestion.' She cocked her head. 'Close enough?'

'You went farther.'

'Oh, leagues. Why don't you sit down, Eve? We'd both be more comfortable.'

'I'm comfortable on my feet.'

'As you like. But a few steps back, if you don't mind.' She

gestured with the stunner. 'I wouldn't want you to try for your weapon. I'd have to use this, and I'd hate to lose such a good audience.'

Eve took a step back. She thought of Roarke, several floors above. He wouldn't come down to seek her out. At least she didn't have that concern. If anything, he'd call down if he locked onto something. So he was safe, and she could stall.

'You're a medical doctor,' Eve pointed out. 'A psychiatrist. You've spent years studying to help the human condition. Why take lives, Reeanna, when you're trained to save them?'

'Branded at conception perhaps.' She smiled. 'Oh, you don't like that theory. You'd have used it to push your case, but you don't like it. You don't know where you came from, or from what.' She saw Eve's eyes flicker and nodded, pleased. 'I've studied all available data on Eve Dallas as soon as I learned Roarke was involved with you. I'm very attached to Roarke, once toyed with the idea of making our all-too-brief liaison into something more permanent.'

'He dumped you?'

The smile froze as the insult hit target. 'That's beneath you, such a petty female hit. No, he didn't. We simply drifted in opposite directions. I had intended to drift back, let's say, eventually. So I was intrigued when he took such an avid interest in a cop, of all things. Not his usual taste, certainly not his usual style. But you are . . . interesting. More so after I accessed data on you.'

She made herself comfortable on the arm of the relaxation chair. The weapon stayed aimed and steady. 'The young, abused child found in a Dallas alley. Broken, battered, confused. No memory of how she'd gotten there, who'd beat her, raped her, abandoned her. A blank. I found that fascinating. No past, no parents, no hint of what made her. I'm going to enjoy studying you.'

'You won't get your hands in my head.'

'Oh, but I will. You'll even suggest it yourself, once you

take a trip or two on the unit I've made just for you. I really hate that I'm going to have to see to it that you forget everything we discuss here. You have such a keen mind, such a strong energy. But it will give us a chance to work together. As fond as I am of William, he's so . . . short-sighted.'

'How involved is he?'

'He has no idea. The first test I ran on the doctored unit was on William. Quite a success, and it made things so much easier. I could direct him to adjust each unit I wanted. He's quicker, more adept electronically than I. He actually helped me refine the design and personalize the one I sent to Senator Pearly.'

'Why?'

'Another test. He was very vocal about the misuse of sub-liminals. He enjoyed games, as I'm sure you've discovered, but he continually pushed for regulations. Censorship, if you ask me. He stuck his nose into pornography, consenting adult dual controls, commercial advertising and its use of suggestion, all manner of things. I thought of him as my sacrificial lamb.'

'How did you gain access to his brain pattern?'

'William. He's very clever. It took him several weeks of intense work, but he managed to hack through security.' She angled her head, enjoying the moment. 'At the top level of NYPSD as well. He injected a virus there. Just to keep your EDD men occupied.'

'And that's where you accessed my pattern.'

'Indeed it is. He has a soft heart, my William, it would pain him horribly to know he had a vital part in coercion.'

'But you used him, you made him part of it. And it doesn't pain you at all.'

'No, it doesn't. William made it all possible. And if not him, there would have been another.'

'He loves you. You can see it.'

'Oh please.' It made her laugh. 'He's a puppy. All men are when it comes to an attractive female form. They simply sit up and beg. That's amusing, occasionally irritating, and always useful.' Intrigued, she touched her tongue to her top lip. 'Don't tell me you haven't used your basic female advantage on Roarke.'

'We don't use each other.'

'You're missing a simple advantage.' But Reeanna flicked it away. 'The esteemed Dr Mira would label me a sociopath with violent tendencies and a driving need for control. A pathological liar with an unhealthy, even dangerous fascination with death.'

Eve waited a beat. 'And would you agree with that analysis, Dr Ott?'

'Yes, indeed. My mother self-terminated when I was six. My father never got over it. He turned me over to my grandparents and wandered off to heal. I don't believe he ever did. But I saw my mother's face after she'd taken the lethal handful of pills. She looked quite beautiful and very happy. So why shouldn't death, taken, be an enjoyable experience.'

'Try it,' Eve suggested, 'and see.' Then she smiled. 'I'll help you.'

'One day, perhaps. After I've completed my study.'

'We're laboratory rats then; not toys, not games, but experiments. Droids for dissecting.'

'Yes. Young Drew. I regretted that because he was young and had potential. I'd consulted with him, rashly I see now, when William and I were working on the Olympus Resort. He fell in love with me. So young. I was flattered, and William's very tolerant of outside distractions.'

'He just knew too much, so you sent him a modified unit and told him to hang himself.'

'Basically. It wouldn't have been necessary, but he didn't want to let the relationship die. It meant he had to, before he lost that glaze infatuation puts over a man's eyes, and looked too closely.'

'You stripped your victims,' Eve added. 'The final humiliation?'

'No.' Reeanna appeared shocked and insulted by the idea. 'Not at all. Basic symbolism. We're born naked, and naked we die. We complete the circle. Drew died happy. They all did. No suffering, no pain at all. Joy, in fact. I'm not a monster, Eve. I'm a scientist.'

'No, you're a monster, Reeanna. And these days, society puts their monsters in a cage and keeps them there. You won't be happy in a cage.'

'It won't happen. Jess will pay. You'll fight to put him there after my report tomorrow. And if you can't make the coercion charges stick, you'll always believe he was responsible. And when there are others, I'll be very select, very careful, and I'll see to it that each subject self-terminates well out of your range. You won't be bothered by it again.'

'You arranged for two in my range.' A sickness churned in her stomach. 'To get my attention.'

'In part. I did want to watch you at work. Watch you closely, step by step. Just to see if you were as good as reported. You detested Fitzhugh, and I thought why not do my new friend Eve a little favor? He was a pompous ass, an irritant to society, and a very poor game player. I wanted his death to be bloody. He perferred blood games, you know. I never met him in person, but matched with him in cyberspace now and again. A poor loser.'

'He had family,' Eve managed. 'Like Pearly, Mathias, and Cerise Devane.'

'Oh, life goes on.' She waved a dismissing hand. 'All will adjust. That's human nature. And as for Cerise, she was no more maternal than an alley cat. It was all ambition with her. She bored me senseless. The most entertainment she ever provided was dying on camera. What a smile. They all smiled. That was my little joke – and my gift to them. The final suggestion. Die, it's so beautiful, it's amusing, and so joyful.

288

Die and experience the pleasure. They died experiencing the pleasure.'

'They died with a frozen smile and a burn on the brain.'

Reeanna's brows drew together. 'What do you mean, a burn?'

Where the hell was her backup? How much longer could she stall? 'You didn't know about that? Your little experiment has a slight defect, Reeanna. It burns a hole in the frontal lobe, leaves what we could call a shadow. Or a fingerprint. Your fingerprint.'

'That's nothing.' But she worried her lip as she considered it. 'The intensity of the subliminal could cause that, I suppose. It has to get in, firmly, to bypass the instinctive resistance, the knee-jerk survival instinct. We'll have to work on that, see what can be adjusted.' Annoyance shadowed her eyes. 'William will have to do better. I don't like flaws.'

'Your experiment's full of them. You have to control William to continue. How many times have you used the system on him, Reeanna? Would continued use expand that burn? I wonder what kind of damage it could cause.'

'It can be fixed.' She tapped the fingers of her free hand on her thigh, distracted. 'He'll fix it. I'll do a new scan on him, study the flaw – if he has one. Repair it.'

'Oh, he'll have one.' Eve stepped closer, judging the distance, the risk. 'They all had one. And if you can't repair William's, you'll probably have to terminate him. You couldn't risk that flaw becoming larger, causing uncontrolled behavior. Could you?'

'No. No. I'll look into this immediately. Tonight.'

'It may already be too late.'

Reeanna's eyes snapped back. 'Adjustments can be made. Will be made. I haven't come this far, accomplished this much, to accept any sort of failure.'

'And yet to succeed fully, you'll have to control me, and I won't make it easy.'

'I already have your brain pattern,' Reeanna reminded her. 'I've already implemented your program. It's going to be very easy.'

'I'll surprise you,' Eve promised. 'And Roarke. You can't manufacture without him, and he'll find out. Do you expect to control him as well?'

'That will be a particular pleasure. I did have to adjust the time schedule. I'd hoped to enjoy him first. A little trip, you might say, down memory lane. Roarke's so creative in bed. We haven't taken time to compare those notes, but I'm sure you'll agree.'

It put Eve's teeth on edge, but she spoke coolly. 'Using your toy for sexual gratification, Dr Ott? How unscientific.'

'And what fun. I'm not the master William is, but I do enjoy a good, creative game.'

'And that's how you met all your victims.'

'So far. Through the loops and the underground. Games can be relaxing and entertaining. And both William and I agreed that processing input from players would help us develop more creative options for the new VR.' She fluffed at her hair. 'Not that anyone had in mind what I was creating.'

Her gaze shifted to the monitor, frowned over the data being transmitted from Roarke's office. He was processing the VR specs now, she noted. 'But you've already got Roarke digging. Not just on young Drew, but on the unit itself. I wasn't happy about that, but there are always ways around inconveniences.' Her smile tilted up at the corners. 'Roarke isn't as necessary as you believe. Who do you suppose will own all of this if something happened to him?'

She laughed again, pure delight, as Eve stared blankly.

'Why, you will, darling. It will all be yours, in your control, and therefore mine. Don't worry, I won't let you stay a widow long. We'll find someone for you. I'll choose him personally.'

Terror froze her blood, iced her muscles, closed frigidly around her heart. 'You made a unit for him.'

'Just completed this afternoon. I wonder if he's tested it yet? Roarke is so efficient, and so personally interested in all of his holdings.'

She shot a stream at Eve's feet, anticipating her. 'Don't. I'll just stun you, and this will take longer.'

'I'll kill you with my own hands.' Eve forced air in and out of her lungs, ordered herself to think. 'I swear it.'

In his office, Roarke frowned over the data he'd converted. *Missing something*, he thought. *What am I missing?*

He rubbed the strain out of his eyes, sat back. He needed a break, he decided. Clear the mind, rest the eyes. Picking up the VR unit on his desk, he turned it over in his hands.

'You won't chance it. If you do, and I stun you, you'll never get to him in time. There's always the hope you can stop it, save him.' Her smile spread again, derisively. 'You see, I understand you, Eve, perfectly.'

'Do you?' Eve asked, and instead of lunging forward, leaped back. 'Lights out,' she shouted, snatching for her weapon as the room pitched into darkness. She felt the slight sting as Reeanna's aim wavered, skimmed her shoulder.

Then she was down, blocked by the desk, and gritting her teeth against the pain. She'd rolled fast, but not well, and had come down hard on her bad knee.

'I'm better at this than you,' Eve said calmly. But the fingers in her right hand tingled and shook, forcing her to switch the weapon to her left. 'You're the amateur here. Ditch the weapon, and I might not kill you.'

'Kill me?' Reeanna's voice was a hiss. 'You've got too much cop programmed into you. Maximum force only when all other methods fail.'

Near the door, Eve told herself, holding her breath, training her ears. To the right of it. 'There's no one here but you and me. Who's to know?'

'Too much conscience. Don't forget, I know you. I've been in your head. You wouldn't be able to live with it.'

Moving closer to the door. That's it, keep going. Just a little more. Try to get out, you bitch, and I'll drop you like a piece of spoiled meat.

'Maybe you're right. Maybe I'll just cripple you.' Weapon gripped, Eve bellied around the desk.

The door opened, but instead of Reeanna rushing out, William started in. 'Reeanna, what are you doing in the dark?'

Even as Eve leaped to her feet, Reeanna's finger twitched on the weapon, sending William's nervous system jittering.

'Oh, William, for God's sake.' It was disgust rather than distress. As he started to topple, Reeanna ducked under him and threw herself at Eve. Her nails scraped viciously across Eve's breasts as both women crashed to the floor.

She knew where to aim. She'd tended every bump and bruise on Eve's body and now battered at them, twisted, jabbed. A knee rammed against that tender hip, a balled fist slammed into the wrenched knee.

Blind with pain, Eve shot out an elbow, heard the satisfactory crunch of cartilage as it connected with Reeanna's nose. Reeanna screamed, a high, female sound, and dug in with her teeth.

'Bitch.' Sinking to the same level, Eve grabbed a handful of hair and yanked. Then, slightly ashamed of the lapse, she jammed her weapon under Reeanna's chin. 'Breathe too hard, and I'll put you out. Lights on.'

She was panting, bloody, her body singing with pain. She hoped there would be satisfaction later at seeing her opponent's beautiful face bruised, smeared with blood that continued to stream out of her broken nose. But for now there was too much fear.

'I'm putting you out anyway.'

'No, you won't.' Reeanna's voice was steely calm, and her

lips curved into a wide, brilliant smile. 'I will,' she said, and twisted the wrist of the weapon hand Eve pinned until the point rested against the side of her neck. 'I hate cages.' And smiling, she fired.

'Jesus, Jesus Christ.' She scrambled up while Reeanna's body still shuddered, shoved William over, snatched out his pocket 'link. He was breathing, but she didn't much give a damn.

She started to run.

'Answer me, you answer me!' she shouted at the 'link as she fumbled it on. 'Roarke,' she ordered, 'main office. Answer me, goddamn it.' Then she bit back a scream as the transmission refused to go through.

Line currently in use. Please wait or retry momentarily.

'Bypass, you son of a bitch. How do you bypass with this thing?' She increased her pace to a limping gallop, not even aware she was weeping.

Footsteps pounded toward her in the breezeway, but she didn't even pause.

'Dallas, holy God.'

'Back there.' She raced past Feeney, barely heard his frantic questions through the roaring sea of terror in her head. 'Back there. Peabody, with me. Hurry.'

She hit the elevator, pounded on the call control. 'Hurry, hurry.'

'Dallas, what's happened?' Peabody touched her shoulder, was jerked off. 'You're bleeding. Lieutenant, what's the status?'

'Roarke, oh God, oh God, please.' Tears were streaming, scalding her, blinding her. Panic sweat flooded out of her pores, soaking her skin. 'She's killing him. She's going to kill him.'

In reaction, Peabody pulled her weapon as they rushed

through the opening doors of the elevator. 'Top floor, east wing,' Eve shouted. 'Now, now, now!' She all but threw the 'link at Peabody. 'Get this fucker to bypass.'

'It's damaged. It's been dropped or something. Who's got Roarke?'

'Reeanna. She's dead. Dead as Moses, but she's killing him.' She couldn't breathe, couldn't. Her lungs wouldn't hold air. 'We'll stop him. Whatever she told him to do to himself, we'll stop him.' She turned wild eyes on Peabody. 'She's not taking him.'

'We'll stop him.' Peabody was through the doors with her before they fully opened.

Eve was still faster, even injured, she gained speed through terror. She wrenched at the door, cursed security, and slammed her hand down on the palm plate.

She all but ran over him as he stepped to the threshold.

'Roarke.' She burrowed into him, would have climbed inside him if she could. 'Oh God. You're all right. You're alive.'

'What's happened to you?' He tightened his grip on her as she shuddered.

But she was jerking back, grabbing his face in her hands, staring into his eyes. 'Look at me. Did you use it? Did you test the VR unit?'

'No. Eve—'

'Peabody, drop if he moves wrong. Call the MTs. We're taking him in for a brain scan.'

'The hell you are, but go ahead and call them, Peabody. She's going to the health center this time, if I have to knock her unconscious.'

Eve stepped back, fighting for breath as she carefully measured him. She couldn't feel her legs, wondered why she could still stand upright. 'You didn't use it.'

'I said I didn't.' He pushed a hand through his hair. 'It's aimed at me this time, is it? I should have seen it.' He turned away, glanced over his shoulder as Eve lifted her weapon. 'Oh, put that damn thing down. I'm not suicidal. I'm pissed. She slipped it right by me. It just started to click five minutes ago. Mindoc. Mind doctor,' he elaborated. 'That's the name she used in her game playing. She's still using it, still playing. Mathias had dozens of transmissions to her in the year before he died. And I took a close look at the data report on the unit. The one they just gave me, and the stats from the files. They hadn't buried those deeply enough.'

'She knew you'd find it. That's why she—' Eve broke off, sucked in air that she could hear whistle eerily in her swimming head. 'That's why she personalized a unit for you.'

'I might have gotten around to testing it if I hadn't been interrupted.' He thought of Mavis, nearly smiled. 'I doubt Ree put much effort into altering data. She knew I trusted her and William.'

'It wasn't William – not voluntarily.'

He only nodded, looked at her ruined shirt, the bright red splashes. 'Did she bloody you?'

'It's mostly hers.' She hoped. 'She didn't want to be taken in.' Eve blew out a breath. 'She's dead, Roarke. Self-terminated. I couldn't stop her, Maybe I didn't want to. She told me – the unit, your unit.' Her breath was wheezing again, hitching, skipping. 'I thought – I didn't think I'd be in time. I couldn't make the 'link work, and I couldn't get here.'

She didn't hear Peabody close the door to give her privacy. She didn't care about privacy. She only continued to stare, blind now, and shudder. 'I couldn't,' she said again. 'I stalled her, all that time I was stalling her, building my case, and you could have been—'

'Eve.' He came to her, gathered her close. 'I'm not. And you did get here. I won't leave you.' He pressed his lips to her hair when she buried her face against his shoulder. 'It's over now.'

She knew she'd replay that endless run, the panic and

the helpless grief, a thousand times in her dreams. 'It's not. There'll be a full investigation, not just of Reeanna, but of your company, the people who worked with her on the project.'

'I can stand it.' He tipped her head back. 'The company's clean. I promise. I won't cause you any official embarrassment, Lieutenant, by being arrested.'

She took the handkerchief he pressed into her hand, blew her nose. 'Be hell for my career, being married to a con.'

'Be easy on that account. Why did she do it?'

'Because she could. That's what she said. She enjoyed the power, the control.' Briskly, she rubbed her cheeks dry with the heels of her hands, hands that were nearly steady now. 'She had big plans for me.' The shudder was hard but brief. 'Kind of a pet, I imagine. Like William. Her little trained dog. And with you dead, she figured I'd inherit all your goodies. You're not going to do that to me, are you?'

'What, die?'

'Leave me all this stuff.'

He laughed, kissed her. 'Only you would be annoyed by that.' He brushed her hair back from her face. 'She had a unit for you.'

'Yeah, we didn't get around to testing it out. Feeney's down there now. I'd better let him know what happened.'

'We'll have to go down. She disengaged the 'link, which is why I was on my way to you when you jumped me. I was worried when I couldn't get through.'

'It's tough.' She touched his face. 'Caring.'

'I can live with it. You'll want to go into the station, I imagine, to clean this up tonight.'

'It's procedure. I've got a corpse – and four deaths to close.'

'I'll take you, after you've been to the health center.'

'I'm not going to the health center.'

'Yes, you are.'

Peabody rapped on the door, opened it. 'Excuse me, the MTs are here. They need to be cleared through security.'

'I'll take care of it. Have them meet us in Dr Ott's office, would you, Peabody? They can examine Eve there before I take her in for full treatment.'

'I said I'm not going in for a treatment.'

'I heard you.' He pressed a control on his desk. 'Clear the medics through, please. Peabody, are you carrying restraints?'

'They're standard issue.'

'I wonder if you might loan them to me so I can restrain your lieutenant until I deliver her to the nearest medical facility.'

'Just try it, pal, and see who needs a doctor.'

Peabody gnawed manfully on the inside of her cheek. A smirk at the moment wouldn't please her lieutenant. 'I sympathize with your problem, Roarke, but am unable to comply. I need the job.'

'Never mind, Peabody.' He scooped an arm around Eve's waist, taking her weight as she limped toward the door. 'I'm sure I can find a substitute.'

'I've got a report to file, work to finish. I've got a dead body to transport.' Eve scowled at him as he called for the elevator. 'I don't have time for an exam.'

'I heard you,' he repeated and simply picked her up bodily and carried her into the elevator. 'Peabody, tell those MTs to come armed. She's liable to make a run for it.'

'Put me down, you idiot. I'm not going.' She was laughing as the doors closed on them.

If you enjoyed *Rapture in Death*, you won't want to miss
J.D. Robb's thrilling next novel . . .


CEREMONY in DEATH

Death surrounded her. She faced it daily, dreamed of it nightly. Lived with it always. She knew its sounds, its scents, even its texture. She could look it in its dark and clever eye without a flinch. Death was a tricky foe, she knew. One flinch, one blink, and it could shift, it could change. It could win.

Ten years as a cop hadn't hardened her toward it. A decade on the force hadn't made her accept it. When she looked death in the eye, it was with the cold steel of a warrior.

Eve Dallas looked at death now. She looked at one of her own.

Frank Wojinski had been a good cop, solid. Some would have said plodding. She remembered him as affable – a man who hadn't complained about the bilge disguised as food at the NYPSD Eatery or the eye-searing paperwork the job generated. Or, Eve thought, about the fact that he'd been sixty-two and had never made it past the rank of detective-sergeant.

He'd been on the pudgy side and had let his hair gray and thin naturally. It was a rare thing in 2058 for a man to bypass body scuplting and enhancements. Now, in his clear-sided view casket with its single spray of mournful lilies, he resembled a peacefully sleeping monk from an earlier time.

He'd been born in an earlier time, Eve mused, coming into the world at the end of one millennium and living his life in the next. He'd been through the Urban Wars, but hadn't talked of them as so many of the older cops did. Frank hadn't been one for war stories, Eve recalled. He had been more likely to pass around the latest snapshot or hologram of his children and grandchildren.

He'd liked to tell bad jokes, talk sports, and had had a weakness for soydogs with spiced pickle relish.

*A family man*, Eve thought, *one who left behind great grief.* Indeed, she could think of no one who had known Frank Wojinski who hadn't loved him.

He had died with half of his life still ahead of him; died alone, when the heart everyone had thought so huge and so strong had just stopped.

'Goddamn it.'

Eve turned, laid a hand on the arm of the man who stepped beside her. 'I'm sorry, Feeney.'

He shook his head, his droopy camel's eyes filled with misery. With one hand he raked through his wiry red hair. 'On the job would have been easier. I could handle line of duty. But to just stop. To just check out in his easy chair watching Arena Ball on the screen. It's not right, Dallas. A man's not supposed to stop living at his age.'

'I know.' Not knowing what else to do, Eve draped an arm over his shoulder and steered him away.

'He trained me. Looked after me when I was a rookie. Never let me down.' Pain radiated through him and glinted dully in his eyes, wavered in his voice. 'Frank never let anyone down in his life.'

'I know,' Eve said again because there was nothing else to say. She was accustomed to Feeney being tough and strong. The delicacy of his grief worried her.

She led him through the mourners. The viewing room was packed with cops as well as family. And where there were cops and death, there was coffee. Or what passed for it at such places. Eve poured a cup, handed it to Feeney.

'I can't get around it. I can't get a hold of it.' He let out a long, uneven breath. He was a sturdy, compact man who wore his grief as openly as he wore his rumpled coat. 'I haven't talked to Sally yet. My wife's with her. I just can't do it.'

'It's all right. I haven't talked to her either.' Since she had nothing to do with her hands, Eve poured a cup of coffee for herself that she didn't intend to drink. 'Everybody's shook up by this. I didn't know he had a heart thing.'

'Nobody did,' Feeney said quietly. 'Nobody knew.'

Eve kept a hand on his shoulder as she scanned the over-crowded, overheated room. When a fellow officer went down in the line of duty, cops could be angry; they could be focused, fix their target. But when death snuck in and crooked a capricious finger, there was no one to blame. And no one to punish.

It was helplessness she felt in the room and that she felt in herself. You couldn't raise your weapon or your fist to fate.

The funeral director, spiffy in his traditional black suit and as waxy-faced as one of his own clients, worked the room with patting hands and sober eyes. Eve thought she'd rather have a corpse sit up and grin at her than listen to his platitudes.

'Why don't we go talk to the family together?'

It was hard for him, but Feeney nodded, set the untouched coffee aside. 'He liked you, Dallas. "That kid's got balls of steel and a mind to match," he used to tell me. He always said if he was ever jammed, you'd be the one he'd want guarding his back.'

This surprised and pleased Eve and simultaneously added to her sorrow. 'I didn't realize he thought of me that way.'

Feeney looked at her. She had an interesting face, not one he'd have called a heart-stopper, but it usually made a man look twice with its angles and sharp bones, the shallow dent of the chin. She had a cop's eyes, intense and measuring, and he often forgot they were a dark golden brown. Her hair was the same shade, cut short and badly in need of some shaping. She was tall and lean and tough bodied.

He remembered it had been less than a month since he had come across her battered and bloodied. But her weapon had been firm in her hand.

'He thought of you that way. So do I.' While she blinked at him, Feeney squared his hunched shoulders. 'Let's talk to Sally and the kids.'

They slipped through the crowd, jammed together in a room oppressed with dark simulated wood, heavy red draperies, and the funeral smell of too many flowers crammed into too small a space.

Eve wondered why viewings of the dead were always accompanied by flowers and draping sheets of red. What ancient ceremony did it spring from, and why did the human race continue to cling to it?

She was certain that when her time came she wouldn't choose-to be laid out for study by her loved ones and associates in an overheated room where the pervasive scent of flowers was reminiscent of rot.

Then she saw Sally supported by her children and her grandchildren and realized such rites were for the living. The dead were beyond caring.

'Ryan.' Sally held out her hands – small, almost fairy-like hands – and lifted her cheek to Feeney's. She held there a moment, her eyes closed, her face pale and quiet.

She was a slim, soft-spoken woman whom Eve had always thought of as delicate. Yet a cop's spouse who had survived the stress of the job for more than forty years had to have steel. Against her plain black dress she wore her husband's twenty-five-year NYPSD ring on a chain.

*Another rite*, Eve thought. *Another symbol.*

'I'm so glad you're here,' Sally murmured.

'I'll miss him. We'll all miss him.' Feeney patted her back awkwardly before drawing away. Grief was in his throat, choking him. Swallowing it only lodged it cold and heavy in his gut. 'You know if there's anything . . .'

'I know.' Her lips curved slightly and she gave his hand a quick and comforting squeeze before turning to Eve. 'I appreciate you coming, Dallas.'

'He was a good man. A solid cop.'

'Yes, he was.' Recognizing it as a high tribute, Sally managed a smile. 'He was proud to serve and protect. Commander Whitney and his wife and Chief Tibble are here. And so many others.' Her gaze drifted blindly around the room. 'So many. He mattered. Frank mattered.'

'Of course he did, Sally.' Feeney shifted from foot to foot. 'You, ah, know about the survivor's fund.'

She smiled again, patted his hand. 'We're fine there. Don't worry. Dallas, I don't think you really know my family. Lieutenant Dallas, my daughter, Brenda.'

Brenda was short with rounded curves, Eve noted as they clasped hands. Dark hair and eyes, a bit heavy in the chin. Took after her father.

'My son, Curtis.'

Slim, small boned, soft hands, eyes that were dry but dazed with grief.

'My grandchildren.'

There were five of them, the youngest a boy of about eight with a pug nose dashed with freckles. He eyed Eve with consideration. 'How come you've got your zapper on?'

Flustered, Eve tugged her jacket over her sidearm. 'I came straight from Cop Central. I didn't have time to go home and change.'

'Pete.' Curtis shot Eve an apologetic wince. 'Don't bother the lieutenant.'

'If people concentrated more on their personal and spiritual powers, weapons would be unnecessary. I'm Alice.'

A slim blonde in black stepped forward. She'd have been a stunner in any case, Eve mused, but having sprung from such basic stock, she was dazzling. Her eyes were a soft, dreamy blue, her mouth full and lush and unpainted. She wore her hair loose so that it rained straight and glossy over the shoulders of her flowing black dress. A thin silver chain fell to her waist. At the end of it was a black stone ringed in silver.

'Alice, you're such a zip head.'

She flicked a cool glance over her shoulder toward a boy of about sixteen. But her hands kept fluttering back to the black stone, like elegant birds guarding a nest.

'My brother, Jamie,' she said in a silky voice. 'He still thinks name calling deserves a reaction. My grandfather spoke of you, Lieutenant Dallas.'

'I'm flattered.'

'Your husband isn't with you tonight?'

Eve arched a brow. Not just grief, she deduced, but nerves. They were easy enough to recognize. There were signals as well, but they weren't clear. The girl was after something, Eve mused. But what?

'No, he's not.' She shifted her gaze back to Sally. 'He sends his sympathies, Mrs Wojinski. He's off planet.'

'It must take a great deal of concentration and energy,' Alice interrupted, 'to maintain a relationship with a man like Roarke and a demanding, difficult, even dangerous career. My grandfather used to say that once you had a grip on an investigation, you never let go. Would you say that's accurate, Lieutenant?'

'If you let go, you lose. I don't like to lose.' She held Alice's odd gaze for a moment, then on impulse crouched down and whispered to Pete. 'When I was a rookie, I saw your grandfather zap a guy at ten yards. He was the best.' She was rewarded with a quick grin before she straightened. 'He won't be forgotten, Mrs Wojinski,' she said, offering her hand. 'And he mattered very much – to all of us.'

She started to step back, but Alice laid a hand on her arm, leaned close. The hand, Eve noted, trembled lightly. 'It was interesting meeting you, Lieutenant. Thank you for coming.'

Eve inclined her head and slipped back into the crowd.

Casually, she reached a hand into the pocket of her jacket and fingered the thin slip of paper Alice had pushed inside.

It took her another thirty minutes to get away. She waited until she was outside and in her vehicle before she took the note out and read it.

*Meet me tomorrow, midnight. Aquarian Club. TELL NO ONE. Your life is now at risk.*

In lieu of a signature there was a symbol, a dark line running in an expanding circle to form a sort of maze. Nearly as intrigued as she was annoyed, Eve stuffed the note back in her pocket and started home.

Because she was a cop, she saw the figure draped in black, hardly more than a shadow in the shadows. And because she was a cop, she knew he was watching her.

Whenever Roarke was away, Eve preferred to pretend the house was empty. Both she and Summerset, who served as Roarke's chief of staff, did their best to ignore each other's presence. The house was huge, a labyrinth of rooms, which made it a simple matter to avoid each other.

She stepped into the wide foyer, tossed her scarred leather jacket over the carved newel post because she knew it would make Summerset grind his teeth. He detested having anything mar the elegance of the house, particularly Eve.

She took the stairs, but rather than go to the master bedroom, she veered off to her office suite. If Roarke had to spend another night off planet as expected, she preferred to spend hers in her relaxation chair rather than their bed. She often dreamed badly when she dreamed alone.

Between the late paperwork and the viewing she hadn't had time for a meal. Eve ordered up a sandwich – real Virginia ham on rye – and coffee that jumped with genuine caffeine. When the AutoChef delivered, she inhaled the scents slowly,

307

greedily. She took the first bite with her eyes closed to better enjoy the miracle.

There were definite advantages to being married to a man who could afford real meat instead of its by-products and simulations.

To satisfy her curiosity, she went to her desk and engaged her computer. She swallowed ham, chased it with coffee. 'All available data on subject Alice, surname unknown. Mother Brenda, nee Wojinski, maternal grandparents Frank and Sally Wojinski.'

Working ...

Eve drummed her fingers, took out the note and reread it while she polished off the quick meal.

Subject Alice Lingstrom. DOB June 10, 2040. First child and only daughter of Jan Lingstrom and Brenda Wojinski, divorced. Residence, 486 West Eighth Street, Apartment 4B, New York City. Sibling, James Lingstrom, DOB March 22, 2042. Education, high school graduate, valedictorian. Two semesters of college. Harvard. Major Anthropology. Minor Mythology. Third semester deferred. Currently employed as clerk, Spirit Quest, 228 West Tenth Street, New York City. Marital status, single.

Eve ran her tongue around her teeth. 'Criminal record?'

No criminal record.

'Sounds fairly normal,' Eve murmured. 'Data on Spirit Quest.'

Spirit Quest. Wiccan shop and consultation center, owned by Isis Paige and Charles Forte. Three years in Tenth Street location. Annual gross income one hundred and twenty-five thousand dollars. Licensed priestess, herbalist, and registered hypnotherapist on site.

'Wicca?' Eve leaned back with a snort. 'Witch stuff? Jesus. What kind of scam is this?'

Wicca, recognized as both a religion and a craft, is an ancient and nature-based faith that—

'Stop.' Eve blew out a breath. She wasn't looking for a definition of witchcraft, but an explanation as to how a steady-as-a-rock cop ended up with a granddaughter who believed in casting spells and magic crystals.

And why that granddaughter wanted a secret meeting.

The best way to find out, she decided, was to show up at the Aquarian Club in just over twenty-four hours. She left the note on the desk. It would be easy to dismiss it, she thought, if it hadn't been written by a relative of a man she'd respected.

And if she hadn't seen that figure in the shadows. A figure she was sure hadn't wanted to be seen.

She walked to the adjoining bath and began to strip. It was too bad she couldn't take Mavis with her for the meet. Eve had a feeling the Aquarian Club would be right up her friend's alley. Eve kicked her jeans aside, leaned over to stretch out the kinks of a long day. She wondered what she would do with the long night ahead.

She had nothing hot to work on. Her last homicide had been so open and shut that she and her aide had put it to bed in less than eight hours. Maybe she'd spend a couple hours glazing out watching some screen. Or she could pick a weapon out of Roarke's gun room and go down and run a hologram program to burn off excess energy until she could sleep.

She'd never tried one of his auto-assault rifles. It might be interesting to experience how a cop took out an enemy during the early days of the Urban Wars.

She stepped into the shower. 'Full jets, on pulse,' she ordered. 'Ninety-eight degrees.'

She wished she had a murder to sink her teeth into. Something that would focus her mind and drain her system. And damn it, that was pathetic. She was lonely, she realized. Desperate for a distraction and he'd only been gone three days.

They both had their own lives, didn't they? They'd lived them before they met and continued to live them after they'd married. The demands of both their businesses absorbed much time and attention. Their relationship worked – and that continued to surprise her – because they were both independent people.

Christ, she missed him outrageously. Disgusted with herself, she ducked her head under the spray and let it pound on her brain.

When hands slipped around her waist, then slid up to cup her breasts, she barely jolted. But her heart leaped. She knew his touch, the feel of those long slim fingers, the texture of those wide palms. She tipped her head back, inviting a mouth to the curve of her shoulder.

'Mmm. Summerset. You wild man.'

Teeth nipped into flesh and made her chuckle. Thumbs brushed over her soapy nipples and made her moan.

'I'm not going to fire him.' Roarke trailed a hand down the center of her body.

'It was worth a shot. You're back . . .' His fingers dipped expertly inside her, slick and slippery, so that she arched, moaned, and came simultaneously. 'Early,' she finished on an explosive breath. 'God.'

'I'd say I was just on time.' He spun her around, and while she was shuddering and blinking water out of her eyes, he covered her mouth in a long, ravenous kiss.

He'd thought about her on the interminable flight home.

310

Thought about this, just this – touching and tasting and hearing that quick catch in her breath as he did. And here she was, naked and wet and already quivering for him.

He braced her in the corner, gripped her hips, and slowly lifted her off her feet. 'Miss me?'

Her heart was thundering. He was inches away from driving into her, filling her, destroying her. 'Not really.'

'Well, in that case' – he kissed her lightly on the chin – 'I'll just let you finish your shower in peace.'

In a flash she wrapped her legs around his waist, took a firm hold of his wet mane of hair. 'Try it, pal, and you're a dead man.'

'In the interest of self-preservation then.' To torture them both he slipped into her slowly, watched her eyes go opaque. He closed his mouth over hers again so that her shallow breaths shuddered through him.

The ride was slow and slippery and more tender than either had expected. Climax came as a long, quiet sigh. Her lips curved against his. 'Welcome home.'

She could see him now, those stunning blue eyes, the face that was both saint and sinner, the mouth of a doomed poet. His hair was streaming with water, black and sleek, just touching broad shoulders roped with subtle and surprisingly tough muscle.

Looking at him after these brief, periodic absences always made something unexpected lurch through Eve. She doubted she would ever get used to the fact that he not only wanted her, but he loved her.

She was still smiling as she combed her fingers through his thick, black hair. 'Everything okay with the Olympus Resort?'

'Adjustments, some delays. Nothing that can't be dealt with.' The elaborate space station resort and pleasure center would open on schedule because Roarke wouldn't accept any less.

He ordered the jets off, then took a towel to wrap around her when she would have used the drying tube. 'I began to understand why you stay in here while I'm away. I couldn't sleep in the presidential suite.' He took another towel, rubbed it over her hair. 'It was too lonely without you.'

She leaned against him a moment, just to feel the familiar lines of his body against hers. 'We're getting so damn sappy.'

'I don't mind. We Irish are very sentimental.'

It made her smirk as he turned to get robes. He might have had the music of Ireland in his voice, but she seriously doubted if any of his business friends or foes would consider Roarke a sentimental man.

'No fresh bruises,' he observed, helping her into her robe before she could do it for herself. 'I take that to mean you've had a quiet few days.'

'Mostly. We had a john get a bit overenthusiastic with a licensed companion. Choked her to death during sex.' She belted the robe, scratched fingers through her hair to scatter more water. 'He got spooked and ran.' She moved her shoulders as she stepped into the office. 'But he lawyered up and turned himself in a few hours later. PA took it down to manslaughter. I let Peabody handle the interview and booking.'

'Hmm.' Roarke went to a recessed cabinet for wine, poured them both a glass. 'It's been quiet then.'

'Yeah. I had that viewing tonight.'

His brow furrowed, then cleared. 'Ah, yes, you told me. I'm sorry I couldn't make it home in time to go with you.'

'Feeney's taking it really hard. It would be easier if Frank had gone down in the line of duty.'

This time Roarke's brow quirked. 'You'd prefer that your associate had been killed rather than, say, gone gently into that good night?'

'You'd just understand it better, that's all.' She frowned

into her wine. She didn't think it wise to tell Roarke she'd prefer a fast and violent death herself. 'There is something odd, though. I met Frank's family. The oldest granddaughter's on the weird side.'

'How?'

'The way she talked and the data I accessed on her after I got home.'

Intrigued, he lifted his wine to sip. 'You ran a make on her?'

'Just a quick check. Because she passed me this.' Eve walked to the desk, picked up the note.

Roarke scanned it, considered. 'Earth Labyrinth.'

'What?'

'The symbol here. It's Celtic.'

Shaking her head, Eve eased closer to look again. 'You know the strangest things.'

'Not so strange. I spring from the Celts, after all. The ancient labyrinth symbol is magical and sacred.'

'Well, it fits. She's into witchcraft or something. Got herself the start of a top-flight education. Harvard. But she drops out to work in some West Village shop that sells crystals and magic herbs.'

Roarke traced the symbol with a fingertip. He'd seen it and others like it before. Throughout his childhood the cults in Dublin had run the range between vicious gangs and pious pacifists. All, of course, had used religion as the excuse to kill or be killed.

'You have no idea why she wants to meet you?'

'None. I'd say she figures she read my aura or something. Mavis ran a mystic grift before I busted her for pinching wallets. She told me people will pay almost anything if you tell them what they want to hear. More if you tell them what they don't want to hear.'

'Which is why cons and legitimate business is very much the same.' He smiled at her. 'I take it you're going anyway.'

313

'Sure, I'll follow through.'

Naturally, she would. Roarke glanced at the note again, then set it aside. 'I'm going with you.'

'She wants—'

'It's a pity what she wants.' He sipped his wine, a man accustomed to getting precisely what he wanted, one way or another. 'I'll stay out of your way, but I'm going. The Aquarian Club is basically harmless, but there are always unsavory elements that leak through.'

'Unsavory elements are my life,' she said soberly, then cocked her head. 'You don't, like, own the Aquarian, do you?'

'No.' He smiled. 'Would you like to?'

She laughed and took his hand. 'Come on. Let's drink this in bed.'


Relaxed by sex and wine, Eve fell peacefully asleep, draped around Roarke. She was baffled to find herself suddenly and fully awake only two hours later. It hadn't been one of her nightmares. There was no terror; no pain; no cold, clammy sweat.

Yet she had snapped awake, and her heart wasn't quite steady. She lay still, staring up through the wide sky window over the bed, listening to Roarke's quiet, steady breathing beside her.

She shifted, glanced down at the foot of the bed, and nearly yelped when eyes glowed out of the dark. Then she registered the weight over her ankles. *Galahad*, she thought, and rolled her eyes. The cat had come in and jumped onto the bed. That's what had awakened her, she told herself. That's all it was.

She settled again, turned onto her side, and felt Roarke's arm slide around her in sleep. With a sigh, she closed her eyes, snuggled companionably against him.

*Just the cat*, she thought sleepily.

But she would have sworn she'd heard chanting.